1

This book is dedicated to my mother, for always being there for me. I love you!

And a special thanks to my sister, April, for helping me with proofreads and edits.

Table of Contents

Chapter 1

Akinia paused at the door to Khee-Lá's room, wondering if she should knock or just turn around and leave. It had been four months since she woke after being rescued from her imprisonment in Jade Enbrilth's base, and nearly as long since she'd last spoken to her uncle.

Finally, she raised her hand and softly knocked.

"Come in," Khee-Lá called.

She hesitated a moment before opening the door.

Khee-Lá seemed surprised to see her there, but didn't say anything.

"I wanted to talk to you," she admitted quietly.

Khee-Lá nodded and motioned for her to sit down.

"I know you're angry with me, and I guess I don't blame you, but how long are going to keep ignoring us?" she asked.

"I can't go along with this when it places you in such danger," he stated, his voice betraying no emotion.

"I'm in no more danger than I was before, but if I stay here, then you and Ko-Pau and Nath will all be in more danger because Jade will try and use one or all of you as bait to get me to surrender myself, and it *would* work. He would kill me if he had to use those measures to get to me, but for now he thinks he can change my mind so I'm safe," she protested.

"Look at yourself, Akinia. Do you see what he's done to you? You nearly died from the wounds you received, do you realize that?" Khee-Lá demanded.

Akinia looked away. She knew perfectly well how close she came to dying, because it had never seemed close enough until she saw Khee-Lá's face when he found her. His presence was the only thing that had given her reason to fight against death.

"You are too important to me, and to the future of the Empire, to sacrifice yourself like this. I can't sit back and allow you to place

11

yourself in this danger," he continued, "I can't let him hurt you again."

"I already told you that I can't live like that again. I had never set foot outside of the orphanage until Ko-Pau came for me; I wasn't allowed to. I hated that life so much because of it. I don't regret you taking me there because I know it was for my own safety, but I won't live like that again," she whispered.

"Do you realize how selfish you're being?" Khee-Lá demanded angrily.

Akinia looked up at him, shocked.

"You're acting like a stubborn child who is too busy thinking about what she wants to even care about how your decisions will affect everyone else. Someone in your position oftentimes needs to make sacrifices of personal comforts to do what's best for the people you're supposed to protect. You are endangering everyone in the Empire and Motúk just because you don't like being told what to do," he snapped.

Akinia stood up quickly. "You're just overprotective and too busy trying to do what's best for me to realize that sometimes keeping me where I'd be safest isn't necessarily what's best for me. I can't be expected to live a safe life here and then be able to kill Jade and Lokita. Maybe if you weren't being so selfish you could realize that you aren't the only one who can decide on a course of action that's best for me. Ko-Pau and Lo-Kí understand that, why can't you?" she yelled.

"Akinia," Khee-Lá called sharply as she turned and stormed towards the door.

She stopped suddenly and turned to face him. "I'm just going to do us both a favor and leave," she snapped. Her vision blurred by the angry tears welling up in her eyes, she stormed into the hallway. She didn't even notice Rofa waiting to greet her. The cub excitedly ran around her legs, tripping her. Akinia landed heavily, with her arms braced in front of her to catch herself.

"Akinia," Khee-Lá gasped worriedly as he ran from his room to help her up.

"I'm not made of glass. I don't break every time I fall down," Akinia griped, snatching her arm away from him. She didn't look back as she stormed down the hallway to her bedroom. Her injuries had left her weak, and she collapsed on the bed, exhausted. She made no attempt to stop the tears from flowing, or to wipe them away, but she cried in silence.

Chapter 2:

It was nearly an hour later when Ko-Pau knocked on Akinia's door. Not receiving an answer, he reached out with his mind to see if she was asleep. He felt her mind inside, but was surprised to find that she wasn't sleeping. When she didn't seem to notice his mind brush against hers, he grew worried. "Akinia?" he called, pushing the door open.

Akinia didn't react to his entrance. She was sitting on her bed, leaning against the wall for support, staring blankly into the far corner of the room. Though she had put on several pounds since her rescue, Akinia still had a malnourished appearance that struck Ko-Pau like a dagger each time he saw her.

He placed a hand on her shoulder and she jumped, startled.

"Oh... Master, I didn't notice you come in," she admitted, shaking her head to clear it.

Ko-Pau sat down beside her. "Are you alright?" he asked, already knowing that she wasn't.

Akinia began to nod, but then shook her head, knowing better than to try and lie to her Master. "I tried talking with Khee-Lá again," she explained simply.

Ko-Pau closed his eyes and sighed. "I assume it didn't end well?" he asked, turning his gaze back onto her face to watch her reaction.

"No, we fought again," she admitted. She related their conversation to her master, ending with her snatching away from him and retreating to her room. "I didn't mean to let it turn into a fight, it just did," she said defensively.

"I don't blame you for what happened, I blame Khee-Lá. He's always had a short temper, especially when he's worried about someone he cares for. You shouldn't let it bother you; he'll come around sooner or later," Ko-Pau advised.

Akinia nodded slowly. "I wish it would be sooner," she murmured.

Ko-Pau stood up and motioned for Akinia to follow him. "Let's take a walk," he suggested.

"Alright," Akinia agreed. She slowly raised herself off of the bed, knowing that if she stood too fast she would get dizzy, and followed her Master out into the hallway. "Where are we going?"

"Nowhere in particular, just walking," he shrugged in reply, "How are you feeling today?"

"I've been better, but I've been a lot worse, too. That fight with Khee-Lá earlier kind of wore me out," she admitted. "Do you think we'll be able to get back to work soon?"

"Not until you're stronger. I can't take you out there like this or you'd be killed," Ko-Pau shrugged, wondering again why Akinia was so eager to get back to the front, when she had hated it before. "And, besides that, you still look like a walking skeleton. You have to start eating more, like Hyaline said."

"I'm trying, but I've never eaten much. It's hard," she complained.

He sighed. "I know, Slick, but you have to get back to a normal weight. You heard Hyaline: it's dangerous for you to be so thin still."

"I know," she promised. "I really am trying."

"You need to try a bit harder before Hyaline starts force-feeding you," he reminded her gently.

Nodding, she reached into her pocket and pulled out the metal cylinders Khee-Lá had given her to practice her control. Stretching out with her mind, she tried to stack the cylinders on top of one another as she walked. "Oh!" she gasped as she felt a burst of power suddenly surge through her mind, throwing all of the disks across the hallway. "That's the third time that's happened this week," she complained as Ko-Pau gathered them again with a quick brush of his thoughts.

"I doubt it's anything to be concerned about," he replied as he handed them to her.

Akinia slipped them into her pocket and leaned against the wall for support. The power surge had left her even weaker. "I think I need to get something to eat," she admitted, growing dizzy.

Ko-Pau wrapped his arm around her and led her silently to the dining hall. He settled her at an empty table and then went to get her

14

some food.

She buried her head in her hands, trying to make the room stop spinning. She barely noticed Ko-Pau's return.

"I think you should stop with the control exercises until you get a little stronger. These surges don't seem to be going away, and I can't have you passing out and injuring yourself," he ordered as he set the tray down in front of her.

Akinia nodded in agreement as she began to eat. "I don't know what's wrong with me," she complained between mouthfuls.

"Nothing is wrong with you except that you're too weak to control your power right now. You'll be fine in a few weeks," he promised.

She continued to eat, slowly and methodically clearing her plate. "I'm going to go lay down. I still don't feel too well," she informed him.

"I'll walk with you," he decided, "Should I get Hyaline?"

"No," Akinia replied, "I'll be fine. I just need to take a nap."

Hyaline, the base medic, was determined to keep Akinia in her room for another few weeks. If she caught wind of this she would have her way; that was the last thing Akinia wanted.

Ko-Pau watched his young apprentice carefully as he walked her back, hoping that she wasn't having a relapse. *Of course*, he grumbled to himself, *she would probably be stronger if Hyaline stopped taking blood every week.*

When Akinia was rescued, Hyaline had discovered that the girl's blood was a type that seemed to be completely unique to her. Ever since Akinia grew strong enough, Hyaline had been taking blood as often as was safe. She wanted to ensure that she had some on hand in case the girl was injured again, as well to send samples off for testing. Akinia had endured it good-naturedly, but her healing had been noticeably slower ever since.

Akinia slipped silently into her room and stretched out on her bed. She was seemingly asleep moments later.

Ko-Pau closed the door and turned to find Khee-Lá standing behind him.

"Is Akinia in there?" Khee-Lá asked awkwardly, shifting uncomfortably as he stood. He didn't know how he would be received after his previous behavior.

Ko-Pau nodded. "She's asleep. She had another power surge

and nearly passed out this time. She was already weak from your spat earlier," he informed his master.

The words were not intended as a rebuke, but Khee-Lá flinched as though they had been physical blows. "I didn't mean to yell at her, I swear it. I especially didn't mean to make her so weak," he promised the younger man.

Ko-Pau's expression softened somewhat. "I know. It isn't entirely your fault," he sighed. "Hyaline took more blood this morning."

Khee-Lá's eyes narrowed. "Why did she take blood? Is she running tests or something?" he asked. He glanced towards Akinia's door worriedly.

"I forgot that you don't know," Ko-Pau apologized, "Hyaline has been taking blood from Akinia the last month or so, that way she'll have some available if Akinia manages to get injured again. Akinia has a rare blood type, remember?"

"Oh," was all he could think to say. Hyaline had told them when she first found out, but he hadn't thought that she would take blood so soon. "Maybe I should just come back later?"

"She isn't angry with you, she blames herself," Ko-Pau informed him before turning and disappearing down the hallways.

Khee-Lá's pain showed clearly on his face as he thought about what his former Apprentice had said.

Chapter 3:

Akinia woke feeling rested, but not strong. The last time that she had felt truly strong was when she had faced Lokita in the Command Center of the Sigidian Battlecruiser. Akinia sat up slowly, trying to keep herself from getting dizzy.

"Mistress, is there anything that you need?" Jaynine asked, walking over to her.

"How long have I been asleep?" she asked as she stretched.

"I do not know when you fell asleep, as I was elsewhere on Paméd, but lunch was served two hours ago," the droid replied.

Akinia froze. She had slept for four hours? Annoyed at herself for having slept so long, Akinia shook her head. "I'm going up to the library. Would you bring me a cup of tea, please?" she asked.

Jaynine gave his standard bow before leaving the room.

Akinia slowly made her way up to the library, careful not to exert herself again. She pulled a book that she had been reading from its spot on the shelf and then settled into one of the plush chairs.

Jaynine arrived a few minutes later gripping her cup in his metal hands.

As Akinia took the first sip, a thought occurred to her. "Jaynine, will you please get me my com-link? I left it in my room," she asked.

The droid bowed and walked off.

How long had it been since she had spoken to Charlotte? The girl had been like a sister to her at the orphanage, and she had completely forgotten about her. *Well*, she decided, *not completely*. She did think of the girl every now and then, but hadn't been able to bring herself to contact her.

Jaynine returned a few minutes later carrying the com-link.

Akinia strapped it onto her wrist and typed in the destination.

The headmistress nearly fell out of her chair when she saw

17

Akinia's face on the screen, and then her eyes narrowed as she saw the cuts and gashes on the girl's too-thin face. "What happened to you?" she asked worriedly.

"Nothing important. I'm fine," Akinia lied.

"I don't believe you."

Akinia smiled. "I didn't think you would, but I don't want to talk about it. I'm going to be just fine."

"Those men didn't hurt you, did they?" she demanded suspiciously.

"No, Headmistress," Akinia promised, "this all happened while I was doing my job, but I *don't* want to talk about it."

Norda struggled for a moment before sighing and nodding in defeat. "How have you been? Are you keeping out of trouble? It's been so long since I've spoken to you," the headmistress asked.

"I'm doing my best to stay out of trouble, but trouble seems to find me," she complained, "But I've been well. I'm actually having a lot of fun. I've gone so many places and seen so much, it's even better than I had imagined it would be." A little lie wouldn't hurt... and it was mostly true, anyway...

"I'm glad you're settling into this life," she said warmly.

Akinia hesitated, wondering whether or not to tell her, before deciding to go ahead. "I found my parents," she admitted. She watched the woman's eyes widen at this news.

"Are they still alive?" Norda asked.

Akinia shook her head. "My mother and father, as well as my twin sister and grandparents, were murdered a month before I was brought to you. It was my uncle who left me at the orphanage," she explained.

"Who were your parents? And your uncle, is he still alive?"

"My uncle is a Najee, the one who trained my Master. His name is Khee-Lá," she paused as recognition blossomed in the woman's eyes. "Do you know him?"

"Do you remember when you were seven and a runaway freight ship was going to crash into our section of the city?" Norda questioned. She waited for Akinia's affirming nod before continuing, "The Najee who stopped it was a man named Khee-Lá Juntoby."

"He never left me for very long. He was afraid I would get hurt if he did. He hated having to leave me there, but didn't think it was safe to try and raise me during the war," Akinia explained, nodding.

18

"What of your parents? Who were they?" the headmistress asked.

"My father was a man named Josiah Zanoratta, he crashed on my mother's home planet, Náto, and couldn't remember where he came from. My mother was Queen Leonora Juntoby," Akinia admitted, grinning at the amazed expression on the woman's face.

"You're a princess, then?" she asked in disbelief.

Akinia gave a single nod.

The headmistress laughed. "I raised a young princess all these years and never knew it!"

Akinia laughed with her for a minute before asking, "May I speak to Charlotte?"

"Of course, give me a moment to find her," Norda replied.

Akinia waited patiently while the woman stood and left the room.

Some five minutes later a young girl ran into the office and, panting, stared at the screen.

Akinia stared at her in shock.

Charlotte was now nine years old. She was taller and thinner than she had been before, and her hair hung several inches longer.

"Shar?" Akinia asked in amazement.

"Akinia, what happened to you?" the girl demanded, openly gaping at the scratches on her face.

"I'm fine, just got cut up a bit. How have you been?" Akinia asked.

The girl's face darkened. "I hate it, Kinny. No one likes me and no one wants to adopt me. I think I'm going to be here for the rest of my life," she complained.

"I bet I know why no one likes you," Akinia said, lowering her voice to a whisper as if to convey an important secret.

Charlotte leaned in closer. "Why?" she breathed.

"I think that they don't like you because you're so pretty and so smart. They're jealous of you," Akinia confided, "Try hanging out with older kids."

"I will. Why haven't you contacted me before?" she demanded.

"I wanted to, Shar, I really did, but I couldn't. I still can't explain why, but you have to trust me. Okay?" Akinia asked.

Charlotte nodded slowly. "I still have your blanket," she admitted.

"Good, every time you look at it you'll think about me, and know that I'm thinking about you," she replied, smiling. Her heart wrenched and she wished she could hold little Charlotte in her arms like she used to...

Akinia, come and eat. You have to keep your strength up, Ko-Pau instructed.

Give me a few minutes, she replied.

If I don't see your face in here in ten minutes, I'm sending Nath after you, he warned before ending the contact.

"Can you come and visit me, Kinny?" the girl asked hopefully.

"I don't know. I probably won't be able to for a long time," she admitted.

The girl's face darkened. "Will you at least talk to me more often?" she asked.

"I have to go now, Charlotte. I'll contact you again soon, I promise," Akinia swore.

"Make it very, very soon," the girl begged.

Akinia gave her a quick wink before disconnecting. She stood, leaving the book on the chair, and made her way downstairs. It only took her a few minutes to navigate the familiar hallways between the dining hall and the library.

As she turned the last corner that led to the dining hall, Akinia froze.

Khee-Lá was standing beside Ko-Pau and Nath just outside the doorway.

Akinia looked from one to the other for a moment before turning to walk back the other way.

Nath glanced at the two older men and then ran after her. "Akinia, come back here," he called as he caught up with her.

"I don't want to fight with him again," she stated as she continued to walk.

Nath grabbed her arm and turned her around to face him. "He isn't going to fight with you. He wants to talk to you, make things better between you," he explained.

"I tried that earlier," she snapped.

"Humor me, just come and talk to him," Nath begged.

Akinia rolled her eyes but allowed Nath to lead her back to where the two men stood. She crossed her arms and warily approached her uncle.

"I want to make it clear that I still don't think this is a good idea," Khee-Lá stated firmly, annunciating every syllable to get his point across.

Akinia glared at Nath as she turned and tried to leave again.

Nath grabbed her shoulders and turned her back around. "Be patient," he whispered.

"I don't want to fight with you again," she stated stubbornly, taking a deep breath.

"I don't want to fight with you, either. What happened earlier made me realize that I've been stupid to ignore you, and I am sorry. I still think that this is a bad idea, but I realize now that I have two options," Khee-Lá apologized.

"What options?" Akinia questioned.

"I can either continue to ignore you and make the both of us miserable without changing anything, or I can recognize the fact that none of you are going to change your stubborn minds and just go along with it," he replied.

"I would recommend the second option," she said pointedly, "And you have no right to call anyone stubborn."

He grimaced, knowing she was right, but otherwise didn't respond to her comment. "My thoughts exactly, but the fact is that you're still too weak to go back to the front. I spoke with Hyaline and she said that it would be at least a couple of months before you were strong enough to begin working again, so I thought we could go home," Khee-Lá explained.

Akinia considered that for a moment. "Just you and I, or are Ko-Pau and Nath coming too?" she asked.

"I assumed that the four of us would go. I need Ko-Pau to be there in case Andrid has me removed again. Of course, this time I think he'll have me kicked off of Náto, rather than out of the palace," he replied.

Akinia remembered Ko-Pau telling her that, when Khee-Lá had told Andrid that he had been forbidden to pursue Jade, Andrid had kicked him out of the palace and wouldn't let him back in for a month. "I agree to go so long as you don't harass me about resting, eating, breathing or anything else related to my health or safety," she compromised. She watched her uncle thinking it over, both amused and wary as she saw him debating with himself.

"I reserve the right to 'harass' you if Ko-Pau agrees that you're doing too much, will that satisfy you?" he offered.

Akinia thought it over. Ko-Pau wouldn't bother her unless she really was overdoing it, and if Khee-Lá wouldn't bother her until he did… "Alright, but only if you both agree that I'm overdoing it," she clarified, "And you can't bug him until he relents, either. That's cheating."

Khee-Lá raised his right hand. "I promise."

"Good. Now let's get some dinner, I'm starving," she grinned, walking past them into the dining hall.

"You sit; I'll get your tray," Nath ordered, pointing to their usual table as he walked past her.

Akinia sighed and made her way to the table. There was no point in arguing with Nath; she couldn't win.

Khee-Lá sat down first.

"I'm sorry about earlier," Akinia apologized as she sat down, "I shouldn't have treated you like that."

"I'm sorry that I yelled at you, again. I just worry so much about you," he explained.

"I know," Akinia replied, just as Nath set her tray down in front of her. "Thanks, Nath."

"No problem," he replied as he stuffed a bite of food into his mouth.

Akinia ate quickly.

"So what have you been doing all day?" Ko-Pau asked.

She swallowed and explained, "I was in the library reading for a while, and then I contacted Charlotte."

"It's about time. You know it's been like a year and a half since you talked to that kid you claim to love so much," Nath said pointedly.

"Yeah, yeah, I know. I just couldn't do it before. I don't know why, I just couldn't," she shrugged, "I think maybe I was trying so hard to concentrate on being a good Najee that I didn't want to be reminded of my life before."

"Probably, but you're a natural, so you shouldn't worry about it. I bet she was glad to hear from you," Nath replied.

"Hang on a minute," Ko-Pau ordered, "Who is 'Charlotte'?"

"A little kid Akinia knew back at the orphanage," Nath answered, before she could.

"I just wanted to talk to her for a few minutes. I can't believe how much she's grown," Akinia added.

Ko-Pau nodded, his mouth full of food.

It didn't take long for Akinia and Nath to wolf down their food. Nath offered to walk Akinia back to her room since Ko-Pau didn't want her walking alone after earlier.

"Goodnight," she said as she slipped into her room.

"Goodnight," he replied, but Akinia noticed a strange shadow crossing his eyes as he watched her.

She had seen it many times before when he looked at her, but only since he had found out about her relation to Jade and Lokita. Her lips twisted into a grimace as she closed the door behind her. Nath tried to hide it, she knew, but he had changed since they told him. Their relationship had turned on some invisible axis, and she couldn't pinpoint exactly what the difference was between them.

Had she been wrong to tell Ko-Pau and Khee-Lá to let Nath in on the secret?

There were times, like now, when she wondered if she wouldn't rather him never have known. A part of her just wanted nothing to have changed, but another part was glad that he knew. Could they ever have had a truly trusting relationship if she had kept this from him? Granted, they both still had secrets from one another, but she felt confident that if she asked Nath those same questions about his past that he had refused to answer during her first year in Ko-Pau's care, he would answer them.

Sighing and trying to put the thoughts out of her mind, Akinia quickly changed into her nightgown. "Would you bring me a cup of tea please, Jaynine?" she asked, noticing the droid in her closet.

"Of course, Mistress," he replied, "Would you like some cream in it today? The kitchen has just gotten a fresh shipment of such supplies."

"Do I ever have cream in my tea?" she snapped.

"Of course not, Mistress. My apologies," the droid replied, startled by her reaction.

Akinia sighed and sat down on her bed. "I'm sorry. I've had a long… I was going to say 'day', but I think 'few months' would be more accurate," she apologized, "I know that's no excuse, but I guess I'm just a bit crabby from being stuck here. I hate feeling so useless. I can't even walk down the hallways by myself now because they think I'm going to pass out."

The droid bowed and left the room. He returned several minutes later and, as Jaynine began to complain about the quality of Paméd's dishes, Akinia assumed she was forgiven.

The Najee smiled as she listened to his rant, while he tidied up the room. As Akinia drained the last drop of the dark liquid, she set the cup on the nightstand and slipped between her sheets. Her eyes closed and she fell into a deep sleep.

Chapter 4:

The thick, leafy foliage of Kineston slowly began to materialize out of the darkness. Small, brown shoots sprang up from the misty ground, growing into massive trees within moments of appearing. Wide leaves crawled out of trembling stems, briskly shaking themselves as they settled into their new forms. Small animals formed from the swirling mists that filled the landscape, releasing a cacophony of sounds as they solidified.

Akinia stared around in wonder, her mouth gaping open. There was a deep peace and beauty there. I am safe, she realized, closing her eyes and taking a deep breath as she savored the feeling. Akinia settled at the base of a massive tree, turning her head up to watch the animals playfully chase one another through the branches.

Hours seemed to pass before a violent, screeching cry tore through the forest. Akinia lurched to her feet as the animals tore off through the brush. Her hands instinctively reached for the wajun at her waist, but it wasn't there. She barely had time to comprehend its absence before a pair of arms roughly grabbed her.

"This time, I'll kill you," Jade whispered.

Akinia woke with a start in the middle of the night, her hands gripping the edges of the bed so tightly that her knuckles shown white in the darkness of the room. The dream had been so real, so lifelike. She jerked upright and wrapped her arms around herself, her heart pounding in her chest. One of her hands lurched up to her ear, still able to feel the moist heat of Jade's breath. "Jaynine," she called softly, barely able to keep her voice from shaking.

The droid walked out of the closet. "Yes, Mistress?"

"I need some water, please," she asked.

The droid seemed to sense the urgency of her need; he left faster than usual to fulfill her request.

It was a nightmare, Akinia, she reminded herself, the hairs on the back of her neck standing on end. *It was just a nightmare; get a grip.*

When he returned, she snatched the cup from him and began to sip the cold water gratefully. Her mouth was dry and parched. The cold water helped to calm her heart and lungs. "Thank you," she murmured to the droid as he took the empty cup from her.

"Shall I get the medic?" he asked.

Akinia shook her head. "No, it was just a nightmare," she replied. *Just a nightmare...* As she lay down, her heart rate and breathing gradually slowed back to normal. Eventually she fell back asleep.

Chapter 5:

Akinia woke early the next morning and quickly climbed out of her bed. Her head throbbed and her vision blurred as she stood. Hesitating for a moment to let her head stop spinning, she made her way to the closet and quickly pulled out one of her mother's old dresses. Her shoulders ached, so she didn't bother to do anything to her hair but brush it. She had just finished brushing and was beginning to stretch, when a soft knock came at her door. "Come in."

Nath slipped inside. "How are you this morning?" he asked.

"I... I didn't sleep well," she admitted, sitting down heavily on her bed. "I had nightmares all night."

"About Jade?" he guessed as he sat down beside her. "You know, you can talk to me if you need to."

Akinia gave a doubtful snort. "You have no idea what you're asking for," she sighed dismissively, as she stood up and walked across the room.

"I saw what they did to you," he reminded her.

She laughed. "You didn't come close to seeing what they did to me, Nath. What you saw was only a shadow of what I went through."

A confused expression took root on Nath's face. "I don't understand?"

"I know," Akinia replied quietly. She slipped from the room, leaving Nath to wonder what she meant.

It didn't take her long to find the meditation pond. She quickly settled into a grassy patch of earth near its edge. She smiled as she watched the fish bump the surface of the glassy water, grabbing what delicacies they could pry from the air-filled world above. She watched insects fly low over the surface, leaving thin rippling trails in their wake. A small bird fluttered its wings as it landed on a large rock not far from her.

"Hello, little one," she murmured.

It trilled a light melody in response.

Akinia laughed softly as it fluffed its feathers up and took off, landing a moment later on the other side of the water.

"Interesting, aren't they?" a familiar voice called from the doorway. Lo-Kí smiled as Akinia turned to face him.

"They're beautiful," she agreed.

"You seem to be doing far better," he mused.

"I feel much better, but I'm nowhere near as strong as I was before," she sighed.

Lo-Kí seemed to think about this as he walked over and settled down onto one of the many stone benches set around the edge of the pond. "Do you speak of physical strength, or mental strength?" he queried.

"Physical," she replied immediately. "If anything, my mental strength has grown since my capture."

He nodded slowly, his aged hand shaking slightly as he placed a stray lock of his long white hair behind his ear. "I see," he said quietly.

Akinia bit her lower lip as she debated whether or not to ask Lo-Kí. After a few minutes of silence, she decided to. "Master Lo-Kí," she began, but then paused.

"What is it, child?" he asked encouragingly.

She hesitated another moment before continuing. "Ever since I came back I've noticed that I felt…well… different," she admitted.

"How do you mean?" he asked cautiously, taking in her worried expression.

"I… I almost feel like… like I don't really belong anymore. I'm just kind of distanced from everyone," she explained reluctantly.

Lo-Kí frowned. "Is this because of your new standing among our brethren, as a survivor of Jade's torture? Or is it something else?"

She sighed and broke off a blade of grass, twisting it between her fingers. "I don't know. I guess that's part of it. I mostly sense it when anyone is talking about my… torture. Except for Khee-Lá, it doesn't seem like any of them truly understand what I went through. They talk about it like I was in just another battle or like I was locked up in a cell somewhere and ignored. It's just so…simple to hear them speak of it. And they offer to talk to me about it, but I just can't. They don't know, and they don't understand, and I don't think they'll ever be able to unless they go through it themselves," she explained haltingly,

28

pausing several times as she struggled to find the right words.

Lo-Kí nodded. "It is not uncommon for you to feel such. I know your uncle felt the same way, and he also came to me to speak about it, after he had tried to deal with it in his own manner for a great while. Our brethren do not understand because, as you said, they have no basis for such understanding. Having not gone through it themselves, they cannot imagine the pain involved with it. Even your dear Nath, honorable as his intention may be, is unable to truly help you overcome your pain."

"How is it that it doesn't feel that way when I talk to you? I mean, it seems like you understand," she asked a bit awkwardly.

"I understand because I have experienced what others have not. No, not at Jade's hand. I suffered as a young man, only Ko-Pau's age. At that time we were not at war with Sigadia, but with a long extinct kingdom called Guryn. Sigadia did not exist; it was a part of our Empire. I was a leading force in the war against them, much like yourself, but was captured by youthful folly rather than accidentally being caught in an ambush. It was the Emperor who had me tortured. I still bear the scars," he informed her. He pulled up the ivory sleeve of his long robes to reveal numerous crisscrossing scars across his wrinkled forearm.

Akinia stared at them in amazement. "How did you escape?" she asked softly.

"The Nrell heard of my capture and, when all other attempts at rescue failed, they emerged from their world and rescued me. It was during that rescue that the Najee joined the fight and one of them, the Master of Masters at the time, killed the Emperor. Which, of course, effectively ended the war. It was by no means immediately over, but that was the beginning of the end," he sighed, pulling his sleeve back down.

Akinia's eyes widened as he spoke of the Nrell and she glanced quickly at his right hand, but both his hands were gloved. Her gaze then lowered to her own hand, which was tightly clenched to conceal the mark that the Nrell had given her.

Lo-Kí raised one eyebrow, but didn't comment.

"I had better be going," Akinia said quickly, "They'll be waiting for me for breakfast." She quickly stood and rushed from the pond. Did Lo-Kí suspect? But certainly he couldn't see the mark, not unless he had one himself... But that was crazy. If Lo-Kí had the mark he would have seen hers before now, wouldn't he? She shook her head to clear it and then laughed at herself for letting her mind jump to these conclusions.

"Good morning," Khee-Lá said pleasantly as she sat next to him in the dining hall. He seemed uncomfortable, as though he still felt guilty about how he had treated her.

Good, Akinia thought snobbishly. She knew it was wrong, but she felt glad that he was beating himself up so badly over it; she had certainly lost more than one night's sleep, herself. "Good morning, Uncle."

Ko-Pau joined them a moment later. "Have you decided when we're leaving yet? I have to let Lo-Kí know," he asked as he sat.

"Hyaline says that Akinia is strong enough to safely travel now, but that she'd rather we wait at least until the end of the week so she can continue to monitor her. Also she wants to get Akinia's file together for the medic on Náto, just in case she were to take a turn for the worst while we're there," he reported.

"So, the end of the week?" Ko-Pau inquired.

Khee-Lá nodded. "If Akinia has no objections…"

"Sounds fine to me," she shrugged. She was eager to see Náto, especially her mother's old home, but she tried to keep a nonchalant attitude.

Nath sat down a moment later. "What sounds fine to you?" he asked.

"We're leaving at the end of the week," she replied, taking another large mouthful of food.

"Cool. It'll be nice to get off this rock," he griped as he began shoveling food into his mouth.

Akinia laughed.

Ko-Pau and Khee-Lá were heartened by the delicate sound.

She hadn't laughed much since her captivity; it hurt too much when she did. Anymore, a quick smile was all they had been able to drag from her.

The Najee were disappointed again when her laughter rescinded into a pained grimace.

Her hand automatically leapt up to the side of her head and she began massaging her forehead.

"Are you still hurting?" Nath demanded, turning slightly to face her.

"I'm fine," she protested, wondering how he had found out. She had told him about her nightmares, but she hadn't said anything about a headache.

"What do you mean, still hurting?" Khee-Lá demanded, anxiously looking Akinia over.

"She had nightmares last night or something and woke up with a headache. She sent Jaynine to the kitchen for a glass of water and then chugged it. The droid said she'd been tossing and turning all night and her head still hurt this morning," Nath reported, edging away from Akinia, and the blow he knew he would receive for telling.

"What, so now you're using my own droid as an informant against me? I'm fine!" she snapped angrily, realizing how he knew. She stood and stormed out of the dining hall, ignoring the three Najee's orders for her to return. Angry tears pricked the corners of her eyes as she stomped down the hallways and up to the library. She passed several Masters who asked her how she was feeling, but she only muttered, "Fine."

Akinia hesitated as she stepped from the lift-chamber, debating on where she wanted to go. A moment later she decided. She had only been to Master Tanlaish's hidden office once, but in her rage she managed to find it as though she visited it every day. She knocked on the hidden door, felt Tanlaish's touch against her mind, and then watched as the door slid open.

"Hello, dear," the old woman welcomed as Akinia walked inside.

She sat on one of the chairs. "Hello, Master Tanlaish."

The woman considered her for a moment. "You've not come to tell me you've opened the box, I suppose?" she mused. Tanlaish had given Akinia a small metal box with a secret combination, in the hope that the young girl could crack the code that her old mind couldn't grasp.

"No… I just needed to get away for a little while," she admitted. Akinia had been working at the box for a while, especially while she was unable to leave her bed, but had still yet to figure out the combination. She reached up and began to massage her head, which had begun to pound fiercely.

"Are you alright, child?" Tanlaish asked.

"I think so. I've had a headache all morning, but that's just because I didn't sleep well last night. Nath managed to get my droid to

31

spy on me and report back to him somehow. Now Khee-Lá thinks I'm sick again, but I'm not!" Akinia was protesting by the end of her explanation.

Tanlaish laughed. "Be grateful you have people so concerned for your safety, young one. A great many of us are alone here, even young apprentices such as yourself. There are a great many Masters who wouldn't care if their apprentice had a broken leg, they would expect the poor child to get to work as soon as it was set," she advised. She put a stack of papers into a folder and carried it across the room to a small locker.

"There has to be a balance in there somewhere, though," she argued.

Tanlaish shut the cabinet and turned to face the young girl. "You went through an ordeal that would have killed most Najee. It quite nearly killed you. I can't name another, barring your dear uncle, who could have survived something like that. They have a good reason to be a bit overprotective of you right now," she admonished.

Akinia ducked her head; she knew the older woman was right. "I just wish they wouldn't be so touchy about every little thing. It's been getting on my nerves. They won't even let me walk around by myself. I managed to escape a few minutes ago," she muttered.

"I know, love," Tanlaish comforted, her voice and eyes much softer now, "but they only care about your well-being. You are too important to take risks with."

Akinia crossed her arms loosely. "Everyone keeps saying that. Sometimes I can't help but wonder if being the Child of the Prophecy is the only reason they worry so much about me," she admitted.

"Nonsense. Your Master and your uncle, and Nath all care a great deal about you. Even if the prophecy were not in existence you would still be a cherished Najee," the older woman corrected.

Akinia smiled weakly. She knew Tanlaish was right, but that didn't stop the thoughts from entering her mind. "I should apologize to them, shouldn't I?"

"That is, of course, up to you. But I should think that it sounds like a good idea," she smiled.

Akinia stood slowly. "Thank you," she murmured, leaving. She knew Tanlaish was right, and that she should apologize, but she wasn't going to go back now.

Pulling a book off of a shelf she passed, Akinia settled into one of the chairs. She had been reading for nearly two hours when her eyes began to sting. Headaches were bad enough, but ones that interfered with how long she could read were even worse. Sighing, she placed the book back on the shelf and made her way back downstairs.

She jumped, her hand automatically leaping to her heart as she opened her bedroom door to find Nath waiting for her. "Don't do that!" she snapped.

"I'm sorry, about everything," he apologized.

"No you aren't," she laughed, rolling her eyes. "You're only sorry I got mad at you." When Nath didn't respond, Akinia knew she had gotten it right. "So anyway, I'm sorry I yelled at you."

"No big deal. I guess I deserved it," he grinned.

"You know you deserved it, getting Jaynine to spy on me," she said pointedly, crossing her arms.

"Chatterbox came to me the first time," Nath defended.

"I don't even want to know how long the droid has been spying on me. I just want to put it behind us, and for you quit listening to him and telling Master and Khee-Lá," she sighed, flopping down on her bed.

"Are you alright?" he asked, perplexed.

"Yeah, I'm fine. I'm just bored. I hate being stuck here, and now Master won't even let me work on my control exercises because I'm too weak," she griped.

"Yeah, well, we'll be at your palace soon enough," he shrugged.

She frowned as she noticed his expression change again; it became clouded and guarded. "I still can't believe that I'm a princess, and that my mom was a queen," she whispered.

"Yeah, well, it's true, Princess, and you'd better get used to it. I'd be willing to bet that you become the center of everyone's attention for the next year or so. You're probably going to have to get another ship just to drag all of their presents home with you. Your mom was the greatest ruler they've had in generations, I hear," Nath warned with a laugh.

"And everyone but me got to meet her," she sighed.

"From what I hear, every other word out of Khee-Lá's mouth when you aren't around is that you're just like her, looks and all. And I'm certain that you'll be pelted with stories and stuff," Nath shrugged.

"Yeah, well, it isn't the same, is it? I mean, someone could come up to you right now and tell you who your dad was, and tell you a million stories about him, but that doesn't take the place of knowing him, does it?" she replied pointedly.

Nath looked away. "I don't care who he is. I don't want anything to do with him even if I did find out who he is," he said slowly.

"At least you have a mom, and sisters. I have a king uncle and queen aunt I've never met, a Najee uncle, an ex-Najee uncle who wants me dead, and a twin sister who was supposed to be a Najee who wants me dead," she laughed.

"And don't forget you have seven cousins, too," he reminded her.

"That I've never met, either," she added.

"Still, you have a great family," he shrugged.

"Did you miss the part about an uncle and a twin sister who want me dead?" she asked pointedly.

"Every family has their little issues," he reminded her, laughing.

"Little issues," she echoed, a distant look growing in her eyes as she remembered the weeks of torture that she had suffered at their hands.

"Snap out of it. You know what Master said; you aren't supposed to think about it," Nath ordered, crossing his arms.

Akinia smiled. "Sometimes I think you know me better than I do," she laughed.

"It isn't that hard to know what you're thinking about when you get depressed like that. There isn't much that upsets you," he explained, grinning. "Why don't you go see what Major Skyler is up to? I've got stuff to do before lunch."

"Alright," she shrugged. She liked talking to Skyler.

"Oh, and your cub is in my room again, sleeping on my bed. Would you mind getting her off before my pillow gets covered in drool, again?" he grumbled as he stood up and opened the door.

"She wouldn't sleep on your bed if you didn't invite her in your room every time you think I'm not around. And the scraps from your plate aren't helping your anti-Rofa policy much, either," Akinia said pointedly.

"Maybe if you fed her more she wouldn't come begging me for scraps," he muttered.

"I feed her plenty, Nath. You just like her and don't want to admit it," Akinia laughed. She brushed past him into the hallway and made her way three doors down to his room. "Come on, Rofa, Nath doesn't want you in here right now," she called in.

The cub huffed and rose up onto her three legs. Her two muscular hind legs were much more developed than they had been when Akinia first rescued the orphaned cub several weeks before her capture. The front leg, set into the middle of the cub's chest, was nowhere near as powerful, since the cub ran only on her hind legs. Already her back was level with Akinia's waist, and there were no signs that she was anywhere near being done growing.

"Let's go see Major Skyler," she suggested, grinning as the cub began to bounce excitedly beside her. She wondered if she should put Rofa's leash on her to keep her from running Skyler down, but then decided that the cub would listen to her well enough… she hoped.

Chapter 6:

"I'm not kiddin', Commander. There's nothin' for you to do," Skyler insisted again.

"Yeah right. There's always something to do," she stated impatiently, crossing her arms.

Skyler sighed. "Look, Commander, I'd love to put ya to work, but if I do I'm gonna get it bad from Ko-Pau and Khee-Lá. They told me I wasn't to let you do anythin'. If they find out that I told you that..." he let his voice drift into silence.

Akinia growled, annoyed, and flopped into one of the chairs in the navigation area of the small TX762 cruiser.

"They're just tryin' to keep you from gettin' worse. You've gotta get well before they'll let you do anythin'," Skyler explained.

"I know," she sighed, "but this is getting ridiculous."

"Just bear with 'em, Commander. They're just worried about ya. They'll get bored with you the next time Commander Nath gets himself into a mess. That shouldn't be too far off," he laughed.

"That's true," she agreed, scratching Rofa's head.

"And after ya get done visitin' your family we'll be back to work. There's plenty of the war to last us," he sighed.

Akinia turned her gaze away as she was reminded again of her relation to Jade. Skyler didn't know... none of her men did. How could she possibly tell them that it was her uncle killing them off one by one? How could she tell them that it was her twin sister who was assassinating Najee left and right? No, none of them could find out. The only ones who could know about this were the ones who already did: Khee-Lá, Ko-Pau, Nath, and Lo-Kí.

"Fine," she sighed, "Can you at least tell me how everything's going?"

"Sure can. Everythin' is 'bout ready. We'll be able to leave by tomorrow mornin'," he reported.

"Alright, don't work everybody too hard. We still have a week, you know," she laughed. Skyler hated leaving things until the last minute, and everyone knew it.

"Commander," Skyler called as she turned to walk away, "I really am sorry, but orders are orders."

She smiled. "I know." She left Skyler to finish up checking the computers.

Rofa tagged along happily at her side.

"Come on, girl, let's go find someone we can bother. Maybe Master will be wandering around here somewhere," she suggested.

The cub enthusiastically began searching around her, as though she had understood her mistress's words. Even so, it was Akinia who spotted Ko-Pau walking down the hallway in front of them.

"Master," she called, darting to catch up with him.

"Stop running Akinia, or I'll let Hyaline lock you in your room," he threatened, stopping to wait for her. "What did you need?"

"Nothing, really, I just was wondering what you were doing," she shrugged.

"I'm trying to get some things taken care of before our journey," he replied, walking again.

"Can I come with you, or am I not allowed to do that either?" she asked pointedly, crossing her arms.

Ko-Pau grimaced. "You went to see Skyler, didn't you?"

"Yes, and he wouldn't let me do anything. Something is up. He always tries to hide what work needs to be done, but this is the first time I've ordered him to tell me what needs to be done that he's still told me there wasn't anything, despite the fact that preparations have just begun. Was it you or Khee-Lá that ordered him not to let me help?" she demanded.

Ko-Pau sighed. "It was Khee-Lá, but Nath agrees as well, and Hyaline insisted on it. I think you should be allowed to do some tech work, but Hyaline and Khee-Lá won't hear of it. Just humor them, please. We're all finally getting along again and I'd like to keep it that way. Oh, by the way, Laani and Master Junop just arrived. Why don't you go visit with her for a while?"

"Alright, I'll see you later," she agreed. "Come on Rofa." Without another word she and the cub veered into the hallway to their right. She extended her mind, carefully avoiding touching Khee-Lá or Ko-Pau's minds, and quickly found Laani in the Dining Hall.

38

Akinia! Laani gasped.

I'm not supposed to be extending, I'll come to you, Akinia replied quickly.

Alright, but hurry, I've missed you!

Akinia laughed. *I'm coming, I'm coming,* she replied teasingly just before severing the contact. She shook her head to clear it as her vision blurred slightly. "What's the matter with me, Rofa?" she murmured, so quietly that she could barely hear herself. She wound her fingers into the thick hair between Rofa's shoulder blades. She leaned against her pet for support, hoping the dizziness would pass soon. If Khee-Lá or Hyaline saw this, she was going to be put back to bed for another few weeks, and she did *not* want that to happen.

She extended her mind slightly to touch her cub's mind, curious why Rofa had a puzzled expression on her face. A smile crossed her face as she realized the cub was concerned about her. *It's alright, Rofa, I'm fine, just a bit tired,* she promised reassuringly, not entirely certain the cub believed her. *Why don't you go and bug Nath? I bet he misses you.* she suggested.

Rofa enthusiastically agreed.

With the cub vanishing around the corner, Akinia finally pulled her mind back into itself as she approached the Dining Hall.

"Akinia!" Laani called excitedly as she saw her friend enter.

"Laani!" Akinia called back with a grin, running to embrace her.

"I was so worried when I found out what had happened!" Laani gushed, concern flooding her voice. "Are you okay? How are you doing? How bad were you hurt? No one would tell me anything! Don't you ever do anything like that again! I was so worried I couldn't sleep most nights. I'm never going to be able to relax when we're on separate missions again!" She pulled Akinia into a tight hug.

"Akinia!" a harsh voice snapped from just behind the Adamian girl.

Akinia rolled her eyes. "The warden's back," she whispered to Laani before turning. "Nath, how are you, my dear friend?" she asked, sweetly.

"Don't you 'dear friend' me, Akinia, you know perfectly well you aren't allowed to run. Give me one reason why I shouldn't tell Master and Khee-Lá?" he demanded, crossing his arms and glaring at her.

39

"Because I will make your life miserable if you do," she threatened in an all-too-innocent voice, an angelic smile on her face.

He snorted, shaking his head. "Good enough," he relented. "Hey Laani," he greeted, giving her a lopsided grin.

The Lyndop girl grinned back and walked over to him. "Hey, handsome, how've you been holding up?" she asked, hugging him.

"Well, you know, Akinia's been making life miserable, but I've been pushing through well enough," he teased, flinching when Akinia hit him.

"What he means is that he's been making a pain out of himself and he's lucky I haven't killed him yet," Akinia corrected.

"Why am I more inclined to believe Akinia's version?" Laani wondered aloud.

"Because you're both against me," Nath sighed, acting dejected. "Hey!" he complained when they both hit his arms. "You see what I mean?" he demanded pointedly, rubbing his arms theatrically, though he could barely feel where Akinia had hit him.

"Don't be such a baby, Nath," a young Núnto apprentice around Nath's age teased as he walked over. "You'd think you'd enjoy the fact that girls are hitting on you for once."

"Shut up, Keer," Nath snapped, rolling his eyes.

"Hey, Keer, long time no see," Laani grinned.

"Hey Laani," the boy grinned.

Akinia regarded him curiously for a moment. Keer was tall, perhaps an inch or two shorter than Nath. He was also built very thinly, almost like he had been stretched, and his arms were a bit too long in proportion to his body. His features did not have the same maturity Nath's did, seeming a bit young in comparison to her co-apprentice, and were partially hidden by his long hair. Keer's hair was around the same length as Nath's, but unlike Nath, Keer let his hang free. So much of it was brushed into his face that Akinia wondered if it was deliberate. He grinned at her, revealing a dimple in his left cheek.

"Akinia, this is Keer. He isn't half as cool as he thinks he is, but he's a pretty fun guy to hang out with if you can shrink his ego a bit," Nath introduced, grinning.

"So he's a lot like you?" Akinia asked innocently.

Laani tried to smother her laughter with her hand, but couldn't entirely hide it.

Nath grinned and gently shoved Akinia's head to the side.

40

"Nah, he just wishes he was more like me," he teased.

Keer rolled his eyes. "Yeah, okay, Nath, whatever you say," he agreed in a patronizing tone. "The only time anyone ever wanted to be Nath was when Ko-Pau showed up with you," he admitted to Akinia, grinning.

"And this suddenly got very strange so Laani and I are going to go catch up while you two stay here," Akinia decided, grabbing Laani's hand and dragging her away. Once they were out of the Dining Hall Akinia whispered, "Is he always like that?"

"Aren't all guys their age? Except Nath, I mean," Laani replied, laughing.

"True," Akinia consented. "So where should we go? We can't spar, so that's out of the question. I'm not supposed to leave the main base area, so walking outside is out of the question…"

"We could go to the meditation courtyard? The one with the pond you like so well?" Laani suggested.

"Sounds great," Akinia agreed. "So what have you and Master Junop been up to these last few months?"

"Nothing special, just the usual run on the front," she shrugged. "For about two months I was dating a Lyndop Full Najee, Jesdin Gare, but then I found out he was also dating a girl from his home world, so I broke up with him. I still don't understand why Najee date and marry non-Najee. I mean, seriously, we're going to live like at least three times as long as any normal people, so why expose yourself to that heartache? I will only ever date or marry a Najee, personally."

Akinia smiled. "Yeah, that sounds like a good idea," she agreed. "I still don't understand why the lives of Najee are so extended."

"Some of the Masters think it's because when we extend our minds we're unifying a bit more with the energy of the universe and it's enough to slow the process of death," she shrugged. "I don't know, personally, and I also don't care. That's the way it is, and I'm just going to accept it and go on with life."

Akinia grinned. "That's all we can do anyway, right?" she pointed out.

"Exactly," Laani agreed. "So tell me absolutely everything that has happened to you since the last time we saw each other."

"There's really nothing to tell," she hedged, "Lokita caught my fighter in a tractor beam, brought me to Jade, he tried to get me to join him, and when I wouldn't he had me tortured until I would agree to fight for him, but I would never agree to that. Khee-Lá, Ko-Pau, and Nath broke into Jade's base, brought me out, and Hyaline has been driving me crazy ever since," she shrugged, her gaze shifting to the ground as she tried not to remember any of the details of her captivity.

Laani was dying to know more, but sensed Akinia's reluctance to speak about what had happened. She put a hand on Akinia's shoulder in a comforting manner before asking, "How are you feeling?"

"Better, but I'm weak," she sighed. "And I'm losing control of my powers."

"Losing control?"

Akinia sighed. "Yeah, I keep getting these *bursts* of power and flinging whatever I pick up. I've been banned from extending until I get well again," she explained, making a face.

Laani laughed. "Well that explains Nath, then. I had wondered…"

"Wondered what?" Akinia asked cautiously.

"You know what," she replied with a wink. "Tell me all."

"There's nothing to tell. There's not!" she exclaimed when Laani scoffed. "We're just friends; that's all. Nothing more or less between us than there was the last time we saw you. I promise."

Laani pursed her lips, disappointed. "It's a shame; he's a great guy," she mused.

"Yeah, well, you're welcome to him," she sighed with a smirk. "It's all I can do to survive him as a co-apprentice!"

Laani smiled and shook her head in amusement, but otherwise didn't comment.

"How have you been?" Akinia asked in an undertone, the thought of Laani and Nath's relationship reminding her of Laani's struggle with depression. How had she been handling these last months?

"Not here," Laani answered quickly, glancing around the fairly crowded hallway. "Come," she beckoned, taking Akinia's hand and leading her down a series of turns in the hallways. Finally, they stopped outside of a small door. Laani opened it and motioned for Akinia to enter.

Akinia was surprised to find a much neglected yard, one whose ancient walls were broken and collapsed in some areas. The grasses, covering so much of Paméd, had completely overrun it. The stone benches were worn by time and weather, and now had the appearance of crude, flat-topped arches. "What is this place?"

42

"In ancient times, before Lo-Kí, even, this was one of the training fields. After the orders to move apprentice training to the fields in view of the Master of Master's study, this field was soon neglected. No one lives in this part of the base anymore, so it was completely abandoned. I like to come here to think and be alone," she explained, lovingly fingering one of the benches. "I never cleaned it because I prefer it like this: wild and free."

Akinia looked again with new eyes, trying to see the beauty her friend saw in the rugged, untamed ruins. After a moment, she *did* understand better what Laani saw. There was a sense of mystery in this ancient place. The overwhelming stillness and silence, so unusual on Paméd, lowered her voice to a hushed whisper and caused her breath to catch in her chest, afraid of disturbing what ancient things lay here.

"Imagine who all must have trained here," Akinia marveled. "It was in use when the Nrell were still among us."

"Could you imagine watching them fight?" Laani sighed. "They are said to be the most beautiful beings; lightning fast and the fiercest warriors in existence!"

"They are very beautiful. Their skin is the palest shade of white, and their eyes are darker than the blackest black you have ever seen. And their hair is so thin and light, it's all but transparent!" Akinia related.

Laani frowned. "How do you know that?"

Silently cursing herself for her loose lips, Akinia quickly covered, "I've seen pictures of them in books. I was very taken with them when I was younger."

"Sounds like you still are," she teased.

"A bit," Akinia relented, smiling. "Now, how are you?" She sat on one of the benches and motioned for Laani to join her.

"It's been hard," she admitted, sitting down. "Master helped me a lot, because I was reluctant to talk to Nath about it. I was terrified for you, and strangely enough, that let me keep my head better than usual. I managed to keep the depression off until just before they left to rescue you, and it wasn't as strong of a fit as usual. Either I'm getting better or mind-numbing fear is good to keep me thinking clearly."

"I hope you're getting better. We're good friends, but if *that's* what it takes to make you afraid enough not to be depressed, I'm going to do my best *not* to help," Akinia mused teasingly.

"Good friends? I thought we were best friends," Laani pouted

43

teasingly.

"Best friends, then," Akinia laughed, "But I'm still not getting captured every time you get depressed!"

Laani pretended to be shocked. "And you call yourself my best friend?" she gasped.

Akinia stuck her tongue out and crossed her eyes. "So how long are you here for?"

"Not long," she sighed, "Master just needed to rest for a few days and order more men to supplement our squadrons. We took heavy losses in the last skirmish. I lost three of my main troop."

Akinia's jaw dropped open in shock. She couldn't imagine losing any of her main troop! "I'm so sorry, Laani," she gasped.

Her friend smiled, but her lips and face were tense. "I'm okay," she promised, in what would have been a convincing tone if her face hadn't betrayed her. "I talked to Nath and he calmed me down before I could get too upset. So how long until they let you out?"

Akinia rolled her eyes. "I get to go home in a week, spend a while there, but they're still talking about waiting several *months* before letting me get back to work!"

"They *do* have good reason," she reminded her. "Besides, they always give you the hardest assignments. I can understand them wanting to wait until you're at full strength again. Seriously, look at yourself; I can hardly believe you're able to walk right now."

"Yeah, yeah, I know," she sighed. In an attempt to change the subject, she asked, "So why did you want to talk here instead of in the hall? I was expecting something really bad from the way you were acting back there."

"Oh, that," Laani grimaced. "Not many people know about my… disability… and I want to keep it that way. Some of the Council Elders, well, they would never rest until I was forbidden from working the front if they found out about it. They aren't all as nice as Master Lo-Kí."

Akinia gave a grim bark of laughter. "I bet they're the same ones that tried to convince them to lock me up here for the next decade."

"Probably."

They fell into a comfortable silence, each drifting into her own thoughts. Both were thinking about getting back to work, but Akinia was thinking mostly of the next time she would face her uncle and sister. Would she be able to hold her own, or were Khee-Lá and the other Masters right?

A part of her wanted so badly to tell Laani, to confide in her friend the truth about her lineage, but how could she? No, as much as she trusted Laani, she could never tell her the truth. Or could she? Would Laani be accepting and loyal to their friendship, or would the information destroy their relationship forever? She sighed and rubbed her forehead with the tips of her fingers.

"Are you alright?" Laani asked, concerned.

Akinia nodded. "Yeah, I'm just… I'm fine," she promised, forcing herself to smile.

"Maybe I should get you back to your room? I'm not supposed to be tiring you out, right?" Laani suggested, concerned. Without waiting for her friend to answer, she stood and pulled Akinia to her feet, wrapping an arm around her shoulders for support.

"I'm fine, really," Akinia protested.

"Sorry, not buying it. You are going to go and rest, and then later we'll talk some more," Laani ordered, gently pulling on her to get her moving.

"And if I disagree?"

"It would be pointless," Laani shrugged, before grinning and adding, "I'd just get your Master."

"That's cheating!" she protested, crossing her arms and allowing herself to be led back through the maze of hallways.

They were nearly to her room when they heard Nath frantically call, "Akinia!" He darted up the hallway towards them and touched her cheek, checking for fever. Turning to Laani, he demanded, "Is she alright? What happened?"

"Hey, relax," Akinia ordered calmly, drawing his attention back to her. "I'm fine, you are all just way too overprotective. I started to get a headache, no dizziness, nothing, but Laani noticed and ordered me back to my room."

"Come on," Nath ordered, wrapping his own arm around Akinia's shoulders, half-leading and half-carrying her into her room.

Laani released her hold on Akinia as Nath took over. She stepped back, watching them with interest.

"Really, I'm fine. I can walk on my own," Akinia protested, but Nath didn't seem to hear her.

He reached out with his mind as they entered and turned down

45

the blankets on her bed. "Lay down and rest, or I'll get Khee-Lá," he threatened.

Akinia sighed and slipped her feet out of her shoes. "Are you going to tuck me in and read me a bedtime story?" she asked in a baby voice, batting her eyelashes as she sat down.

"I'll tuck you in, but I don't do bedtime stories," he laughed. "Now lay down."

Sighing again, she pulled her legs up onto the bed and laid back on her pillow. "Are you satisfied?" she asked, glaring at them both.

"We'll check on you later," Laani promised from the doorway, where she stood with her arms crossed.

Nath pulled her blankets over top of her, making a point of tucking them up around her chin. "Sleep well, Kiddo," he grinned, turning to leave. He hesitated in the doorway and added, "By the way, I wouldn't recommend trying to leave, because I'll be watching you."

Akinia stuck her tongue out at him, annoyed at them both. "I'll get you for this someday, you know I will," she threatened.

Nath grimaced. "Yeah, I know," he sighed as they left, closing the door behind them.

She settled in to a more comfortable position and closed her eyes. *One of these days...*she griped to herself before falling asleep, contemplating *exactly* how she would get her revenge on them.

Chapter 7:

It had been two days since they left Paméd. Today they would arrive on Náto and, for the first time, Akinia would see her home world. She spent more time dressing than usual, taking special care to make certain her dress sat correctly. She felt the ship shudder as they came out of hyper-space, and took it as her cue to join the others.

"You look nice," Khee-Lá complimented as she finally emerged from the changing room. He was examining stats on several small monitors.

Akinia tried to smile, but her nerves turned it into a grimace. She approached the windows on the port side of the ship. "Thanks," she managed, taking several slow, deep breaths as she looked at the small planet.

She had looked forward to returning home for so long, so why did she suddenly feel as nervous as she had when she was leaving the orphanage? A lump rose in her throat as she gazed out the viewing panel at the beautiful green planet beneath her. White clouds swirled over its surface, and large blue patches interrupted the delicate green of the foliage-covered earth.

Khee-Lá seemed to sense her apprehension, even from the other side of the command center. He walked over and squeezed her shoulders. "Don't be scared," he whispered.

"I'm not scared. I'm just… worried," she replied, sighing.

"You don't have anything to worry about," he reminded her.

"I've not seen these people since I was a baby. I don't know them, I don't know what they're like. For all I know, they'll kick you out and then spend my entire visit comparing me to my mother," she complained.

"And there is nothing wrong with being compared to your mother. Leonora was…"

"I know, I know, she was 'the kindest queen in our history, and the most beloved by our people'. You've told me a million times," she interrupted.

"Hey, Princess, you busy?" Nath called from the other side of the small ship.

"No, what do you need?" she replied, moving quickly towards him before Khee-Lá could draw her back into conversation.

"I don't need anything, just wondering if maybe you could remind me why we're spending the next few weeks in a palace?" he complained, tugging at the tight collar of his shirt.

"That looks like the same shirt you wore to lunch with Alania our first day on the Capitol Planet," she said accusingly. She slapped his hand away and then straightened his shirt collar, fixing the button that had made it only halfway through the hole.

"Thanks, and it is," he sighed.

"Did you try to braid your hair?" she demanded, glancing at the tangled mess laying down his back.

"Why? Did I mess it up bad?" he grimaced.

She rolled her eyes. "Turn around," she ordered. She quickly began trying to untangle the mess. "Well, if you'd hold still I wouldn't be pulling it so much," she chastised as Nath pulled away from her, complaining that she had pulled his hair.

He crossed his arms and sighed before allowing her to continue. "Last time I try to braid it," he grumbled.

"Good. Next time just come to me," Akinia ordered as she continued to try and untangle his hair. Once she got it undone, she quickly plaited it and then fastened it with the elastic band she had pulled from somewhere in the middle of the mess. "There, all done."

"Thanks," he said reluctantly. He grinned at her. "I'm surprised you haven't got your hair all done up fancy. I mean, you *are* supposed to be a pampered palace brat now."

"Watch it, boy," Khee-Lá said, laughing.

Nath turned crimson. He'd forgotten that his grandmaster had been raised a 'pampered palace brat'.

"Having not lived in a palace since I was a baby, I can hardly be a palace anything. I've been working hard my entire life, so that cuts out pampered. And I am not a brat, Nathaniel," she pointed out, crossing her arms.

"She's got you there," Ko-Pau called, laughing. "Strap

yourselves in, we're entering the atmosphere."

They landed a few minutes later. Khee-Lá had to get up to speak with the atmospheric guard, to explain who he was so that they could get through. "Alright, you two get the ship settled in, I'll take Akinia up to the palace," he decided.

"Don't you think she ought to wear her cloak if you're planning on walking through the city to get there?" Ko-Pau said pointedly, crossing his arms.

"Yes, I suppose you are right. We wouldn't want the people running around, terrified that they were seeing Leonora's ghost, would we?" he agreed, chuckling softly.

Akinia darted down the hallway to her small room and pulled out her black cloak. She fastened it around herself and lifted the hood to where it mostly blocked her face. "Better?" she asked, returning to the main area beside the door to the outside.

"Perfect, now come. We should get out of here before the workers come to move the ship," Khee-Lá said quickly.

"We'll see you soon, we just have to do some paperwork," Ko-Pau promised.

"Just remember to keep your hood up," Nath called, stopping himself as he reached to tug at his collar again.

"Alright," Akinia said in a blanket response. She quickly darted after Khee-Lá, who had already stepped outside. Her jaw dropped in amazement as she gazed around at the city. The buildings were elegant and regal; the simple, curving architecture displaying timeless beauty. "I've never seen anything like it," she said, delighted.

Khee-Lá smiled. "Yes, you have; it was just a very long time ago," he corrected. "Come on, we should get moving."

Though her uncle tried to hurry her along, Akinia found herself stopping every few yards, looking at the wares that the shopkeepers had out on little stands in front of their stores. There were some with displays of jewelry, others with clothes, still others with mounds of books stacked both outside and just inside the doorways of the shops.

Khee-Lá snatched something from one of the jewelry stands and tossed a couple of coins to the shopkeeper. He looked it over a moment before nodding in satisfaction.

"What is that?" Akinia asked, motioning to the trinket.

"A gift to help me apologize for behaving like a fool," Khee-Lá sighed.

"Surely they won't be too mad at you? I mean, you were acting on orders and trying your best to keep us all alive," she protested, again.

Khee-Lá smiled. "I was not referring to them, and they are quite capable of growing angry with me. Not everyone has your gift of serenity, Sweetheart," he laughed, guiding her farther up the path. "No, I got this for you." He stopped walking and turned to her. "I'm sorry I was so irritable, and that I wasn't around until recently. I know that you understand why that was, but that doesn't make it right. I hope that you'll forgive me," he asked, proffering the trinket.

"We've already gone over this, Uncle. I'm not mad at you," she protested.

Khee-Lá shook his head, laughing. "So much like your mother..." he muttered. He took her hand and pressed the trinket into it, folding her fingers overtop of it. "Take it, please," he asked, pushing her closed fist back towards her.

"Alright, but you've got to quit apologizing for it. I know you were upset, just let it go," she admonished with a soft smile. She opened her hand to reveal a slender bracelet. Three small charms hung from it, each a strange symbol she did not recognize and each carved from a precious gem. "What are these?" she asked, fingering the charms.

Khee-Lá took it from her and fastened it onto her wrist. He then placed his hand on her back and guided her farther up the path. "Well, as legend goes, in the beginning of the Nátoan people, when only a handful inhabited this planet, a young man named Veron set out to discover what lay past the horizon. No one would go with him, terrified as they were of the monsters they heard howling at night, so one morning he set off alone. By nightfall he had walked so far that the Nátoan settlement was no longer in sight. He debated on whether to make camp or try to keep moving. That's when he heard the monsters howling again. Now, he had reached a place on Náto where ancient trees grow tall, hugging the sky as well as the earth. He found a low branch and pulled himself up into the tree, trying to escape the vicious monsters.

"That is when he realized that the monsters were howling from above him. He leapt to the ground, breathing heavily with fright before realizing that it was merely the wind howling through the branches. He relaxed and began to laugh at himself for being so frightened of the wind. Suddenly, there were several dark-clothed figures on all sides of him. They spoke with a strange, raspy voice in a strange tongue that made the hair on his neck stand on end. They began to move closer to him, and he knew he was going to die. He saw a long, thick branch lying on the ground at his feet. He picked it up and swung it around, viciously attacking the figures until he drove them off. He sat with his back to the tree trunk and his hands wrapped around his faithful staff all night long. He fell asleep shortly before the dawn. When he woke, he saw this symbol burned into the tree above his head," he paused as he fingered the first charm, "It was a symbol that had not been there the night previous. In fact, the tree was still smoking when he saw it. He called it 'courage', for it was the skill he had been forced to call upon, and he carved it into his staff.

"Three days passed with no special events or sightings of the strangers. And then, with the dawn of the fourth day, he saw more of them. They carried strange weapons, carved staffs with blades at each end, and stood in a line guarding what seemed to be the only pass through the tall ridge mountain that ran from horizon to horizon blocking his path. Veron was frightened of them. He traveled, well-hidden in the brush, up and down the line of rocks; one day down, one day back, and one day up, before returning to the pass. The wall was impenetrable everywhere else. His heart was torn. He wanted to continue on his mission and discover what else lay on the planet, but he was frightened that the creatures would kill him. Then he came up with a plan.

"He scouted around some more until he found what he was looking for, a small cave barely large enough for him to crawl into, which was blocked from sight by several thick bushes. He cut limbs from them. These he set back in front of the entrance to block it again from sight. Satisfied that they would work, he laid them down to where all he would have to do is jump into the cave and pick them up, and then they would be in place. So he hid his staff among the bushed near the pass and then showed himself to the cloaked figures, who began to scream and shake their weapons at him. He called them forwards, provoking them by drawing closer and darting back until they all began to chase him in anger. He led them around for several minutes, careful to let them get close, but not too close, before darting a little bit ahead of them as he led them past the cave. He leapt into the cave and lifted the branches, waiting hidden until their footsteps dimmed as they ran the other way.

"He slowly lowered them and looked around. Once he was

convinced that they couldn't see him, he ran from his hiding place, grabbed his staff, and darted through the unguarded pass. He stopped on the other side as another tree smoked with a symbol burnt into it. He called this one 'wit' for that was the skill he had called upon to make it through the pass. He carved this symbol into his staff as well," Khee-Lá said, fingering the second symbol. "Veron continued his journey until he came to this very plain. That is when he found this place, and discovered that the area was fertile, and well suited to start a more permanent settlement. Excited by this news, he ran back to the ridge finding, to his surprise, that there were several ways to get on top of the ridge from this side. He climbed to the top and traveled a day's journey down it before repelling to the bottom with use of a rope he had brought with him.

"He ran back past the ancient trees where he had been attacked and returned to the small settlement. He told them all about his discovery, and of the chance to create a new community on the plain, but no one wanted to go with him. No one, that is, but a young woman who had just lost her parents and siblings to a fatal disease that was running rampant through the colony. At her acceptance another mark appeared, this time burnt onto the wall of one of the little shacks that they had been living in. Veron did not have a chance to name the last mark, as the hooded figures approached the settlement at that moment. One lowered its hood and it was discovered that these were the last handful of an ancient race, one thought long extinguished.

"The figure that lowered his hood was said to have but a single eye set into the middle of its face, a small mouth, and no apparent nose or ears. It approached Veron, who held his staff in front of him defensively. The other colonists were frightened and ran away, but Veron stood strong, and the woman with him. When the figure spoke, it spoke in their tongue and said, 'Behold, one worthy of this land. For many who settle here have gained one or two of the marks, thou hast earned the three. Courage, wit, compassion: the three great gifts. Thy bloodline is worthy.' It then pulled its hood back up and led its fellows into the woodlands, to be seen again only in time of great need.

"This woman, Aseera, became the first queen on Náto. Veron became the first king. Veron brought Aseera back to this place, building a small home for her. He left her there and returned to find the other settlers, but his search resulted in nothing. Either they had died of the illness, or they had been destroyed by wild animals as they ran in fear, or they gave up and left in one of the small ships. One ship was left and, though it could not fly, its communication devices were still workable. They called for more to join them, and that is how the small colony became a great civilization. Veron and Aseera, as you may already have guessed, began a line of rulers traceable to you and I," Khee-Lá finished.

Akinia thought about the story for a moment, pausing as she realized how close they were to the palace. She looked up at the beautiful building, her eyes widening as she realized that the enormous balconies were covered with flowering vines, which sent off a brilliant perfume richer than anything she had ever smelled before. Yet, somehow, the scent was vaguely familiar. She grinned. "That smell, I remember it."

Khee-Lá smiled, and then frowned. He sighed. "Come on, we should get inside. I've delayed long enough." He led her to its base and through a set of wrought iron gates that stood open, towering over anyone who stood beneath them.

They stepped into a long hall that seemed to stretch from one side of the palace to the other. The floors seemed to be a solid sheet of smoothly polished marble, and the walls and tall support pillars looked to be granite. On the walls, surrounded by flowing draperies of red silk, hung portraits of the royal families that seemingly dated back the last several thousand years.

"We have to replace one of the oldest ones every now and then, but they are substituted with exact copies," Khee-Lá explained, watching her gaze at them with wonder.

Akinia nodded and quickened her pace, hoping to find one in particular. Nearly halfway down the massive hall, she found what she was looking for. Draped in black silk, rather than red, the portrait held four people. The man, the woman, and the two small babies smiled out of the picture as though they could see her standing there. A sob stuck in her throat as she realized that Khee-Lá had been right: Akinia was nearly identical to her mother, except for her nose. If the picture was anything to judge by, the young Najee decided, she had received that from her father.

Her eyes glanced quickly to the babies, one held in her father's arms, the other held by her mother. She noticed that their necklaces were peeking out of the blankets they were wrapped in. Lokita lay in their father's arms, Akinia in their mother's. *How ironic*, Akinia thought to herself, *that father was holding Lokita, and mother holding me, when just days later mother's brother took me away and father's brother took Lokita.* A tear streamed from her eye as she noticed something else about the two babies: the hands closest to each other were extended, and they were grasping each other by their fingertips. It was as though that was the most natural thing in the world, that they were happy so long as they could touch.

Khee-Lá stood silently several paced away, not wanting to intrude upon this moment as Akinia saw her family for the first time since she was a baby. He shifted uncomfortably, wondering how long he should wait and allow her to stare at the picture before continuing. The decision was made for him when she wiped the tears away and walked back to him. He wrapped his arms around her for a moment before guiding her to a stairway a short way further.

She was quiet as she walked, seeing nothing but her parents' faces, and her sister's. Who would have thought that that beautiful baby girl would become the vicious monster feared by all? Who would have thought that the twins who were holding each other's hands, as though terrified of being apart, would be living a vicious battle to end each other's lives? She stopped as Khee-Lá did.

He opened a door and waved her inside. The suite was not unlike the one on Kineston, except that it was much, much larger.

She walked around, exploring the enormous room. She found the bedchamber first. The mattress was enormous, and impossibly high. A thick curtain could be drawn around it to shut out the light, but there was also a thin gossamer curtain.

"It's beautiful," she decided, having looked at all of the other small rooms, too. The enormous library was her favorite part.

"It was your mother's room," Khee-Lá informed her. "No one had the heart to touch it after she died, so it remained the same as always. The servants keep it clean and useable, but no one else has been in here in fifteen years. It is, by all right, yours now."

"This was mother's room?" she echoed, her voice a whisper.

"I have to go and find Andrid and Katarina, and explain to them…" his voice trailed off, and Akinia easily picked up the note of fear it held.

She placed a hand on the side of his face, stretched her mind to engulf his, and allowed her confidence to flow into him. "It's going to be alright," she promised before kissing his other cheek. Satisfied that he was okay, she lowered her hand and released his mind. She kept a small tendril of though attached to his, just for the emotional support that she knew he would need.

"You scare me at times," he admitted, laughing.

"Good," she replied smugly. "I wouldn't have it any other way."

Khee-Lá laughed, shook his head a couple of times, and left. His niece was a sweet child, but more than that she was a brave warrior and a strong woman. The combination was so perfect and so absurd, sometimes he couldn't help but smile as he thought of it. But then other times, such as this, it also disturbed him.

Chapter 8:

He met none of the servants as he walked to the throne room. Of course it *was* the middle of the day. At this hour very few worked. Most merely relaxed and waited for the cooler evenings to finish their daily chores. The king and queen would be no exception, though they would be speaking to the diplomats in their throne room over a nice bowl of Jeetó freeze.

The guards to either side of the throne room door bowed as he approached, instantly recognizing their prince. "I shall announce your arrival, my lord," one said, turning to enter.

"No, Kell Tran-Jeck," he ordered, stopping the young officer. The makings on his uniform told the Najee that this young man ranked a Kell, the third highest ranking in the Imperial Guard, and the name badge gave him the surname Tran-Jeck. "I wish to enter unannounced."

The Kell bowed and returned to his position. "As you wish, my prince."

Akinia watched this interaction through her uncle's thoughts, but the more intently she watched, the deeper into his mind she reached.

Sweetheart, stop. Touch my mind, don't inhabit it, he chastised.

She pulled away, uncertain how she had gotten so deep. *Sorry, I'll just wait for you to get back. Let me know before you come,* she requested before cutting off the contact.

Khee-Lá sighed and pushed the ornate double-doors open, wishing that Akinia hadn't completely severed her mental connection to him. He found himself in dire need of the steady stream of courage and comfort she had been pouring into him.

The room he entered was a long ornate hall, with wide pillars that supported the delicately sculpted arched roof. The floor was beautiful marble, inlaid in various patterns of stars, with the three marks of Veron hidden here and there. Thick hand-woven rugs of the softest fleeces covered various sections of the floor, bringing patches of bright color to the room. The walls were covered in tapestries of various plants and animals native to Náto. At the end of the grand hall sat two large thrones, one considerably smaller than the other.

The largest throne held a tall man with dark brown hair, unlike the golden-blonde hair shared by Khee-Lá and Akinia. His gray eyes sparkled and morphed to a soft blue color as he caught sight of Khee-Lá.

The smaller throne next to him held a thin and willowy woman, her stomach round with a child. Her thin arms and slender hands wrapped delicately around the bulge as though to gently hold the baby within. Her copper hair was pulled up into a loose bun, from which long sections of hair hung down freely about her shoulders. Her lips quivered in delight as she saw her brother-in-law, and her green eyes brightened. Ignoring all manner of Court etiquette, she pushed herself up from the throne and ran to the Najee, throwing her arms around him. "Khee-Lá! Oh, how wonderful to have you back, again!"

Khee-Lá smiled and kissed her cheek before pulling back to place a hand on her swollen stomach. "I see you and my brother are still on speaking terms," he teased. "This one will make, what, eight?"

"And nine, brother, and nine," Andrid added, walking towards them in a more dignified fashion. He held his hand out as though to shake Khee-Lá's, but the older brother pulled the younger into a tight hug.

"It has been too long, Andrid," he smiled. "Did I just hear you say your wife is having twins?"

"Ah, yes. According to the medic, this pair will be identical. I was so afraid we would get another set of fraternal. We have some ideas for names, but we would like to speak it over with you privately first," Andrid explained.

"We have much to discuss, then, brother. Send your guests and guards away so we can speak privately for a time. I am afraid that this cannot wait," he ordered, his face growing dark as he remembered why he was there.

Andrid and Katarina both seemed confused by his attitude, but nodded. "I would like you all to excuse us, please. We will reconvene tomorrow at this time to finish our discussions," Andrid asked of the dozen diplomats assembled. Once they had left, he dismissed his guards, including the two stationed behind the velvet draperies behind the thrones.

"Khee-Lá?" Katarina questioned worriedly, "Something has happened. What is it? What's the matter?"

Andrid frowned. "Answer her," he ordered, concern flooding his voice as well.

Khee-Lá took a deep breath to steady himself, and then another. "I," he began, but then he stopped as he tried to figure out how to continue. All of the speeches he had practiced in his mind for the past several years, and especially over the past several months, fled from his mind, leaving him with nothing but his guilt and anguish. His eyes frantically searched theirs, hoping for some trigger that would allow him to speak the words he knew he must say.

"You what?" Andrid demanded, watching him warily. He had only once seen his elder brother act this way, and that was when he had returned to tell them the Council forbade him to hunt down Jade. So what news could he bring now that affected him so? "Khee-Lá, tell me," he requested, his tone kinder, yet more cautious.

"So many ways I saw myself doing this," he murmured, "Yet none of them seem to be the right way now." He turned away from them, heaving out a sigh as he struggled to find words. They remained that way for several long agonizing moments before he finally turned to face them again. "Forgive me," he begged, his voice barely a whisper, "I have wronged you, and I beg your forgiveness."

"What is this about, brother?" Andrid demanded, frowning.

Khee-Lá's hands balled into fists and his eyes closed tightly, before cracking open again; his lips parted slightly, and then closed once more; his mouth felt dry and blistered as he tried to force out the words that didn't want to come. "Akinia lives," he managed to whisper, his voice soft enough that neither Andrid nor Katarina could understand him.

"Come again?" Katarina requested.

Having gotten the words out once, the second attempt came through much clearer and so much louder that it was nearly a yell, "Akinia lives!"

The silence was shattering. Their soft breath seemed as loud as a thundering waterfall in the complete deadening absence of any and all sounds. A needle dropped at the end of the hall would have resonated throughout the enormous marble chamber with shocking volume and clarity. No one moved, no one spoke, and no one blinked.

Finally, Katarina whispered, "What did you say?" Her breath was ragged and all the color had drained from her face. She looked quite nearly on the verge of fainting.

Khee-Lá swallowed heavily. "Akinia lives," he repeated once more. "The night Jade attacked the palace, I took her. I hid her on Paméd for a short time before I was ordered to take her away and hide her somewhere. I never left her unguarded. Jade attacked Náto searching for Akinia, seeking to kill her. If I had allowed you to know of her survival, word would have spread and it would eventually have reached Jade's ears. As it is, he only recently has discovered that she was not killed in the attack. I beg your forgiveness, and your understanding. It was the only way to keep her alive."

"You," Andrid began, but he stopped and paced several steps away. He turned sharply and came at Khee-Lá, landing his fist squarely on the Najee's nose, but Khee-Lá never tried to dodge his brother's fist. The crunch as Andrid broke his brother's nose resonated throughout the hall.

"Andrid!" Katarina gasped, shocked. She placed a hand over her mouth, but made no move to assist her brother-in-law.

"How dare you?" Andrid demanded. "How dare you keep her hidden from us? Where is she?"

Khee-Lá stood upright again and straightened his crooked nose before it could set. "Leonora made me her Protector. I had a duty to keep her alive, no matter what. And with Jade trying his best to kill her, even being so bold as to attack an Imperial palace, I had to make everyone believe she had died that night," he explained, again.

"Where is she?" Andrid demanded again, his voice bordering on a growl.

"She looks exactly like Leonora," he whispered, his voice barely carrying to them. "They could pass for one another, easily, were Leonora still with us."

"Which she may have been if you hadn't run off with Akinia instead of protecting your family!" Andrid growled, his hand balling into a fist again, though he resisted the urge to hit his brother again.

Khee-Lá's eyes opened wide, and then narrowed in anger. "How dare you insinuate that I would leave my parents and sister to die? How dare you try to make me out to be the villain here, Andrid? By the time I was able to locate Mother, Father, Aki, Josiah, and Leonora, it was too late. I watched them die by Jade's hand, and I had to spend the last sixteen years of my life reliving that in my dreams every night! My only comfort was in knowing that I was able to save one member of my family, and I was still tormented by the knowledge that you could never know she had survived. You think that you felt pain when you lost them? You haven't even begun to know pain," he growled, his voice a low hiss by the end of his speech.

Andrid snorted. "And there you go again with that excuse. Oh, poor Khee-Lá, you weren't even able to find your family in this place, something I've seen you do in seconds. Don't feed me that idiotic story again, I've had it enough. You were only thinking about Akinia when you left the others to die. Don't deny it: you know it's true," he sneered.

"Boys, please," Katarina begged, tears streaming from her eyes. Leonora's daughter lived?

Khee-Lá shook off the hand Katarina had placed on his shoulder. "So that's what you think?" he demanded. "You think I left our family to die? Maybe you are more of an idiot than I thought. If giving my life would have saved them, I would have died a thousand times over. There was too much commotion, too many people, and I was young and inexperienced. In the time it took me to realize that the Sigidians had broken through, our troops were unprepared to deal with a catastrophe of that magnitude, and our family was in danger, I had only moments left in which to search for them, hoping to be able to get them out. The only one I found was Akinia, but I kept searching. I searched until I found them, and I found them just as Jade took their lives. When I found them, Akinia was the only one left."

Both men stood facing one another, breathing heavily, each trying to come up with something suitable to say, and neither having any luck. Katarina stood between them, a hand on each of their chests, hoping they would make up quickly and without any more bloodshed.

Finally, Khee-Lá sighed, "I should never have come here. I'll get my things and we'll leave." He turned and walked towards the door, but Katarina grabbed him and turned him to face her.

"Where do you think you're going?" she demanded.

"I was wrong to bring her here, Katarina," he sighed. "Akinia is expecting love and joy at her return, not this," he motioned to Andrid. "I need to get her away from here while she still has a happy picture of her family in her mind."

"Wait," Andrid ordered, holding one finger up in front of him. "Akinia is here?"

Khee-Lá nodded. "She's in Leonora's old room. I thought it appropriate," he explained.

Andrid pushed roughly past him. "You have an hour to leave," he called as he walked away, "But Akinia stays. You aren't stealing her from us again."

Khee-Lá flicked his hand towards the doors and they slammed shut, the locks clicking into place a moment later. "Akinia stays with me. End of story."

Andrid spat in the direction of his brother. "By the signs of Veron!" he swore, "She stays, Khee-Lá! I won't let you steal her from us again. As the King of Náto I order you to leave, and I order that Akinia stays."

Khee-Lá crossed his arms stubbornly. "As a Najee Warrior, under full authority by the Najee Council of Masters, and on behalf of Akinia's Master, I now remind you of Article 57, Page 13, Paragraph 2, Line 1: No ruler of any principality under authority of the Elderian Empire, under rule of the Princeshian line, renewed under the authority of Princess Alania, may give an edict that will directly interfere with the duties of a Najee of any rank enlisted in the service of the Najee Council of Masters and/or the personal service of the current ruler of the previously indicated Elderian Empire."

Andrid raised an eyebrow. "And what has that to do with *my* niece?"

"*Our* niece is a Najee Apprentice in service of the Najee Council of the Masters and she is currently in my authority. Any order forcing her to remain behind while I leave is impeding her duties as she is currently ordered to assist me. Your edicts cannot touch her," he explained, a note of arrogance in his voice.

Andrid cursed and began pacing, his hands on his hips. But before he could think of something to say, Katarina shoved them both.

"Both of you shut up," she ordered harshly. "Leonora's *baby*, our last living link to *your sister* is sitting upstairs waiting to meet her aunt and uncle, and all the two of you can do is sit here arguing over who owns her! Now Khee-Lá Emmeda-Juntoby you let me out of this room *now* so I can see my niece for the first time in fifteen years, and Andrid Emmeda-Juntoby you *will* leave him alone and let him bring us to Leonora's little girl. Am I clear to you both?"

Khee-Lá grinned at her, while Andrid glared at the floor. "I was hoping one of you would say that," he informed her.

"Wait one moment," Andrid ordered. "Before we go to see her I must know one thing: Where has she been all these years? You said you only had her at Paméd for a short time?"

"Hidden among hundreds of other children, in an orphanage as far into the Empire as I could find. I guarded her from a distance, enlisting other Masters I trust to guard her when I had to return home or when I was ordered on other missions. Of course, none of them knew why they were guarding that area. She was never in danger," he promised.

Andrid's lips moved, mouthing 'an orphanage?' before his jaw locked and his fist balled again.

"Enough," Katarina ordered sharply as she noticed his behavior. "The important thing is that she is home. Khee-Lá, take me to her. Now."

Khee-Lá, smiling again, bowed deeply at the waist before rising again and lazily flicking his hand towards the doors. They opened, seemingly of their own accord. He offered his arm to his sister-in-law, which she pointedly refused as she brushed past him. Sighing, he hurried to catch up with her, Andrid sulking as he reluctantly followed.

Chapter 9:

A lump rose in her throat as she looked around, seeing the room with this new information in mind. *Mother*, she sighed to herself. She walked into the adjoining room and gently fingered the thick comforter on the bed. She wondered if it was the same one her mother had used. It was childish, she knew, but she couldn't resist pulling up the edge of the comforter and pressing it to her nose, inhaling deeply. The smell was warm and comforting, ringing a familiar chord somewhere in the back of her mind, the way the flowers outside had. A bit regretfully, she smoothed the comforter back down into its place.

Would she have been sitting here with her mother and Lokita if Jade hadn't attacked the palace that day, or would she be off somewhere on a mission with Nath and Ko-Pau?

Khee-Lá contacted Akinia. *Brace yourself, sweetheart, they are coming*, he cautioned.

Who broke your nose? I swear if I ever find them I'll-, she growled back, feeling the pain through their link.

Hush now, I only got what I deserved. Andrid has broken my nose many a time in our lifespans. I can almost guarantee this will not be the last time, and that I have deserved it every time he has, Khee-Lá soothed. *He'll be over it in a few hours. Now, sit up straight, smile, and be your charming self.*

As you wish, Uncle, she replied tartly, still bitter over her uncle's nose. She pulled the contact away to compose herself. Even though she was expecting it, she still jumped when the door opened and Andrid and Katarina hesitantly walked in. She stood and waited for them to speak, suddenly nervous beyond the ability to force words from her mouth.

They came to a stop mere feet in the doorway and stared open-mouthed at Akinia. Andrid seemed to be going into shock. "Leonora," he whispered, his soft voice carrying in the silence.

Khee-Lá smiled from the doorway, where he had paused unseen to watch their first meeting. "Andrid, Katarina, allow me to introduce our niece, Akinia Núro Leonora Kheelita Juntoby-Zanoratta," he introduced, walking over to stand by his niece.

Andrid temporarily came out of his haze as his brother walked past. "I told you to get out of here!" he snarled, charging Khee-Lá as though to hit him again.

Akinia ran to stand between them, her presence effectively stopping Andrid's charge. "He stays, or I go with him," she said quietly, but firmly.

"By the Signs of Veron, she even sounds like your sister," Katarina murmured.

"Yes," Andrid agreed, stepping back to stand by his wife, "And she's just as blatantly stubborn and clearly always takes Khee-Lá's side just as Leonora did."

As he moved away, Akinia took several steps to the side, letting Khee-Lá face his brother again.

"Come off it, Andrid," Khee-Lá sighed. "You know Leonora remained neutral in our arguments unless one of us was being incredibly unreasonable."

Andrid gave him a half-hearted smile. "Then she often thought I was the one being unreasonable."

Katarina ignored her husband and brother-in-law's conversation and stepped closer to Akinia. "I wonder if you are real," she admitted, reaching hesitantly to touch the girl's shoulder. Her hands moved to brush Akinia's cheek, and then to shift a stray strand of hair behind Akinia's ear. As her fingers traced Akinia's face, she marveled at the crisscrossing wounds showing on her bared skin. "What happened to you?" she whispered, her fingers lightly tracing a particularly long gash on her cheek.

The tension radiating from Khee-Lá was strong enough that even Andrid and Katarina could feel it thickly in the air.

"What is it?" Katarina demanded, turning to Khee-Lá.

But it was Akinia who answered, "I was captured by Enbrilth. He wanted me to join him, but I wouldn't."

"Jade did this?" Andrid demanded of his brother, motioning to Akinia.

"And more," Khee-Lá sighed and looked away in shame.

"Akinia heals fast, but her wounds were great. We nearly lost her."

Akinia blushed and pulled away from Katarina to walk over to Khee-Lá. "Thanks to you and Master and Nath, I'm alright now," she beamed, standing on her tiptoes to give her uncle a kiss on the cheek. She turned to smile at Katarina and Andrid, "Master and Nath distracted Jade while Uncle Khee-Lá found me. Then he and Master held Jade off while Nath snuck me out of the base and onto our ship. We were home to Paméd soon after."

"I want to know how you were captured in the first place," Andrid demanded, glaring at his brother. "After all, if Khee-Lá was watching you so closely…"

Khee-Lá opened his mouth to speak, but Akinia put a hand on his shoulder to stop him.

"I was captured doing my job," she explained. "Jade caught my fighter in a tractor beam while my squadron was trying to push his troops back enough to allow us to escape with Princess Alania and Princess Inzan. There's nothing anyone could have done to prevent it, but it was rectified quite nicely, I think. But can we please find a more pleasant topic? I've had more than enough of this one over the past several months."

"Yes, I agree," Khee-Lá decided, nodding. "Where are the children? I'm certain she would enjoy meeting them."

"The younger are on an outing, but Rignon and Amalli are here," Katarina sighed. "Amalli has some guests over, but I will have her send them away. Rignon is in his room studying."

"Let me get them, please?" Khee-Lá requested. "You can stay here with Akinia and get to know one another."

"As you wish," Katarna replied tersely, wrapping her arms around her niece.

Are you sure you want to leave me? Akinia asked a bit worriedly, leaning into Katarina's hug.

They'll be more pleasant with me gone. I told you they would be angry with me. Just enjoy this, sweetheart, he recommended. "I will return soon."

"Take your time," Andrid muttered.

Please hurry, Akinia requested.

Nath will be here soon, within minutes. He'll come, he promised as he walked out of the room. Without another word he severed the contact.

Her stomach twisted, tensing in uncertainty. She opened her mouth slightly to speak, but found herself unable to. Her eyes drifted from her aunt to her uncle and in a fraction of a second she took in his appearance. He was about the same height as Khee-Lá and, while still built thickly muscular, had a slightly thinner physique. His hair was dark and slightly wavy and his eyes seemed to be the same changing-color she and Khee-Lá shared. His nose was not overly large, nor overly small, and the tip was slightly hooked. Overall, he was a very handsome man.

She hesitated a moment as he reached for her hand, before willingly slipping hers into his. She couldn't help but marvel at the gentleness in his thick, stocky fingers. An uncertain smile crossed her lips.

Andrid pulled her hand to his lips and gently kissed her fingers. "I never thought I would have the pleasure of seeing you grown," he admitted, his eyes searching hers.

"Come," Katarina urged, gently pulling on Akinia, "Let's sit down."

Akinia nodded and let her aunt lead her to the large, plush couch. Katarina sat on her right and Andrid on her left. "This all seems surreal," she admitted.

Katarina smiled and took Akinia's hand in her own. "It does to us as well," she promised. "We never imagined that you might be alive, after all these years…"

"How long have you been a Najee?" Andrid asked solemnly, frowning.

"A little over a year," she admitted, "But I only found out about all of *this* after Khee-Lá rescued me from Jade." She motioned around her as she said 'this'. "I couldn't wait until I was well again and could come here. It is very beautiful."

Katarina fingered the charms on Akinia's bracelet. "Did Khee-Lá tell you the story of these symbols?" she wondered.

Akinia nodded. "He told me as we walked here. I enjoyed hearing it," she smiled.

An awkward silence overcame them again as each wondered what to say next. Finally, Andrid shifted slightly and asked, "How long will you stay?"

"I'm not sure," she admitted, "Until Uncle Khee-Lá says to leave, I suppose. Master and Nath are here as well." Her eyes shifted to look at Katarina's swollen stomach. "How long?" she wondered, her eyes brightening.

Knowing exactly what she was talking about, Katarina answered, "Three months."

"A boy or a girl?" Akinia wondered next.

"Twin girls," she smiled, absentmindedly placing a hand on her stomach.

Akinia beamed; she loved children! As the door opened, all three stood and turned their attention to the three who entered.

Khee-Lá walked in first, silently encouraging the two hesitant children walking behind him.

The boy, whom Akinia assumed to be Rignon, walked in first. Her first impression was that he looked a great deal like Nath. He was thin and pale, except for a splattering of freckles across his nose; and he had long dark hair that he kept tied back in a ponytail. The thirteen year old was much shorter than Nath, however, standing an inch or two shorter than Akinia. His eyes seemed to be the same as the other Juntobys, and a small red birthmark was visible on the right side of his neck. He seemed very wary of Akinia, and stopped as soon as he was inside of the doorway.

The girl seemed near his same age, but her eyes flashed from blue to dark green and seemed to show a greater wisdom and age than her brother's did. Her shoulder length copper-red hair, the same shade as her mother's, was streaked through with golden highlights the same shade as Akinia and Khee-Lá's hair. Her skin, like her brother's, was very pale, but her face and arms were covered in a thick splattering of tan freckles. A dark, diamond-shaped birthmark was visible on the back of her right hand. She paused a half-step behind her brother, frowning as she caught sight of Akinia.

Her scrutiny made Akinia feel a bit self-conscious. She hesitated before offering a reluctant smile, which the children did not return.

Khee-Lá smiled and urged them forwards with a gentle push. "Akinia, allow me to introduce your cousins, Prince Rignon and Princess Amalli Krann-Juntoby. Rignon, Amalli, this is your cousin Princess Akinia," he introduced, laughing at their shocked expressions.

"Aunt Leonora's daughter?" Amalli demanded suddenly, turning sharply to look at her uncle. "I thought she was dead."

"Amalli!" Katarina chastised, shocked by her daughter's lack of

69

manners.

Khee-Lá cut in, "No, Katarina, she's quite right. They deserve to know the truth. I wronged them as much as I wronged you, and I need their forgiveness just as surely." He turned to them and gave them a quick explanation of how Akinia had survived, and asked again for their forgiveness.

"Of course, Bashka," Rignon said at once, though he still seemed quiet and reserved.

"Of course, Uncle," Amalli seconded a moment later, even less enthusiastically than her brother.

"Bashka?" Akinia questioned.

"I am Rignon's Protector as well, sweetheart," Khee-Lá explained. "Bashka is a traditional endearment for one's Protector."

She frowned, "Oh."

Amalli bit her lower lip. "She is come home, to stay?"

"Only for a time, sweetheart," Khee-Lá sighed. "I would like for her to be able to remain, but our duty will only leave us time for a short visit."

"Duties?" Rignon asked, puzzled.

"Yes," Khee-Lá said proudly. "Not only do you have an Uncle who is a Najee, but a cousin as well."

Amalli smiled for the first time. "I'm glad you're home, Cousin," she greeted warmly. She hugged Akinia with a true delight that confused the older girl even more.

Andrid watched his children with amusement. "You suspicious child," he laughed at Amalli, pulling her into a hug. "You thought she was going to take the throne from Rignon, didn't you?"

"The thought crossed our minds, father, though I would have surrendered it if it was rightfully hers," Rignon asserted quickly. His cheeks flamed slightly at the acknowledgment.

Andrid shook his head, laughing, as he released his daughter. "Well, I hope that will be the end of your disdain, because it is truly a miracle to have our little Akinia back from the dead."

"I never held disdain, Father, only concern for my brother," Amalli corrected crossly. "But now my concern is gone, and I can truly enjoy my cousin's presence. Come, Akinia, let me show you around. And I'll introduce you to my friends, I do think they'll adore you!"

"Not so fast," Khee-Lá interrupted, just as Akinia began to accept her outstretched hand. "Akinia cannot leave this room until your father announces her return. Otherwise, people are likely to think she's Leonora's ghost!"

"Quite right," Andrid agreed, nodding. He was reluctant to even acknowledge his brother right now, but couldn't deny the truth of his words.

"Then go and announce it, Father, please," Amalli begged, taking her father's hand.

Rignon nodded eagerly. "Yes, Father, please!"

"Not yet," Katarina decided firmly. "We must reveal it privately to the children tonight, and then in the morning to our closest friends. It is only proper that they know before we release a public announcement."

"Then what is Akinia to do during mealtimes until then?" Amalli asked, shocked.

"I can eat here, or I could return to the ship. I'm certain Skyler wouldn't mind me joining the men for meals," Akinia suggested helpfully.

The door opened and everyone jumped, none of them having expected anyone else. Ko-Pau and Nath walked in, shutting the door behind them.

"Bashka!" Amalli cried excitedly, running to him.

Ko-Pau snatched her up and spun her around a couple of times before setting her down. "Hello, baby girl," he laughed as he set her down. "I've got a present for you."

Amalli laughed and eagerly took the small package from him. She ripped the paper, squealing with delight as she revealed an intricately designed necklace charm on a slender silver chain. "Bashka, it's beautiful!" she gasped, hugging him again.

"Here, let me put it on you," he offered, taking it from her.

She turned around, twitching with delight as she waited for him to fasten the clasp. "Mother, look!" she implored, running to her mother.

"Gee, maybe I should have brought gifts," Nath mused mournfully. "Then I might have gotten a 'hello' from her."

Akinia laughed. "It couldn't just be that she likes Master more, could it?" she teased, giving Nath a quick wink.

Nath pretended to be shocked. "Now how could anyone like Master more than they like me?" he asked, perplexed. "I'm younger, stronger, and far better looking."

"I think Nath may have hit his head coming out of the ship," Akinia confided in a carrying whisper as she walked over to Ko-Pau and hugged him.

How has it gone so far? Ko-Pau asked as the room erupted in laughter.

Let me show you? Akinia requested, sharing a flood of memories with him.

He only hit Khee-Lá once? I'm impressed, he teased.

Akinia pulled back and scowled at him. *That isn't funny!*

Smiling, Ko-Pau pulled her into another hug.

"Bashka, you're making me jealous!" Amalli teased, returning to him.

Nath grinned. "I bet that's the first time a couple girls were fighting over you, Master," he teased.

"Nowhere near the first," he disagreed, an arm around each of them, "but they certainly are the prettiest."

"Bashka! Don't tease!" Amalli chastised, laughing.

Akinia grinned. "Oh, no, let him go on! I don't mind a bit of flattery."

"Then why do you hit me every time I flatter you?" Nath asked, sounding offended.

Akinia ignored him as she looked back to her aunt and uncles, smiling at them. "I never could have imagined this," she sighed happily.

"What?" Nath wondered curiously.

Akinia took Amalli's hand in her own and leaned her head onto Ko-Pau's shoulder. "My family. I've been alone so long I never honestly believed I had any relatives left. Now I'm being overrun with them!"

Everyone laughed except for Andrid, whose face contorted into a scowl. "You should never have had to endure that," he growled, glaring at his brother.

Akinia instantly regretted what she had said. "Please don't misunderstand: I have no regrets about my upbringing. It was the only way to keep us all safe. At any rate, the past can't be changed, and we're all together now," she corrected quietly.

"Well said," Ko-Pau seconded, kissing her forehead.

Katarina took Andrid's hand suddenly, her other clutching her stomach. "I need to go rest. I feel unwell," she sighed reluctantly, her brow furrowing. "You should go and summon the children."

"Are you alright? Is it the baby?" Andrid demanded anxiously.

Amalli began to move towards her mother, but stopped as Katarina smiled and shook her head. "I'm just a bit nauseous, and my head aches. I will be fine once I rest," she promised.

"We'll leave and let the kids have a few minutes to themselves," Khee-Lá said firmly, looking at both Ko-Pau and Nath.

Andrid was visibly struggling to decide whether or not to heed his wife's instruction.

Katarina smiled at him. "You also should decide which of our friends we need to tell first, and then have them come in the morning."

He sighed and nodded in agreement. "You are quite right," he agreed.

They all moved towards the door at the same moment, only Akinia, Amalli, and Rignon remained where they were. Andrid and Katarina each kissed her forehead as they passed her, holding her tightly for a moment before releasing her.

Khee-Lá touched Akinia's mind just before he left. *I'll be close by if you need me, but you should do fine on your own. They really want to know and love you.*

So long as I don't want to take the throne from Rignon?

Yes, well, refrain from that and you should get along fine, he laughed.

Akinia smiled and watched them leave before turning back to her cousins. They both seemed reluctant to speak, so she took a deep breath and said, "Let's sit. We have a lot to talk about."

Chapter 10:

"And so, you recovered and returned to us," Amalli finished, as Akinia described the details of her upbringing, ending with her recent rescue.

She had told them nothing of Lokita, fearing they would recognize her name, and did not tell them about Jade's terrible revelation, but all else she had freely offered up. Though she skittered over the details of her torture, the little she did tell them caused Amalli to gasp and caused both children's eyes to widen in amazement of her resiliency. "Yes," she agreed, smiling wryly. "I recovered, and came home."

"And you are really friends with Princess Alania and Princess Inzan?" Rignon asked, amazed.

Akinia laughed and nodded. "Yes, I suppose I am."

His face brightened. "What are they like?"

"Both are very kind, very charming women. I really enjoyed meeting them," she reported. "Alania was very kind to me, even before she knew that I was, well... To her I was just an orphan child who happened to become a Najee, and yet she still treated me with as much respect and kindness as she did Master Lo-Kí. That alone should tell you her character."

Amalli smiled at her brother's mystified expression. "Uncle Khee-Lá said as much, you shouldn't be surprised by our cousin's testimony," she chastised with a laugh.

"Have you never met her?" Akinia wondered.

Rignon shook his head with a sigh. "I will not travel to the Capitol until next year, for my first Senate meeting."

Amalli smiled. "And I am certain you will enjoy it."

Akinia frowned. "Will you not go with him?"

"Of course not!" Amalli laughed. She quickly realized how

ignorant Akinia was of Nátoan politics, so she explained, "This trip will, for Rignon, be a very important time. He will travel with a Senator and with one of our Senator's daughters of his or our parents choosing, and no one else shall accompany them except for the servants, of course. Many times a young Heir ends up marrying the girl who accompanies him, if only because they develop a close friendship on the trip."

Rignon turned red and pointedly looked away, but Akinia was very curious. "Is the Heir the first son, then?" she wondered.

"The firstborn child, girl or boy, unless the firstborn renounces their title to the next in line, in which case the second eldest become the Heir," Amalli corrected. "If a girl is the Heir, then a young man accompanies her."

Akinia smiled. "Tell me about your siblings," she requested, leaning forwards in anticipation.

Amalli smiled. "Our brother Anlix and sister Lanzi are twins, but ever so different. Lanzi could not be gentler or sweeter while Anlix… well, he is a bit of a handful and enjoys scaring the rest of the children. He doesn't dare try it with me, and I can usually make him mind, but he is incurably mischievous and detests his studies. He does nothing but dream of joining the Imperial Army and fighting Sigadia, though I do hope the war is well over by time he comes of age. They are only ten, but both are so eager to take their places in society.

"Then there is our sister Schran, who is eight. She does nothing but sit in the garden and read day in and day out. Many nights I have to drag her in to go to sleep because she doesn't want to stop reading! She loves animals dearly and enjoys listening to the birds sing, which is one reason she chooses the garden to read in.

"Our brother Noregh is seven, but he looks a bit older than Schran. He has no particular interest or ambition, though that isn't surprising at his age. He simply flitters from one thing to another, enjoying it all with equal fervency.

"Our jewel, though mother says not to say such things, is our baby sister Karanne, who is recently five years of age. She is an angel and rarely leaves my side. She is a bit shy to those she does not know, but once she gets used to your presence she will chatter away until you fear your ears may fall off! She finds reading difficult, though she enjoys being read to, and she loves to play catch-and-chase in the gardens," she finished, her face lighting up at mention of her youngest sister.

Akinia smiled. "I hope they return soon."

"As do I," Amalli agreed.

"Akinia," Rignon began curiously, "did you ever think about us? I mean, not us specifically, of course, but your family in general? Did you ever imagine we might exist?"

She frowned and averted her gaze. "When I was young I did, but as I grew older I stopped believing it could be possible. I had contented myself with being alone, and later with having the Najee as my family. You cannot imagine how it felt when Khee-Lá told me the truth about who I was, and all of the family I still had," she smiled, looking back at them.

Amalli shuddered. "I cannot even begin to imagine feeling so alone..." she murmured.

"You'll never have to," Rignon said quickly, putting his arm around his sister.

They shared a smile full of such love and admiration for one another, it caused Akinia's stomach to turn in pain. She and Lokita would never have a bond like that. Fate had separated them, only to reunite them years later as mortal enemies. What would it be like to have a sibling with whom she could share such love? Forcing those thoughts away, she turned her attention back to her cousins. "And what about you?" she wondered. "What do you enjoy?"

Amalli smiled. "My brother enjoys helping Father, learning more about becoming king in his place. We also like to play shess. I love to paint and to sew; I made the waistbelt Rignon is wearing now," she explained, motioning to her brother.

Akinia, for the first time, noticed what her young cousin was wearing. His slacks and short-sleeved shirt were the same shade of black, and a single glance at his calloused feet revealed he wore no shoes. Around his head was a simple circlet of plain polished gold. Around his waist hung the item Amalli was so proud of: a wide sash-like belt of rich blue silk, the ends of which hung down to his knees after having been tied in an intricate knot at his hip. "You made this?" Akinia asked, impressed.

Amalli beamed. "I made his and Father's, as well as our brothers'. I enjoy it immensely, though my friends think it a waste of time and energy when we could as easily order them made."

"Nothing that you enjoy so much is a waste of time," Akinia

asserted, smiling, "especially not something this beautiful!"

Blushing, Amalli ducked her head and murmured her thanks. "I also enjoy riding Skyretts," she managed a minute later. "Perhaps once you are able to wander Náto, I will introduce you to Nilek and Insheff?"

"What is a Skyrett? And who are Nilek and Insheff?" Akinia asked curiously.

"Skyretts are large flying reptiles native to the Southern Plains," Rignon explained before bitterly adding, "They are very dangerous, but my sister insists on riding them. Nilek and Insheff are a mated pair of them that the Representative of the Southern Plains gifted to her when he discovered she cared for them."

Amalli smiled. "They are perfectly gentle, otherwise he would never have dared give them to me," she asserted gently. "I think you would greatly enjoy riding them, though you will have to ride Insheff; Nilek is my favorite and I dote upon her, though Insheff is just as gentle and pleasant."

Akinia smiled. "And I must introduce you to my Rofa. I am certain she isn't far. Perhaps I'll have Nath bring her here tonight?"

"Who is Rofa?" Rignon wondered a moment before Amalli opened her mouth to speak.

"My ceffre cub," Akinia explained. "I found her on a mission last year; she had been orphaned by the Sigidians, and all of her littermates had perished. I took grief from my men and from Nath, but I couldn't leave the poor thing to starve to death or be eaten."

Their eyes opened wide. "We have only heard of ceffres, from visiting dignitaries," Amalli gasped. "They are said to be very dangerous, vicious creatures."

Rignon nodded his agreement. "I cannot imagine my Bashka allowing such a dangerous animal on Náto."

"Nor my Bashka," Amalli agreed, frowning.

Akinia laughed and shook her head. "They are not dangerous or vicious when they have been raised with love and care. On the planets where they are fought and killed by the locals, only the vicious survive, and they teach their offspring to be vicious. There are, I believe, four systems where Ceffres are raised as companions and working beasts; even the children are allowed to play with them! They are very intelligent creatures and respond remarkably to kindness and love. My Rofa is a favorite of Princess Inzan, and even Princess Alania is somewhat partial to her," she explained quickly.

Amalli's eyes widened further. "She has been to the Capitol with you?"

"Yes, with Master Lo-Kí's blessing. He gave me permission to keep Rofa, despite the enormous size she will grow to, though I believe his generosity was encouraged by Rofa's having saved mine and Nath's lives the day I found her," she mused. In response to their curious gazes, she added, "The cub disabled a sniper neither of us had noticed, and held him long enough for us to take him into custody."

"Goodness!" Amalli gasped. "Is that why you decided to keep her?"

"No, not exactly," Akinia hesitated. "When I found her she was alone and injured... I pitied her, so I fed her from my rations and carried her to the safety of our ship. I couldn't leave her to die."

"I think that I would very much like to meet her," Rignon decided thoughtfully.

Amalli nodded her agreement.

"And I think I would like to meet Nilek and Insheff as soon as I am able," Akinia smiled. "Do you have any pets, Rignon?"

He smiled. "No," he replied with a sigh. "I suppose I could have one if I wished, but I never took the time to find one."

"I imagine if he ever gets a pet it will be some sort of bird," Amalli laughed. "Rignon enjoys watching them fly about the palace."

Akinia smiled. "They are beautiful," she agreed. "We used to have a small flock of Terlings that lived in the outer crevices of the orphanage; I enjoyed watching them through the library windows while I read."

"Terlings?" Rignon questioned.

Akinia nodded. "They are about the size of my fist, crème-colored, and have little black dashes all over them," she explained. "They sing very prettily, too."

"How queer!" Amalli exclaimed, a distant look in her eyes as she tried to imagine them.

"I haven't seen any since leaving the orphanage, but I've had little time to look at birds," she laughed.

Rignon's head cocked slightly to the side. "What is it like, to be a Najee?" he wondered.

Akinia frowned. "It is very rewarding, knowing the lives you've saved and the people you've helped; but it is also very difficult at times to live with the things you have to do in order to do your job. The most difficult, most terrifying part is putting your mission and the lives of others before your own safety. Telling Nath to leave me to Jade was the most difficult thing I've ever done, but it was necessary," she sighed.

"How…" Amalli began to ask, but she hesitated and swallowed before continuing. "How did you keep from going crazy?"

"Honestly? I don't know…" she admitted, grimacing. "But let's not talk about that any more, please… I've had more than enough conversation about that since my rescue."

"Of course," Amalli agreed, nodding.

Rignon echoed her agreement a moment later. "Tell us about yourself," he requested.

Where to begin? Akinia wondered. Her mind flashed through a list of information she wouldn't share: her heritage, her destiny, her loss of control… "I enjoy reading," she began, "and I was a medic's apprentice of sorts at the orphanage. Now I mostly read, sleep, and play with Rofa in my time off."

Amalli pursed her lips. "Do you not play shess?"

"I know the rules, but I never had a partner. None of the other orphans enjoyed it much," she shrugged.

"We must be certain to play with you while you're here. I am certain Uncle would be thrilled to have a partner while he is away from Náto. Neither Ko-Pau nor Nath play," Amalli decided.

"That sounds wonderful," Akinia smiled.

There was no time for either of her cousins to respond before the door cracked open. Akinia barely registered Nath's face before a dark, furry blur raced into the room. "Rofa!" Akinia laughed, standing to catch her excited cub.

Though she had bolted into the room, Rofa calmly settled at Akinia's feet, happily gazing up at her mistress.

"I missed you, too," Akinia promised, laughing as she scruffed the ceffre cub's head.

Amalli and Rignon rose to their feet, hesitantly watching the cub.

Nath laughed, shaking his head, as he stepped into the room. "Sorry about that, Kiddo. She got away from me," he apologized, grinning.

"Actually, we were just talking about Rofa," Akinia informed him, still stroking the cub's thick fur.

Nath turned to Amalli and Rignon, his grin widening at their uncertain expressions. "You've never seen a ceffre, have you?"

"No," Amalli replied warily, "we have not."

Akinia gave them an encouraging smile as she knelt down beside her pet. "She's really very gentle," she promised them.

Rignon hesitantly glanced between Akinia and Amalli for a moment before cautiously approaching the cub.

Seeing him approach, Rofa rose to her feet again and excitedly approached the young prince, eagerly licking his hand.

The prince was startled, but quickly regained his composure. A small smile crept onto his lips as he hesitantly petted the ceffre. He turned to his sister, giving her an encouraging nod.

Given confidence by her brother's approval, Amalli eagerly made friends with the cub, which basked in the attention.

Well, they seem to like her, Nath noted, grinning to Akinia.

I think she likes them, too, Akinia laughed in reply.

"I hate to cut the fun short," Nath commented loudly, "but aren't you guys supposed to be getting ready for a dinner or something?"

Akinia gaped at him in surprise. "Since when are you Mr. Responsible?"

Nath grinned. "Since Master Khee-Lá sent me to remind you guys that it was almost dinner time," he explained. "Come on, you two get out. Akinia has to get dressed, too."

Rignon puffed up defensively. "You shouldn't speak to us that way; I'm a prince of Náto!" he chastised, somewhat teasingly.

"Yeah, you are, and I'm one of Princess Alania's Najee," Nath laughed. "Now that we all know our social standings, get out." He playfully head-slapped the young prince, gently shoving him towards the door.

Rignon turned back towards Nath, laughing as he rammed into the Najee.

The two boys playfully wrestled for a few minutes before Nath grabbed the prince in a loose headlock.

"Fine, I give up!" Rignon relented, unable to break free of the Najee's grip.

Nath laughed as he released the boy. "It's about time," he teased. "Go on, get out of here."

Rignon turned to leave, but Amalli stayed firmly planted where she stood. "You would never dare try something like that with me," she decided.

"You're right, I wouldn't," Nath agreed, grinning. He extended his arm towards the young princess, and then raised it slightly.

Amalli gasped, laughing as she rose a foot off of the floor. "Nath, let me down this instant! This is not dignified!"

"You lost the right to dignity when you refused to walk out," Nath grinned. He turned to Akinia. "See you later, Kiddo." Without another word, he followed Rignon from the room, Amalli floating behind him, protesting the entire way.

Is it always this way between you three? she wondered.

Basically, Nath affirmed. *You've got about half an hour until dinner. Master's gonna come for you.*

So I am eating with everyone tonight?

Yeah. There's some private dining room or something; they think you won't be noticed there.

Is it really going as well as I think it is? Akinia wondered, a shy note to her thoughts. Some of her previous anxiety over meeting her family flowed through their mental link.

Better, Nath promised reassuringly.

Pleased, Akinia strengthened their mental embrace for just a moment before pulling her mind away from his, enveloping her thoughts within themselves once more.

Chapter 11:

"The children are in the dining room, waiting for you," Ko-Pu informed Akinia as she stepped out into the hallway to join him. "Khee-Lá is helping Andrid and Katarina explain."

Akinia nodded, a bit nervously. She tried to return Ko-Pau's smile, but only managed a grimace.

Ko-Pau frowned, concerned. "Are you okay, Slick?"

The Apprentice nodded again. "I just wish all of the introductions were over," she admitted.

"I know," he assured her, smirking. "Come on, this is the last round of family introductions, and we've already gotten through the hard ones."

"You're right," she agreed, returning his smirk with a small smile. She extended her mind to touch his, and he willingly lowered his defenses and let her in.

You really are nervous, aren't you? Ko-Pau noted, surprised, as he felt the tension in her thoughts.

Akinia hesitated. *A bit*, she finally admitted.

Ko-Pau wrapped his arm around her shoulders.

Smiling, Akinia leaned into his side. *Thanks.*

Any time, he laughed.

She took a deep and calming breath as they stopped in front of a large, ornate door. Akinia felt Khee-Lá's mind touch her own, and, through their link, she could feel him touch Ko-Pau's as well.

The door swung open.

Akinia stepped inside the small dining room. She recognized Andrid, Katarina, Rignon, and Amalli, and she also noticed Nath and Khee-Lá standing against the far wall, but she only recognized the five children lined up in front of her by the physical similarities they all possessed.

All five had honey-gold hair, and beautiful silvery eyes which, as she watched, flickered between blue and green in color. Nervous smiles crept onto their lips as they stared wide-eyed at their cousin.

"Akinia," Andrid said, breaking the deafening silence in the room, "These are your other cousins. Next to Rignon and Amalli, the eldest are the twins, Anlix and Lanzi," he paused and motioned to the boy and girl who seemed to be about ten years old. "Then there are Schran and Noregh," he paused and motioned to the girl who seemed to be about eight years old, and the boy who looked to be about a year younger. "Then there is little Karanne, she's the youngest, for a few more weeks," he laughed, motioning to the girl, who seemed to be about five years old.

Karanne hid shyly behind Noregh for a moment, but, as Akinia smiled at her, she darted over and wrapped her arms around Akinia's legs.

Akinia laughed and knelt down to give the girl a proper hug. "Hello, Karanne," she greeted.

The girl grinned and shyly buried her face in Akinia's shoulder.

Her smile widening, Akinia stood up again, lifting the little girl into her arms as she did so.

"You *do* look like Aunt Leonora," Anlix decided, his eyes widening.

Everyone laughed, amused by his observation.

"Come," Andrid said loudly, "let's have our dinner."

As everyone made their way to their seats, Karanne clung to her cousin's arm, successfully acquiring one of the two coveted seats next to Akinia. Amalli sat on Akinia's other side.

The long table in the middle of the room had already been set with everything that the family could need. The food was piled high on silver platters, and a dozen crystal pitchers sat around the platters to supply the drinks. Andrid placed food onto his plate and poured himself a drink, and then Katarina followed suit. Only afterwards did the others fill their plates.

Conversation was awkward and arduous as the meal began, but as everyone gradually relaxed, the room erupted into cheery conversation. Most of the questions were directed at Akinia, who happily answered whatever her cousins asked of her, except for questions about her time in captivity. Nearly three hours passed in that manner before no one could procrastinate the end of the meal any longer.

Andrid and Katarina stood, inciting everyone else to stand a moment later. "We should let Akinia get some rest; she's had a long journey," the king told his children firmly. "And you all are awake far past your bedtimes. Goodnight."

A chorus of goodnights from the seven youngest were heard, and they began to file from the room, stopping only a moment to hug and kiss everyone goodnight. Karanne clung to Akinia when she came to give her older cousin a hug goodnight. "Will you tuck me into bed?" she begged. "Please?"

Akinia smiled as she looked to her aunt, uncles, and Master for permission.

Khee-Lá nodded in encouragement. "Go ahead," he urged. "We'll come and say goodnight later."

"Speak for yourself," Katarina laughed. "I am going to go to sleep. Goodnight, Akinia."

Akinia gently detached herself from Karanne as she walked over to her aunt, carefully hugging the pregnant woman. "Goodnight, Aunt Katarina," she smiled. Turning to Andrid, Akinia hugged him as well. "Goodnight, Uncle Andrid."

"Goodnight, Akinia," he smiled, before kissing her forehead.

"Goodnight, Uncle Khee-Lá. Goodnight, Master. Goodnight, Nath," Akinia bade, hugging them each in turn. She took Karanne's hand and allowed the little girl to lead her out into the hallways, pausing only a moment in the doorway to glance back at her family.

Chapter 12:

"Will you sing me a song, please?" Karanne begged as Akinia started to leave.

Akinia smiled and sat down on the edge of Karanne's bed. "I've already told you two stories, don't you think you should go to sleep now?" she teased. "Your mommy won't be happy if I keep you up too late."

"Just one?" the five-year-old pleaded.

"Fine," Akinia relented, smiling. "But only one."

Karanne grinned and settled more deeply into her blankets.

Akinia thought for a moment. "I used to sing this one to a little girl I knew before I came here. Her name is Charlotte," she informed her cousin. She cleared her throat slightly and then began to sing:

"Hush little one, now go to sleep,
Hush little one, don't cry.
Lay down your head, now go to bed,
I'll be here when you rise.

"Look up above, child, you will see
The stars shining way up high
All through the night they shall shine their light
And I'll be here when you rise.

"Soon morn shall come and once again
Light shall dwell in the skies
But while night is here, child, do not fear
For I'll be here when you rise."

Akinia started to sing the verses over again, but stopped when she saw that Karanne was fast asleep. Smirking, she carefully stood and quietly crept out of the girl's room. She jumped as she saw Khee-Lá in the hallway waiting for her. "You startled me!" she quietly admonished.

He laughed softly. "I didn't mean to," Khee-Lá assured her. "I just came to check on you; you've had a busy day."

"It has been busy, hasn't it?" she laughed.

Khee-Lá wrapped his arm around his niece's shoulders and led her down the hallway. "Is it everything you hoped for?" he wondered. "Our family, I mean."

"More," Akinia corrected, grinning. "Are they always this sweet?" she wondered. "I mean, it isn't just because I'm home, is it?"

"Always," Khee-Lá promised, amused. "Actually, Andrid is usually a lot nicer, but you saw a fair representation of everyone else's personalities."

Akinia nodded slowly as she considered it, her mind wandering to a distant future when she and her cousins would all be old, and their children would be grown... *I won't be old*, she corrected, realizing the fallacy in her daydream. *I'll still be young... but what will happen then?*

"Let's sit here a while," Khee-Lá suggested as they neared a padded bench in the hallway.

Akinia nodded as they sat down. She leaned her head against her uncle's shoulder. "We'll live for thousands of years, won't we, Uncle? If Jade doesn't kill us first, I mean," she asked, adding the last as an afterthought.

He nodded slowly. "Our lives will be extended, but for how long no one knows. Some, like Lo-Ki, live for eons. Others live only a few years more than is normal. The more powerful a Najee is, and the more they use their psychokinesis, the longer their lives seem to be," he mused.

"But we won't be able to keep returning here forever, will we?" she murmured knowingly. She sat up slightly to look him in the eyes. "If we could, then there would be others like us, wouldn't there? There would be other Nátoan Najee visiting here regularly."

Khee-Lá frowned. "It doesn't do to dwell on such things," he reprimanded, "But I suppose you must realize that there will come a time when we will have to remove ourselves from Náto long enough that the people will forget who we are, but it will be long after your cousins are gone."

"Are there any other Nátoan Najee still alive, on Paméd?" she wondered curiously.

He sighed and shook his head. "When the war began, the Najee were decimated beyond anything previously seen. Thousands of our people were slaughtered in the first handful of years. Despite what the public believed, the Empire was losing the war. Your arrival on Paméd was the turning point, the reason we're able to hold our own, but it came too late for those killed in the beginning. There had been five Nátoan Najee, besides myself, still fighting when Jade first attacked, and none survived the first three years except for me. I later discovered that at least one of them was one of our distant ancestors."

Akinia frowned. "But I've done so little!" she protested. "How could those few battles have turned the war around?"

Khee-Lá smiled at her. "You gave us hope, the likes of which we hadn't had since the first attacks. We were inspired by your strength, your courage, and the promise of your future," he explained. "Now you should get some rest. Go on."

Akinia stood and kissed his cheek, "Goodnight, Uncle."

"Goodnight, sweetheart," he replied, giving her hand a quick squeeze before he released it. "I love you."

Her cheeks flushing with pride, Akinia smiled. "I love you, too."

Chapter 13:

Khee-Lá's thoughts gently brushed against Akinia's, silently urging her to wake.

Akinia stirred slightly, vaguely aware of the sunlight on her face. *Uncle?* she questioned uncertainly, still too asleep to be certain it was him.

Good morning, Sweetheart, he greeted, amused. *You need to wake up and get dressed: our friends will begin arriving soon, and you'll be expected to join us as soon as they find out about you.*

Though she did not voice her desire to sleep longer, her uncle could feel it through their telepathic link. *It isn't funny,* she groused, feeling his silent laughter.

Yes it is, he assured her. *You'll think so, too, as soon as you wake up enough to put some thought into it. Come on, get up.*

I am, she sighed, forcing herself to sit up.

Khee-Lá pulled his mind away after gently brushing her thoughts once more.

"Come on," Akinia yawned to Rofa, who lay stretched out on the floor near the bed. "If I have to wake up, so do you."

Rofa yawned, stretched her legs, and then sighed as she closed her eyes and settled back into a semi-sleeping state.

"Oh, no you don't," Akinia laughed, climbing from beneath her covers. "You're getting up, too. Come, Rofa."

Heaving a sigh of irritation, the cub forced herself onto her feet, stretching the toes of her single front leg in a very feline manner. She followed Akinia to the closet, flopping onto the floor again just inside of the doorway.

Akinia laughed, shaking her head. "You are the laziest creature I have ever known," she teased, kneeling down to kiss the cub's forehead. "And I've known some really lazy ones."

Rofa licked Akinia's chin, without warning.

"Rofa!" Akinia protested, laughing as she wiped the drool away.

"Mistress," Jaynine's voice called from just outside of the closet, "I have laid a dress out for you already. Would you prefer a different one?"

Nath must have brought him in last night, Akinia realized, startled to hear the droid's voice. "I didn't even see the one that you laid out," she admitted.

The droid turned and walked out into the main room. "I put it on the sofa," he explained, lifting the dress and holding it up for Akinia's inspection.

"It's beautiful," Akinia mused, gazing at the elegantly simple gown. As the light hit the shimmering blue silk, the hues of the cloth ranged from a light sky blue to a deep royal, enhancing the watery appearance of the flowing fabric. She reached out and took the dress from the droid. "Thank you, Jaynine," she smiled. "Would you bring me some tea, please?"

"Of course, Mistress," the droid replied at once, bowing at the waist before turning and leaving.

Akinia returned to the closet, stepping over Rofa, who was still lying in the doorway. It only took her a few moments to remove her nightgown and slip into the beautiful dress. *It fits perfectly,* she noted, both amused and a bit grim. *What would this place have been like, with you here, Mother?*

Shaking her head to clear it, Akinia returned to the main part of her room, sitting down at the vanity. She carefully brushed out her hair with the silver brush lying on the top of the vanity.

Jaynine returned just as she set the brush back down.

"Perfect timing," Akinia laughed, watching as the droid set an ornate silver tea service on the low tea table in the sitting area.

The droid did not respond as he quickly poured a cup of tea for her.

"Thank you," Akinia smiled, taking the cup and saucer from him.

"Is there anything else I may do for you, Mistress?" the droid asked.

Akinia thought for a moment. "Not right now, Jaynine. Thank you."

92

The droid bowed and walked away, busily cleaning the immaculate room.

The Apprentice smirked as she watched him. She sat down on one of the plush armchairs, tucking her legs up around herself. Closing her eyes, she inhaled the gentle scent of the tea, which rose in steamy plumes from the dark liquid's surface. Yawning, Akinia wondered if she would be awake in time to meet Andrid and Katarina's friends.

Are you ready, Slick? Ko-Pau asked her, as she took the first sip of her tea.

I think so. Are they ready for me, yet? she wondered, a bit nervously.

You can finish your tea; they're still showing up.

How many are there?

Only six so far, and there aren't many more coming, he promised.

Alright, Akinia sighed. *Master, do you think everything went alright yesterday?*

I think everything went perfectly, Ko-Pau replied at once, hesitating a moment before adding, *Except for the part where Andrid broke Khee-Lá's nose. That was slightly less than ideal.*

Uncle Khee-Lá acted like it happened all the time.

In a sense, it does, Ko-Pau laughed. *They're constantly fighting, but Khee-Lá doesn't usually fight back because he knows he could hurt Andrid pretty badly, and Andrid is usually satisfied if he gets one good punch in. They are your uncles, after all.*

Akinia smirked in response to his teasing tone. *You say that like I take after them.*

Just a bit... maybe... Actually, sometimes they really remind me of you and Nath, the Master laughed.

We are nowhere near that bad, she quickly asserted.

Ko-Pau considered it for a moment. *No, I suppose you aren't,* he relented. *Enjoy your tea. I'll come and get you when it's time.*

Alright, Akinia sighed, a moment before he pulled away.

It was nearly half an hour later when Ko-Pau finally knocked on her door. "You should probably leave Rofa here," he suggested as the cub tried to follow Akinia from the room.

"Stay, girl. I know, but I'll be back soon," Akinia promised, touching the cub's thoughts with her own to reinforce the words.

Rofa heaved a sigh as she plopped down onto the floor, sulking.

"Are you ready for this?" Ko-Pau asked, smiling, as the door slid shut behind his Apprentice.

"I hope so," Akinia replied, an undercurrent of nervousness eating away at the confident façade she tried to display.

Ko-Pau chose not to acknowledge it. "It's this way," he informed her, turning and heading up the hallway.

Akinia easily kept pace with him, the ball of nervousness in her stomach growing with each step.

Ko-Pau's thoughts gently brushed against hers, and she welcomed the contact.

Thanks, she said simply, feeling his silent reassurance through their mental link.

Anytime, Slick, he replied. "Here we are," he said a few minutes later, as they stopped in front of a set of large double-doors. "This is the throne room."

"Aren't you coming?" she asked, frowning, as he made no move to open the doors.

"Not this time," Ko-Pau smiled. "They just want you right now. Khee-Lá is waiting inside for you."

Akinia hesitated, and then nodded. She forced herself to smile. "Well, here goes," she sighed. She reached for the handles of the doors, but then they swung open, seemingly of their own accord.

Good luck, Ko-Pau bade, giving her a reassuring wink.

His apprentice smiled in response, and then stepped through the doors. Besides her aunt and uncles, a dozen people stood in the throne room; Akinia's cousins were nowhere to be seen.

Every eye turned on Akinia as she entered, and twelve distinct gasps could easily be heard.

"Dear friends," Andrid began, proudly motioning to Akinia, "please allow me to introduce my niece, Princess Akinia Juntoby-Zanoratta."

Each of the six couples bowed and curtsied to Akinia, the looks of shocked amazement never leaving their faces.

Khee-Lá smiled at Akinia. "Come here, Sweetheart, don't be nervous," he beckoned, motioning for her to come to him.

Akinia managed a smile for the strangers as she quickly made her way to her uncle's side, suddenly self-conscious under their intense gazes..

Andrid silently beckoned to his guests. Each of the couples

approached one at a time, and Andrid introduced them to Akinia as they did so, giving each couple a moment to speak with her before moving on to the next couple in line.

The guests stayed for more than an hour, eager to discover all that they could about their missing princess, before Andrid finally asked them to excuse Akinia. "She had a long journey to come here, and she needs her rest," he informed them.

After a round of goodbyes, which lasted another half-hour, the twelve diplomats dispersed, leaving the Juntoby family in peace.

"There now, that wasn't so bad," Khee-Lá teased, hugging his niece.

Akinia couldn't help but laugh, relieved that it was over.

"We'll make the public announcement later this morning," Andrid promised her, pointedly ignoring his brother. "Once that occurs, then you will be able to explore Náto all you like."

"The palace, at least," Katarina corrected. "It would still be far too soon for you to wander the streets. Let the excitement of your return calm some before you venture into public."

"That sounds wonderful," Akinia agreed, smiling.

Chapter 14:

Despite Andrid's assurances that it would be later that morning when the public announcement would be made, it was early afternoon before the King and Queen's statement was released to the people of Náto.

Akinia watched from her balcony as the crowds gathered in the streets, surrounded the holo-projectors that now created three-dimensional images of Andrid and Katarina. The girl was too far away to hear the words that the holographs spoke, but she knew exactly what was being said.

"Fifteen years ago," Andrid began solemnly, "our planet was surrounded by Sigidian troops. Led by a man we once considered to be our ally, our protector, the Sigidians invaded our streets and our homes, slaughtering our people. Among those we lost, as you all well know, were my father and mother, my sister, Leonora, her husband, Josiah, and their twin daughters, Aki and Akinia. We still mourn our losses, and we shall continue to mourn them until the end of time, but today we have been given a miracle. Princess Akinia Juntoby-Zanoratta, once believed to have been massacred with so many others, has returned to us, alive and well. Let us all celebrate!"

The crowd visibly reacted as a third holographic image joined the first two, this image showing Akinia standing with her aunt and uncle.

The real Akinia smiled as she watched the Nátoans run through the streets, cheering and celebrating. *They really loved her, didn't they?* she asked Khee-Lá, who was wandering in another part of the palace.

I never knew anyone who could spend more than five minutes in a room with your mother and not love her, he replied, a sad note to his thoughts.

Unable to think of an appropriate response, Akinia strengthened her mental bond with her uncle, letting him feel all of her love for him pouring through their link.

He gratefully returned the gesture, and Akinia could feel him smiling.

They were interrupted a moment later by Katarina hesitantly opening the bedroom door. "Akinia? May I have a moment?" she requested.

"Of course," Akinia replied at once.

I will let the two of you talk, Khee-Lá decided, pulling his thoughts away from his niece's before she could reply.

Katarina smiled broadly as she entered, motioning to one of the plush chairs as she sat on another one.

Akinia sat where her aunt indicated. "Is everything alright?" she asked uncertainly.

"Yes, of course," Katarina replied hastily. "I just wanted to speak with you for a few minutes, about the ball."

"Ball?" Akinia echoed uncertainly.

The queen smiled. "A princess of Náto has returned home after fifteen years of being thought dead. If I don't throw a ball in your honor, what kind of a queen does that make me? Or an aunt, for that matter?" she teased. "Do you know how to dance?"

Akinia hesitated. "In theory, yes; in practice, not at all," she admitted, blushing slightly.

Katarina pursed her lips slightly as she contemplated her niece's answer. "Well, that won't do," she finally decided. "I will have to teach you. Not today, of course. Today you are going to explore the palace and enjoy being home. I think we'll try tomorrow, and see how you do."

"That sounds wonderful," Akinia agreed, smiling.

They sat in silence for several long moments, neither sure what to say next. It was Katarina who broke the silence. "Akinia," she began hesitantly, "I know that you don't have any memories of your mother, and it breaks my heart to think of the way that you were raised. I know that it was necessary, and I have forgiven Khee-Lá for keeping you hidden from us, but no child should grow without a mother's love. I'm only your aunt, and we've only known one another for a very short while, but I'm a mother to your cousins, and a mother's heart always has extra room to welcome another child in. If you ever need anything, please know that I am here, and I will always be."

Akinia's eyes grew wide as she listened to her aunt. She

98

hesitated, uncertain how to respond, before standing and walking over to her.

Katarina stood as Akinia approached, searching the girl's eyes with her own as she tried to determine what the girl could be thinking.

"Thank you," Akinia said gratefully, carefully hugging the heavily pregnant woman.

The queen enthusiastically returned her niece's hug, holding her tightly for several minutes before she loosened her hold. "Come, why don't I give you a tour now that the announcement has been made?" Katarina suggested.

"Alright," the princess happily agreed.

Their exploration was not overly long, Katarina grew ill and had to rest again, but Akinia's seven cousins were more than happy to take over.

As they wandered the hallways, the servants followed as discreetly as they could bear to, all straining for a glimpse of the once-dead princess.

Amalli and Rignon tactfully directed their cousin and siblings to venture down the lesser-used hallways, especially as the diplomats began arriving; Katarina had made it very clear to them all that Akinia's introductions were to be saved for the ball.

Akinia was kept mostly hidden from the Nátoans for the four days leading up to the ball, and Katarina lived up to her promise of teaching Akinia how to dance. With Khee-Lá as her partner, Akinia quickly learned the three series of complicated dance steps that were most commonly used.

However, the young Najee was still very weak, and the lessons tired her, so Katarina decided to use the time to teach her niece diplomacy; it was an area that Akinia excelled in, much to her family's delight.

"Alright, that's enough for today," Khee-Lá finally said as the music drew to a close. "She needs to sleep at some point tonight."

Akinia thought to argue, but decided against it as she yawned. "I think Uncle Khee-Lá may be right," she sighed, giving Katarina an apologetic smile.

"He is," Katarina agreed, nodding. "Go on and get some rest."

Smiling, Akinia hugged each of her uncles and her aunt before leaving. Ko-Pau, Nath, and all seven of her cousins had already gone to bed for the night. *Do you think that I'm ready for tomorrow?* she asked

Khee-Lá as she wandered to her room.

I think that you are going to do wonderfully, he promised.

Goodnight, Uncle, Akinia smiled, strengthening their mental embrace.

Goodnight, Sweetheart, Khee-Lá replied as he pulled his thoughts away from hers.

Chapter 15:

Akinia stretched as she lay in bed, though she was still half asleep. She could feel the warm sunshine creeping through the open window to lie across her face, and she could feel the thick pillows and comforter that enveloped her body... a small part of her, the part that was beginning to wake, sighed in contentment. *I could lay here forever*, she decided, nuzzling her face deeper into one of the fethera pillows.

She rolled onto her stomach, feeling a chill on her face as the sun's warmth was suddenly stolen from it. It wasn't cold in the room, or even close to it, but the sun had been slightly warmer... She sighed again, but this time in frustration; she was more awake than asleep now, and in a few minutes she would have to crawl out of bed and get dressed. For now, though, she simply burrowed her face into the comforter and pretended she was still asleep.

"Rofa!" she chastised as the ceffre cub leapt on top of her, startling her into sitting upright. She couldn't stay mad at her pet for very long, though. A smile crept onto her face as she began to scruff the cub's massive head. "What am I going to do with you?" she laughed.

As Rofa leapt back onto the floor and darted out onto the balcony, Akinia swung her legs off the bed and let her feet hang a few inches from the floor. She glanced after her pet, noticing with surprise that the sun was already very bright... *How late did I sleep?* Akinia wondered absentmindedly as she began to walk towards the closet.

My wajun! she suddenly remembered, turning to walk along the far side of the bed and retrieve it from the nightstand where she had left it.

She only made it part of the way there when a soft electronic voice commanded, "State your name."

She jumped, startled, and looked around for its source.

"State your name," it repeated.

Frowning, she turned towards the bare wall, where the voice seemed to be coming from. She slowly raised her hand and began to feel around the wall, hoping to find some small indicator of whatever wished to know her name. For a moment she felt nothing, but then she could barely discern a small ridge beneath her fingers. *A door*, she realized, amazed. *Could my mother have had a private study, like Headmistress had in her room?*

"State your name," the voice commanded once more.

"Akinia," she quickly replied, watching the ridge carefully to see if it would open.

"State your *full* name," it specified.

Frowning, she tried, "Akinia Juntoby."

"State your *full* name."

It would know the name my mother knew for me, my legal name, if it knows anything, she decided. "Akinia Núro Leonora Kheelita Juntoby-Zanoratta," she stated confidently.

"State your *full* name."

Could it possibly know? She reached out with her mind, to check that she was alone, before barely whispering, "Akinia Núro Leonora Kheelita Juntoby-Enbrilth."

A red light traced a rectangle on the wall that was slightly taller and barely wider than Akinia's figure, following the thin path she had traced with her fingertips. The moment the light finished tracing, the rectangle sunk slightly into the wall and slid to the side. Akinia cautiously walked through the doorway to see what lay on the other side.

The room was gray and dimly lit, but as she passed over the threshold, a series of small lights suddenly turned on. The room was empty of furniture, barring a metal desk and a simple metal chair in the middle of the room. On top of the desk were two small silver chests. A folded piece of paper sat on top of each of the two chests and a single word in beautifully scrawled calligraphy was penned on the upper flap. One of the two words caught her eye as she approached.

Akinia's hands shook violently as she picked up the folded paper upon which her name was written. She didn't notice the thick layer of dust that covered every surface of the room, including the letter. She didn't even notice the door slide shut behind her as she struggled to open the paper and see what it said.

102

My dearest Akinia,

The fact that you are reading this letter means two things: the first is that you survived the attack on our palace, and second is that I did not. I write this in haste because I do not know if I will survive and I wish you to know how much I love you in the event that I am not there to tell you myself. I also wish to apologize to you for not being there with you now as you grow up.

I know that since you have figured out how to get into this room, my private study, you know the truth about your father. I beg you not to hate us. Someday you will know how the heart pulls you to love certain people, even those who your mind tells you are wrong to be with.

I hope you never have to read this letter, but if you do I hope that you know that I love you and your sister more than anything else. Never forget that.

I am leaving now to find you. I pray that your uncle will keep you safe, since you are with him, but I cannot remain here while you and your sister are apart from me. I could not forgive myself if either of you did not survive while I hid away here. I am leaving this for you, in case I am killed before I can give it to you myself. Keep it safe, and remember that you and Aki are all that each other has. Love and protect one another, for I know that you will both grow to be powerful and important Najee as Khee-Lá has told me. My sweet girl, remember always that you are my heart and my hope.

Farewell, my dear one,
-Mother

Akinia read the letter once, twice, and again a third time. Each time she absorbed the words deeper into her mind and her heart. Each time a different part stood out to her.

The first time she read, she realized that Leonora's death had not been the sudden and brutal attack that she had envisioned. Her mother had known that she would likely die, and had gotten her things in order hastily for her children if she did. What was it like to realize that you were going to die? How did it feel to write a letter knowing that it would only be read after you were long dead?

The second time she read, her heart nearly stopped beating. She knew about Josiah? She knew that she was marrying the younger brother of the man trying to destroy the Empire and she didn't care? Khee-Lá had told Akinia that Leonora's heart had been her greatest downfall, but did he understand how true of a statement that had been? Khee-Lá had always assumed that Leonora never knew Josiah's true identity, but this letter proved that he was wrong. Leonora knew, and she had loved Josiah anyway.

The third time she read, her blood boiled. Her mother had been safely locked away in here, and yet she had left to find her daughters. She could have lived if she had stayed here. But Akinia knew what happened next. Leonora had left to find her daughters, but knew they were separated. She had gone to find Lokita first, probably because Lokita wasn't with a Najee. Tears rolled down Akinia's face as she realized that Leonora would have lived had she gone to find Akinia first, because Khee-Lá would have rescued her also instead of allowing her to run off and be killed.

She found another surge of hatred for her twin rising up. If her mother hadn't gone looking for Lokita, she would be alive. If it weren't for Lokita, Khee-Lá would have hidden Akinia with Leonora somewhere. But no, it wasn't Lokita's fault. How could the innocent baby be blamed for being loved by her mother? At that time, she wasn't trying to kill Akinia or destroy the Empire. She was still an innocent child at that point, and not responsible for the evil that took her that night.

Akinia re-read her mother's words about Lokita. "Remember that you and Aki are all that each other has," she read, her voice barely a whisper, "Love and protect one another, for I know that you will grow to be powerful Najee as Khee-Lá has told me." *I'm sorry, Mother,* Akinia sighed to herself, *I know that it would hurt you to see us like this, as enemies. I would change it if I could, but I can't. In a way I'm glad you're gone, so that you don't have to see what Lokita has done to me, but I wish you were here! Why did you have to leave this room? Why did you have to go to Lokita, and not to me? Why did you leave me? Why couldn't you have just stayed alive for me? If you couldn't have done it for yourself, you should have stayed for me!*

Tears began to fall rapidly from her eyes, until it seemed as though a steady stream of water was falling. She felt the pain and frustration and desolation that she had seen in the eyes of the other orphans for years at the orphanage. The feeling of abandonment that the others had all felt had never surfaced in her before, until she read her

104

mother's letter. It felt as though she had found and lost her mother in the same moment. It was like she could have touched Leonora if she had just stretched her hand out a bit farther, but her mother was snatched away before she could act on the realization.

Bitterness welled up inside her, against her mother. All of the anger and frustration and hate she had felt seemed to hurdle itself at the image of her mother. *Why couldn't you have stayed alive for me? You couldn't have helped Lokita! You didn't do her any good by being there when she was taken! But you could have helped me, mother. You could have been there for me instead of leaving me without any parents, to be raised by a stranger along with thousands of other children! Why couldn't you have stayed alive for me? Didn't you love me enough to want to stay alive, to be with me? You said you did, but then you went to Lokita! You went to her, and it killed you!*

A part of her wanted to rip Leonora's letter to shreds, and then burn what remained. A larger part recoiled from the idea, holding the letter close with such ferocity that it seemed almost a sacred item. A third part seemed to remember that there was a box beneath the letter which held something that her mother had left specifically for her.

Gently setting the letter to the side, and wiping the tears from her cheeks with the back of her hands, Akinia hesitantly unfastened the simple latch that held the lid down. As she lifted it, she gasped. Lying inside of the box, on a cushion of red velvet, sat the circlet Leonora had worn in her portrait in the Grand Hall. Khee-Lá had told her about this circlet: it was the lost diadem that had been searched for, unsuccessfully, for the past fifteen years.

Her hands shook as she lifted the circlet from the box. She gently traced the gold double-band that looped in the front to encircle the large teardrop-shaped sapphire that hung from a golden chain three links long. She followed the double-band around until her fingers touched the opposite side of the sapphire. No dust had entered the box, and none tarnished the beautiful circlet. Akinia hesitantly bit her lower lip for a moment before lifting the circlet to her head. The loop that held the sapphire rested on her forehead. The outer edges of the double-loop touched each of her eyebrows, and the topmost edge brushed her hairline. The sides of the circlet sagged down along the sides of her head before rising back up to sit near the top of the back of her skull.

It fit perfectly. Had Akinia not been brushing the smooth gold with her fingers, she would have sworn that the circlet wasn't on her head. Every curve, every angle, everything was synced perfectly to the contours of her skull. "Identical to Leonora," she mused grimly, "Uncle, you have no idea..."

She fingered the circlet for a while more. Her mind was empty of coherent thoughts, but a random jumble of emotions and images flooded through her. *Why?* Sighing, she pushed herself to her feet and reluctantly peeled the circlet away from her head. She turned it this way and that, watching the light reflect off of the gold bands and the crystalline jewel. With great reluctance, she placed it gently back into its box and closed the lid.

Her hand lay on the top for a while as she debated whether or not to take it out again. *No, Akinia*, she sighed, picking the letter up and carefully folding it, *no one can know about this...not yet...* Hesitating a moment, she put the letter back where she found it. *How do I tell Uncle Khee-Lá? How do I show this place to him without him finding out that Mother knew? I can't bring Andrid or Katarina here, and definitely not the children... Maybe I should tell Master? No, he would tell Khee-Lá... Or I could...no, not Nath...*

Or maybe...well, I'll figure out what to do later, after the ball, she decided. She gently fingered the hastily inscribed letters on the outside of the paper, reluctant to leave it sitting there. "Mother," she whispered, the tense layers of her voice betraying the confusion and pain the word now brought to her.

A deep furrow carved itself into her brow as she forced herself to turn and leave the little room. She hesitated in the doorway a moment, but then stepped back into her bedroom and allowed the door to slide shut behind her. *Did that just happen?* Akinia wondered, uncertainty creeping up on her. *Don't be silly... Even you couldn't have imagined something like that,* she chastised herself.

A painful, rapid throbbing began to pound inside her head as her frustration mounted. As her vision began to blur slightly, she crawled onto her bed and curled up in the center, pulling the thick fethera comforter over top of herself. *Mother,* she sighed, closing her eyes to try and ward the headache away.

She sat up abruptly several minutes later. *This isn't working.* She rubbed her forehead for a moment before pushing herself to her feet. Her mind shot out across the palace, touching the vaguely familiar minds of her newest family as well as the familiar mental embraces of Ko-Pau and Khee-Lá. It took her a moment longer to find Nath in the

106

palace gardens.

What's going on, Kiddo? he asked as he felt her close her mind off to everyone but him.

Nothing, she lied easily, *wait for me, I want to walk, too.*

Nath's smirk translated through their mental link. *I'll meet you in the hall. I was headed inside… I escaped from your cousin a few minutes ago*, he reported, an image of Noregh surfacing in his thoughts.

Akinia considered chastising him, but thought the better of it and just said, *I'm coming now.* She pulled her thoughts away from his, enveloping her mind within itself. Shaking her head with a semi-amused smirk, she pushed herself to her feet and slipped into the hallway, hoping she could make it all the way to Nath without being noticed.

She rounded a corner and stopped short, seeing Nath casually lounging against tall archway overlooking the gardens. She watched him silently for a moment, the way his eyes shined and the corners of his lips twitched as he smiled… "What are you looking at?" she asked curiously.

He didn't jump at the sound of her voice, but glanced back at her out of the corner of his eyes. "Your cousins," he explained simply, motioning with his shoulder to the garden below.

Akinia stepped closer, pausing just beside him to watch Anlix and Noregh playing catch-and-chase. Not far from them, Lanzi could be seen crossing her arms and scolding them for not getting ready for the ball.

For the barest fraction of a second Akinia found herself truly happy. All of her concerns and fears melted away as she watched the children, as she sensed Nath's warm presence beside her, as she breathed in the sweet familiar scent of Náto… but a shadow seemed to grow inside of her heart, pushing away the good feelings and making the confusion and pain rise up inside of her again. She could feel her forehead crease as she turned away from the window. Giving a sigh, she began to stroll back up the hallway.

"You don't look so good," Nath noted, concerned, as he turned to follow her.

Her eyebrows arched slightly. "Thank you, Nath," she replied dryly. "That's what every girl wants to hear."

He rolled his eyes. "Come on, you know that's not what I meant… Are you okay?"

A grim smile crept onto her lips as she nodded. "I guess," she shrugged.

"I'm taking that as a 'no'," he stated, puzzled. He wrapped one arm around her shoulders and gave a slight, comforting squeeze.

She laid her head against his side, her pace slowing them both until they finally stopped. "I think this is the first time we've walked like this since..." her voice trailed off and she bit her lower lip, blushing.

He frowned. "Is it?"

Unwilling to speak, she just gave a slight nod that he felt more than saw. She tensed as she felt the odd mix of emotions radiating from him. She could feel anger, pain, fear, and even a trace of resentment; it was the latter that hurt her the most. *He'll never see me the same way again*, she thought bitterly, unable to determine who she hated the most for that fact: Jade, Nath, or herself. A sharp twinge of pain cut through her, but it wasn't caused by her physical wounds...

"I hadn't even thought about it," Nath sighed, "but I guess it makes sense. You have no idea how bad you looked when we brought you back; I was scared to look at you too hard for a while."

She grimaced and pulled away slightly to look at him. "I looked better than I felt," she admitted quietly. She buried her face into his chest as he pulled her close and held her in his arms.

"It that what's bothering you?" he asked without pulling away. "What happened, I mean?"

It took Akinia a moment to clear her head enough to answer. She had forgotten how nice it felt just to have him hold her; of all the things that had seemed to have changed between them these last months, this wasn't one of them... "No," she answered decidedly. "No, I actually haven't thought about that much since coming here."

"What, then?" he asked, this time pulling away slightly to look her in the eyes. "Tell me."

"It's nothing... everything... I just... my mother..." her voice broke, and she pulled away as she tried to regain her composure; the last thing she wanted was to start crying.

"Akinia..." he murmured gently, his voice laced with almost as much pain as hers.

"Don't tell my family, especially my uncles," she begged, turning sharply to face him. "Please."

"Fine," he agreed, "but I think you should talk to-"

"-not Master either; I mean it, Nath, please don't. You know how much they all overreact," she half-asked, half-ordered.

He visibly struggled between his loyalty to Ko-Pau and his loyalty to Akinia, but her wide-eyed pleading seemed to win out because he sighed, nodded, and muttered, "Fine."

Akinia smiled and opened her mouth to thank him. Before she could speak, though, he held up a hand to silence her.

Amalli is here, he informed her quickly, not bothering to pull his mind away from hers.

Amalli? Isn't she supposed to be getting ready for the ball? Or wrangling my cousins into preparing?

Nath didn't respond farther than a shrug; there wasn't time for any other answer.

Amalli rounded the corner in the hallway, a wide smile spread across her face. Her pale skin had a rosy appearance, as flushed as she was from her excitement. Her copper hair hung loose around her shoulders, the golden highlights catching each ray of light and magnifying it enough that each strand seemed to glow. It was a beautiful backdrop to her sandy-brown gown. In her usual style, the half-sleeved top was intricately beaded down to the thick burgundy ribbon belt that wrapped around the empire waist of the plain floor-length skirt. Her hands were behind her back, obviously hiding something from sight. "Oh, Nath, there you are," she breathed, relieved. "I've been looking everywhere for you!"

Nath smiled as he turned to talk to her. "Hey, kid, what's up?" he asked, crossing his arms and leaning back against the wall.

"What do you have there?" Akinia asked curiously, wondering what could make her young cousin so excited.

"Oh, Kinny, you're going to love it!" Amalli gushed, walking forwards to embrace her cousin with one arm, the other holding whatever it was safely behind her back still. She gave Akinia a quick kiss on the cheek.

Noticing her diverted attention, Nath quickly snatched the bundle of cloth from Amalli's hands and held it up above his head.

"Hey!" she protested, laughing as she reached for it. "Nath, that isn't nice, give it back!"

Akinia laughed, too. "You may as well tell him what it is, he'll never give it back... Unless you'd like me to *make* him."

Nath rolled his eyes. "Yeah, like you have that power," he scoffed with a wink.

She stomped the foot nearest to him, laughing when he jumped. "I would say that I do," she said pointedly, elbowing him in the ribs. "So what is it, anyway?"

Amalli smiled proudly. "It's a gift for Nath," she explained. "Remember how you told me a few days ago you didn't have a waistbelt to wear to the ball? Well, I made you one. Here, look," she ordered, snatching it back as Nath lowered it. She unfolded the cloth and held it up for Nath to see.

"Oh this is very nice," Akinia praised, fingering the seams. *Now try to get out of it, Nath, dear*, she grinned.

A little help, please, he begged.

Not a chance! This is far too amusing, she laughed. *Besides, I did warn you that I would make you pay...*

Nath glared at Akinia, but only for a moment while Amalli wasn't looking. "How, er, how did you know what size to make it?" he asked, but Akinia knew he was still trying to figure out how to get out of it.

"Bashka told me," she explained.

Nath rolled his eyes. "Ko-Pau knew about this?" he asked, slightly annoyed.

She nodded. "Yes. Bashka said what size to make it and he said you would absolutely love it when I showed him earlier. He said you would be sure to wear it," she said proudly. Her smile turned into a frown as Nath rolled his eyes again. "You don't like it," she realized, upset.

"No, of course I like it, Amalli," he promised quickly.

She doesn't believe you; be more convincing, Akinia ordered.

How am I supposed to be more convincing? I don't like it! I'm surprised I managed to be even this convincing, he growled. "I really do like it, kiddo," he promised, again.

"So you'll wear it to the ball?" Amalli questioned hopefully.

Nath grinned. "Absolutely," he promised. *Shut up, Akinia*, he growled as he heard her silent laughter through their mental link.

She beamed again. "Oh good!" she gushed, "I made it to look like Bashka's, it's even the same color. Generally that is reserved for family lines, but then you've always said that Bashka is like a father to you so I decided it would be appropriate. I should probably go and make sure the children are getting ready. The last time mother hosted a ball they didn't even get dressed until it was nearly time to join the party! Which reminds me, Akinia, mother wants to help you get ready. She said to inform you that she would be waiting in your room. I would bet that she is there now."

Akinia grinned at Nath as her cousin sped off. "I had best get to my room, then," she decided. "I'm sure Ko-Pau will be delighted to help you tie that if you run into trouble," she added as she darted away.

"You think you're funny, don't you?" he demanded, annoyed, as she left.

I know I am, Nath dear, she laughed, rounding the corner.

He growled through their mental link. *I'm going to go and find Master, and then I'm going have a nice long talk with him about why I don't like coming to Náto,* he decided. He pulled his mind away from hers, but Akinia pointedly pushed to keep a brushing contact between them. *Okay,* he relented with a sigh. He knew his presence reassured her, and wouldn't rob her of that.

Akinia didn't comment on the direction his thoughts had taken him, but it was a struggle to bite back the smart remark that had come to mind. She tried not to annoy him when they were tenuously linked like this.

Could have fooled me, Nath laughed.

Shut up, she ordered, laughing as well. She pulled her mind away from his as he located Ko-Pau, not trusting herself to be able to restrain from commenting as they spoke. Also, she had just arrived at her own door and doubted it would be prudent for them to remain linked while she dressed. A slight blush rose in her cheeks, but she hoped Katarina would attribute it to her nervous excitement.

"Oh, Amalli found you, excellent!" Katarina noted as she walked in, beaming at the sight of her young niece. She met Akinia halfway across the room and grasped her hands, leading her to the metal dress form that held her gown. "Well," she prodded, "what do you think of it?"

Akinia's mouth fell open as she saw the dress. Yards and yards of purple silk billowed to form the long skirt, gathered just beneath the bodice of the empire waist. The top was a sweetheart neckline with gold cord forming a halter top, the ends of which would fasten between her breasts. Another gold cord, this one with tasseled ends, would be tied loosely around her natural waist, flattering her figure. The lower hem of the skirt would brush the ground.

"I don't know what to say," she gasped, gently fingering the intricate gold embroidery curling around the hem of the skirt. "I've never seen anything so beautiful!"

Katarina laughed, pleased with the praise, and willingly accepted Akinia's embrace. "It belongs to you now, my dear," Katarina informed her as she gently brushed a stray strand of hair behind the girl's ear. "I have another gift for you as well. Close your eyes."

Though uncertain what to expect, Akinia did as she was told. She felt her aunt playing with her hair for a moment before she was instructed to look in the mirror.

"It was your mother's," Katarina explained proudly.

Akinia couldn't reply as she gently fingered the silver circlet. It dipped down in the front, as Amalli's did, and a large teardrop-shaped diamond hung between her eyebrows. "My mother's?" she echoed.

Katarina nodded. "She never took it off when she was your age. She even slept in it most nights," she laughed. "I once asked her why and she told me that this circlet represented her people and her planet, without them she was nothing and she couldn't bear to remove it for even a moment."

Akinia smiled, but a tear fell from her eye. "She loved this place so much..."

"She loved you even more," Katarina promised, holding her young niece in her arms. "I only wish that you could have known her now that you are old enough to remember her."

"As do I," she sighed, leaning into her aunt's embrace.

They held each other for several long minutes before Katarina gently pulled away. "Let's finish dressing you, shall we?" she suggested.

Several hours later, Katarina finally left her.

Akinia's head was sore from the dozens of hairstyles that had been experimented on her, and her face was red and sore from all the times her makeup had been scrubbed away so that they could start with a fresh canvas. Finally, Akinia put her foot down and scrubbed her face clean, refusing to allow any more makeup to be put on her. She had fought long and hard with Katarina and her maids over that one, but had ultimately won.

Now Akinia sat alone, savoring her victory as she counted the seconds since her aunt had left. Finally, when she thought it was safe, she stood. "Akinia Núro Leonora Kheelita Juntoby-Enbrilth," she whispered as the electronic voice asked for her name. She hesitated a moment before stepping inside.

"Mother," she whispered, "I wish you were here with me now!" Feeling tears begin to prick the corners of her eyes, she started blinking rapidly to clear them away. If she arrived at the ball with her eyes red and swollen, Katarina would never forgive her.

Her fingers trembled slightly as she took her mother's letter in her hands and read it again. As she read the last word, her eyes closed and she savored each syllable. Finally, she sighed and set the letter aside. She gently lifted the lid of the box and stared down at the circlet within it.

An idea began to form in her mind and, before she could talk herself out of it, she switched her com-link on. "Jaynine, come to my room. I need your help with something," she ordered.

"Of course, Mistress."

Chapter 16:

The music that had been playing at a pace suitable for dancing suddenly slowed and began at a much higher, much more delicate melody. Khee-Lá, Ko-Pau, and Nath, as well as the guests and the royal family, all looked to the head of the stairs as the large, ornate double-doors opened.

On the other side, Akinia took a deep breath to calm herself as she made her appearance. She paused a moment at the top of the stairwell before descending slowly, her footsteps light and smooth.

Soft gasps were heard as the guests took a look at her, and recognized her resemblance to the dearly departed Queen Leonora. Even Khee-Lá, Andrid, and Katarina had to stare at this young beauty, a nearly perfect match to their lost sister.

Her honey-golden hair hung loosely around her shoulders. The double-loop of her mother's old circlet peaked out from underneath her golden locks as it hung over her forehead. The clear crystal that was encrusted into the center of the smaller loop seemed to bring out the sparkle that shone in her eyes, which now seemed to glow bright blue. Her bright red lips curved into a slender smile as she paused at the turn in the staircase.

All of the male guests got down on one knee, and the female guests lowered themselves onto both knees as they bent forwards at the waist in respect. Even the royal family and the Najee bent forwards slightly.

Akinia's cheeks quickly turned pink.

Khee-Lá stood erect before the others as he walked three-quarters of the way up the lower flight of stairs and offered Akinia his arm. "We're going to have a nice long talk later," he whispered as she slipped her arm around his.

Akinia gave a quick nod that was so slight, only Khee-Lá

noticed it; she had been expecting that ever since she found the circlet and her mother's letter. As they reached the bottom step, everyone rose.

As she was introduced to the various officials and their spouses, as Princess Akinia Juntoby-Zanoratta, she did her best to keep the names and faces together in her mind.

Khee-Lá watched with pride as she politely answered their many questions.

Just like her mother, Akinia was a natural.

She politely inclined her head as each couple bowed, keeping her aunt's instruction at the forefront of her mind. The most common query was where she had hidden these many years, to which she always replied, "In the care of my Protector, deep within the Empire, where I could be safe." This ended most of the queries, as there was not time for the diplomats to inquire further in this initial introduction, but Akinia had a distinct feeling that certain people were not satisfied with her answer. She resolved immediately to avoid them as much as possible.

Finally, the long line of introductions came to an end. Half the names, she had already completely forgotten; the other half, she could vaguely remember whose name started with what sound… it was a very rare few whose name she could *actually* remember. She was shamefacedly pondering this when Andrid approached her.

"May I request the honor of your hand for the first dance?" he asked, bowing and holding his right hand out to her.

Feeling every eye in the room watching her, she curtsied deeply, a smile tracing her lips. "I would be honored, Uncle," she replied, blushing as she placed her hand in his and allowed him to lead her out to the center of the floor.

No one else danced as the orchestra began their song. The entire assembly seemed content to watch the king dancing with his long-lost niece, marveling at her grace and beauty, so similar to that of their late queen.

The faces of the crowd blurred together as Andrid led Akinia through the intricate steps of the dance, twirling her around and around. She kept her eyes firmly directed onto his face, afraid that she would get dizzy if she tried to look anywhere else.

"You are very beautiful, my dear," he praised, smiling.

Akinia's blush deepened. "Do you ever get tired of flattering me?" she wondered, biting her lower lip to keep from laughing.

"Never," he answered seriously. "It is an uncle's privilege to flatter his nieces and toughen his nephews; your uncle, Khee-Lá, never gave me the opportunity. I had hoped… Ah, well, this is no place for such a discussion… What do you think of your aunt's handiwork?" His eyes drifted around the room as he asked, leaving no doubt as to what he was referring to.

"It is amazing," Akinia sighed fondly. "Does she do this often, or just when her long-lost nieces return home?"

Though his lips tightened in anger, as they always did, when she made the joke, he managed to smile and reply, "Yes, quite often. She always enjoyed balls, even as a young girl. I'll never forget the time she invited the three of us over to her house for a tea party, and then proceeded to play a recording of music and coerce us all to dance. She could have been no more than ten at the time!"

Akinia allowed herself to laugh softly at the tale, perfectly able to imagine her aunt doing such a thing. They fell silent, simply enjoying the moment as the dance slowed to its finale. The assembly clapped softly, respectfully, as the dance ended. A blush rose to Akinia's cheeks as she allowed herself to look at their rapturous faces.

"I thank you for the dance, my dear," Andrid smiled, bowing deeply.

Akinia curtsied low in response. "Thank *you*, Uncle."

No sooner had Andrid walked away than Khee-Lá approached. "May I beg the next dance?" he asked with a quick wink. He bowed and held out his hand to her.

Once again Akinia curtsied. "You may have as many dances as you wish, Uncle, and you don't need to beg," she teased as she drew herself upright again and placed her hand in his. As the music began to play once more, they took their positions and began a much slower and less dizzying dance.

This time other couples began to trickle onto the dance floor, still giving the young princess a great deal of room in the center.

Akinia opened her mind to her uncle, gently caressing his thoughts with her own.

Are you glad we came here? Khee-Lá wondered.

She smiled. *Very much so*, she assured him.

I suppose the story of how you found my sister's circlet is too long to be covered at present?

Much too long, she sighed. *I will tell you when we can escape from everyone for a while… I do intend to tell you, but you can never tell anyone else.*

His puzzlement was easily felt through their mental link, but he decided to respect her wishes and be patient. *In all honesty, do you feel well?*

Uncle, you promised, she complained, sensing an undercurrent to his thoughts that felt a little too possessive.

He sighed. *I know, but I would feel better if you could honestly assure me that you feel well; I don't want you getting ill again because you overdid it!*

I feel perfectly fine, she promised, a twinge of annoyance seeping through to him. *I promise that if I feel unwell I will rest; will that satisfy you?*

I suppose so... for now... Though, I will most likely ask you again several times before the night is over. Bear with an old man's fretting?

Akinia laughed. *Perhaps when I have an old man's fretting to bear... for now I'll practice with yours.*

Flattery will get you everywhere, he teased. The song ended just then and he bowed to her once more, kissing her fingers as he did.

She curtsied in response, giving him a quick kiss on the cheek as he walked past her. *I love you.*

I love you, too, Sweetheart, he replied softly before pulling his mind away from hers with a last, gentle caress.

Another familiar mind brushed up against her own, and she turned to see Ko-Pau standing behind her.

"May I?" he asked simply, bowing and offering her his hand.

"Of course, Master," she replied, smiling, as she curtsied.

I'm not very good at this, despite Katarina's many attempts to train me, he teased and apologized as he stepped on her foot.

I won't tell if you don't, she bargained, quickly relating her dismay at being unable to remember most of the names.

His silent laughter rang through their mental link. *I wouldn't worry too much about it, Slick; I've been coming here for years and I still haven't learned half their names!*

She pursed her lips thoughtfully. *Should that make me feel better, or worse?*

Hey! Ko-Pau exclaimed, still silently laughing. *I think you've been around Nath too long; you're turning mean!*

It was just an innocent question, she teased.

Innocent? he echoed, flabbergasted.

She made a face at him, carefully chosen so that it would look cute to any onlookers, but Ko-Pau would know the intent behind it.

He grinned, immediately catching on. "It has been a pleasure to dance with you, Your Highness," he said seriously as the dance came to an end. He bowed again and walked away.

Your turn? Akinia guessed dryly, touching Nath's thoughts.

I'm afraid not, he grinned. *I've never liked dancing.*

I don't want to hear a word out of you about hating to dance; you aren't the one Katarina put into four-inch heels! she spattered, feeling his silent laughter in her mind.

As the music began once more, she was approached by a man, whom she recognized as being one of the Senators, though his name was lost to her. As they danced he made a few gentle inquiries after her health, notes about the pleasant weather, and a handful of mentions about how happy he was to have her safely on Náto once more.

The next several dances were all claimed by various Senators, and it was partially with amusement and partially with annoyance that she noted their attempts at conversation almost mirrored his.

Nearly two hours into the dance, a young man, perhaps sixteen, approached her. He stood several inches taller than Akinia, though he was nowhere near as tall as Nath. Despite his thin build, his features were somewhat rounded, and they had a nobility and dignity to them which defied his young age. "May I have this dance, Your Highness?" he requested, bowing and offering her his hand.

Akinia felt her cheeks warm slightly, and her humiliation at the realization only caused them to turn a brighter shade of red. "Of course," she replied, hesitantly placing her hand in his. "You'll forgive me if I sound rude, diplomacy is still very new to me, and I'm sure I'm going to offend somebody tonight without meaning to, but I don't recall having met you earlier?"

The boy smiled as he began to lead her through the complicated dance steps. "I arrived late," he explained. "My Master and I have only just returned from Sigadia; the invitation was waiting for me when I arrived home this evening."

"You're a Najee?" Akinia gasped, a bit surprised. "Are you Rheighton Tor-Karr? Forgive me, my Master and Uncle both told me of you."

His smile widened. "I'm glad to know they think so highly of me," he laughed. "I've only spoken to them once or twice; I'm rarely in the Empire, and even more rarely when they happen to be here."

"I'm glad that you were able to come tonight. I-I mean, I didn't expect that I would get to meet you so soon," she hastily clarified, laughing at herself.

Rheighton joined in with her quiet laughter, but then stopped and looked over his shoulder.

"May I?" Nath requested of the younger boy, holding his hand out for Akinia's.

After a moment's hesitation, Rheighton bowed and placed Akinia's hand into Nath's. "Of course," he relented, without protest. Turning and bowing to Akinia, the young Najee disappeared into the crowd of guests.

"I thought you hated dancing?" Akinia questioned, eyeing Nath suspiciously.

"'Hate' is a strong word," Nath teased. "Besides, I just thought about how you had to dance in those suicide shoes Katarina stuck you in, and suddenly dancing didn't seem so bad in my nice, flat-soled boots."

Are you sure it's that, or were you just jealous? she accused, grinning.

Jealous? Nath laughed. *Now why would I be jealous of him?*

I don't know... Why would you cut in his dance with me?

I don't have to be jealous to want to dance with you, Kiddo. Besides, I get to be around you all the time, while he's stuck on ten-month runs in Sigadia; why would I be jealous of a three-minute dance?

Were you jealous? Akinia wondered curiously, the teasing tone gone from her mental voice.

Not in the least, Nath answered at once, before grinning and adding, *but, as your older co-Apprentice, I am obliged to scare away every guy who falls in love with you. It's a rule.*

What kind of rule is that? Akinia demanded bitterly, feeling her entire torso turn red.

Nath grinned, slowing them to a stop. He pulled her fingers to his lips, winking as he gave them a gentle kiss. *Mine.* Without another word, he pulled his mind away from hers and walked away, disappearing into the crowd.

Akinia continued to blush profusely as she glanced around at the couples still dancing around her.

120

"Kinny!" Karanne called excitedly as she darted amongst the swirling couples. The five-year-old girl eagerly grabbed Akinia's hand with both of hers. "Come here, come here," she urged. "Amalli wants you."

"Alright," Akinia laughed, her blush fading some as she allowed the girl to lead her across the ballroom. "I'm coming."

Chapter 17:

"She's a natural," Andrid commented to his brother.

Khee-Lá didn't miss the fact that it was the first time since Akinia's return home that Andrid had spoken entirely kindly to him. Perhaps all would be well, after all. "She most certainly is," he replied. He glanced over to see his niece dancing with one of the senators. As the song changed the senator bowed and stepped away. A young man, perhaps a year or so older than Akinia, stepped over and gave a quick bow before offering the princess his hand. She took it willingly and allowed him to lead her through the complicated dance steps. Khee-Lá smiled as he realized that it was young Rheighton Tor-Karr, the only other Náto born Najee. His smile disappeared as he noticed them both laughing. "That looks like it could be trouble," Khee-Lá commented under his breath.

Andrid laughed. "No, I think trouble is coming from the other direction," he said, motioning with his head to the far right of the room. Nath was walking over towards the dancing Najee with a determined look on his face.

"Personally, of the two I would prefer it be Nath," Khee-Lá admitted.

Andrid was confused. "But Rheighton is Nátoan," he protested, "How could you prefer Nath over one of our own?"

Khee-Lá gave a quick laugh as Nath tapped Rheighton's shoulder and took over the dance. He possessively placed his right hand on Akinia's waist and took her hand in his left. "Easily: I can keep a closer eye on Nath and have much more control over him," he explained. He crossed his arms and watched interestedly as the two danced. They didn't appear to be talking, but Akinia was blushing and smiling. As much as it disturbed him to see the two of them together, Khee-Lá knew that Nath was a good kid; Akinia wouldn't be able to find much better.

It wasn't that Rheighton was a bad kid, but Khee-Lá didn't know him very well and had absolutely no power over him off of Náto. He caught himself smiling, but his smile once again faded as the song ended. Nath pulled Akinia's hand up to his mouth and gently kissed her fingers before winking and disappearing in the crowd. Akinia blushed crimson and looked after him a moment before she was interrupted by little Karanne running over and tugging on the Najee's hand. Akinia smiled and followed willingly as she was led across the ballroom.

Chapter 18:

They found Amalli in the corner of the grand ballroom, in the midst of a small group of girls. All of them were chattering excitedly, but they fell into a hushed and reverent silence as Akinia approached.

"Cousin Akinia," Amalli greeted, smiling broadly. She motioned to the other girls. "Please, allow me to introduce Aimma Kol-Nerr; the Ishlas Meghren Fehl-Krinn, Turra Ish-Baen, and Lonya Myk-Traan; and the Jeertan Kolla Tír-Mahn, Kree Tren-Hye, and Malle Hrish-Venn."

Katarina had already explained to Akinia what the honorifics 'Ishla' and 'Jeerta' meant: an Ishla was the child of a Nátoan diplomat, with no formally declared plans to follow in their parent's footsteps; a Jeerta was a child, generally the child of a diplomat, who had formally requested to be trained in diplomacy, and had received the royal family's blessing in the endeavor.

Each of the girls curtsied deeply to Akinia as Amalli introduced them. The eldest appeared to be around sixteen; the youngest could be no more than twelve. The only girl without a title was Aimma Kol-Nerr, who seemed to be about thirteen years old.

That puzzled Akinia for a moment, before she remembered Khee-Lá telling her that Amalli had a handful of friends who were not born into Nátoan political circles. She found herself wondering if any of the Jeertan that Amalli had just introduced were from non-diplomatic families. "It's nice to meet all of you," she replied, after only a moment's hesitation. She even managed to smile.

"These girls are my closest friends," Amalli explained. "I am certain that they will absolutely adore you!"

Before anyone else could say anything, another senator approached. He bowed and asked Akinia to join him for a dance…

After several hours, as the excitement began to wear down and the guests began to leave, Akinia asked Katarina's permission to retire for the night.

The queen hesitated, but then nodded. "You've had a long day," she agreed, giving her niece a fond smile.

Returning her smile, Akinia hugged her aunt, and then located the rest of her family to say 'goodnight'. It was nearly an hour later that she found herself standing in the doorway of her bedchambers.

Akinia breathed a sigh of relief as she stepped into the main room and closed the door behind herself. "Jaynine, please?" she asked simply, noticing the droid.

Jaynine bowed and left.

Stretching her tired arms, Akinia wandered to her closet to find a nightgown. A few minutes later, she returned to the main parlor area and sat down on the couch. She closed her eyes, and was very near to falling asleep, when a knock at the door startled her. Frowning, she stretched her mind towards the doorway.

Whoever was standing there was no Najee; they didn't react to her touching their thoughts.

Her frown deepening, Akinia stood up and walked to the door, slowly opening it. "Yes?" she asked, realizing that it was a maid.

The young woman's eyes opened widely as she saw Akinia, but she recovered quickly. "I was asked to deliver this to you," she explained, offering a sealed letter to the Najee.

Akinia took it and quickly ripped it open.

Princess Akinia Juntoby-Zanoratta,

it began,

I would be very honored if you would consent to joining me for a walk tomorrow afternoon.
We will not go far from the palace.
Please send your response with the maid; she knows where to find me.

Yours, loyally,

-Apprentice Rheighton Tor-Karr

Akinia read it twice before the words fully sank in.

The maid wordlessly offered her a pen.

"Thank you," Akinia said absentmindedly as she took it. She stepped inside of the room to use one of the small tables to write on. It only took her a moment to decide what to say.

Apprentice Rheighton Tor-Karr,

I would be glad to walk with you. Thank you for the invitation.

-Princess Akinia Juntoby-Zanoratta

She pursed her lips, sighing as she read the short note that she had scribbled onto the back of his. Uncertain what else there was to say, she folded the paper, slipped it back into the envelope, and handed it to the maid.

The maid curtsied and left, just as Jaynine returned with Akinia's tea.

Akinia thanked the droid as she curled onto her bed to drink the hot beverage. *Rheighton Tor-Karr asked me to walk with him*, she told herself, careful to make sure no one was eavesdropping on her thoughts. A small smile crept onto her lips. *I wonder why he did?*

Chapter 19:

A soft and contented groan escaped from Akinia's lips as she woke just enough to feel the warm sun on her head. She buried her face more deeply into the sunbaked comforter, enjoying the sensation of the soft, warm fabric. *I should have been awake hours ago*, Akinia realized, sighing, though she made no move to rise.

The Najee lurched upright, startled, as Rofa leapt onto the bed. "Rofa," she groaned, half-heartedly shoving the cub away.

Rofa whimpered happily and excitedly licked Akinia's face.

"You're lucky that I love you," Akinia growled, though a smile played on her lips as she spoke. She held the cub's head firmly in place as she kissed Rofa's large forehead. *I do love you, sweet girl*, Akinia sighed, placing the words directly into the ceffre's thoughts. She smiled as she felt the affection pouring back to her through their mental link. "Come on," she sighed, scruffing her pet's thick fur. "I guess I'd better get dressed, since you woke me up. I could have slept a lot longer, you know."

Unconcerned, Rofa licked Akinia's hand as they walked towards the closet.

Laughing and shaking her head, the young Najee quickly slipped her nightgown off before pulling a simple tunic-style gown over her head. She gently fingered the red silk, absentmindedly wondering how often her mother had worn this particular dress. Turning to Rofa, she commented, "Hyaline is going to kill me: I've been forgetting to exercise."

Akinia sighed as she walked back out into the main portion of her room. "I guess I'd better do them before I forget again," she mused, walking over to one of the small nightstands beside her bed. She set her right hand on the top of it and took a deep breath… Akinia jumped as the door to her suite opened and Nath walked in. "You startled me," she admonished.

Nath grinned. "Payback?" he suggested. "You startle me all the time."

Rolling her eyes, Akinia turned away from Nath and put her hand back on the nightstand. She rose up onto her toes and lifted her right leg to cross behind her left so that it didn't touch the floor. Extending her left arm for balance, she proceeded to slowly lower and raise herself by bending her ankle and knee, always careful that her bare heel didn't touch the floor.

"What are you doing?" Nath asked, sounding as though he was suppressing laughter.

"I'm exercising," she replied, never missing a stride. Up, hold, two, three. Down, hold, two, three. Up hold, two, three. Down, hold, two, three.

"That hardly looks like it would be a workout for anyone, especially you."

"Ha!" she laughed. "I would love to see you try doing this for an hour a day, even one day. Hyaline ordered me to do it and half-a-dozen others every day. This one helps to strengthen my legs, and my ankles as well. It also helps with balance. You know, you could do with some assistance in that area."

"Hey!" he protested. "Not all of us are as graceful as you, Princess."

Akinia held her lowered position for a moment before allowing herself to stand normally. She turned to face Nath. With a teasing grin she reminded him, "You seem graceful enough when you're dancing."

"What, like this?" he asked, suddenly grabbing her and dragging her through the first few steps before she settled into the dance and allowed herself to be led.

Her laughter rang through the room, echoing off of the walls. She let her head fall back and watched in joy as the ceiling above her spun and twisted, an entirely different world than the one she saw in everyday life. Her feet and Nath's seemed to flow effortlessly together in perfect timing, even without their conscious guides.

"Hmm, I see what you mean," Nath noticed suddenly.

"About what?" Akinia asked uncertainly.

He grinned, "You are much lighter on your feet today." He stretched his mind towards her, and she welcomed it.

She embraced his consciousness and let it meld together with

130

her own, every facet of hers matched to some area of his. Their feet seemed to move of their own accord as they broke from the ranks of ordinary dance. They twirled and stepped, the movements perfect and seemingly rehearsed.

Time ceased to have meaning as they ducked and twirled around one another. They only stopped when, exhausted, Akinia's knee gave out on her. Nath caught her before she could fall, and quickly set her in a chair. "Are you alright?"

She began laughing again as she held her hand against her head, lightheaded. The laughter began as soft chuckles and quickly turned hysteric as Nath looked on incredulously.

"Um, should I assume you aren't alright?" he asked uncertainly.

That set her off again.

This time, Nath joined in. "W-what are w-we laughing a-at?" he finally managed to stammer as he slid down to sit on the floor beside her.

"I-I don't know!" Akinia laughed. Tears began streaming from her eyes. Slowly they settled into shaking sobs of mirth. "That was fun," she commented as she rubbed her temples with her thumbs.

"Hey," Nath said, taking her hand and pulling it away from her head. "Can I help? Do you need anything?"

"Just for you to swear that Ko-Pau and Khee-Lá will never find out about any of this," she replied viciously. Her eyes narrowed into a piercing glare.

"Deal, unless you collapse or something and the medic needs to know," he bartered, releasing her arm.

Nodding, she pushed herself up from the chair. "So what kind of dance was that? I don't remember ever having learned it."

Nath shrugged. "How should I know? I thought you were leading."

"You know I don't dance!" she laughed. "How could I have been leading?"

"I've never even seen a dance like that before, how could I have been leading?" he countered.

"I haven't either," she reminded him.

Nath smirked. "There's no telling," he shrugged.

"I guess not," Akinia agreed, smiling.

"Well, come on, everyone's waiting for you," he informed her. "It's time for lunch."

Akinia gaped at him.

Nath grinned. "You may have overslept, just a little bit."

Chapter 20:

Akinia sighed as she prodded the vegetables on her plate. The majority of her food remained untouched.

Are you okay, Slick? Ko-Pau asked, a bit concerned. He was careful to keep his expression even, so that none of the others would notice their silent conversation. *I haven't seen you play with your food like this for months.*

The Apprentice hesitated, uncertain what to tell him.

Ko-Pau frowned slightly as he read more deeply into their mental link. *What are you waiting on?* he wondered, sensing a tremor of anticipation in her thoughts.

Akinia hesitated again, and then silently showed her master the memory of Rheighton's note. She mentally winced as she felt his surprise. *I know that I should have asked you first; I'm sorry,* she apologized.

You should have, he agreed at once, *but I'm not angry. You know that you will have to be escorted by a handful of Nátoan guards, right?*

Why? Akinia wondered, shocked. *I can take care of myself.*

Ko-Pau hesitated, amused, as he tried to figure out how to explain it to her. *You are not just a Najee now; you are a princess of Náto. I know that you can take care of yourself, but you also have to respect the customs of your people.*

Why can't one of you just walk with us? she wondered, wordlessly conveying her annoyance at the prospect of being followed by the guards.

His silent laughter reverberated through their mental link. *Do you really want your Master or your uncle to walk with you? I suppose I could always send Nath; I'm certain he would love to give you a running commentary of your conversation with Apprentice Tor-Karr...*

Akinia grimaced. *I see your point…*

You may want to tell your uncles and your aunt before *the boy shows up.*

Mentally wincing at the idea of telling Khee-Lá, or Andrid, she hesitantly asked, *Will you tell him?*

You'll stand up to Jade Enbrilth, but you won't ask Khee-Lá's permission to go on a walk?

Which one of my uncles are you *more afraid of?* she retorted, trying to suppress a painful twinge in her chest as she thought the words.

Ko-Pau hesitated, wordlessly debating whether or not to address the pain he felt through their link. *I see your point,* he admitted. *Fine, I'll tell him. When is Rheighton supposed to be coming?*

Sometime this afternoon, so it could be any time, or it could be later today, she offered.

I should be a lot less understanding about this… You're only fifteen, he mused, inwardly grimacing.

I walk with Nath all the time, she protested.

That's different!

How?

It… just is…

Master, Akinia laughed.

He smirked in response. *I know, you're right… but I worry about you.*

Trust me?

I do trust you, completely, Ko-Pau assured her, *but I don't know Rheighton well enough to trust him.*

He's a Najee, she reminded him.

Ko-Pau hesitated. *Being a Najee doesn't necessarily make someone a good person, Akinia,* he said gently.

They both winced as a picture of Jade flashed through the back of Ko-Pau's mind.

"What are you two talking about?" Khee-Lá wondered, watching them curiously.

Ko-Pau pulled his mind way from Akinia's. "Nothing, Master," he assured the older man.

Akinia winced as she watched Khee-Lá's expression change, realizing that Ko-Pau must be telling him. Her face reddened slightly as she turned her attention onto the food on her plate, but she wasn't certain *why*. Every now and then, she could feel Khee-Lá's eyes on her.

Lunch was nearly over when Khee-Lá cleared his throat and asked, "Akinia, when is your friend arriving?"

"Friend?" Andrid questioned.

Khee-Lá smiled, giving Akinia a reassuring wink as she met his gaze. "Yes, Brother," he agreed, nodding. "It seems Akinia made a friend last evening: Rheighton Tor-Karr. They are going to walk this afternoon."

Andrid frowned, glancing back and forth between Akinia and Khee-Lá. "Who agreed to that?" he wondered.

When were you going to tell me about this? Nath asked, disgruntled.

When I got back, Akinia replied, grimacing. She could feel his irritation as he pulled his thoughts away from hers.

"Ko-Pau, as her Imperial guardian, agreed, and then I, as her Nátoan guardian, added my consent," Khee-Lá said patiently, but firmly.

Andrid hesitated, and then nodded. "Very well," he agreed. "I will have an entourage arranged."

"A discreet entourage?" Katarina prodded, giving her husband a stern look.

The king smiled and nodded. "Yes, dear."

Akinia touched Khee-Lá's mind as they all resumed eating. *No offense, but since when are you the understanding one?* she asked, semi-teasingly.

Khee-Lá only smiled.

Chapter 21:

'Understanding one', Akinia silently groused, resisting the urge to roll her eyes at her uncle and Master. *I should have known better...*

"And how long do you think you'll be gone?" Khee-Lá asked of Rheighton, a threatening undercurrent to his innocent tone.

Rheighton hesitated only a moment to consider his answer. "We should be no more than two hours, Your Highness," he replied confidently. His smile faltered as he saw the expression on Khee-Lá's face, and he quickly corrected, "Forgive me, I meant one hour."

A slightly more pleased expression crossed Khee-Lá's face, and Akinia felt a strong urge to slap his arm, as she often did to Nath.

Akinia, Ko-Pau said warningly, having touched her thoughts just in time to catch the semi-coherent contemplation.

I wouldn't actually do it, she promised, her irritation very apparent to the older Najee. She bristled as she felt her master's silent laughter through their mental link.

"An hour's walk can take you some distance," Ko-Pau observed contemplatively. "Where were you planning to go?"

"Not far, I promise you," the apprentice answered at once. "I thought perhaps to the market?"

Khee-Lá and Ko-Pau exchanged a glance, and this time Akinia could not resist the urge to roll her eyes.

"There are a lot of people in the market," Ko-Pau said solemnly.

"A lot of dangers," Khee-Lá added. "Akinia is weak; her captivity stole a great deal of her strength, which she hasn't fully regained. It may be more difficult for her to sense when she is in a dangerous situation."

Uncle! Akinia protested, a pleading note to her thoughts.

"I expect that you'll take extra caution to watch around you both?" the Nátoan prince finished, ignoring his niece's objection.

"I will bring her back safely," Rheighton swore.

Ko-Pau and Khee-Lá both nodded slowly. "Yes," Ko-Pau said simply, "you will."

"May we go now, Master?" Akinia requested, silently adding, *I thought that you were on my side.*

I am, her master replied pointedly. "Yes, I think so. Khee-Lá and I will escort you down to the side gate; your entourage is waiting there," he informed them.

Khee-Lá nodded his agreement and waved Akinia and Rheighton out of the small parlor and into the hallways.

The group walked silently through the palace, and Akinia was extremely aware of Khee-Lá' and Ko-Pau's gazes on her as she walked beside Rheighton. *Is this all really necessary?* she demanded of her master.

No, I just enjoy torturing you, he replied, a hint of sarcasm barely detectable. *Yes, of course it's necessary. I've told you before, Slick, I don't know Rheighton well enough to trust him with you. A little fatherly threatening can work wonders on a boy, though.*

You sound like you speak from experience, Akinia remarked, dryly.

Ko-Pau grimaced. *I do,* he admitted, suppressing a handful of less-than-pleasant memories.

In spite of herself, Akinia smirked.

When they reached the side gate, neither Khee-Lá nor Ko-Pau spoke. They simply kissed Akinia's forehead as they left, and gave Rheighton a stern glance.

Rheighton chuckled nervously. "I feel like I should be afraid," he admitted.

"You should be," Akinia sighed, managing a half-smile to let him know that she was, at least partially, teasing him. She didn't bother to close her eyes as she extended her mind around them. It was slightly more difficult to maintain her composure when she felt the minds of her guards... all *fourteen* of them!

Her companion didn't seem to notice her shock. Hesitantly offering her his arm, he led her off of the palace grounds and into the crowded marketplace.

Akinia had pulled her hood up around her face, so that no one could recognize her.

They walked in silence at first, before Rheighton began the conversation. "I understand that you lived on a trade world in the Edging?" he prodded uncertainly, using the slang term for the star systems on the outer edge of the Empire.

A soft smile crept onto Akinia's lips as she nodded. "Uncle Khee-Lá thought I would be safest there," she explained.

"What was it like, if I may ask?" he wondered. "I've never been to the Edging."

"I don't really know," Akinia laughed. "We were never allowed to leave the orphanage."

Rheighton's eyes widened slightly. "Never?" he echoed, shocked. "You must have felt trapped."

"Sometimes," Akinia admitted, grimacing. "I always looked forward to leaving. When I was little, I used to dream about being adopted, but as I grew older I realized that I never would be. Once I accepted that, I started looking forward to my seventeenth birthday; I was going to the System Capital for medical training."

"You wanted to be a medic?" he echoed, impressed.

She nodded, smiling. "I always helped the medic in the orphanage. It was something that I enjoyed, and I was good at it," she explained. "My headmistress always hoped that I would change my mind and decide to become a lady-in-waiting for a noblewoman, but that never really interested me."

Rheighton laughed, a bit timidly. "And now you're a Nátoan Princess, and you could have ladies-in-waiting if you wanted to," he explained, in response to her curious look.

"I suppose I could," Akinia mused. The thought had never occurred to her before. She looked at him curiously. "What about you?" she wondered. "What were your plans before you were chosen?"

"I never wanted to do anything else," he shrugged.

"Never?" Akinia asked, surprised. "You always wanted to be a Najee?"

"When I was little, I used to dream about working with Master Khee-Lá," Rheighton admitted. "He was my prince, and the only Najee from Náto. I'd be no more than four or five when I would use sticks as wajun and pretend to be a Najee Apprentice training under him. I knew that Ko-Pau was working with him as his Apprentice, but I was just so *certain* that once he learned of a boy from his home-world becoming a Najee, he would fight to be allowed to train me."

Akinia smiled. "Little did you know, while you were dreaming about him becoming your Master, he was dreaming about becoming mine. He had to fight and fight before he was even allowed to give me to Ko-Pau, and that was just a compromise the Master of Masters agreed to so that Khee-Lá wouldn't take me and hide until my training was completed."

"He would really have gone that far?"

"To protect me? He would have done anything, Rheighton. He told my family that I had been killed, just so that no one would know where I was and put me into danger. He tried to lock me on Paméd until it was decided that I was able to kill Jade and Lokita if they faced me, just because he was scared of me getting hurt again. He hid my existence from everyone we had contact with, even giving them false identities for me, just to keep word of my survival a secret from everyone. He wouldn't even tell me my own name or history until Jade told me a twisted version first," she admitted, immediately regretting that she had spoken.

"How did Jade know who your family was?" he demanded, surprised.

"It's obvious, isn't it?" she asked, hesitating a moment as she decided exactly how it was obvious. "He had come here specifically to kill me because he knew that I was the child of the prophecy. He knew exactly who I was and where I lived, and then he knew exactly who I was when I became a Najee."

"And how did he twist that around?"

"He told me that they had only given me part of the prophecy, the part that said I would drive a great evil from the land. He said that he had come to take me so that I could fulfill my destiny and destroy the Empire. According to him, there was another part of the prophecy that told something about turning my back on the evil surrounding me to join him and finish the job he had started. It was all ridiculous, of course. But then he told me that the Najee had lied to me, and kept my family a secret from me. I tried not to believe, but when Khee-Lá admitted that it was true... Well, then Khee-Lá explained to me the real story of my past, no secrets, no lies," she smiled, but a shadow crossed her eyes as she remembered the other part of that revelation, a part she would never share with anyone.

Rheighton didn't seem to notice. "I know you can't like to talk about this, so if I'm prying too much, just tell me to leave you alone,"

140

he instructed, "but I can't even imagine living through something like that. How did you hold on for so long before they came for you?"

Akinia frowned and looked away.

"I'm sorry, I went too far, forget it," he apologized quickly.

"No," she sighed, "you didn't... The truth is, I didn't hold on. I wanted them to kill me, just to be free from it. It was Jade and Lokita that kept me alive. They would torture me to the point of death, revive me, and then bring me back to near death. I just laid there, hoping that this time they would take it too far and they wouldn't be able to bring me back."

Rheighton swallowed loudly as he watched her face twist into a mask of pain as she remembered her captivity. "I can't even imagine pain that bad," he murmured. "But if it was so horrible, then how could you just come back, like nothing had happened? They say that you never cry, that your mind is as whole as it was before. Even Master Khee-Lá was bordering insanity for nearly a year before he recovered, and he only spent a week in Jade's power."

Akinia gave a single bark of dry, humorless laughter. "What would be the point?" she asked, plucking a leaf from a nearby bush and twisting it in her fingers. "I have things that I have to do, people that I have to be strong for. I can't afford to lose my mind, or give myself over to the pain. The more time I spend dwelling on the past, the less time I have in the present to prepare for my future. This past is a distraction, and I can't afford to be distracted."

Rheighton stopped walking and turned to face her. "Princess Akinia," he began, "No one expects you to be that strong. Actually, the fact that you survived is more than anyone expected of you. Don't be so hard on yourself."

She gave him a pitying smile. "I've lived through the pain once, and I don't want to live through it again. Every time I think about it, I'm living it again. As to no one expecting me to be that strong...well, no one would expect *you* to be that strong, or Master, or Khee-Lá, or any other Najee. I *am* expected to be strong, to be unscathed. I am the Child of the Prophecy, who has the ability to destroy Jade. He isn't supposed to destroy me, in any form. And in a way, I'm grateful for those expectations, because they've allowed me to keep my sanity."

Rheighton turned and they began walking again. "You are a very strange girl. That's a good thing," he assured her hastily, realizing how that must have sounded. "I've never met anyone like you before."

"And you'll never meet anyone like me again," she grinned.

"I'm alright with that, as long as the original sticks around," he smiled, a curious and thoughtful expression on his face.

Akinia blushed. "We should probably keep moving; our escorts are getting a bit unsettled."

Rheighton's ears reddened as he nodded in agreement. "You're right."

Even though they had agreed to be gone for an hour, Rheighton led her back to the palace gates a full ten minutes before the settled time.

Khee-Lá and Ko-Pau were standing in the gateway, waiting for them.

"I appreciate your punctuality, Rheighton," Ko-Pau said approvingly.

"As do I," Khee-Lá agreed, nodding. He even managed a slight smile for the boy.

Master, Akinia complained.

Not another word, he replied firmly.

Rheighton bowed at the waist. "I thank you for allowing Princess Akinia to walk with me," he said gratefully.

Akinia smiled, unable to keep a slight blush from rising in her cheeks. "I enjoyed it," she managed.

This is the point where you would invite him to join you for tea one afternoon, Khee-Lá reluctantly advised. *Do not set a date; that is for Ko-Pau and I to do.*

She made certain that her uncle felt her gratitude through their link before voicing, "Would you like to join me for tea one afternoon?" *I feel silly saying that out loud*, she admitted to her uncle and Master.

Their silent laughter reverberated through their mental link, though their faces remained stoic.

"I would like that very much," Rheighton agreed, looking to Khee-Lá and Ko-Pau.

The two Masters exchanged a look. "We will consider the matter and discuss it with you at a later time," Khee-Lá decided in a tone that was neither encouraging nor discouraging.

Rheighton bowed again. "I look forwards to hearing your decision," he replied. He bowed to Akinia and then left.

Once the Apprentice was well out of earshot, Ko-Pau laughed, "If he bowed any more, he would break his spine."

"He was far worse when he first met us. Do you remember?" Khee-Lá asked, grinning.

"You are both absolutely horrible," Akinia reprimanded, unable to keep a smirk from crossing her lips.

Ko-Pau laughed as he wrapped his arm around her shoulders and began to lead her into the palace. "You'll thank us, someday," he assured her with a wink.

Khee-Lá fell into step on her other side, also wrapping one arm loosely around her shoulders. "Just think, we could have let Nath escort you," he reminded her. "Or, worse, we could have allowed Andrid to arrange things."

Akinia's eyes widened in mock horror. "You're right," she relented, sighing.

"But you did have a nice walk?" Ko-Pau wondered.

She nodded, trying unsuccessfully to hide her smile. "It was nice," she admitted, carefully gluing her eyes to the far end of the hallway. "Other than Nath and Laani, I've never really enjoyed a conversation with someone so close to my own age."

Akinia didn't notice the knowing glance that her Master and her uncle exchanged.

And so it begins, Ko-Pau noted dryly, carefully hiding his thoughts from Akinia.

I suppose it does, Khee-Lá agreed, grimacing. *Is it too late to lock her away?*

Far too late.

Khee-Lá smiled wryly. *I was afraid you'd say that.*

Chapter 22:

Akinia's skin shimmered with sweat, despite the fact that the crescent moon gave little light in the darkness. She tossed and turned as the nightmare caused her body to shake in panic.

Khee-Lá, sitting awake in his room, could easily feel her distress as he glanced over that wing of the palace with his thoughts. He gently stroked her mind, trying to calm her, but the moment he touched her thoughts, she became defensive.

An iron shield, ten times stronger than any she had produced before, sprang up effortlessly around her mind as another tendril of thought shot out from behind her defenses and began attacking Khee-Lá.

He shrank back in pain and quickly put up his walls, but she broke through them as though they weren't even there. *Akinia, stop!* he managed to call, but her subconscious mind paid no attention.

She was so lost in her nightmare that she didn't register him as a friend.

Wake up! he screamed to her.

After a few more frantic calls, Akinia woke, immediately pulling back into herself in horror as she registered what had been occurring. She tried to contact Khee-Lá, but his walls were up around his mind, and he flinched at the touch of her thoughts. Hastily wrapping her robe around herself, Akinia ran down the hallways to his room.

Pushing the door open without bothering to knock, she ran in and to her uncle's side. "Are you alright?" Akinia demanded breathlessly, laying her hand on his shoulder.

He was sitting on the edge of his bed, panting heavily as he held his head between his hands, rocking back and forth in pain.

"What happened?" she asked, her voice a hoarse whisper as she struggled to comprehend what had occurred.

With a bit of effort, he managed to take his hands away from his head, though he still panted and rocked in pain. "I'll be alright. You were having a nightmare and I suppose when I tried to calm you, you thought I was someone else and attacked me," he soothed, placing his hand on top of hers and giving it a gentle squeeze, even managing to give her a tense smile. "What were you dreaming about?"

Akinia looked away quickly. "It was nothing. It isn't important," she replied hastily.

"Tell me?" Khee-Lá asked again. His breathing began to slow and he didn't rock nearly as fast as he had before.

"It's not that hard to guess," the girl sighed, grimacing.

Khee-Lá nodded slowly. "Go back to bed," he ordered gently, giving her hand another squeeze.

"And do what? Sit up all night? You know I won't be able to go to sleep after what I did. What if I attack you again?" Akinia retorted. She tried to make herself sound angry, or irritated, but her voice just came out scared.

"I'm not going to bother you again. You didn't attack me until I touched your thoughts. Just go back to bed," he soothed.

"Please don't act so calm about this. You know as well as I do that I could have, and would have, killed you if I hadn't woken up," she begged, standing and pacing back and forth, her arms crossed tightly over her chest.

Khee-Lá stood up and put his hand on her shoulder, but she jerked away from him.

"I don't want to hear it! This isn't the first time I've lost control since you rescued me. Something is wrong with me and I don't know what it is. Until I do, I want you all to leave me alone, no matter what's happening," she ordered. Without another word she stormed from the room.

Khee-Lá touched her mind, trying to figure out where she was going, but she put her walls up as strong as she could. He was surprised to realize that they weren't as strong as they had been while she slept, despite the fact that she was putting all of her strength into them.

He leaned back against his doorpost, rubbing his temples. *I need to tell Lo-Kí, ask his advice*, he mused to himself. *Akinia is right: something is wrong.*

Chapter 23:

The next morning Khee-Lá found Akinia on the balcony in her room, staring out over the city below with a troubled look on her face. "You missed breakfast," he noted. He came to stand beside her, leaning against the handrail.

"I wasn't hungry," she replied simply.

"Your aunt was worried about you, but I told her that you hadn't slept well last night and that you were probably still asleep," he informed her.

Akinia nodded.

"The rest of us were worried, too," he added quietly.

"You didn't tell them," she accused, "I was serious when I said that I wanted them to leave me alone."

Her uncle sighed. "Sweetheart, you can't run from your power just because it scares you. You have to learn to master it or it will grow to a point that it's out of your control completely," he cautioned.

Akinia turned to look at him. "I nearly killed you last night; I won't do that again. I can't control myself anymore," she reminded him, "I can't risk your lives just to learn to kill Jade and Lokita."

"If you let it grow out of your control, these little power bursts could grow as well. What would you do if one of them injured or killed somebody? You must use your powers to tame them. Otherwise you're only allowing them to grow more dangerous to everyone around you, as well as yourself," he insisted.

Akinia looked back out over the city and didn't reply.

Khee-Lá sighed again and began to walk away.

"I never wanted this," Akinia sighed, her voice so low that Khee-Lá nearly didn't hear her.

"You never wanted what?" he asked, when she didn't continue.

Akinia swallowed heavily, turning to face him. "I never wanted

147

to be a Najee," she admitted. "Hurting people, killing them; I never wanted any part of it, even if it meant that I could protect the people around me."

"None of us wanted this, sweetheart," Khee-Lá promised her. "At least, not that part of it."

"I know that," she assured him, before hesitating and sighing. "But now I do want it, and that scares me. I *want* to kill Jade, I *want* to kill Lokita; that's not who I am… That's not who I *was*."

Khee-Lá hesitated before he spoke. "I wish that I could say something, to make you feel better, but I can't," he sighed helplessly.

"Please, say *something*," she pled, her voice trembling. "I nearly killed you."

"That was just an accident, Akinia," her uncle quickly assured her. "That's all, just an accident."

"An 'accident' that only happened because I'm not strong enough to control my psychokinesis, because I'm too weak to protect you from myself," she argued, hastily blinking away the haze of tears forming in her eyes. "How am I supposed to protect the Empire from Jade when I can't even keep myself from hurting the people I love?"

Khee-Lá pulled her into his arms. "You stopped yourself," he reminded her. "When you woke up, you stopped yourself. You *are* strong enough."

Akinia swallowed heavily as she leaned into his hug. "What about the bursts, when I throw things? I'm awake then."

"Physical weakness, not mental," he clarified. "Ko-Pau assured me that they're happening less frequently as you recover more fully from the physical traumas."

"I'm scared," she admitted, the words tasting bitter in her mouth. Even so, she couldn't deny the truth in them.

Khee-Lá pulled back slightly to kiss her forehead. "Don't be," he soothed. "You'll get through this, like everything else."

Akinia nodded slowly, even managing a weak smile for him.

"Come on, let's go enjoy what's left of our visit," he suggested.

"I think I need a few more minutes," she admitted. "I'll meet you later?"

Khee-Lá gave her a reassuring smile and kissed her forehead again. "Of course, Sweetheart," he agreed. "Let me know if you need anything."

"I will," Akinia promised as her uncle turned and left. She

sighed. *I need to talk to Master Tanlaish, and to Master Lo-Kí. I'm sure one of them could tell me what's happening to me, how to fix it...*

She glanced down at her right hand and began to trace the mark on it with her left index finger, thinking back to when the Nrell, Antia of the Emran clan, had given it to her; it had been only a few minutes after the Nrell rescued Akinia from her crashing fighter...

Excitement and hope welled up inside of her as a thought entered her mind, *What if I could speak with Antia?* Surely the Nrell would know what was wrong with her, if anyone did... but her excited grin faded as she realized that there was no way she would be able to get away from Ko-Pau, Khee-Lá, and Nath long enough to go and visit the Nrell.

If she could even find one of the other Najee that bore the mark, maybe they would know a way to contact the Nrell... but, after all these months, she still had yet to see a Najee with the mark.

Dejected, Akinia pushed away from the handrail. "Jaynine?" she called, looking around her suite for the droid.

"Yes, Mistress?" he replied as he walked slowly over to where she stood.

"Please bring me a cup of tea, and ask Nath if he wants to join me," she ordered. The droid bowed and walked away. Surely talking with Nath would take her mind off of her troubles, as it always did.

"You alright, Princess?" Nath asked as he walked into her room several minutes later, "You don't usually miss a meal."

She nodded, but Nath wasn't convinced.

He reached towards her with his mind and was surprised as he felt her recoil behind her thick mental defenses. "Why are you blocking me out?" Nath demanded, confused; the two of them had always talked freely with one another through their mental link.

"It isn't safe for you to touch my thoughts anymore. I nearly killed Khee-Lá last night when he did," she admitted, "He was supposed to tell you to keep away from me, but he thinks that I need to just ignore the fact that I keep losing control of myself like this."

"Wait," Nath said, raising a hand to stop her, "What do you mean you nearly killed Khee-Lá?"

Akinia sighed and related the events of the previous night. "I don't know why it happened, but until I can control myself I need you and Master and Khee-Lá to just stay away from my mind. It isn't safe," she pled.

Nath nodded. "I'll make Master stay away, but you don't have a chance of keeping me out of your head," he warned, "I come so close to matching your strength that it would be no problem for me to defend myself against you if you turned on me. I'll just stay out at night."

"You are so stubborn," Akinia complained, but she smiled and let her defenses down. Nath was right: if anyone was safe within her mind it was him.

He carefully reached towards her, touching her mind with his own. *See? Nothing's gone wrong*, he teased.

Yet, she warned.

He could sense her anger, her frustration. *It'll be alright. You have more power over yourself than you know. You won't hurt me.*

I wish I could believe you, but if I could attack Khee-Lá, then what's to stop me from hurting someone else?

Look, you were having a nightmare. It isn't uncommon for us to attack in self-defense under those circumstances. I've lashed out at Master once or twice myself. It's alright, he assured her, but even as the words left his mind he felt a flash of fear and a partially coherent plea. *No! Don't even think like that! You are not turning into him, or her. You are just going through some problems because you're still weak. Don't you ever think that again!*

Nath... her mental voice trailed off as she struggled to find words. Instead, her mind sent a jumbled collection of images and emotions. *He is in me, whether I like it or not. How can I help but wonder?* She stood and walked onto her balcony, resting her arms upon the handrail, and lowering her head to lie atop her arms. *Who am I, Nath? Am I Leonora Juntoby's daughter, or Jade Enbrilth's niece? Or is it possible that I can be both at once? I don't know anymore.*

Nath walked out onto the balcony to join her. "Who you are, and who your family is, are two different things."

"Two different things that add up to the same person, Nath," she corrected with a heavy sigh. "And in my case my family's identity could ruin me, and put my life in greater danger than it was in before."

"You know, no one that knows thinks any less of you, and none of the Najee would," Nath promised, gazing away from her and out over the city.

"*You* know that isn't true," she corrected quietly. She crossed her arms loosely and walked to the other end of the balcony.

"What are you talking about?" he demanded, looking back at

150

her suddenly as he heard the double-meaning in her words.

"You know perfectly well what I'm talking about, Nath," she sighed. Her gaze softened and her lips curved into a soft smile. "I know you were trying not to show it, but I could tell. You haven't looked at me the same way since you found out. You haven't talked to me the same way. To be honest, you don't even sit or stand or walk in my presence the same way as you did before." She turned around to look straight at him. "I don't blame you, I expected it. But if it's changed you this much, you of all people, imagine what everyone else would do if they found out?"

"Akinia, I..." he began, but she interrupted.

"Nath, you don't have to explain anything. It isn't anything more or less than I expected," she promised, partially relieved to have finally mentioned something to him.

"But Akinia..."

"I said just let it go. Don't worry about it," she shrugged, turning back around to look out over the city again. A part of her was now beginning to regret acknowledging his change.

"Would you please let me talk?" he growled, pulling gently on one of her shoulders to turn her around. "I think it's time you knew the truth about me, and I need you to just listen, okay?" he begged.

Akinia was puzzled, but she nodded in agreement.

"When I was little, my mom told me who my dad was. Yes, she knew, and I knew. She made me swear never to tell anyone the truth, because it would place us in danger. When I was seven I had to get a job to feed my mom and my two younger sisters, one of which had literally just been born. On the trade world where I was raised, the only job I could find was working for a smuggler named Deek Berrion. He taught me how to pick pockets and sent me out every day to get what I could get, and in exchange he made sure my mom and sisters ate. I, on the other hand, had to forage for whatever I wanted to eat. And that was fine because I was a very good thief.

"That's what I was doing when Master found me. I was thirteen and making my usual run and was literally running when I literally ran into him. I saw an opportunity to pick the pocket of an off-worlder who was obviously dressed decently, and I took it. He didn't notice until I had run out of sight. He reached out and touched my mind, trying to figure out where I was going, and I recoiled from the contact. So he asked around, found out where I lived, and offered to take me in.

151

"By then I had three sisters to support along with my mother, so I refused until he offered to get my mom a job as a housekeeper for a rich farmer much farther into the Empire. She would be safe and happy, and my sisters would be fed and educated, so I agreed," he stopped and sighed, "But before we left my mother warned me again of the dangers about telling anyone who my father was, especially a Najee. She didn't think that Ko-Pau believed her when she said she didn't know who my dad was, and she was right. He questioned me extensively those first few months, and nearly tricked me into telling him the truth a few times."

"So who was your father? And why have you been telling everyone that you don't know?" she asked curiously when he didn't continue.

He sighed again. "You have to swear to me that you won't tell anyone, anywhere, at any time, under any circumstances," he told her.

"That's a very big blanket promise. I won't tell anyone, anywhere, at any time, under any circumstances, except those in which the information would save one of us from being killed or something. Alright?" she bargained, crossing her arms.

Nath thought about it for a moment. "Alright. That will work. I wouldn't even be telling you except that I think you have a right to know this, especially now," he informed her. He paused and took a deep breath.

Akinia watched him closely and curiously. She had never seen him like this before, and it frightened her.

His shoulders sagged forwards and his eyes darted around nervously, as though looking for someone he was afraid to see. Several times he attempted to speak, but then the words seemed to catch in his chest and he would hesitate again.

She placed a hand on his shoulder and gave him a cautious smile, hoping it would urge him to speak.

He seemed to gain a bit of strength from her silent encouragement and finally managed to choke out, "My father... my father was Josiah Enbrilth. That's why I was so shocked when I found out who you... I had never imagined... I had never thought it possible that you might be... that anyone might be... I'm sorry that you thought... but I couldn't tell you while we were on Paméd." Looking humiliated and as though the words had given him a sour taste in his mouth, he turned away from her and looked out over the city. A distant

152

look grew in his eyes and tears seemed to well up in them, tears that he quickly blinked away, leaving only a troubled expression.

Akinia looked at him, her face blank with shock. Was he being serious? She took a deep breath to calm herself, and struggled to find her words. "You're my brother?" she whispered, the words tasting foreign on her tongue. Her mind tried to reject the term, since she had never had use of it.

"Half-brother, but yes," he sighed, turning to look at her again. "Akinia, you are my little sister. That's why I was so shocked when I found out who you were. That's why I've changed towards you. I don't love you *less* because your father was Josiah Enbrilth, I love you *more* for it."

A thousand questions wrestled to break free of her mouth, to be answered and laid to rest, but she found herself unable to speak for the longest few minutes of her life. "Why have you never told Master this?" she finally managed to ask.

"When I first agreed to work with him, it was only for my mother and sisters. There was no other reason. I had been trained by Deek Berrion to hate Najee and avoid them whenever possible. I was raised to believe that they were these evil beings trying their best to throw people like me in prison, or have us killed. I didn't trust him, at all. It was a bit more than a year later before I really began to realize that all I had been told about the Najee were lies. By then Master had stopped asking about my father," he paused and sighed. "It's just gotten too easy to keep my secret, since no one asks anymore.

"If he asked me now, I might tell him, but then again I might just continue to deny it. I never wanted to claim any relation to Jade, especially not after learning about Leonora and the twins. I should have recognized the necklace when you showed it to me that first day, I had seen it enough times looking at our *sire*'s picture in the Hall, but I didn't. If I had...I don't know if I would have told you or not, but I wouldn't have hurt you like this.

"I just want to forget about them, but I never want to lose you now that I've found you. I love you, but we can never tell anyone the truth. Just keep to the story of Josiah Zanoratta, and forget Josiah Enbrilth. Not everyone is as accepting of it as Master and Khee-Lá. Promise me, please," he begged.

Akinia nodded. She reached for him as the first tears began to flow.

"Shh, it's alright," he comforted, holding her closely. He rubbed her back with one hand as the other cupped the back of her head.

"Does Jade want to kill you, too?" Akinia asked quietly.

"Jade doesn't know that I'm his nephew. So far as he knows, it's only you and Lokita, I think," he sighed.

Akinia nodded slowly. "I hate him," she confided.

"Who?" Nath asked, pulling back slightly to look at her.

"Josiah," she replied bitterly, "I hate him for marrying my mother knowing Jade was after him, I hate him for what he did to you and your mother, and I hate him for creating Lokita and I."

"What?" he demanded angrily. He reached for her mind and saw a quick succession of images in her thoughts. He felt what she felt as she attacked Khee-Lá, he felt the horror and self-loathing that had overcome her as she realized that she had nearly killed him, he saw the frustration in her heart as she struggled to understand why she could no longer control her powers.

She pulled her mind away from him abruptly. "Do you see?" she demanded angrily, shaking in a powerful and terrifying mixture of fear and rage as she backed away from him. "Do you understand? I nearly killed my own uncle because I couldn't control my powers! What will happen if I don't wake up next time? If I can't stop myself... I'm almost as dangerous to our side as Lokita is, and I hate him for making me this way!"

Nath slapped her face before he realized what he was doing. "Don't you ever say anything like that again! Do you understand me?" he ordered harshly, pointing his finger at her face.

She nodded meekly, holding her cheek with her hand and too stunned to speak. Her mouth opened slightly, and then snapped shut again. The rage left her, and now she trembled only from fear of herself.

"You are not a danger to us. You're just having a little bit of trouble because you're still weak from your captivity. In a few weeks you'll be fine!" he continued.

Akinia nodded faster. "I'm sorry," she whispered, a lump in her throat. She tried unsuccessfully to stifle a sob, and then a tear fell from her eye, followed by a steady stream of tears. "I'm sorry, I'm so sorry."

Nath's eyes widened and he pulled her close. "No, I'm sorry. I shouldn't have hit you, or yelled at you," he murmured. "I love you."

She didn't respond as she leaned her head against his chest, letting him hold her.

154

Chapter 24:

Akinia closed her eyes and breathed in deeply, savoring the sweet, honey-like scent of the flowers blossoming along the garden paths. The bell-shaped ivory blossoms had an ethereal glow in the moonlight. Even the trees and shrubbery, with their green and purple leaves, were bathed in liquid silver. The young Najee gave a tense smile as a cool evening breeze blew across the courtyard. She lowered herself onto one of the many stone benches that lined the gravel paths. Her eyes drifted shut as she leaned her head against the thick trunk of a tall hardwood tree.

Despite the occasional gust of cool air, the night was warm and peaceful. A chorus of insects softly chirped and chittered in the thick shrubbery. Even the hard stone bench was surprisingly comfortable to sit on. Akinia could feel herself starting to drift off to sleep...

No! she sharply chastised herself, lurching to her feet and staring at the bench in betrayed horror. *I must not go to sleep... I cannot go to sleep...*

"Akinia?" Ko-Pau called softly.

She jumped, startled to hear her master's voice.

As he walked closer, Ko-Pau gave her a smile that was both pitying and reassuring.

Akinia watched him uncertainly. "How long have you been standing there?" she wondered.

"Long enough," he sighed, walking past her to sit on the bench that she had just left. He motioned for her to join him.

The young Najee hesitated a moment before sighing and sitting down next to him. She curled her legs up onto the bench, clinging to his arm as she laid her head on his shoulder.

Ko-Pau shifted his seat slightly, and moved his arm to where it was around her shoulders. He gently kissed the top of her head. "You know you can't lie to me, right, Slick?" he asked gently.

Unwilling to speak, Akinia simply nodded.

"Good. Now, tell me what's bothering you," her Master ordered gently. "Why are you out here in the middle of night?"

"I couldn't sleep," she replied simply. It was *entirely* a lie…

Ko-Pau sighed heavily, the sound laced with patient frustration. "Was it that you couldn't sleep, or that you *wouldn't*?" he asked knowingly.

Akinia sat up slightly, turning to look him in the eyes. "Does it really matter?" she asked pointedly.

"I want you to listen to me, very carefully," Ko-Pau ordered slowly. "What happened with Khee-Lá was not your fault. It was an accident; that was all. You cannot go the rest of your life without sleeping."

"I can't let myself hurt you, either," she argued, pushing herself to her feet. As she turned to walk away, Akinia sighed, "Goodnight, Master."

Ko-Pau frowned. "Don't walk away from me. We aren't done talking about this, yet," he ordered.

Akinia paused and turned back to face him. "What else is there to say?" she asked, grimacing. "Ever since you came for me, you've been telling me how strong I am, how much more powerful I am than the rest of you. Now, I can't control that power. Master, I'm dangerous, and we both know it. Pretending that I'm not isn't going to do anything but put us all in danger."

The older Najee's mouth closed and opened a dozen times as he tried to find something to say to comfort her. He sighed and held his arms out to her.

Giving him a grim smile, Akinia quickly returned and let him hold her.

"We'll figure this out," Ko-Pau promised, gently kissing the top of her head.

"I hope so," Akinia sighed as she pulled out of his arms. "Goodnight, Master."

Ko-Pau managed a troubled smile for her. "Goodnight, Akinia." He sighed as he watched her walk out of sight down the garden paths, a part of him knowing that she wasn't going to go to bed. *I hope we can figure this out, if only for her sake.*

156

Chapter 25:

Akinia smiled as she gently fingered the well-worn spine of a book. The volume was one of thousands which filled the palace library. The comforting, familiar scent of aging cloth and paper had kept her company for the rest of the night. Now, as the sun began to rise, spreading a blanket of gold across the magnificent display of books, Akinia could feel her need for that comfort lessening. *I won't fall asleep now, not during the day,* she reminded herself. It had been hard from time to time to force herself to stay awake, especially since she had grown used to sleeping through the night, but she had somehow succeeded.

"You are up rather early," Andrid noted, startling Akinia by suddenly appearing behind her.

I've grown too used to using my thoughts to watch around me; I would never have let him sneak up on me before! "I have too little time left here to waste it asleep," she laughed, giving him a warm smile.

Andrid hesitated, a shadow crossing his features at her mention of leaving. "Do you know how long you have left? Khee-Lá hasn't mentioned a date of departure to me," he asked, a poor façade of idle curiosity coloring his tone.

"He hasn't, but I'm certain that it will be soon," Akinia replied, silently adding, *but nowhere near soon enough... I need Lo-Kí, and Tanlaish!* "I'm almost strong enough to return to the front; they need every Najee they can get."

The king nodded slowly. "I won't waste my energy or what little time we have left in trying to convince you to stay; I can see that you're determined," he sighed. A wry smile crossed his lips as he mused, "You remind me so much of my brother. More of Leonora, naturally, but a great deal of my brother, as well."

Akinia smirked in response. "I'm certain that there are parts of you, and of my cousins, in me, as well," she mused.

Andrid laughed. "Let's hope that there is far less of me than of either of my siblings, or any of my children. I'm afraid my most definable quality is my temper, and you certainly don't want that," he teased.

Uncertain how else to respond, Akinia only laughed and shook her head.

After a few moments, their laughter drifted into silence. Andrid cleared his throat slightly. "Amalli tells me that you enjoy shess?" he questioned.

Akinia nodded. "I haven't played it very many times, but I think it's fun," she agreed.

"Would you care to play a game with me?" the king offered.

A smile crept onto Akinia's lips. "I would love to," she replied happily.

Andrid smiled in response and wordlessly offered her his arm. He led her over to a small game table which was set up against the far wall, pulling the chair out for her as she sat down. "I usually play with Rignon or Amalli, and generally in my study, but a change of scenery feels nice from time to time," he mused, pulling open a small drawer in one of the table's legs and removing the game pieces from it. "This is generally where Rignon and Amalli play against one another; I understand why they chose the library."

"It's beautiful," Akinia agreed, smiling as she set the black pieces up along the checkered squares on her side of the tabletop.

"And quiet," Andrid added with a laugh. "Most of my younger children aren't overly fond of the library."

Laughing softly, Akinia suggested, "Perhaps when they get older?"

"Perhaps," her uncle agreed, sliding one of his soldiers forward two squares. "Make your move."

Akinia took only a moment to counter his move, matching it by moving a soldier of her own. "Uncle," she began curiously, a stray thought taking root in her mind, "does Aunt Katarina have any family on Náto? I don't remember meeting any of them."

Andrid nodded slowly as he contemplated his next move. "Yes, she does. Her mother, older sister, and younger sister all live on Náto, and her older brother lives at a military base further into the Empire," he explained simply.

"Why haven't I met them?" she wondered.

"None of them are actually on Náto at the moment," her uncle explained. "Katarina's mother is very active as a Senator. She, Katarina's young sister, Trena, and Trena's husband, Senator Ashe Ko-Beck, are at the Capitol for Senate meetings. They won't be back for at least another two months. Alla, Katarina's older sister, is a Representative in Motúk; she won't be back from her tour for at least another year. Katarina's brother, Jocquen, is a Colonel in the Imperial Army. He and his family live at a training base further into the Empire; we almost never see them, anymore."

Akinia nodded slowly as she countered her uncle's move. "I hope I get to meet them all," she mused.

"You will," Andrid promised, laughing. "It may be another visit or two from now, but you will certainly get to meet them."

If I'm not killed in the meantime, the young Najee thought grimly. *And if I don't accidentally kill my family...* She forced the thoughts out of her mind, making herself focus intently on Andrid's next move. Her focus was so intense, that she jumped when Nath touched her thoughts.

Kiddo, get up here, now, Nath ordered, without preamble. A dark solemnity tainted his thoughts.

Fear immediately flooded Akinia. *What's the matter?* she demanded. Nath was never so solemn.

Katarina's in labor; the medic is really worried. You need to hurry.

Is she going to be alright?

Nath hesitated. *I don't know.*

We're on our way, Akinia promised, feeling the blood drain from her face.

Nath didn't respond, he just pulled the contact away.

"Are you alright?" Andrid demanded, concerned, as he watched his niece pale.

Akinia swallowed heavily. "Uncle, we need to go."

Chapter 26:

Akinia kissed the top of Karanne's head as she held the little girl on her lap, gently rocking back and forth to comfort the child. No one seemed to notice; they were all too wrapped up in their shared anxiety to pay too much attention.

She'll be alright, Ko-Pau silently assured Akinia. He didn't move or even glance over at her from where he stood on the other side of the room.

Master, please stop touching my thoughts; it isn't safe, Akinia requested, trying to gently push him away.

You don't need to be alone with your thoughts right now, he countered.

Akinia hesitated, trying to think of a rebuttal, but she couldn't. She just sighed and stopped pushing his consciousness away from her own. *I feel so helpless.*

We all do, her Master reminded her.

The girl hesitated, and then let a handful of memories from her captivity surface. *I have the power to help, I just don't know how*, she explained, grimacing. *I feel like I should have been trying harder to learn.*

Ko-Pau silently absorbed the memories of Lokita healing her twin's wounds. An unsettled feeling crept across their mental link to Akinia as they watched the memory play in her mind. *I doubt it would have been of much help in this situation, Akinia*, he comforted, still somewhat disturbed by the memory that she had shared with him.

I could be doing something, instead of just sitting here, waiting.

A tendril of thought gently embraced Akinia's consciousness. Nath felt somewhat surprised to notice Ko-Pau's thoughts connected with her, as well, but he quickly extended his mind to embrace his Master's thoughts as well. *How are you holding up, Kiddo?*

I'm tired of just sitting here, doing nothing, she sighed. *I wish I could do something to help.*

You are, Ko-Pau assured her. *You're taking care of Karanne; that's a lot of help.*

I've never seen her so calm, Akinia mused, a worried undercurrent to her thoughts. *I kind of want to take her outside...*

But you don't want to miss anything that happens? Nath guessed.

Akinia let her silent affirmation pass through their link.

I can take her, Nath offered. *Schran and Noregh, too. It'd be good for them to play outside for a while, get their minds off of their mom.*

Should I go, too? Or should I wait here? Akinia wondered.

Ko-Pau hesitated. *That would be completely up to you, but I have a feeling you'd want to be here when we found something out.*

You're right, she sighed. *Nath, keep a contact with me, okay? I'll let you know what's going on.*

Absolutely, he agreed. *I was actually going to ask if you'd mind.* He stood up from his chair on the other side of the room. "Come here, Kar," he said gently, reaching for Karanne. "Let's take a walk."

"I want to wait here," the little girl protested as he scooped her into his arms. "I want Mother."

"I know, Sweetheart," Nath soothed, "but we need to walk around for a few minutes. Schran and Noregh are coming, too."

The prince and princess exchanged puzzled glances as they heard their names. "We are?" Noregh asked, perplexed.

"Yep, you are," Nath smirked. "Come on, we'll be back in a few minutes. We need to walk around for a bit." He walked out of the room without waiting for a response.

Schran and Noregh hesitated before following him out.

Several more minutes passed in silence. Everyone jumped as the door opened and a young medic walked in.

"How are they?" Andrid immediately demanded.

The young woman hesitated, her large hazel eyes widening as they darted from the king to the floor. "I'm very sorry, Your Highness," she began hesitantly, "but the eldest twin was stillborn; we could do nothing. The younger is alive, but barely; I don't know if she will make it or not, but we are doing everything that we can. The queen is weak, as well, but she will most likely recover; it was a very hard delivery."

The king nodded slowly, his face paling.

Khee-Lá placed a comforting hand on his brother's shoulder.

"I want to see them," Andrid said, his voice hoarse.

"I'm sorry, but that isn't possible. The medics are still working on them both," the young medic replied. Without another word, she left the family to grieve the loss of the baby.

Master, Akinia managed, feeling her heart sink and tears well up in her eyes.

Come here, he replied soothingly, meeting her halfway across the room.

The Apprentice leaned her head against her Master's chest as he held her. A moment later, she felt a second pair of arms around her. Barely turning, she realized that it was Khee-Lá.

I'll keep the kids out here, Nath quietly commented, giving Akinia's thoughts a comforting caress.

Good idea, Akinia and Ko-Pau both responded.

Khee-Lá kissed the top of Akinia's head. "I'm so sorry that this had to be your first experience being home," he whispered.

Akinia only nodded in response. *Amalli*, she suddenly thought, gently pulling out of their arms.

Amalli's eyes were red and swollen as she tried to fight the tears back. She held Anlix, Lanzi, and Rignon in her arms.

Akinia quickly crossed the room to join her cousins, pulling the entire group into her arms.

"I am afraid," Amalli confided in her cousin.

"They will be alright," Akinia whispered in response, holding them more tightly. "The medics are taking care of them. I'm sure they'll be alright."

You are certain, aren't you? Ko-Pau noted, somewhat surprised, as he read more deeply into her thoughts.

Akinia hesitated a moment, puzzled to realize that, though she was upset, she was extremely certain. *I am... I wonder why?*

Hopefully for the same reason that we knew where you were going to be taken, Nath quietly commented.

She hesitated, her thoughts flooding with confusion. Her wordless curiosity flooded their mental link. Could she be a Gifted?

Chapter 27:

Several anxious days passed. There were several moments where Katarina's death, and the death of her surviving infant, seemed very likely. Then, one morning, much to the relief of the entire family, and the entire planet, the medic released Katarina to rest in her chambers. The infant, a beautiful girl named Leena, was released to the nursery, as well. Though everyone tried to persuade Katarina to let the governess care for the infant, she insisted on taking care of Leena herself.

Akinia breathed a sigh of relief as she entered her bedchambers, lying on the long sofa in the parlor. She had spent the last several days with the youngest children, caring for them and reassuring them. Karanne would wake in the night, crying, so Akinia sat up by her bedside so that she could comfort her. In part, it was to help Karanne, but in part it was to keep herself from falling asleep. She had dozed off once or twice, but each time she had quickly woken again.

A smile crossed Akinia's lips as she thought of how Nath had chastised her for it when he found out what she was doing. They had argued, and eventually came to the reluctant agreement that Nath would watch her while she slept, to make sure her subconscious mind didn't stir. It was a sweet gesture; Akinia could only hope that it would work.

She jumped as she heard a knock on her door. "Come in," she called uncertainly.

The door opened and Khee-Lá entered. "May we talk?" he asked, without preamble.

Akinia frowned and sat up. "Of course," she replied at once. "Is something wrong?"

"No, not at all," her uncle quickly assured her. "I just wanted to talk."

Her frown deepening, all that Akinia could think to say was,

"Oh."

Khee-Lá sighed. "I've been meaning to ask you about this since the ball, but things kept coming up, and then your aunt..." his voice trailed off as he sighed again.

Akinia's eyes widened in understanding. "Mother's circlet?" she guessed.

Nodding, Khee-Lá asked, "How in the worlds did you find it, and where?"

"Mother had a secret study," Akinia explained, motioning to the far wall with her head. "I guessed the key, and there were two boxes and two letters on a table inside, one for me and one for... Aki."

Astonishment covered Khee-Lá's face. "How did you guess the password?" he demanded, amazed. "We've been trying to guess it for years!"

"It was my name," she explained simply. "My full name."

"But I don't understand," Khee-Lá protested. "We tried your full name, assuming it may be the key, and the door wouldn't open."

Akinia hesitated before reaching to his mind. *The key was not Akinia Núro Leonora Kheelita Juntoby-Zanorrata*, she admitted reluctantly.

That's impossible! She didn't know anything about Josiah being related to him! Khee-Lá gasped, shocked.

Apparently she did, Uncle, or she wouldn't have used Enbrilth as my surname, she whispered, *I'm sorry.*

What are you sorry about? You don't have anything to be sorry for, he snapped.

I'm sorry that you had to find out. This can't be easy for you; I know it wasn't for me, Akinia murmured. She stood and walked over to sit beside him. Placing a hand on his shoulder, she kissed his forehead. *She loved him. In her letter she told me that one day I would know how the heart pulls you to love people that your brain knows are wrong to love, and that I would understand then why she still loved him. Her love for him stopped you from pulling his memories from his mind, and her love made her see past his relatives to him. But that isn't even what hurts the most.*

What hurts the most, then?

She could have lived. If she hadn't gone to Lokita, she would have lived. If she had just stayed in her study, they could never have found her. What hurts the most is that now I know how close we came to

166

having her here with us, and yet her heart made her leave her study to find her children. As you told me once before, her heart was her downfall. That is what hurts the most, she sighed.

Khee-Lá didn't answer, but took Akinia's hand in his own. She knew his silence was an agreement. She knew how much it hurt him to realize that his sister might not have died if her own choices hadn't pulled her from safety.

"I want to keep it," she whispered.

"What?"

"Mother's circlet. She gave it to me, and somehow it feels like a part of her. I'd like to keep it," she admitted.

Khee-Lá smiled. "Sweetheart, no one is going to take that circlet away from you. It is yours, by all rights. Besides, you look so like your mother with it on that none of the Juntoby family would dare ask you to surrender it."

Akinia smiled and kissed his forehead once more. "I'm going to go and steal that baby from Aunt Katarina," she decided. "I mean, I'm going to go and let Aunt Katarina have some rest, even if that means I have to take the baby for a while," she sighed, looking and sounding so dejected that Khee-Lá laughed.

"Yes, I'm sure it will be such a sacrifice for you to spend the afternoon looking after a baby. It isn't as though you enjoy it at all," he grinned.

"Yes," she grimaced, "I'll be thoroughly bored all afternoon, but Aunt Katarina deserves some rest. I won't enjoy it at all, though." She grinned and winked at her uncle before darting out into the hallway.

Chapter 28:

It didn't take her long to find Katarina, who was relaxing on her balcony and trying to quiet the newborn.

"Oh, Akinia, I'm so glad you're here," Katarina smiled. "It seems like I haven't seen much of you since the baby was born. I was beginning to think you were ignoring me!"

"I have come to see you, but you've been asleep every time I came in! Here, give me Leena," Akinia laughed, reaching for the baby.

"I don't know, she's awfully fussy today," Katarina cautioned uncertainly, absentmindedly tightening her grip on the infant.

"Here, let me try to calm her. I'm good with babies, honestly," she promised, reaching for the baby again.

Reluctantly, Katarina passed Leena to Akinia. "Mind her head," she cautioned.

Akinia smiled. "Hi Leena," she cooed, "Don't cry, there now, you are a little grumpy aren't you?"

"Try singing to her," Katarina suggested, sitting on one of the lounging couches.

"Would you like me to sing to you, Leena?" she asked as she sat on the other lounging couch.

The newborn continued to cry.

Akinia rocked back and forth and began to sing,
"Hush little one, now go to sleep,
Hush little one, don't cry.
Lay down your head, now go to bed,
I'll be here when you rise.

"Look up above, child, you will see
The stars shining way up high
All through the night they shall shine their light

And I'll be here when you rise.

"Soon morn shall come and once again
Light shall dwell in the skies
But while night is here, child, do not fear
For I'll be here when you rise."

Akinia let her voice drift off into humming as she finished the last verse, but Leena had stopped crying by the end of the first verse. She looked over to Katarina and saw that her aunt's eyes were closed and she had stretched out on the lounging couch. Still humming softly, Akinia carried Leena back inside to let her aunt sleep.

"Katarina, I…" Andrid began as he entered, but stopped when he saw Akinia.

"She's asleep on the balcony," Akinia said, smiling at the baby, "I came to get Leena from her for a while so she can rest."

Andrid walked closer, to look at his daughter. "Hello, Leena," he murmured, gently brushing her cheek with his fingers before turning to Akinia and asking, "You say Katarina is asleep?"

"Yes, she fell asleep while I was singing to the baby. I'm glad. She looks like she could use the rest," she confided.

"Well, I won't disturb her. Senator Meriven and his wife had come by to see them both, but if you would be so kind as to bring Leena to the throne room so they can meet her?" Andrid asked hopefully.

"Of course, Uncle," she replied, smiling.

"Thank you. I'll be there in a few minutes. I just want to check on a few things before I join you," he replied. He leaned down and kissed Leena's forehead, and then he kissed Akinia's.

"Come on, Leena," Akinia murmured, "Let's go and see Senator and Lady Merivan, shall we?" She carried Leena out into the hall, jumping when Nath suddenly appeared beside her. "Don't do that!" she chastised, checking quickly to make sure she hadn't upset Leena.

"Now if this isn't a pretty picture," Nath grinned, looking down at Leena. "Hey, cutie. Is your cousin dragging you all around the palace? Not even a week old and she's already bugging you. Poor kid…just imagine what it's like when you get my age."

"Ha-ha very funny," Akinia growled, rolling her eyes. "Actually, Uncle Andrid asked me to bring her to the throne room to

170

meet Senator and Lady Merivan. So, if you'll excuse me…" She pushed by Nath and continued up the hall.

He caught up with her quickly. "Hey, wait up. I'll come with you," he called as he got near.

"Is it me you want to come with, or have you caught baby fever, too?" she teased.

"Baby fever?"

"Yes, baby fever," she said seriously, "It's extremely contagious, especially when you're exposed to children under the age of two. Women are more likely to contract it than men, but there have been quite a few reported cases of men coming down with it. It's incurable and completely terminal; once you've caught it, it stays with you until you die."

Nath laughed. "You are so weird sometimes," he noted.

Checking quickly with her mind to make sure no one was listening, she quietly retorted, "I guess I just take after my big brother."

He made a face at her, which caused her to laugh. "One of these days, Kiddo," he said fondly, "One of these days."

"One of these days what?" she asked mischievously, "You'll grow up?"

He snorted. "You've always got a comeback, don't you, Kiddo?"

"Would you please stop calling me 'kiddo'? It's degrading and annoying. If you have to give me a nickname, can you just call me Kinny?" she requested.

"Nope, I'm afraid that just won't work, Kiddo," he grinned. "Though I am curious why Master is allowed to call you 'Slick' and I can't call you 'Kiddo'?"

"Master is Master, he can call me what he likes, firstly. Secondly, 'Slick' is a nickname with positive connotations and 'Kiddo' is just degrading. And thirdly, when you call me 'Kiddo' I want to hit you because you are only three years older than I am, and besides that we both know I'm a lot more mature than you are," she listed.

He shrugged. "I guess that depends on what area we're talking about," he countered.

"Pretty much any area of life," she stated dryly. "Hang on, Leena, we're almost there. Don't get fussy, at least until the senator and his wife leave, please?"

"Hey, you know good and well that when it comes to courtship, for one, I've got a lot more experience than you do," he protested.

"Alright, that's it. Conversation over. Nath goes away now," Akinia stated pointedly.

"Ha! You know I'm right and you just don't want to admit it!" he said proudly.

"Nope, I have no problem admitting that you've got more experience in the area of courtship than I do, I'm just not going to discuss romance in any form with you," she shrugged.

Why not? My other sisters do, he reminded her.

I can't help that. They may feel comfortable with it, I don't. I'm not going to discuss my love-life or lack thereof with my brother. It just isn't going to happen, she stated firmly.

Hey, that's fine. But you do have to promise me one thing, he demanded, suddenly serious.

What's that?

If anything important happens, I want you to tell me. I'm your brother and I want to be there for you, but mostly I want you to trust me with whatever is going on. Promise?

Akinia smiled, blushing, and bit her lower lip. She had never really considered that side of this new facet of their relationship. It seemed like Nath was trying to adopt every stereotype of the overprotective big brother that had ever surfaced.

You know that I am, he agreed seriously. *Just promise me that you'll trust me enough to tell me if anything happens, please?*

Who else would I tell? she countered.

Nath grinned. *Glad to know we're so close.*

Well, mostly I just know that you're the only one scared enough of me to realize that I'd kill you if anyone else found out anything that I wanted kept secret, she grinned.

Nath shook his head. *You're crazy, you know that?*

Yep, and I wouldn't have it any other way, Akinia replied smugly. "Now, are you coming in here with me, or are you going to run before too much diplomacy can wear off on you?"

He gave her a crooked grin. "I think I'll get out of here before I get sucked into a formal dinner or something. I'm not as good at getting out of invitations as you are."

"Good thing you aren't as good at getting them, too, so you don't have to worry too much about it," she retorted as he started to walk off.

"Alright, that was a good one," he admitted.

"I know," she grinned. "Come on, Leena, let's go meet Senator Merivan and his wife." As she rounded the corner, the two young Kell guarding the door bowed. She inclined her head in response, a slender smile gracing her lips, before walking through the doors.

Senator and Lady Merivan were waiting near the center of the room, talking to one another in an undertone and smiling. They quickly turned at Akinia's approach and both bowed deeply to her. "You're Highness."

Akinia blushed and curtseyed, as Katarina had taught her, before righting herself again. She gave a cursory glance at the Senator and his wife, noting their appearances.

Senator Merivan was a heavyset man in his late fifties or early sixties. He was not tall, being an inch or two shorter than Akinia, but his bearing was dignified and regal. He had a pleasant smile, though his lips were fairly thin. His eyes were dark, but they sparkled pleasantly. His hair was also dark, and was cut rather short. All in all, he had a very pleasant and cheerful appearance, and seemed quite relaxed.

Lady Merivan was a bit taller, and fairly slender. She had beautiful hazel eyes with an intelligent gleam in them that Akinia instantly liked. Her sun-blonde hair hung loose around her shoulder, outlining the proud, yet kind, features of her face. Though she must be near the same age as her husband, she had an overall appearance of youthful vitality that contrasted greatly with the wrinkles around her eyes and the slender streaks of gray in her hair. When she smiled, her entire face seemed to glow.

Akinia smiled. "Senator Merivan, Lady Merivan, how nice to see you both again," she greeted, vaguely remembering that they had been among those introduced to her at the ball.

"And you, Princess," Senator Merivan replied earnestly, bowing at the waist once more.

Akinia inclined her head in acknowledgment. "May I introduce my cousin, Princess Leena?" she introduced, turning the baby that they might see her better.

"She favors her mother," the Senator noted, pleased.

"May I?" Lady Merivan asked, reaching for the infant.

After a moment's hesitation, she passed the child into the woman's arms and was delighted to watch her eyes brighten upon holding the child. "My aunt was too ill to come herself, but the medic says she will recover fully given time."

"And the child?" Lady Merivan queried.

"Leena is healthy, though she will never be as strong as her siblings," Akinia reluctantly admitted. "My uncle knows more than I do of the particulars. He will be along in a moment."

Senator Merivan smiled as he stroked the sleeping baby's cheek. "Such a precious child," he murmured.

Akinia smiled. "She is one of the most beautiful children I've ever seen," she agreed.

Lady Merivan tore her gaze away from Leena to look at Akinia. "Princess Akinia, I had hoped to extend this offer to you and Princess Amalli together, but perhaps you may carry my request to her? I would be greatly honored if you would both consent to joining us for dinner tomorrow evening," she offered.

"I will certainly be glad to ask her for you, Lady Merivan. Provided neither she nor my Master protests, I would be glad to come," she answered, surprised and honored to have received the invitation.

The doors opened once more and Andrid entered, slightly breathlessly, to join them. "Senator, Lady," he greeted quickly with a slight bow.

They quickly bowed, even more deeply than they had bowed to Akinia, as he approached. "You're Majesty," they greeted.

"You will both forgive my absence, but I had to attend to my wife. She woke for a few moments, but she is once again resting peacefully," he apologized and reported.

"That is perfectly understandable, my king," Senator Merivan quickly assured him. "Your niece has been most diligently attending to us."

Andrid smiled. "I had no doubts that she would," he assured them proudly. He took Akinia's hand in his own, kissed it gently, and then added, "She has been a most excellent pupil to my wife's instruction. We are quite pleased with her, and are certain Leonora is being well represented by her daughter."

Akinia blushed crimson, the color flooding not only her face, but also her shoulders and arms. She mumbled a short word of thanks, averting her eyes. "You are too kind to me, Uncle," she protested.

"On the contrary, my dear," he laughed, amused by her reaction to his praise. Turning back to the Senator and Lady, he asked, "Will you care to join us for dinner tonight?"

174

"You will forgive us, milord," Lady Merivan apologized, "but we are expected at the house of Senator Gnack-Ishban tonight."

"Then you must, of course, keep your appointment," Andrid relented without a fight.

"And you must also forgive us for leaving so soon. We had but a moment to come and see how the Queen and young Princess were doing," Senator Merivan apologized.

The Senator and Lady bowed, first to the King, and then to Akinia, before handing Akinia the baby and turning to leave. "Princess Akinia, do be certain to send word when you know for certain if the Princess Amalli and yourself will be able to accept our offer," Lady Merivan requested.

"I will," Akinia promised, gently rocking the baby.

They bowed again and left.

"Offer?" Andrid questioned once they were gone.

Akinia nodded. "They invited Amalli and I to dine with them tomorrow night. I told them I would have to ask my cousin and my Master before I could accept."

"Well done," Andrid praised. "It is such a shame that you didn't have the opportunity to grow up here. I can hardly imagine what your diplomatic skills would have been."

A bitterness underneath his friendly jesting compelled Akinia to reply, "Ah yes, but I would still have been a Najee by now, and my dear cousin would have missed out on years of having been trained to take over for you. I think it has all worked out for the best." She kissed her uncle's cheek and offered to take Leena with her to find Amalli and Ko-Pau.

"By all means," he agreed. "Katarina is in no condition to care for her right now, at any rate."

"Would it, perhaps, be best for me to keep Leena at night as well? I used to do so for the babies at the orphanage when they were ill or in overwhelming number," she offered, not unaware of his discomfort at the thought of her working in an orphanage during her childhood.

"If your aunt is still unwell by tonight, then I will consider your offer," he hedged, "But the children's governess is perfectly able to care for her."

"I know she is, but I'll have so little time with Leena before we leave, and I miss caring for the little ones," Akinia laughed, gently stroking her young cousin's cheek.

"I will consider it," Andrid repeated. "Go on and find Amalli. I'm certain she will be thrilled to discover the invitation."

Akinia smiled. "As you wish, Uncle," she agreed, tightening her hold on Leena slightly. She gently rocked the baby in her arms as she left. She had never seen a child this tiny!

Her little hand, barely able to wrap around Akinia's pinky finger, reached out of the blankets as she began to stir. Though she cried for a moment at having woken, as her delicate hand touched the bare skin of Akinia's forearm, Leena quieted again and settled into a calm and restful sleep. Her lips fell slightly open as she slept, adding to the charm and beauty of this frail little creature.

Akinia hummed quietly, the same lullaby she had sung to Karanne, as she walked. She wandered aimlessly, not caring where she was going, and only slightly concentrating on finding her cousin. Her thoughts were far away. So much had happened these last months! A mother, and father, three uncles, an aunt, eight cousins, a half-brother, a twin sister... Never had she imagined such a family, nor such a family feud! How could she have?

And then there were her power surges, and now her subconscious attack on Khee-Lá... What was she to do about that? How could she trust herself now that she had nearly killed him? Would she ever be able to trust herself enough to use her powers again? Even now, as her walls surrounded her mind more thickly than ever before, it was nothing compared to the power she had felt that night upon waking. If she could summon such power while she was awake... *No! I mustn't,* she chastised herself. *I could not control it, I would hurt them, hurt little Leena.*

Still... if she could summon half as much power while awake as she had possessed that night, could she finally hold her ground against her uncle and twin? Would that be the extra bit she needed to be able to defeat them, once and for all? She frowned as she realized that Lokita held the same power, and had spent many years perfecting its use; how could Akinia stand up against that? How could she ever defeat the experience and knowledge her sister possessed?

She came to a stop as she realized she had arrived at the palace library. Perhaps Amalli would be in here? Still rocking the baby, she walked in and wandered around the rows of books, looking for her cousin. "Amalli, Rignon, there you are," she greeted happily as she saw them, pushing away all thoughts of her twin. "I've been looking for you."

They sat facing one another at a small table, each focusing intently on the shess board before them. At the sound of Akinia's voice, they both rose from their game to greet her. "Is all well?" Amalli asked worriedly, seeing her youngest sister in Akinia's arms.

"Yes, I was just giving your mother a chance to rest," Akinia explained, smiling. "I had come to tell you that I just saw Senator and Lady Merivan. They invited you and I to dine with them tomorrow night, if you were willing."

"You should go," Rignon asserted quietly as Amalli began to protest.

"But mother will need me," Amalli said worriedly, "And besides that, who will watch the children?"

Rignon gave her a wry smile. "They have a father and an older brother, as well as their governess to keep them in line. I believe we will manage long enough for you to go to dinner," he promised.

"Rignon is right," Akinia agreed. "I think it would do you good."

"There now, you see? It is settled: you will go," he decided. "Now, I believe it is my move." He sat back down to the table, ignoring his sister's uncertain expression, and proceeded to move one of his Skyscrapers.

Amalli reluctantly sat down to finish their game. "Will you join us?" she asked as she moved one of her soldiers.

Akinia shook her head. "No, I still need to find Master and get his permission, and then you will need to contact Lady Merivan and let her know for certain that we are coming."

"You are the one she extended the invitation to, you will reply," Amalli corrected. "If you are uncertain what to say, I will assist, but Mother has given me strict instructions to ensure you do as much of your own diplomacy as possible. She says that it is vitally important to you, given your friendship with Her Highness."

"You won't change your mind, I suppose?" Akinia mused.

"Never."

"In that case, I'll try," she sighed. Noticing it was Rignon's turn again, and suddenly noticing a move on the board that would benefit him, Akinia reached over and moved his senator to take Amalli's queen.

"Akinia!" Amalli protested. "Rignon, you can't keep that move;

that's cheating."

"Thank you, Cousin, I hadn't noticed that," Rignon beamed.

"You are quite welcome," Akinia replied, curtsying. She flashed Amalli a mischievous grin and teased, "Enjoy your game." Without another word, she turned and left to find her Master, ignoring her cousins' debate as to whether or not Rignon should be allowed to keep that move.

Chapter 29:

Getting Ko-Pau's permission had been even more easy than Akinia had thought that it would be, and the following evening found Akinia and Amalli in a transport, speeding across the face of Náto.

Akinia fidgeted with the hems of the poet sleeves of her gown, fingering the delicate lace that trimmed them.

"You are going to wear the threads away to nothing," Amalli laughed.

Grimacing, Akinia forced herself to look out of the swiftly-moving transport.

Amalli watched her curiously. "You act as though you are nervous," she mused, a bit surprised. "It is only a dinner, and only with Senator and Lady Merivan; you've dined at the Capitol, with Her Highness!"

"That was different," Akinia groused. "Alania was already my friend."

"So are Senator and Lady Merivan; you just don't know it yet," the younger princess promised.

Akinia turned back to her cousin, unable to stop a smile from spreading across her face. The smile disappeared, however, as the transport pulled to a stop.

"For goodness' sakes, Akinia, smile," Amalli teased, stepping out of the transport. "It is only a casual dinner."

Why did I agree to this? Akinia wondered, sighing as she followed her cousin out of the transport.

The Merivan estate was a beautiful, rolling meadow. Tall, evergreen shrubs lined the short white gravel walkway that led to the front entrance. A myriad of beautiful exotic-looking animals grazed on the rolling pastures. Merivan Manor itself was a beautiful white marble building, which displayed the same timeless elegance as the rest of

Náto's architecture. The smooth lines and arcs seemed almost liquid.

"It is very beautiful, is it not?" Amalli sighed, smiling at her cousin's awestruck expression.

"It is," Akinia agreed simply.

Amalli grabbed her cousin's hand and pulled her forward a step. "Come we should keep walking," she suggested, releasing Akinia.

A nervous smile creeping across her lips, Akinia nodded in agreement and followed her cousin up the stairs. As they reached the top step, the massive wooden doors swung open and Senator and Lady Merivan stepped outside to meet them.

The Senator and Lady bowed deeply to the princesses. "Thank you very much for joining us, Your Highnesses," Senator Merivan greeted, offering the girls a pleasant smile.

"Thank you for extending the invitation," Amalli replied happily. "I feel that I so rarely get to see you both. I wish that you would visit us more often, like you used to."

Lady Merivan smiled pleasantly, dimples appearing in her cheeks. "I would enjoy that very much. The Senate has had us away from home far too much in recent months," she agreed. "Please, come in. Our dinner is being laid out as we speak."

Akinia tried unsuccessfully to keep from gazing around the interior of Merivan Manor. *I once thought the palace at the Capitol was the most beautiful place I had ever seen, and then the Nátoan Palace was even more beautiful, but Merivan Manor might be even more beautiful than that!* Akinia realized, amazed.

The interior of the manor was even more elegant and beautifully sculpted than the exterior. Marble statues decorated a myriad of shelves at different heights and depths in the walls. Here and there, elegant waterfalls were carved out of the white marble walls, and even out of the columns that supported the roof. Trenches crisscrossed the floors, filled with water from the waterfalls; tiny, golden fish swam through the miniature rivers. Wide, arched bridges, elegantly carved from the same white marble as the rest of the manor, allowed for easy crossing of the streams.

The dining room that they entered was far more simple than the rest of the house. The room was plain white, and contained nothing but the carved wooden table and a dozen intricately wrought chairs. An elaborate feast was strewn across the top of the dining table, and, though there were only to be four people dining, a place setting had been placed at each seat.

Senator Merivan settled at the head of the table, while Lady Merivan sat to his right, and Princess Amalli sat to his left. Akinia hesitated only a moment before remembering that she was supposed to sit next to Amalli.

Akinia and Senator Merivan talked very little during the course of the dinner; they simply listened to the animated conversation that Amalli and Lady Merivan were sharing, occasionally laughing at a funny story.

Finally, Amalli grew tired of Akinia not participating in the discussion, and drew Akinia into it by mentioning her friendship with Princess Alania.

The Senator and Lady were both very surprised and impressed by the information, and they began questioning Akinia about her experiences in the Capitol.

"Amazing," Senator Merivan would comment from time to time, shaking his head and laughing.

Despite her initial concerns, Akinia found herself somewhat disappointed when the evening drew to a close.

"Thank you again for coming, Your Highnesses," Lady Merivan bade in the doorway of the Manor.

"Thank you for the invitation," Akinia replied earnestly.

Amalli nodded her agreement. "Yes, and you must both come to dine with us next week. Shall we say a week from today?"

"We would like nothing more, Princess Amalli," Senator Merivan assured her, smiling as he bowed to them both.

A few minutes later, Akinia and Amalli were back in the transport, speeding towards the palace. "You win; that was a lot of fun," Akinia admitted.

Amalli only smiled.

Chapter 30:

Akinia laughed as she watched her youngest cousins race up the garden path.

They shrieked excitedly as they ran from Anlix.

The Najee smiled as Leena's tiny hand emerged from the bundle of blankets that the infant was wrapped in, amazed at the strength with which the baby could grasp Akinia's finger.

"I told you that the dinner was nothing to worry about," Amalli teased, falling into step beside her cousin, somewhat out of breath from chasing after her siblings.

The older girl smirked. "This is all so new to me, still," she shrugged.

Amalli frowned. "But you've dined with Her Highness, at the Capitol!" she protested.

"Yes, but I was just a Najee, then; now I'm supposed to be a princess, too. It feels like people expect more of me," Akinia explained.

"I suppose so," Amalli agreed, after a moment's thought. "Hello, Leena," she cooed, leaning closer to kiss her baby sister's forehead. "You won't be here much longer, will you, Akinia? Uncle Khee-Lá rarely stays this long."

Akinia nodded slowly. "I don't know when we'll leave. I'm getting stronger, and I have to get back to the front as soon as I can," she mused. "I'm sure it won't be long until I can come home again, though."

"Sometimes Uncle Khee-Lá is gone for more than a year," the younger princess sighed.

"Let's just enjoy the time we have left, and not worry about how long I'll be gone, alright?" Akinia suggested.

Amalli smiled. "Of course; you're right," she agreed. They walked in silence for a couple of minutes before Amalli turned sharply towards her cousin. "You still haven't met Nillek and Insheff!" she realized, horrified.

"You're Skyretts?" Akinia asked uncertainly.

"You must ride them before you leave," Amalli insisted.

Akinia laughed at her cousin's expression. "I would love to," she relented.

Amalli pursed her lips as she thought. "We must go tomorrow. I will have Father arrange a transport for us. Speaking of pets, where is Rofa? I haven't seen her for several days."

"She keeps sneaking off, and I always find her asleep in a corner somewhere," Akinia explained, laughing. "You would think that she's exhausted, but she's just gotten lazy these last few months. Come on, I don't hear the children anymore; that can only mean trouble."

Her cousin laughed. "We should find them," she agreed.

Chapter 31:

Akinia glanced at her cousin uncertainly as they stepped out of the transport. It had been three hours since they had left the Capitol City, and there were no buildings in sight. The empty plains stretched out for miles in most directions, but the massive cliff face that loomed above the two princesses interrupted the vast emptiness.

"Welcome to Cair Tyon," Amalli laughed, amused by her cousin's awestruck expression.

A large shadow swept across the ground, dropping from the top of the cliffs and sweeping over the two girls.

Fighters, Akinia instinctively thought, her hand dropping to the wajun on her waist. She began to turn, trying to keep herself between Amalli and the threat, before she realized what was flying above her. Her eyes widened in shock, even as a wave of relief swept through her. "That's a Skyrett?" Akinia asked, disbelief tainting her voice. *They're huge!*

Amalli nodded, watching the beast fly. She didn't seem to have noticed her cousin's initial reaction.

A half-dozen more shadows launched from the top of the cliffs, joining the first Skyrett in its lazy, circling flight. The brilliant glow of light which radiated from the creatures, reflecting from the massive red-gold rays of the early morning sun, made it difficult to determine anything about the creatures, except for their massive size.

They watched the creatures fly for a handful of minutes before Amalli raised an arm and waved.

Two of the massive creatures let out a loud, shrieking cry in response, and then began hurtling towards the ground at breathtaking speeds. They landed only feet from Akinia and Amalli, hitting with enough force that the ground vibrated beneath the girls' feet.

As she looked the Skyretts over, memorizing their appearances,

185

Akinia only vaguely noted the presences of the two men that had been riding the creatures.

The Skyretts were immensely tall; at least six feet at top of their shoulders, not counting the height of their long, serpentine necks. From the ground to the tops of their heads, the creatures must have been at least ten feet in height! Their bodies were slightly shorter than they were tall, not including the length of the tails. The tails, alone, were more than ten feet long. Two pairs of enormous wings, covered in long, feather-like scales, sprouted from the Skyretts' backs, one over each of their four legs. Despite being so large, the creatures were very slender and elegant in appearance. Thin, sinewy, rippling muscles were easily visible beneath the thick layer of tiny scales that covered them. Though a rainbow of colors were visible on both creatures, one was predominantly a soft yellow color, while the other was mostly a pasty blue.

Amalli laughed happily as the light blue one anxiously clawed at the ground, the five massive talons on each of its feet digging trenches into the dirt. "Akinia, this is Nilek," she introduced, motioning to the blue Skyrett, "and this is Insheff," she finished, motioning to the yellow one.

"They're beautiful," Akinia managed.

Insheff lowered his massive head, curiously looking her in the eyes. He had a long, slender face, which dished in slightly at the muzzle. Like Nilek, Insheff had a pair of long, slender appendages growing from the back of his skull; Akinia remembered Amalli referring to them as 'leftre'. They hung limply down beside his neck, reaching all the way to his shoulders. His eyes were large and hazel, with deep, black pupils. Several moments passed before he pulled away from her, a satisfied gleam in his eyes.

"I think he likes you," Amalli decided, pleased. "He doesn't normally approach anyone but me, or Keepers Till-Meff or Sherr-Meff," she added, motioning to the two men that had been riding the Skyretts.

Hearing the same second-surname given for each man, Akinia forced herself to tear her eyes away from the beautiful animals. The older man, Keeper Till-Meff, had been riding Nilek. He was a large man, though not overly tall, and seemed to be in his late fifties or early sixties. His brown eyes were bright, and pleasant. In contrast, Keeper Sherr-Meff was tall and thin, and seemed to only be in his late twenties.

He had bright blue eyes, but a sour expression; it surprised Akinia to see him smile when he bowed.

"We have not seen you for some time, Princess Amalli," Keeper Till-Meff said pleasantly. "It's nice to have you here again."

Amalli smiled in response. "I would have come far sooner, but I couldn't bear to be away from my cousin," she explained, motioning to Akinia. "She has come to ride with me today."

Keeper Till-Meff nodded in understanding. "I had wondered why you had asked for both of them to be saddled. It's a pleasure to meet you, Princess Akinia," he added, bowing again to Akinia.

"And you, as well," she replied, smiling.

"You've never ridden a Skyrett before, have you?" he stated, more than asked.

"She has not," Amalli interjected, "but I've told her how. Besides, she is a Najee; she will be fine."

The two Keepers exchanged an uncertain glance, but they seemed to decide the better of arguing. "Very well," Keeper Till-Meff sighed, nodding. "We'll leave you to it."

Amalli thanked him.

The two men bowed again and walked towards the cliff face before disappearing into the crevice-like mouth of a cave.

Amalli turned to her cousin, giving her a broad smile. "Come, let's fly," she offered temptingly, before darting to Nilek's side. She placed a gentle hand on Nilek's shoulder, and the giant beast settled down onto its stomach. With only a small effort, Amalli clambered onto the small hollow between the two pairs of wings. It took her only a moment to take hold of the leftre.

Hesitating only a moment, Akinia cautiously approached Insheff. She placed her hand on Insheff's shoulder, and for a long moment, nothing happened. Then, the massive beast let out a sigh and slowly sank onto his belly. Smiling, Akinia carefully climbed up onto his back. It took her a long moment to find her seat in the hollow of his back; the thin cloth saddle did little to help her grip the creature's slick scales. When she did find her seat, she carefully grabbed Insheff's leftre. Akinia was surprised to find that, though they were covered in the same tiny scales that covered the rest of the Skyrett's body, the leftre had a far more rubbery texture, which was much easier to grip.

"Are you ready?" Amalli asked.

Akinia nodded in response.

"Just remember to grip him with your thighs, or else you'll fall off. Touch his sides with your heels to make him go faster, and guide him by the leftre," Amalli reminded her.

"Alright," Akinia replied, a ball of nervous excitement forming in the pit of her stomach.

Without another word, Amalli urged her Skyrett into the air.

Nilek's powerful talons left deep gouges in the earth where she pushed off. Her massive wings created a violent gust of air that struck Akinia; it only took a few powerful strokes to send the Skyrett and rider airborne.

Akinia followed on Insheff only moments later. She gasped in shock as Insheff's powerful launch nearly unseated her. The alternate flapping of the front and back pairs of wings created a wave-like motion on the Skyrett's back as they slowly gained altitude. Akinia closed her eyes as the ground rapidly shrank beneath her. *I'm going to be sick*, she realized, only moments after they launched.

Just as Akinia felt that she was going to vomit, the sickening rocking motion suddenly stopped. Forcing her eyes open, Akinia gazed around. Her breath caught in her chest as she saw the distant horizon, and the ground that they had just left. *It's beautiful*, she mused.

Insheff had stopped flapping his wings, content to glide on a current of air.

Akinia hesitantly tried moving the leftre, curious how the creature would react.

With even the slightest movement, Insheff would adjust his wings by a minute amount to go in the direction his rider indicated. The more drastic the movement, the more drastic his response. Now that they were aloft, the movements were much smoother, and far less choppy than the initial flight had been.

Nilek swooped and dove in a variety of ever more complex maneuvers around them.

Akinia knew that her cousin was showing off. Feeling a bit more confident on Insheff's back, she began to direct him to copy Nilek's every move. It was a beautiful, but dangerous, dance as they twisted and lurched in increasingly complex patterns. Akinia nearly lost her seat a handful of times, but she didn't let it discourage her.

Soon other Skyretts joined in on the game. Though none had riders, they seemed more than eager to fall into line behind Insheff, following Nilek's lead.

Akinia almost wished that she was on the ground, so that she could watch the spectacle.

They flew for several hours, only rarely pausing the game to let the Skyretts rest, drifting along a warm updraft of air. Finally, as the sun began to set, Amalli waved to catch her cousin's attention. She motioned downward, and then directed Nilek into a sharp descent.

Somewhat disappointed, Akinia patted Insheff's neck and then directed him down as well. Their descent was far slower, a lazy spiral that took several minutes to reach the ground. With a dull thud, Insheff carefully settled onto the ground by Nilek's side. "That was a lot of fun," Akinia informed her cousin, grinning.

"I knew that you would enjoy it," Amalli laughed in response. "I wish that my brother did; he and I would have a lot of fun flying together."

"How can he dislike it?" Akinia wondered, surprised.

Amalli laughed. "I think that he's afraid of falling," she explained. "Come, we should go. Mother and Father will be worried about us."

Akinia frowned. "Don't we need to give Nilek and Insheff back to the Keepers?"

"No, they'll fly up to the roost in a few minutes; they'll care for them then," the younger girl explained. She gave each of her pets a tight hug around the neck before leading Akinia back to the transport.

"We should come flying again on my next visit," Akinia suggested, glancing over her shoulder as she climbed into the transport behind her cousin.

Amalli grinned. "Or we could go flying again before this visit is over?" she suggested slyly.

"That would be wonderful," Akinia agreed, smiling.

Chapter 32:

A wave of relief rushed through Akinia as she settled onto the plush sofa in her bedchambers. She murmured a quiet word of thanks to Jaynine as the droid handed her a cup of tea. A soft smile crept onto the girl's lips as she watched the steam rise up from the surface of the dark liquid, swirling in elegant patterns before it dispersed. The long day flying had left her legs sore and tender; it felt nice to simply relax.

A quiet knock sounded from the door. "Akinia," Khee-Lá called softly, "may I come in?"

Sighing, Akinia set her teacup aside and rose to her feet. It took her only a few moments to cross the room and pull the door open. "Please, come and sit down," she offered, returning to the sitting area. "Would you like some tea?"

"No, thank you," he replied, giving a troubled sigh as he settled onto a nearby armchair. "I just needed to speak with you for a few minutes, if you don't mind?"

Akinia frowned as she saw the troubled expression on his face, and then she sighed. "We're leaving, aren't we?" she asked knowingly.

Khee-Lá hesitated, and then nodded.

"When?"

"Two weeks," he replied, grimacing. "I'm sorry, Akinia. If we could stay longer, we would, but you're stronger now, and the Council needs us all back on the front."

She managed to force a smile onto her lips. "We've been away too long," she agreed. "None of us has been on a mission since I was captured; we can't afford to be down even one Najee, let alone four."

"Least of all, you," Khee-Lá mused.

Akinia swallowed heavily, her eyes drifting away from her uncle. "I don't know how much help I'm going to be," she admitted, grimacing.

"Sweetheart, you're going to be just fine," he promised. "We'll work through this, and you'll come through it even stronger. Don't give up on yourself, not after everything that you've gone through to get here."

"Have you told Uncle Andrid and Aunt Katarina that we're leaving?" she wondered, changing the subject.

Khee-Lá hesitated a moment, debating on whether or not to allow her to change the subject, before he shook his head. "Not yet, but I'll tell them tonight," he sighed. "Actually, I should probably go and talk to them now, before they retire for the night. I wanted to tell you first."

Akinia stood as her uncle did, setting her teacup aside. "I love you, Uncle," she informed him, embracing him and kissing his cheek.

He wrapped his arms around her in return. "I love you, too, Sweetheart," he replied. "Sleep well."

"You, too."

Without another word, Khee-Lá left.

As the door slid shut behind him, Akinia sighed and settled back into her seat. *Two weeks*, she mused, grimacing. *Only two weeks left... I know that I need to go home to Paméd, but I don't want to leave Náto, either.*

What are my cousins going to say when they find out?

She didn't have to wait long to find out; by breakfast the next morning, all of her cousins were aware that she was leaving. The two weeks passed both painfully slowly and impossibly fast. Her family presented her with many beautiful gifts; one even arrived from Katarina's mother, Lady Leena Fange-Ellis, who had only just received word about Akinia's survival. Despite the rush of activity surrounding their imminent departure, Akinia even managed to find a few minutes one afternoon to contact Charlotte.

Then, one morning, Akinia found herself slowly walking up the ship's entryway, sharing one last look with her family before the doors closed and the ship launched into the sky.

"Are you okay?" Khee-Lá asked, coming to stand beside his niece as she looked out of the port, watching Náto rapidly disappear.

Akinia smiled and kissed his cheek. "Of course, Uncle," she promised, before she paused and sighed. "Is it strange that I already miss them?"

He laughed. "Not in the least," he assured her. "I miss them, as

192

well; but I also miss Paméd."

"Me, too," Akinia confided, her stomach twisting. *You have no idea how much*, she silently added, keeping her thoughts carefully shielded from all of her companions as she contemplated her dangerous lapses in control. *At least on Paméd I can sleep; there are enough Masters to keep me from hurting anyone.*

Hopefully Master Lo-Kí or Master Tanlaish will know how to help me.

Chapter 33:

Akinia sighed as she stretched out across her bed. Had Paméd always been this boring? Her heart sank as her thoughts drifted back to her family. If only she could have had more time there! *I can't just lay around, feeling sorry for myself. Paméd was enough to occupy me before, it's enough to occupy me now. Master doesn't want me to spar yet, but I can always go to the library...*

Sighing again, she pushed herself up off of the bed. It didn't take her long to navigate the familiar passageways that led up to the library. She searched through shelf after shelf, row after row, of books and holo-orbs. She paused as she reached up to pull a book off of a shelf above her head. It sounded like Lo-Kí and Khee-Lá were talking on the other side of it. She walked around to the end of the row, meaning to talk to them, but she then realized that they were talking about her. She paused, half-hidden, to listen.

"But it's getting so much worse than accidentally flinging bits of metal at a wall, Lo-Kí," Khee-Lá protested angrily. He stormed back and forth through the small resting area where Lo-Kí sat.

"What do you mean?" the old man asked in response.

"She was having a nightmare the other night, and I reached out to calm her, she nearly killed me without realizing it," Khee-Lá reported, "She was so powerful while she slept, she knocked my defenses away as though they were nothing. I've never felt so much power, even from Jade. If she hadn't woken when I screamed her name, she would have killed me. There was nothing I could do to get away from her. I doubt there's anything anyone could do to get away from her if she attacked someone again."

He sank into one of the chairs, burying his face in his hands. Lo-Kí seemed greatly disturbed. "You say she was powerful when she slept, is she as powerful while awake?" he demanded.

Khee-Lá shook his head. "Her walls were still strong after she woke, she refused to allow Ko-Pau and I to touch her mind after that, but they were nothing compared to the walls she had put up while she was unconscious. I don't know what to make of it, what to do about it," he replied, worried.

"I want her to be kept isolated while she sleeps, as she seems to lose control easier in her unconscious mind," Lo-Kí ordered.

"She's scared of herself and, frankly, I'm beginning to be afraid of her as well," Khee-Lá admitted, lowering his voice slightly. "I try not to show it, but I think she knows. Ko-Pau feels the same way. Nath is the only one who isn't scared of her, but that's only because his power nearly matches her own and he thinks he could hold his own if she attacked."

Lo-Kí rubbed his chin thoughtfully. "Go and get her, bring her back here," he ordered. "I have a proposal for her."

Akinia took a deep breath to calm herself. So Khee-Lá *was* scared of her. "There's no need for that," she called as Khee-Lá began to stand, "I'm right here."

Khee-Lá looked over at her, startled and ashamed. "I…" he began, but Akinia held a hand up to stop him.

"You're scared of me, I don't blame you. You have no explaining to do," she stated calmly before turning to Lo-Kí, "I apologize for eavesdropping. It was not my intention."

"You are forgiven," he replied simply.

She sat on the couch beside her uncle. "You said you have a proposal for me?" she prodded after a moment.

Lo-Kí nodded slowly. "Emperor Caylon has requested a prisoner exchange, no Najee involved. Obviously we do not trust him enough to send so many of our soldiers and our prisoners to his palace without a Najee guard, so you will disguise yourself as a soldier and attend the exchange," he reported, "We need you to go as you are one of the least known Najee, as well as one of the most skilled. It would give you a chance to learn to control yourself, where you wouldn't have to be afraid of hurting your loved ones."

"I can't condone sending her into Caylon's palace, Lo-Kí," Khee-Lá warned.

"I'll go," Akinia said simply.

"What if Lokita or Jade shows up, you aren't capable of defeating them yet!" Khee-Lá protested.

"I'll deal with that if the situation arises, but I remember hearing someone mention that they are supposed to be at the front for the next several months," she replied stubbornly.

"Are you fully certain that you understand the risks, Akinia?" Lo-Kí demanded.

She nodded. "If I am caught, I will likely be killed or strapped to another torture device. It is too far into Sigadia to even think about getting a rescue. I would be completely alone if something were to go wrong," she recited.

"So long as you know the risks, you may go if you wish," Lo-Kí replied.

"No!" Khee-Lá growled. "Lo-Kí, this is madness. How can you condone sending a frightened child who can't even control her own powers into the heart of Sigadia by herself?"

"You will do well to watch your temper, Khee-Lá," he reprimanded softly. "Would you rather that I keep her in the Empire where your niece is in danger of being found by Jade and Lokita and being killed? They know she will be here and they know she will be kept close to us after this. They would never suspect that I would send her so far from Paméd considering what has happened. I must do what is best for all of you, even if it seems more dangerous on the surface. I believe this will help her to remain hidden as well as to gain better control over her powers, and it will keep you out of the way if she were to lose control again. She will go, and you will say nothing more on this matter."

Fuming, Khee-Lá stormed away.

"Here we go again," Akinia muttered. Turning her attention back to Lo-Kí, she asked, "When is this mission taking place?"

"You will leave in six weeks. Until then, you will go where your master wishes you to, only be certain you are back in five weeks that we might get you fully prepared," Lo-Kí replied.

"I will be," she promised. Recognizing that she was dismissed, she stood and left. Her feet guided her back down the lift-chamber and hallways and into her private chamber. Her mind ran a thousand light-years a minute. Khee-Lá was frightened of her, by his own admission. He had told Lo-Kí that Ko-Pau was frightened of her as well. In a way, she was glad that they were frightened. After all, hadn't she wanted them to be cautious?

Still, her stomach sank as she realized that, despite all of their verbal assurances, they really didn't trust her. But she didn't trust herself, so that made her feel slightly better.

Jaynine entered the room, pausing as he noticed Akinia sitting on the foot of her bed. "May I get you anything, Mistress?" he offered.

"Tea, please," Akinia said simply, needing the soothing comfort of the warm drink.

The droid bowed. "As you wish," he replied before turning and leaving.

As the droid left, Akinia slipped her shoes off of her feet and crawled up to the head of her bed, curling against the mound of pillows stacked near her headboard. *What have I done?* she wondered to herself. *Am I strong enough for this? What if Jade or Lokita find me?*

Shaking her head, she quickly pushed the thoughts away. *No, I have to do this. I can't use my psychokinesis around the Najee; I'll hurt someone. This is the only way for me to figure out how to control it.*

I have to do this.

Chapter 34:

The hair on the back of Akinia's neck prickled as she nervously peeked around the corner. She breathed out a sigh of relief when the hallway was empty. It felt profoundly wrong to be sneaking around the lesser-known hallways in Paméd, but it was better than running into Ko-Pau or Khee-Lá. It had been a week since Lo-Kí had given her the mission, and a week since the last time she had spoken to her Master or her uncle without the conversation turning into an argument.

Finally, she found herself standing in the doorway that led to her favorite meditation pond. Satisfied that she was alone, Akinia sat down on the pond bank and closed her eyes. She didn't allow her consciousness to reach out; she simply focused on calming her breathing and letting herself relax. It was minutes, or maybe hours, later when a quiet voice interrupted her concentration.

"I thought I would find you here," Nath said simply, sitting down beside her.

Akinia jumped slightly, subconsciously leaning away from him. *Why did it have to be Nath? I would have preferred Ko-Pau or Khee-Lá...* Nath was worse than anyone else. With him, it never became an argument, it just left Akinia feeling guilty. His words were only ever accepting, but his entire demeanor had changed. He was worried, resigned, dejected; Akinia often wondered if she would rather him be angry. "Have you been looking for me?" she wondered.

Nath nodded slowly. "Yeah," he sighed, falling silent as he plucked a small pebble from the ground near his knee, lightly tossing it into the pond.

"Did you want to tell me something?" Akinia prodded when he didn't speak.

He nodded. "Yeah," he sighed, again, "I do." Turning slightly to face her, Nath continued, "I know that it doesn't matter what I say, you're still going to go, and that's why I haven't been arguing with you, but I don't want you to. As your brother, I'm asking you to stay."

Akinia swallowed heavily. "Nath, you know that I can't," she replied quietly, looking away from him. "You know *why* I can't."

"You really think that you're just going to magically get control over yourself if you disappear into Sigadia for a couple of weeks?" he asked, giving her a pitying smile. "You aren't even going to be able to use your abilities while you're gone; you're supposed to be pretending you don't have any."

"I can't get control of them here," Akinia argued. "I can't let myself hurt you. I'm afraid. As much as I hate to admit it, I'm afraid." She sighed trying to ignore the sick feeling in her stomach; she was weak, and she hated being weak.

Nath sighed. "Stay, Akinia," he asked. "I'll help you, I'll work with you. I'll be by your side while you practice, and I'll keep you in control if you feel yourself start to get out of hand. This mission is suicide, especially in the state you're in."

Akinia forced herself to turn and look at him again. "I let you into my mind, and even then I'm afraid that I'm going to hurt you," she agreed, "but I can't let you be around me when I'm trying to use my abilities. I'm too strong. You didn't feel my power that night, and I can't control it. If I got another burst, with all of that power, and you were too close… I can overpower you with what I can consciously control, but that other power was easily a dozen times stronger. I would kill you; I almost killed Khee-Lá."

His eyes widened slightly. "I didn't realize it was that strong," he murmured, somewhat distracted by the thought.

"It is," she replied simply, hoping that this would be the end.

They sat in silence for several minutes before Nath spoke again. "I still wish you would stay," he said quietly.

"I can't," Akinia replied, her voice equally as quiet.

"If you go," he began, before pausing and sighing. "If you go, I may never see you again… You have no idea how dangerous this mission is; Caylon will kill you."

"No, he won't," she argued, her heart twisting as she realized how frightened Nath really was. "I'll come home, safely; I promise."

Nath swallowed audibly. "I hope so," he said simply. Without another word, he pushed himself to his feet and left.

Akinia felt her cheeks get tight and her eyes begin sting as the tears began to form. She took a handful of deep breaths to try and calm herself down, but knew that it was a pointless exercise. She quickly typed a code onto her com-link. "Jaynine, please bring tea to my room," she said simply, not waiting for a response before she ended the connection. Pushing herself to her feet, she quickly made her way back to her room.

Chapter 35:

Akinia jumped as the door to her room slid open

Ko-Pau stepped inside, closing the door behind himself. "It's just me," he assured her, seeing her jump. "We need to talk."

The Apprentice frowned. "Is everything okay?" she wondered.

A grim smile crossed Ko-Pau's lips as he sat on the corner of the bed. "No, it isn't," he replied, "and that's what we need to talk about."

"Is it Khee-Lá?" she asked, sighing heavily as she sat on the bed.

Ko-Pau nodded slowly. "It is."

"He's not happy with me," she grimaced.

"You see, that is where you are wrong," the Master corrected. "Khee-Lá was 'not happy' with us when we circumvented his order for you to stay here; now he's *angry* with us for agreeing to this suicide mission you accepted."

"So you do agree with it?" Akinia asked hopefully.

"Not in the least," Ko-Pau replied at once. "However, you and Master Lo-Kí have both made up your minds, and I'm not going to waste what little time I have left with you arguing about it."

Akinia gave him a wry smile, which the Master returned.

"Now, back to what I came in here for," Ko-Pau said suddenly, clearing his throat. "I think it might be best if you and I took a little trip."

"Where to?" Akinia wondered, frowning.

"My home," he replied simply.

Akinia's frown deepened. *Ko-Pau has a home off of Paméd?*

A wry smile crossed Ko-Pau's lips as he watched the confused expression take hold on her face. "I'm not just a Najee, Akinia," he reminded her. "I have a personal life outside of all of this; most Najee

203

do."

"You never told me about it," she countered. "I never would have guessed that you had a home anywhere else. I've never heard you talk about a home-world, or about your family... Do you have any family?"

Ko-Pau nodded slowly. "My father is a merchant in Motúk, but I haven't seen him in at least twelve years-"

"You're a Motúkite?" Akinia demanded, shocked. *I always thought he was Imperial!*

"No, of course not," Ko-Pau laughed. "My father just trades there."

Akinia's brow furrowed as she considered this. "What about your mother?"

The Master sighed. "I don't know," he admitted. "She walked out on us when I was four; I don't really remember her."

"I'm sorry," she apologized, grimacing. "Do you have any other family?"

He hesitated a moment and then nodded. "I have an older brother, Kevdon; he's a Major in the army, posted at an outer station in Quadrant 826, and then there's Alaeia, and Anton, Kaldonn, and Gevra," he finished, a small smile crossing his lips.

"You're brother's wife and kids?" Akinia guessed uncertainly.

Ko-Pau shook his head. "Mine," he corrected.

Akinia stared blankly at him for several long moments. "You're married?" she asked, shocked.

Her master smirked. "Is it so hard to believe that I'm married?" he wondered teasingly.

"You're a father?" she questioned, still struggling to comprehend the information.

"Well, I'm not sure how much of a father I am," he grimaced. "I haven't seen my kids in over a year, and it's been almost as long since the last time I talked to them."

Akinia frowned. "Why?"

Ko-Pau sighed. "I try to keep them all as far away from this part of my life as I can," he explained. "It's dangerous to be related to a Najee, especially one with such a tangible connection to Jade. He and my Master were best friends; his family, your family, have received a lot of threats because of it."

She contemplated his answer for a while before asking, "Why

did you never tell me about them? Nath and I never talk about his family, but at least he told me he had one."

"I should have," Ko-Pau agreed at once. "It just didn't seem to be a relevant topic and first, and, as time went on... There's no excuse; I should have told you, a long time ago."

"When do we leave?" Akinia asked, grinning.

"In two days," the Master replied, smiling as well. "I'm forgiven, then?"

Akinia pretended to consider it for a moment. "I'll think about it," she decided, teasingly. "Does Nath know when we're leaving?"

Ko-Pau nodded. "Yes, he does. He also knows that he isn't coming with us," he informed her casually, watching her closely as he said it.

Her jaw dropped slightly. "Nath isn't coming?"

"We've been a trio, or a quartet, rather, ever since you joined us," Ko-Pau explained. "I've had plenty of one-on-one time with Nath over the years, but I don't think we've ever had any time that was just you and me. Well, except for part of that one short mission, but that doesn't really count since we were undercover the entire time."

Akinia hesitated as she thought back over her time with the Najee. "You're right," she realized, a bit amazed.

"It's settled then," Ko-Pau grinned. "Nath will stay here, while you and I go to stay with my family."

"How long will we be there?"

"Until a few days before you have to leave on your mission," Ko-Pau sighed. "That will give Khee-Lá enough time to calm down before we get back, I hope."

Akinia nodded slowly. "I hope so, too," she sighed.

Ko-Pau gave her an encouraging smile before rising to his feet. "I'll leave you to rest," he decided.

"I'm well; I don't need to rest," she protested.

"I never said you weren't well," he countered, laughing. "All I said was for you to rest. We have a long journey ahead of us, and a very long visit. Besides, I don't think any of us have recovered from our visit with your family."

Akinia smirked, feeling her heart swell with pride as Ko-Pau referred to the Juntoby clan as being *her* family. She rose to her feet and darted over to Ko-Pau, wrapping her arms around him in a tight hug.

He kissed the top of her head as he returned her embrace. "Rest well, Slick," he bade before leaving.

I can sleep here, she reminded herself as she slipped her shoes off and climbed into her bed. *The Masters can keep me under control… but what will I do at Ko-Pau's house, especially without Nath?* She quickly typed in the code on her com-link. "Jaynine, bring me some tea, please," she requested.

"As you wish, Mistress," the droid replied at once.

Akinia shifted as she climbed beneath her fethera comforter, savoring the billowing softness that surrounded her. *How can I ever trust myself not to hurt them?*

Chapter 36:

The two days passed quickly. Unwilling to chance an encounter with her uncle, Akinia spent much of the time helping to prepare the ship for the journey. Though it was only three days' journey to Ko-Pau's homeworld, a small trade planet named Mishtor, the men packed enough food and supplies to last them for a full month.

"We aren't going directly to Mishtor," Ko-Pau explained, when Akinia asked him why.

Akinia frowned. "Why not?"

Ko-Pau hesitated a moment. "Come here, let me show you something," he beckoned, walking to the far side of his bedchambers. He pressed a short code into a keypad on the wall. A panel fell away, revealing a detailed, multi-dimensional, system map. As he input another short code, the map slid out on a low axis, becoming a small holo-table. The Master used his fingers to manipulate the interactive map, pulling up an image of Paméd. "We are here," he said simply, before manipulating the map again. The view changed to show a small, grey planet. "This is Mishtor," Ko-Pau informed her. He put both of his hands on the map and pushed them together, watching as the image zoomed out to include both planets, as well as the planets around and between them, in the projection. "Right about here," he informed her, touching a point about halfway between then, which began to glow red, "is a Sigidian blockade."

"In the Empire?" Akinia demanded, shocked.

The Master nodded, grimacing. "Yes, however we do not need to concern ourselves with that; there are several Najee working on it at the moment," he assured her. "It won't last long, but it also won't be gone before our journey tomorrow. We're going to make a detour, a couple of systems wide; I won't chance having you that near to Jade again."

Akinia nodded in response. "Where did you get this?" she asked, motioning to the map.

Ko-Pau laughed, recognizing the longing in his Apprentice's voice and eyes. "You'll get one," he promised her. "As soon as you're a Full Najee."

Grimacing, Akinia nodded in acknowledgement.

The next morning found them boarding the ship. Though Khee-Lá did not come to say goodbye, Nath stayed with them until the last possible moment, his mind closely linked with his sister's. *Stay safe*, he half-requested, half-ordered.

You, too, she replied, giving his consciousness one more gentle caress before pulling her thoughts away from him.

Ko-Pau spoke little as they programmed the coordinates into the ship's navigation system and set the auto-pilot. In fact, he spoke less and less the closer they got to Mishtor.

Akinia began to worry about him. Finally, on the fourth day of their journey, she asked, "Master, are you alright?"

He smirked. "Yes, I'm fine," he promised her, a distracted air to his voice.

"You seem worried," she pressed, unwilling to let the subject drop.

The Master sighed and pulled her into his arms. "I am," he agreed. "I don't know how they'll react to my coming back, not after I've been gone for so long."

Akinia laughed softly. "They'll be glad to see you, especially after you've been gone for so long," she assured him.

Ko-Pau pulled back to look at her, managing a smile for her. "I wish that I could be as certain as you are, but I never know how I'll be received. Sometimes, they're relieved that I'm alive; other times, they hate me for not having come home or contacted them sooner. I've never been away this long before," he explained.

The Apprentice hesitated, unsure what to say. "Will you tell me about them?" she asked curiously.

Sighing heavily, Ko-Pau wandered to one of the chairs. He motioned for Akinia to sit, as well. "What would you like to know?"

She thought for a minute. "How did you meet Aleaia?" she finally asked.

Ko-Pau smiled, his eyes growing distant. "I was just an Apprentice, around Nath's age," he informed her. "I was on a mission on Ish-Ló, a small trade world near the Motúk border. I noticed her, started showing off, and ended up making a complete fool of myself. She thought it was the funniest thing that she had ever seen and started mocking me; I couldn't even get angry at her for it. One thing led to another, and we were married a year later, after I became a Full Najee. Anton was born soon after."

"How did you manage?" Akinia asked curiously.

"What?"

"Being a father, and a Najee," she clarified.

He sighed, grimacing. "I was a lot better at it in the beginning," he admitted. "I was home frequently, and I contacted them almost every day when I was gone."

Akinia frowned when his voice trailed off. "So what changed?" she prodded gently.

"The war," he replied. "The fighting got worse, I was needed farther away and for longer, it got more dangerous to contact my family. To be honest, I never even noticed it happening."

Unsure what to say, Akinia only grimaced.

Ko-Pau made more of an effort to be cheerful after that conversation. Most of the last three days of their journey was spent telling Akinia funny stories about his three children.

Akinia was almost disappointed when the navigation equipment beeped, and a quiet, mechanical voice announced, "We have arrived."

Chapter 37:

The small Asteroid Navigator touched down heavily on the ground as it landed.

Akinia stood up, making her way to the door in the rear of the ship, but paused as she noticed that Ko-Pau hadn't moved. "Master?" she questioned. "Are you alright?"

He nodded slowly, turning slightly and giving her a weak smile. "I'm fine," he promised. "Just a bit nervous, I guess."

Nodding in understanding, Akinia wordlessly walked over to him and gave him a hug.

"I know, Slick," Ko-Pau sighed, standing to give her a proper hug. "Come on, let's gab our bags and get this over with."

Akinia nodded and quickly slipped the strap of her large bag over her shoulder. Her knees buckled under its weight for a moment before she adjusted to it. "Remind me to kill Jaynine the next time he packs my bag this full," she groused. "I won't need half the things he packed, and it's going to kill me before I get the chance to wear the other half!"

Ko-Pau laughed as he slung his own pack onto his shoulder. "I can just see it now: you survive six weeks in Jade Enbrilth's torture chamber, only to be killed by your luggage after your rescue," he teased.

Laughing with him, Akinia followed her master out of the ship.

The landing field was a barren expanse of artificial rock, worn from years of use. It was surrounded on all sides by ramshackle buildings, whose architecture and enormity hinted at past greatness. Despite the rather abundant populace walking the streets, the city seemed abandoned and neglected.

Akinia hesitated uncertainly. *This is nothing like I expected*, she mused to herself, staring around in surprise. *Maybe I was on Náto too long...*

Ko-Pau smirked, as though guessing where her thoughts had taken her. "They're here to hide," he reminded her. "Mishtor is entirely safe, but it's also an excellent place to blend in with the populace."

"Is *anywhere* entirely safe?" she wondered absently, mostly talking to herself.

The Master sighed, wrapping his arm around her shoulder as they walked. "It won't always be like this," he promised her. "Someday we won't have to look over our shoulders, have battle strategies in place so that we can take a trip home. One day you'll wake up, open your eyes, and just lay in your bed all day, relaxing, just because you can, because there's nothing left to be afraid of."

Akinia gave him a wry smile. "That sounds like a fairy-tale," she mused.

"It isn't," Ko-Pau laughed. "I remember those days. I was just a boy, not even Apprenticed yet, but there *was* peace. Someday you'll know what it is, and so will my sons, and my daughter. Someday it won't just be a fond memory."

"I would like that," Akinia agreed, smiling. A shadow crossed her face as she considered what that peace would cost, what it would require of her... She shook her head slightly to clear her thoughts, letting her gaze wander around the city as they walked.

Ko-Pau drew to a stop in front of a row of small houses, each one identical to those around it, with a small area fenced in behind it. "Here we are," he sighed, gazing at it with an expression falling somewhere between delight and terror. "Come inside; I don't think Alaeia and the children are home yet."

The door creaked loudly as Ko-Pau pushed it open, and Akinia hesitated before she followed him inside, stepping through a long archway and into the main room. As her master deposited his bag on the floor next to the wall, Akinia followed suit. She gazed around the room in wonder. *So this is Master's house...*

"Just wait here. I'm going to make a quick trip up the street. Make yourself comfortable," Ko-Pau told her, leaving her to wander around the house.

"You're leaving?" Akinia asked, suddenly anxious.

"Only for a moment," the master soothed. "You'll be fine. Just make yourself at home, explore the house, do whatever you like, short of destroying the house." Without another word, and without waiting for her reply, he left.

Despite Ko-Pau's assurance that she could explore the house, Akinia stayed in the sitting room, gently fingering the delicate figurines carefully positioned on the wooden shelves. The design of the room was so simple, so warm; she wondered if Ko-Pau had a hand in designing it or if it was solely his wife's work.

Sighing, she turned to the long couch and sat down. She stretched out with her mind and used it to pull the hood of her cloak down around her shoulders. She gently touched the circlet on her brow, as if to remind herself that it was there.

A strange feeling in the pit of her stomach caused her to glance anxiously at her wajun, and then to gently finger the handle. She started as the front door creaked open.

"Anton, I told you to fix this door," a woman snapped.

"Sorry mom, I'll do it later..." the boy's voice trailed off as he stepped into the archway dividing the entryway from the sitting room and spotted Akinia.

Another boy trotted up to see what his brother was staring at. "Wow," he mouthed, his eyes widening.

"Who are you? What are you doing here?" the woman demanded angrily, pushing another child, a small girl, behind her protectively. Her brown hair was disarrayed and her clothes looked as though they had been worn through a stressful day.

Akinia stood up quickly. "Please, don't be alarmed. I am Akinia Juntoby, Ko-Pau's apprentice. He brought me home to meet you all," she explained. *Where is Master?*

"You lying sneak-thief! My husband's apprentice is a boy," the woman, whom Akinia now knew to be Aleaia, snapped, pulling her sons back into the entryway. She pulled a small blaster from her sleeve and aimed it at Akinia.

Akinia opened her mouth, startled, trying to explain.

The door quickly opened and Ko-Pau walked in.

"Daddy!" the little girl exclaimed, running to him.

He swooped her up and hugged her tightly before giving each of his sons a firm handshake and a hug. "Hello, dear," he said, smiling, to his wife.

"This girl says she's with you, that she's your apprentice," Aleaia said hurriedly, pointing to Akinia with a smug grin, as though certain the young girl would now be getting her punishment.

"It's alright, sweetheart. Akinia was assigned as my new apprentice. I had to bring her home to keep her safe for a little while," Ko-Pau explained soothingly, rubbing his wife's shoulders. He leaned forwards and gave her a quick kiss on the cheek. "Kids, I'd like you to meet Princess Akinia Juntoby, Khee-Lá's niece," he introduced, waving them forwards.

"Princess?" the oldest boy questioned. When his father nodded, he bowed forwards slightly. "Pleased to meet you, Your Highness."

"You must be Anton," she said smiling, "Please, just call me Akinia. I get enough of the 'princess' bit from Nath." She looked past the boys to the young girl. "And you must be Gevra. Your daddy told me you were pretty, but I wasn't expecting such a beautiful young lady," she smiled. The seven year old girl smiled back shyly. Akinia looked at the younger boy. "So that must make you Kaldonn."

"Yep, but everyone calls me Kal," he grinned. He extended a hand and Akinia shook it. "Nice to meet you, Akinia."

"And Aleaia, I'm really sorry about that misunderstanding. I thought you knew Master had another apprentice," she apologized.

"No, my dear husband never mentioned it. How long did you say you've been working with him?" the woman demanded, crossing her arms.

"About a year and a half now, isn't it, Master?" she asked.

"Yes, that sounds about right," he agreed, a bit self-consciously.

"Father, where is Nath?" Anton asked.

"He didn't come this time. Akinia and I had to sneak off of Paméd in the middle of the night and fly unseen past Sigidian blockades," he replied dramatically.

"Tell us about it, Father, please tell us!" Kal begged.

Aleaia broke in. "After we get supper going. You boys still have chores to do, now get with it," she ordered, shooing them away. "Gevra, go and clean your room, please."

"Can Akinia come and help?" the girl asked shyly.

"I don't think she wants to go and clean your room, now get on with it," she replied firmly.

"It won't hurt Akinia to spend a few minutes picking up toys. I think she's missed doing it, haven't you?" Ko-Pau asked knowingly.

She grinned. "Sounds like fun, just like old times," she laughed. She took the young girl's hand and allowed herself to be led down a hallway and into a bedroom.

"What is going on, Ko-Pau?" Aleaia demanded, crossing her arms and turning to glare at her husband. "I haven't heard from you in months!"

"I know, sweetheart, I know. Please, sit down and let me explain," he sighed, motioning to a chair.

Akinia didn't hear anything else they said as she followed Gevra.

"So you really work with Daddy?" the little girl asked as they walked into a cluttered room.

"Yes, your daddy is a very brave man. He saved my life several times," she replied as she began picking toys up and putting them into the multi-colored storage units labeled 'toys'.

"That's something I'd like to hear," Anton stated from the doorway.

Akinia turned to see him standing there, leaning on a broom. "You had best get to work before you get into trouble. There will be plenty of time for stories later," she admonished.

"Can't you just think my chores done? That's what Nath does when he comes," he begged.

Akinia gave him a half-hearted grin, laughing to herself at the boy's definition of their powers. "I would, but I think your parents want to talk right now. We had better just go through it like normal," she explained, hoping he wouldn't push her to use the gifts she was so anxious to ignore right now.

"How come we haven't met you before now?" Anton asked.

"Like I said, there will be time for stories later, now get to work so we can talk," she laughed.

Anton sighed and walked away.

"Can you tell me while we work?" Gevra asked mischievously.

"That wouldn't be fair to your brothers, would it?" Akinia asked in reply.

"No, I guess not," the girl sighed. Gevra prodded Akinia several more times for information, but the older girl just smiled and told her to be patient.

Chapter 38:

The mystery of the big secret motivated all three of Ko-Pau's young children to quickly complete their chores. The tasks that normally took them an entire afternoon were now completed in a bit more than an hour!

"We're going out now," Anton announced as he and Kal paused in the doorway of Gevra's room.

"We'll come with you; we're done now," Akinia decided, rising to her feet. She reached down to help Gevra up, and then motioned for the children to lead the way.

Ko-Pau and Alaeia were arguing, their voices a low undertone, but stopped as soon as they saw the children enter. "All done?" Ko-Pau asked.

"Yes, father," Kal replied happily.

Ko-Pau gave them one of the stern looks he usually reserved for Nath, "Are you sure?"

Anton sat down, his brother and sister following suit. "We finished everything, I promise," he assured them.

Akinia hesitated a moment, uncertain where to sit. All of the seats were taken: the three children sat on the couch, and Ko-Pau and Alaeia each occupied one of the plush armchairs.

"Come here, Slick," Ko-Pau laughed, motioning to the wide arm of the chair he was sitting in.

Unable to avoid smiling in response, she obediently sat where he indicated. Her eyes darted to Alaeia, disconcerted by the furious expression on her face. She quickly looked back to the children, smiling as she saw the similarities between them and their father. Little Gevra favored Ko-Pau the most, but all of the children wore expressions and sat with a body language that mirrored their father's perfectly. As she marveled at their similarities, she couldn't keep a somewhat disturbing thought from crossing her mind: *I wonder if I act anything like my father…*

"So what have you been doing? We haven't heard anything from you since you contacted us to tell us you were better. And how did you get hurt? You never told us," Anton demanded.

"Slow down, I can only answer one question at a time," he laughed.

Aleaia glared at the floor, her fists balled so tightly that her knuckles were white.

Ko-Pau didn't seem to notice, but continued to say, "To start with, I was injured when I was battling Lokita."

"Well, he means that he was injured when he was saving my hide from Lokita," Akinia laughed, feeling her face turn red as their eyes darted to her. Glancing back to her Master, she smiled at the animated look he had on his face as he began to tell the story.

"We were fighting back and forth. I nearly had her beat. She was scared. I would have killed her if I hadn't tripped over her cloak. She took the chance to stab a needle into my neck, the syringe full of poison. Akinia and Nath were completing the mission, rescuing three diplomats from the clutches of the Sigidians. Lokita left me there, unconscious, to go after Nath and Akinia," he said, using his hands to depict the battle.

Akinia knew by the look on his face that it was her turn to add to the tale. "Nath and I found the captives and managed to extract them from the Sigidians' hands. I took the first one we rescued to the hanger and fought our way through to an imperial ship. Then I hotwired it and had it ready while Nath brought the other two. We got the ship into the air and I realized that we hadn't heard anything from Master since we left him with Lokita. I leapt out and fought my way back through the lines of soldiers. I found him lying in a crumpled heap on the floor and dragged him back to the hanger, terrified that he wasn't going to make it. Nath helped me drag him onboard and then I brought him and the injured captives back to Paméd. Hyaline and I worked all night, but finally managed to stabilize him. The truly scary part was when Lo-Kí sent Nath and I out by ourselves until Master woke up," she added, laughing.

"So, you saved his life?" Kal said, eyes wide.

"You're the reason Father came home to us," Anton added gratefully.

218

Akinia blushed. "It wasn't anything he wouldn't have done a thousand times over for Nath and I. It wasn't anything he hasn't done a thousand times for Nath," she added as an afterthought.

"When I woke up, Akinia and Nath had just been assigned to their most challenging mission yet. Lo-Kí was sending them to the Capitol to escort Princess Alania and Princess Inzan to Motúk. We had only a handful of chances to talk, but I was still so weak from the effects of the poison that our talks were never long," Ko-Pau added. "We never imagined the adventure waiting for her on such a simple mission!"

Akinia again knew it was her turn. "We spent several days in the palace, talking to the princesses; I had really missed their company. We hadn't spoken since we escorted them from Paméd to Alania's ship nearly a year previous. Finally, it was time to go. The princesses were in grave danger, as usual, so we left four days earlier than expected with no one knowing they were aboard. My own doing," she grinned, but then her grin faded into a troubled frown.

"What happened next?" Gevra demanded worriedly.

"Someone knew our plan. Someone knew that we would be leaving early and they were waiting for us. Lokita and her men had planned an ambush. Our ship lurched suddenly as we were dragged out of hyperspace. I got to the fighters immediately and took all three of our squadrons out to fight her off enough that we could escape. We thought it was working, but then my fighter jerked suddenly to a stop. My head slammed against the dashboard.

"Then I knew my fighter was caught in a tractor beam, it was slowly sucking me into the bowels of Lokita's ship," she paused dramatically. "Nath was panicking, trying to get me out of it, but there was no chance. I was caught too securely and there were too many of Lokita's fighters out around me. It was all I could do to make him get the princesses and leave before we were all captured. The last thing I saw before the hanger bay doors closed in front of me was the *Hailing Comet* making the jump to safety."

"He of course immediately contacted the Council, and we were all panicking as we tried to figure out how we could save Akinia. Lo-Kí was the only one who managed to keep a level head," Ko-Pau interjected.

"Lokita's soldiers dragged me up to the command center of her ship, where she was waiting for me," Akinia continued, her voice growing soft and pained.

"Wow, you actually saw Lokita?" Kal asked, his eyes growing wide.

"Oh, I did much more than that…" she promised. She took a deep breath. "Lokita stood, taunting me, telling me of how the Najee would rally together and charge Jade's base, trying to save me. She told me that they would be ready for them, and they would place bombs in ideal locations. Not a single Najee would be left alive by time they got through with them. I knew I had to do something, so I convinced her to let me contact the Council and tell them not to come, because I knew that they would have a plan and they would make it through to me. It would be the end of Lokita and Jade, but too many Najee would die and it would kill me that they died for my foolishness. The stupid girl actually believed me. I contacted the council and begged them not to send a force after me, I begged them not to send a group to save me."

"We, of course, thought she was insane, and no one listened to her," Ko-Pau laughed.

"I was getting very annoyed as I continued to repeat my request in different ways, finally, Khee-Lá caught on. He agreed to what I asked, and then Lokita cut off the communication. I was sent down to a prison cell to await when I would be brought before Jade Enbrilth," her eyes widened, adding to the drama of the moment.

"The Council was in shock over Khee-Lá's agreement. Some were quite literally ready to kill him. It was then that he explained to us what Akinia had been saying. She managed to send a secret message to us, standing right beside Lokita, to send only one or two Najee in, because they could penetrate Jade's defenses, whereas a large force would have been destroyed," Ko-Pau said proudly.

"It was four days' journey before I was brought to Jade's base, and then only moments before I was brought before Jade Enbrilth. He tried his best to convince me to join him, but I refused. It was then that he sent me to be tortured to the point of death, revived, and then tortured to the point of death again for the rest of my natural life or until I relented and begged him to allow me to serve him by Lokita's side," she shuddered as she thought of her torture, a distant look growing in her eyes as she was brought back to that moment, to the pain. Her legs began to throb violently.

Unbidden images flashed across her vision. She saw the sliverwhip slicing mercilessly through her flesh. She heard the machines running as they summoned the jolt of electricity that would course through her veins a moment later, nearly killing her. She felt the snap as her leg was shattered, again. She felt the violent burn that ran through her body as Lokita healed her…

Ko-Pau's voice brought her out of it as he continued with the story. "We were flying in low over the surface of the planet Jade's base resided on. The vegetation was so thick our scanners were useless, we didn't dare stretch out with our minds for fear of touching Jade or Lokita's and alerting them to our presence. It was then that Akinia suddenly touched all of our minds, guiding us in without being seen or suspected by anyone. We landed and Nath and I went around the front to create a diversion. Khee-Lá snuck in through the ventilation systems to find Akinia."

"I was strapped to a torture device, one designed to electrocute me every few minutes to weaken me. When the fight began, Lokita summoned my guards to assist in driving them away, I believe she was punished severely for that after we escaped. Khee-Lá dropped in through the ventilation shaft in the roof and cut me out of the shackles that held me, but not before the machine began to work. I had to use the last of my strength to push him away enough with my thoughts that he wouldn't be caught in the current," she continued. "I fell unconscious again as I caught sight of Jade in the hallway ahead of us once we had caught up to Master and Nath."

"We fought our way out of Jade's base and back to the ship. It only took us a few minutes to launch into hyperspace, just as Jade's troops got their ships into the air behind us. Akinia remained unconscious for a month after we brought her back to Paméd," Ko-Pau finished.

"So she is just now able to safely travel?" Aleaia demanded.

"No, but that is another story entirely, my dear. I'm afraid that we haven't time for it right now seeing as how our dinner is on the verge of burning," Ko-Pau replied, laughing. Aleaia started to jump up, but Ko-Pau put a hand on her arm to stop her. "I've taken care of it, just tell me how much lactose you wanted added to it."

"I'd rather do it myself," she snapped. She pulled out of his grip and walked past him into the kitchen.

Ko-Pau gave Akinia a pleading look and she motioned for him to follow her. He nodded and walked after her.

"Oh, no you don't. Just let them talk," she murmured to Gevra

221

as the little girl jumped up to follow her father.

"Why is mom so angry with him?" Kal asked his older brother.

"Because he's never home. He's always off fighting the war and she hardly ever gets to see him. She doesn't like it," Anton sighed.

"That's enough for now, boys," Akinia warned, motioning with her eyes to Gevra, who was frowning worriedly.

"So how did you become a Najee, anyway?" Anton asked.

"I was claimed for the Najee before I was born. Uncle Khee-Lá brought this with him when he came home to be with my mother when she gave birth to me and my twin sister," she paused and pulled the necklace from her shirt, "It belonged to the first Najee, a Nrell named Akinia. That's how I got my name. Then when Jade Enbrilth attacked my palace three months after I was born, he killed my parents, my grandparents, and my sister. I escaped only because Khee-Lá and your father were there. They fought their way off of Paméd with me, and then they brought me to an orphanage where I would be safe. Fourteen years later Master returned for me and I've been with him ever since."

"So they know you're going to be a Najee and they tell your parents when you're born?" Kal asked, disappointed.

"No. That was just me. I'm a very powerful Najee, because of all the Najee in my family, and so they could tell I would be one," she assured him.

They all stopped and turned to the kitchen as Aleaia shrieked, "I'm sick of hearing this!"

"Anton, Kal, take your sister outside to play," Akinia ordered quietly.

"But we want to stay in here," Anton protested.

"Do as I said, and later I'll tell you more stories," she offered.

"Alright," the boys agreed reluctantly.

"Come on, let's go play," Anton offered, taking his sister's hand.

Akinia waited until they were gone before she edged closer to the kitchen.

"You know I want to stay with you, more than anything, but I have duties, Aleaia. You knew this when you married me. You knew I would be gone most of the time, especially with the war escalating," Ko-Pau protested.

"I'm sick of being here alone with the kids all of the time. I'm sick of not being able to do everything I need to do because I'm trying

222

to be a mother *and a father* to them. I'm sick of hearing Anton and Kal's non-stop talk about how they're going to be Najee like you when they grow up, and refusing to listen to reason when I tell them that if they were Najee we would know about it by now. I'm sick of Gevra not knowing who her father is because you haven't been home in two years. I'm sick of people thinking I'm a widow, or an unwed mother, or divorced because you are never here," she sobbed.

"I don't know what you want me to do about it. I don't have the option of just quitting being a Najee and coming home to live with you. I have to take Nath and Akinia into consideration," Ko-Pau replied, pained.

"And then that girl is another matter!" she announced. "I don't understand you, Ko-Pau. You're putting that girl, who is of no relation to you or me or any of us, before your own children. They miss you, don't you understand that? They never get to see you!"

"That girl, as you call her, is the only thing that's keeping Jade from destroying the Empire and Motúk," he informed her solemnly.

Akinia listened harder.

"What do you mean?" Aleaia demanded, her curiosity temporarily driving back her anger.

"The girl is the only one of us who can face Jade and live to tell the tale. Khee-Lá escaped by luck, and luck only. No one else has ever lived. Akinia has repeatedly been in Jade's power, and escaped. She is the child of an ancient prophecy, which tells of a girl who will come and destroy a great evil and restore peace to the galaxy. Without her we are all doomed to death," he explained.

"Even so, there must be another who can care for her? And Nath is all but on his own now," she stopped as Ko-Pau cut her off.

"On his own and still getting into as much trouble as he managed to before. He's still a boy, Aleaia. And what do you propose I do, give Akinia away? She has been abandoned enough in her lifetime. I love you, and that is part of the reason I must be away so much. I have to protect you, and the kids. The only way I can do that is by keeping Akinia safe as she tests her wings preparing to battle the most powerful enemy in recorded history, without assistance from us. If she is not kept safe, our children will either be killed along with octillions of others, or they will be sold as slaves to the Sigidians. Our empire will not stand without her," he explained, begging her to understand.

"And you cannot make time for us anywhere? You cannot take

your children on a short trip with you, just a week or so, to make them happy? Is this the price of freedom?" she retorted.

Ko-Pau didn't answer, but sighed in frustration. Why could she not understand?

Akinia darted back to the couch, settling in silently just as Aleaia rounded the corner.

"Where are the children?" she demanded.

"Your argument was getting loud, and Gevra didn't understand. I sent them outside until you stopped. I'll go and get them," she offered.

"Do. Not. Move. Akinia. Juntoby," Ko-Pau ordered sternly, stressing each word into its own sentence.

Akinia froze where she was, halfway between sitting and standing, and became tense. She knew that tone of voice... and it was never good.

"Sit," he ordered.

She sighed and lowered herself back down.

"What exactly was going on in here?" he demanded, taking a seat himself. Aleaia stood beside him, crossing her arms and watching their interaction with interest.

"Nothing, it's just that the kids heard you two arguing, I didn't think it was good for Gevra to be listening to it, since it was already making her upset, so I told the boys to take her outside to play," she shrugged.

"While you stayed in listening?" he guessed, raising an eyebrow.

"I didn't mean it for the purpose of listening in, I was worried about you and was wondering if I could help," she clarified shyly.

Ko-Pau gave her a weak smile, amused by her sudden shy attitude. Shyness was one trait he had only rarely seen in her. "That was kind, sweetheart, but there's nothing you can do. We've been having these arguments for years, haven't we, Aleaia?" he laughed, taking her hand.

"And you see how far I've gotten," Aleaia grumbled, a thin smile tracing on her lips.

"Exactly what all did you hear?" Ko-Pau demanded, suddenly worried.

"Just about everything after Aleaia yelled that she was sick of hearing this," she admitted.

"You and I are going to make a run down to the market. We're out of bread again," Ko-Pau ordered, motioning for her to follow. "Aleaia, why don't you let the children play until we get back? We won't be long."

Akinia sighed and followed him out of the front door, accidentally giving Aleaia a pleading glance that made the older woman wonder what Ko-Pau was going to do.

Chapter 39:

"Master, we aren't out of bread, are we?" she accused as they shut the front door and started walking up the cobblestone street. There were only a handful of people walking around, and none seemed interested in them.

"No, we aren't, but you and I need to talk about what you heard," he said pointedly.

"Oh, that," she said, embarrassed. She looked away. "I'm sorry I was eavesdropping again."

"I don't mind that," he assured her. "No, what I'm worried about was the part where I was explaining to Aleaia why I couldn't stay home with her. I didn't want you to get the wrong idea."

"I know that it's because of me, Master. I've always known," she admitted. She wrapped her arms around herself, knowing that the chill she was getting had nothing to do with the weather.

Ko-Pau stopped, placed a hand on each of her shoulder, and turned her around to face him. "Look at me," he ordered when she continued to avert her gaze. "You are not to blame for my personal problems, Akinia. My family is in danger because of me, and because of what I am. I am only rarely home because I don't want anyone to know that I am related to them, so that the Sigidians do not find out and harm them. I was only using you as an example for why I couldn't stay home, and I apologize for that. I meant nothing of it."

Akinia searched his eyes, and then stretched her mind towards him curiously. He lowered his mental walls and allowed her to examine his thoughts about the matter. Their minds were joined together as she searched him, their eyes were locked into one another as she examined them for the truth as well. She felt all of his love for her, his fear for her fate, and his love for his family as it molded and formed his perception of events. Accepting that he was telling the truth, she pulled her mind away from his and nodded in agreement.

"So I see you've gotten over your fear of touching my mind," he noted as he motioned for her to walk again.

"No, but I had to know," she corrected with a sigh, strengthening her walls again.

"Did you think I would lie to you?"

She gave him a wry smile. "I think that you care enough for me to try and make me feel better when I'm upset, whatever that may take."

"You know me well then, Slick," he teased, echoing her response to his own teasing comment when she had first arrived on Paméd. "Shall we walk a while more, or do you want to go back to the house?"

"It makes no difference to me," Akinia shrugged, "but I think that you want to return to the house. You don't get to come home often."

"Very true," he sighed, his eyes getting a distant look in them.

Akinia smiled and hugged him. "You go on back to the house. I think I want to explore a bit longer. I can find my way back," she urged.

"I don't feel comfortable leaving you here alone," he hesitated.

"I have my wajun," she reminded him patiently.

He regarded her for a moment before sighing. "You *will* contact me if you need me, right? No hesitation because of your own fear?"

She hesitated before giving a single, curt nod. "I will… if I need you," she promised.

He still seemed reluctant to leave her. "Are you certain…?"

"All of your assurances that Mishtor is safe are seeming less and less true," she said pointedly, her voice tainted with laughter. "Either it is truly safe here, and I can walk around by myself, or it isn't and I need to stay with you."

"It *is* safe here," he asserted. "I'm just not certain if you are well enough to be alone, so far from me. What if you were to pass out again?"

"That hasn't happened in several weeks, Master, and you know it," she laughed.

"But it *has* happened, Akinia," he argued. "I don't want you hurt again, especially not with the mission coming up… You need your strength…" His voice trailed off and his eyes darted away from her as his thoughts turned back to the mission.

Akinia grimaced. "If it is this important to you, I won't wander off, not quite yet," she relented.

He gave her a wry smile. "Since when do I ever win our arguments?" he teased.

"If I didn't let you win once in a while you'd stop letting *me* win," she grinned.

"So I *let* you win our arguments, do I?"

"Of course," she agreed instantly. "But, in your defense, I'm *very* hard to deny. It's probably because I'm just so very sweet."

"I wonder what Nath would say to that?" Ko-Pau wondered, amused.

"Whatever it is, I'm certain I would smack him for it," she laughed.

"Probably," he agreed, nodding. "Though I'm certain Khee-Lá would add that your innate charm helps your case a great deal."

"And it's *just like Leonora*," Akinia mimicked, her face acquiring a very impish expression.

Ko-Pau laughed and offered her his arm, which she accepted silently. "There *are* worse people to be compared to," he reminded her. "I don't remember Leonora well, but I do remember she was a very sweet woman."

"That does seem to be the general consensus," Akinia sighed, leaning her head against his shoulder. It amazed her once again how close she and her Master had grown over the past year. How quickly he had gone from a stranger, to a teacher, to a friend, and even a father! Khee-Lá was her legal guardian, her legal father, but he had always been more of an uncle than a father to her. No, Ko-Pau was the man she considered her father, and Nath had always been her big brother, since the day they first met.

She smiled wryly as she considered how natural their relationship had always seemed, the revelation of their shared blood had only strengthened their close companionship. She wished so much that Ko-Pau and Khee-Lá could know! Even if no one else knew, just to share this joyous news with her closest family would be such a pleasure...but she gave her word to Nath, and she could never betray his trust.

She sighed as she thought of Nath and Khee-Lá. When would she see them again? Khee-Lá would not likely be back before she left on her mission, and Nath was still furious with her for accepting it...it was unlikely he would forgive her any sooner than her safe return from

Sigadia, and it may even be a fair length of time afterwards before she was fully forgiven.

"Are you alright?" Ko-Pau asked, concerned.

She nodded. "I was just thinking of Khee-Lá and Nath," she explained with another sigh.

He nodded in acknowledgment. "You should contact them before bed, let them know we arrived safely. I'm certain that Khee-Lá especially would like to hear from you."

"I will," she promised simply.

They fell silent again as they walked. Akinia looked around at the people passing them on the street. The diversity of races still amazed her, even after so many missions to mixed-race planets. For fourteen years she had never seen a being other than an Adamian, and now she was in the presence of at least a dozen races!

But as amazing as she found the full-blooded individuals, it was the mixed-blood beings that earned the majority of her attention. One man caught her attention: a cross between Lyndop and Crystallion. His green skin was fairly translucent, but nowhere near as clear as a pure Crystallion. Even his hair, fiery orange as it was, hung thick and tightly curled around his head, though the strands were almost invisible as a Crystallion's were; it gave him the appearance of having a smoky orange aura around his head and shoulders.

And as amazing as the diverse races were, the diversity of clothing was even more incredible! Dozens of star systems, hundreds of planets, had influenced the array of clothing that attired the crowd. Any one being could be wearing styles from a dozen different cultures, combined to form an entirely new look. Some people looked so bizarre she wanted to laugh, others looked so beautiful she simply wanted to gape at them as they passed, but the majority were somewhere in between, their clothing looking ridiculous enough to be humorous, yet fitting together perfectly enough that she dared not laugh.

She grimaced as they approached the house, wishing she could see more, but knowing that she needed to stay near Ko-Pau for his own comfort. She thanked him quietly as he opened the door for her.

"You forgot the bread," Alaeia noticed suspiciously.

"Is that what we went for?" he teased. "I knew we had forgotten something, Akinia!"

Akinia smiled, but otherwise didn't comment.

Alaeia scowled, but let it go. "The children are waiting for you in the yard. They want you to play," she told him. "Akinia can help me finish dinner."

"I'd be glad to," Akinia said quickly as Ko-Pau opened his mouth to argue. She looked at him pointedly. "Go and play with them," she urged.

He sighed in defeat. "I can barely hold my own against one of you, let alone both of you," he grumbled pleasantly.

Akinia laughed. "Then don't try to argue, just go on," she recommended.

He nodded, grinning at them both, and quickly left.

"Alright," Alaeia sighed, "let's go ahead and get to work." She walked into the kitchen and Akinia followed silently. "We'll process the beans on the front step; it's much more pleasant than the kitchen."

Akinia nodded and grabbed one of the bowls of pod-beans from table as Alaeia took the other. "I've never done them before," she admitted. "You'll have to show me what to do."

"It isn't hard," Alaeia said bitterly. "Even Gevra can do it."

Though she detected the insult in the comment, Akinia smiled and said, "Then it shouldn't take me long to learn."

Alaeia gave her a curt nod and led the way to the front step. As they sat, she pulled one of the beans from the bowl. "Break off each of the tips, pull the string running down the side, and break the bean into the pot. Throw the ends and string into the street," she instructed quickly. "The animals will eat them this evening."

Akinia nodded and began to do as she said.

"Not so much," Alaeia chastised. "Just break the very tip off."

"Sorry," Akinia apologized, blushing. She broke the second tip of very close to the end and looked to Alaeia for approval.

The woman nodded once before turning to her own bowl. "So what did my husband want with you?" she asked nonchalantly.

Akinia grimaced. So *this* was what she wanted… "He just wanted to make sure I hadn't misunderstood anything I heard, and that I knew I wasn't the reason you were fighting," she admitted.

She nodded again. "He was always very good with Nath… Why do you think he didn't tell me of you?"

She hesitated, uncertain whether or not to tell her the truth. Finally, she sighed and explained, "I don't know for certain, but if I had to guess then I would say that it was for my safety. Jade Enbrilth wants me dead; my uncle faked my death fifteen years ago to protect me, when Jade killed my parents looking for me. Master was under strict orders not to let anyone know I was alive until I knew the truth about my past, which wasn't until a few months ago."

Alaeia nodded slowly, causing Akinia to assume that Ko-Pau had informed her of that. "And did my husband ever speak of me? Or his children?" she asked, a strong note of bitterness tingeing the otherwise careful façade of innocent curiosity.

"Not to me," she admitted. "But then, no one ever really talks to me about anything outside of the Najee. We did talk at length on the journey here, and before leaving Paméd. He loves you all so much... I hope I'm lucky enough to be loved that much...someday." Her cheeks reddened and she wondered absently if Katarina would classify that statement as 'meddling'.

Alaeia's lips clenched together tightly. "Do yourself a favor: don't ever marry a Najee, no matter how much he loves you, or you love him. Najee or not, you'll find yourself at home alone with the kids more often than he's there..."

Several replies came to Akinia's mind...All of them were either too close to an agreement, or too close to being rude. Instead, she simply kept her mouth shut and processed the beans in silence.

It was several long minutes that that Alaeia sighed and said, "Bring those beans in when you finish, and don't be too long with them." Without another word she stood and darted back into the house, leaving Akinia alone on the steps.

Sighing, Akinia hurried to finish. She found herself bitterly wondering why she had agreed to come here... *I could be with Uncle Andrid and Aunt Katarina, my beautiful cousins...How did Ko-Pau ever marry that selfish woman?* Instantly, she regretted her harsh evaluation of Alaeia. *Rude*, she chastised herself, *terribly rude!*

Still, she couldn't entirely deny that her first impression of the woman had gravitated towards Alaeia being a selfish, bitter, insensitive woman, with a short temper and little regard for Ko-Pau's responsibilities as a Najee. Yet, at the same time, Akinia also understood the tense relationship that stood between them. It must be very difficult to maintain a close and loving marriage when Ko-Pau had gone so long without talking to his wife, and hadn't even bothered to mention his new apprentice to her! Maybe Alaeia's selfishness wasn't as much to blame as her circumstances...Akinia began to wonder if she would behave the same way in a similar predicament...

Shaking her head to clear it, Akinia snapped the last of the beans. She paused a moment as she stood, stretching her cramped muscles, before going into the house. *I'll be as kind to her as I can*, she decided. *Maybe she'll warm up to me by the time we leave...*

Chapter 40:

Despite Akinia's efforts to get along with Alaeia (a hopeless struggle soon attempted only for her Master's sake) the woman did not warm up to her, nor did she seem any more willing to forgive Ko-Pau for being gone so often. If anything, her behavior worsened during the course of the visit. She didn't speak to Ko-Pau unless necessary, she was harsh and short-tempered to her children, and she seemed to be consciously *trying* to make Akinia hate her…

The happiest parts of Akinia's visit were the rare moments she was alone with the children or her Master.

Ko-Pau loved to play games with the kids, but he especially loved to simply sit and watch them all play together. Akinia had almost as much enjoyment out of watching him play with the children as *he* had from watching her play with them! She especially loved to see him with little Gevra, who quickly learned that she had a power over her father that her brothers didn't have: whatever Gevra wanted, Gevra got; whether it was a hug or a partner in a silly game or a pretty doll from the marketplace, she was soon the most spoiled child in existence.

It also quickly became apparent to Akinia that the boys, both so independent and hard-headed, seemed to idolize Nath more than she had initially thought. Every action and every mannerism which could not be directly attributed to their father *could* be attributed to Nath. They entertained her, almost daily, with dramatic portrayals of glorious battles they imagined themselves fighting in, using a pair of greatly-abused sticks as wajun.

She got a great deal of enjoyment out of watching their antics, but spent the majority of her time playing with Gevra. She was a dark-haired green-eyed little girl with a plain face and delicate features that hinted at future beauty, but she had a mature wit and charmingly childish manner that intrigued Akinia to no end.

Yet there was something else about her... something so strangely familiar in her eyes... It gave Akinia an unsettled feeling that ate away at her for the duration of the visit. It was both far too soon and just in the nick-of-time that Ko-Pau announced they would be leaving in a couple of days...

"Sing me a song?" Gevra asked, batting her eyelashes at Akinia as she crawled into bed.

Akinia smiled and tucked the blankets up around Gevra's chin before sitting at the foot of the bed. "What should I sing for you?"

The little girl thought for a moment, her lips pursing as she concentrated, before she decided, "Something your mommy used to sing to you."

Akinia could feel herself frown, though she forced herself to smile again for Gevra. "I know a very pretty song. If you promise to close your eyes and try to go to sleep, I'll sing it to you," she offered.

This time it was Gevra that frowned. "Daddy says you're leaving soon," she pouted. "Can't I stay up longer? I won't get to see you again for a long time."

"No," Akinia smiled, "you need to sleep. We still have a few more days to spend together. Besides, if you don't sleep now, then you'll be too sleepy to enjoy tomorrow!"

A crease formed between Gevra's eyes, making her look almost identical to her father for a moment. "Fine," she agreed with a sigh, "I'll go to sleep... but I still don't want you to go. You and Daddy could stay here?"

"That does sound like fun," Akinia admitted, stroking a strand of hair behind Gevra's ear, "but we have to go back. We have to do our job and keep you safe."

"You could keep me safe here," she protested.

Akinia laughed. "Yes, we could, but we have to keep lots and lots of other people safe, too. It's a part of being a Najee," she explained. "Now close your eyes and no more talking. We both need some sleep tonight, alright?"

"Okay," Gevra sighed.

A strange look came into Gevra's eyes, the same one that Akinia had noticed before... she still had that little crease between her eyes, too... she looked just like Ko-Pau... Akinia's eyes widened just as Gevra's closed. So *that* was what she had seen! She frowned, but tried to push her uneasy feeling away long enough to sing little Gevra to

236

sleep.

She repeated the song, the same one that she had sung to Karanne, three times before Gevra finally fell asleep. Akinia watched her, smiling, as her eyes fluttered and her lips curved into a peaceful 'o'. Yet, after a while, her smile faded into a troubled frown. *I need a cup of tea*, she decided, standing carefully so as not to jostle the bed. She hesitated a moment before bending down and gently kissing Gevra's forehead.

The strange look she had seen in Gevra's eyes came into her mind, and her stomach began to churn. *How will I tell Ko-Pau?*

Chapter 41:

Akinia pulled the door shut softly enough that it made no noise. She jumped as she turned to walk back down the hallway, her hand on the handle of her wajun. "You scared me!" she admonished in a hushed voice.

Ko-Pau grinned. "Sorry, Slick," he apologized.

She crossed her arms and made a face at him. "No you aren't," she accused. She grinned and hugged him, if only to ensure that he knew he was forgiven for having snuck up on her.

"I won't deny that it was funny, but I *am* sorry," he laughed, pulling away a moment later. "Come with me." He wrapped an arm around her shoulders and led her down the hallway and into the kitchen. "You sit, I'll make us some tea. We're out of yours, so it won't be the same as you are used to. My wife drinks a different type than you do. Some sort of sweet grass she gathers outside of the city makes a nice calming tea, but it's a very light color when it finishes brewing."

"Astermint?" Akinia guessed.

Ko-Pau turned to face her, the small pot he had been holding moved itself to the spigot and began to fill with water. "You know, you scare me sometimes," he admitted, crossing his arms. "How on earth did you know about the astermint? Never mind... You don't have to answer. It's either from a book or a holo-orb, I know."

"Actually, it isn't," she corrected. "The medic back at the orphanage used to use it to settle the young children when they were ill and needed to rest, or when one of us couldn't sleep. It didn't work well on me, so I only tasted it a couple of times," she shrugged. She smiled at her master's amazed, and slightly amused, expression. "What?"

"Nothing," he promised, smiling, "I had just forgotten about that source." The pot moved from the spigot to the heating chamber.

Akinia bit her lip and stared down at the metal table as she traced invisible patterns with her finger. Should she tell? What would he think? She hoped he wouldn't be angry, as she knew Alaeia would be, but how could she be certain? Ko-Pau knew as well as she did how much danger little Gevra would be in once it was discovered.

"You seem troubled," he noted, concerned, as he reached into the heating chamber to pull out the now-boiling water.

Akinia remained silent as he poured the water into two mugs and added the tea leaves. As he handed her cup to her and set his own on the table, she sighed and struggled for a moment to speak before she managed, "I don't know if you want to hear this, but you should know."

Ko-Pau frowned and sat down. "Tell me what's bothering you, Akinia," he ordered gently, wondering what had upset her so much. What did she think he did not want to hear?

She bit her lip again for a moment. "It's Gevra," she finally sighed, but paused, uncertain how her news would be taken.

Alarmed, Ko-Pau demanded, "What is it? What's the matter? Is she alright?"

"She's fine," Akinia assured him, "It's just..." she paused and sighed. "Gevra is one of us. A Najee, I mean...I'm sorry." She apologized hesitantly.

Ko-Pau froze, shock coursing through him, then pride, and then concern, each emotion overtaking his expression completely. He finally asked, "Why do you apologize?"

Akinia blinked in surprise. "I thought that you didn't want your children to be Najee? Alaeia-"

"-Alaeia has never wanted me or our children to be Najee, as you well know. I agree with her only because I know it allows her to sleep at night to think they will never be in the danger I place myself in. I had always hoped that one... But how do you know? Has she done anything? Touched your thoughts or moved something?" he asked eagerly.

She shook her head and he seemed disappointed. "No, she hasn't done anything."

His confusion was obvious. "Well then, how do you know?" he asked curiously, and a bit dejectedly. "If she hasn't done anything then there is no way to know."

"It's her eyes," Akinia admitted. "Haven't you seen them?"

Ko-Pau stared at her blankly. "What?" he asked, confused.

"There is something in her eyes... It's the same thing I see in the eyes of the others, including you. I only see it in Najee, never in anyone else. I can't describe it. Have you really not seen it?" she wondered, amazed.

He smiled, finally understanding. "Akinia, dear child, very few have ever seen what you see. That is a skill of the Gifted Ones, to know a Najee before they display powers. That's one of the ways they found you so many years ago. Lo-Kí warned me that this might happen. Before too much longer you will begin to have dreams of children you have never seen, and you will see that same look in their eyes. Sometimes you will know where they are, other times you will not. In any case, when you start having these dreams you must tell me because we need to get you to a Master with experience in that so that you can control the dreams and learn more about the children. This is how we find most of our new Apprentices."

Akinia's jaw dropped. "So I will have to search for Najee children?" she questioned, uncertain what he was implying.

He shook his head. "No. Once your control training with the Gifted Ones is finished, you will merely be asked to report these dreams and the children's locations. There are other Masters and Apprentices who are in charge of searching for the children. Do you know when Gevra will begin showing signs?"

"It shouldn't be too much longer. She was almost aware of me touching her mind today," Akinia replied before she really knew she had spoken. "I would guess within the next year or two." She frowned as she realized that she hadn't meant to say any of that. Somewhat frightened, she looked at her master, hoping he would offer an explanation without her having to voice her fear.

"Don't be scared," he soothed, recognizing that she was startled. "Lo-Kí warned of this, too. It's merely part of the same gift. You know what you should not know. If it were another child you would know their name and where they lived as well without having ever met them."

Akinia frowned. "Will this happen often?"

"I have absolutely no idea," he admitted, shrugging. "For your sake I hope not, as that can be an added hassle on top of your already pressing responsibilities, but perhaps it will. You should drink your tea before it gets cold."

Akinia nodded and sipped at the pale liquid. There had been no sugar or honey added, and yet it was amazingly sweet. The color was a slight yellow tint, but nearly as clear as plain water. She tried not to look at the color, since she was so used to dark teas that it seemed to have not been brewed all the way. Instead she tried to memorize the patterns and shapes of the leaves: an unsuccessful ploy to keep her mind off of her newfound talent. "Will you tell Alaeia?" she wondered, her voice nearly a whisper.

"Not yet. I'll wait until Gevra is showing signs. It will be easier to convince her that way," he sighed. "Besides, I will be the one who 'discovers' that Gevra is one of us. I don't want her to be angry with you."

Akinia shrugged. "She doesn't like me anyway, so it makes little difference," she laughed, but her laugh was troubled.

"Pay her no mind," Ko-Pau soothed. "She's really just angry with me, only it spills over onto you."

She snorted. "If this is just spilled over..." she mused, shaking her head in amazement. "Let's talk about something else?"

He smiled. "Alright, what do you want to talk about?"

She hesitated, supposing that all uncomfortable topics should be addressed at once, before biting her lip and observing, "You're scared for me, for what's coming."

Ko-Pau openly gaped in shock at the question. This was not the sort of change he had been expecting. His surprise was such that he didn't even notice he had dropped his cup.

It would have shattered on the hard floors, but Akinia caught it with her thoughts, silently praising herself for having kept such good control. Each droplet that had spilled on its way down was safely returned to the cup before being contaminated by the floors; the effort took only the barest scrap of attention, rather than the fierce concentration normally required.

She carefully returned it to the table before hiding her consciousness behind her shield again. Why did she keep reaching beyond herself, when she had sworn she wouldn't? What if she had lost control of herself again?

Finally, after a few moment's silence, Ko-Pau swallowed audibly and asked, "How could I not be?"

Her cheeks flaming in shame, for she knew the pain she was putting him through, she asked, "Can you understand why I chose to go?"

"In all honesty? No, I cannot," he asserted, a hint of resentment lacing his words.

The bitterness, so obvious to her, sliced Akinia to the core. Her face heated over again and it was several long, tense moments before she could arrange her thoughts properly. "You know my fears as well as I: I can no longer trust myself to be near the people I love. I need some time to gather my thoughts and work through whatever it is that's hindering me in my control. Until I do, I am more dangerous to you than Jade is," she managed, haltingly and without meeting his eyes.

Ko-Pau sighed and turned away, running his fingers through his hair. "Can you understand why, in spite of the danger, I wish for you to stay?" he asked, turning back to her a moment later.

"Yes, I really do," she vehemently asserted, searching his eyes with her own earnest gaze, trying to convince him of the truth in her assurance. "I know that you are scared, and that there is good reason. This will be the most dangerous thing I've attempted, even if *they* don't show up unexpectedly. I know that you are afraid I won't come back."

"Again," he added, his voice barely a whisper. "I am afraid that you will not come back, *again*." His eyes shimmered and he turned away, it was several moments before she realized that he was *crying*.

The revelation shocked her. Until this moment, she had never truly grasped how terrified he had been during her captivity. Leaving her tea on the table, she quickly dashed to his side, fighting back tears of her own as she leaned into his arms.

He silently held her, one hand stroking the back of her head. It was several minutes before he was able to speak again. "Do you remember what you said to me before you left with Nath that day?" he wondered quietly.

She gave a wry smile. "You asked me to be careful and not to get hurt, and I said 'no promises'," she recalled, not in the least surprised he would now remember that bit of teasing.

He gave a single bark of laughter. "That isn't what I was referring to," he corrected with a sigh. He tightened his hold on her slightly and kissed the top of her head. "I thanked you for coming back for me, and you told me that you couldn't very well have done anything else because I was the closest thing to a father you've ever had. What you did not realize, and still seem to be unaware of, is that the feeling is mutual."

Akinia pulled back, partly in shock and partly in pride, to look up at her Master. Her brow furrowed in contemplation, even as a

243

pleased half-smile crawled onto her lips, and she resisted the urge to remind him that it had been a conversation from the day *before* they left.

Without pausing, Ko-Pau continued, "You and Nath are as much my children as Anton, Kaldonn, and Gevra. If you were hurt or…"

Akinia swallowed and, in part to hide her own tear-blinded eyes from his sight, nuzzled her head into his shoulder and wrapped her arms tightly around him.

Ko-Pau, unable to even voice the fear that she may be killed, let his voice trail off as she leaned back into his embrace. He tightened his hold on her, wishing that he could change her mind, while at the same time recognizing that the Juntoby stubbornness would never allow her to re-think a decision once it was made with such fierce determination as she now possessed.

Both would have been content to remain there, and neither was particularly keen to release the other, but the ever-prudent Akinia pulled away a short time later. Alaeia probably would not approve should she walk in on them, and Akinia was already far enough dislodged from her good graces to risk any further hatred. She planted a quick kiss on her Master's cheek before returning to her tea. "I cannot stay," she finally whispered, not daring to look at him for fear of losing her determination, "but I will return, safely. I can promise you that, without reservation." And then, to lighten the mood, she teased, "I would never force you back to being alone with Nath."

Despite his doubts, and somber fears, Ko-Pau had to laugh in spite of himself at her last comment. "Well," he laughed, playing along with her, "it must be a mark of your affection that you care enough about me to share in Nath's company."

Akinia smiled, but then frowned and her brow furrowed again.

"What's the matter?" Ko-Pau asked, uncertain if he truly wanted to know. He would likely be up the whole night thinking of her imminent departure, and any concern of hers on the subject might prove too much for him to be able to accept.

"It's nothing," she said hastily. In truth, her mind was far away, worrying about what she would do if she were unable to learn enough control in the short time she would have on this mission. What else could she do? Lo-Kí would surely know, or did he think this mission sufficient? Would he send her to the Nrell next, begging them to teach her as they hadn't done for millennia? Or would he simply keep her to herself, forbidding others to come near her?

Ko-Pau pretended not to notice her wandering mind. *She will speak when she is ready*, he decided, though it was all he could do to restrain the burning desire to demand that she tell him what was the matter. "It's late," he finally observed, taking both of their now-empty cups and putting them into the cleaner. "Go and rest, Slick," he ordered gently.

Akinia sighed and nodded, barely seeming to have noticed his order, and rose from her chair. "Goodnight, Master," she whispered, her voice layered with tension that betrayed her muddled thoughts.

Sleep well, he wished, though he dared not touch her mind, not after how angry she had gotten the last time. It depressed him to think how she hated herself, and how she truly believed herself to be more dangerous than Jade. For a time he had worried that she might do something rash, but now he simply feared her distraction would get her injured, or worse…

Shaking his head, he forced himself to stop thinking of such things. He was home, for the first time in nearly two years. This was supposed to be a happy time, despite the imminent separation that awaited them when they returned to Paméd. Taking another deep, slow breath to calm himself and fully clear his mind, he took his own advice and went to bed.

Chapter 42:

Akinia lay awake staring at the ceiling of the small bedroom. A smile graced her lips as she listened to Gevra's steady, even breathing, but the rest of her features were laced with troubled anxiety. Even as her eyelids grew heavy and nearly impossible to keep open, she fought against sleep with every fiber of her being. It was not a conscious fight, but a subconscious battle that stemmed from her fear of hurting Ko-Pau the way she had hurt her uncle. It had been nearly a month since the attack, and yet she still feared the moments she fell asleep. And now she no longer had Nath to protectively hover over her, waking her if her subconscious mind began to stir.

After nearly an hour of silently battling herself, Akinia sighed and rose from the cot. She grabbed her wajun, belt and all, from the nightstand and then grabbed her discarded clothes from that day. It took her only a moment to dress again, and to buckle the belt around her waist. She fiddled with it for a moment until it sat in just the right spot before taking a piece of paper and penning a quick note in case anyone noticed her absence.

Unable to sleep.

...she began simply...

I am taking a walk. If I am not back by breakfast, please be worried, and not a moment sooner.
-Akinia Juntoby

It was with a fair bit of satisfaction that she signed her name. Everyone knew who she was of course, she probably hadn't even needed to sign her first name, but seeing 'Juntoby' tacked onto the end of her name gave her a feeling of pride and a sense of belonging that had always escaped her before. It was a simple enough reminder that she was no longer without home or family, as she had been her entire life, but it meant the universe to her.

Setting the note on her pillow, she crept from the room with absolute silence. Blinking rapidly a handful of times to clear the sleep away from her eyes, she slipped out the front door and onto the street. Though the surrounding buildings were all houses, she vaguely recalled the direction of the merchants' shops.

None would be open, she was certain, at this time of night, but the buildings and booths themselves always lent an intriguing air to any location. Perhaps that would be enough to clear her mind of such dark thoughts? Willing to try, she wrapped her arms around herself and navigated deep into the heart of the small town.

She jumped and looked to her left as she caught movement in the corner of her eye. A soft laugh escaped her lips as she realized it was only a small rodent darting across an alleyway. She watched the creature skitter about for a moment before continuing her walk. *Rofa*, she sighed, wishing her cub was with her. She always felt safer with Rofa around, and her presence always brought the girl comfort.

She thought back to the day she first found the orphaned ceffre… It was hard sometimes to believe that she had once been able to hold Rofa in her arms! Her heart gave a strange lunge as she felt herself wishing once more for the comforting presence of her beloved pet.

The faces of Khee-Lá, Nath, and even Jaynine also ran through her mind as she mourned their absence. What wouldn't she give to hear Jaynine complain about something? Or to fight with Khee-Lá over her rapidly improving health? Even to hear Nath's teasing would be a welcome comfort at this moment…

And what of her cousins on Náto? Did they miss her now as much as she missed them? What would they be doing now, if she were still on Náto with them? A smile came to her lips as she considered each of them.

Rignon would probably be asking her more questions about Alania and Inzan, or the Capitol. He might be in the library, pouring over books as they spoke, trying to learn everything he could about the lengthy history of his home planet, system, and even the entire Empire! Or perhaps they would be playing shess, drinking hot tea from large mugs as they tried to outwit the other amidst their distracting

248

conversation…

Amalli would, no doubt, be with Akinia. Perhaps they would play shess, or continue the sewing lessons Akinia failed so dreadfully at! Or perhaps Amalli would be with her mother, painting intricate miniatures while Akinia watched in amazement. Or she might be chasing after her younger siblings, keeping them in line for her ill mother…

Anlix would be trying to scare Akinia, or puzzling out how she always knew where he was hiding…

Lanzi would be sitting high in the uppermost branches of one of the ancient trees in the gardens, probably with her little pumen, Asha, lying on a branch near her. She would be reading or staring into the sky, making pictures in the clouds…

Schran and Noregh would be playing catch-and-chase in the gardens, if they managed to elude their tutors or finish their day's schooling…

And little Karanne, precious little Karanne, would be tagging along behind Akinia, clinging to her skirt or to Amalli's. She would say little or nothing, or perhaps she would chatter away and not let anyone else get a word in edgewise, but she would always be near! Akinia could never have imagined how lonely she would feel without the darling child around her…

Akinia wrapped her arms around herself, wondering if the chill racing up her spine was from the soft breeze or her own despair. Little Gevra and the two boys were wonderful companions and very fun, but they were not her family.

Sighing, she looked up at the dark night sky, enjoying the beautiful stars that shimmered and winked. Here and there she noticed small ships, but they were merchant transports rather than the massive Sigidian warcrafts she had so often seen since becoming a Najee.

In spite of herself, she began to relax here on this strangely peaceful planet. How many times had Ko-Pau assured her that she was in no danger here? She did not know, but the number was high. Still, her wajun was never far from her hand, and her eyes darted here and there across the landscape, waiting for the attack that habit told her was coming.

Now, though, as she began to grow more comfortable here, her eyes searched less and her wajun-hand traveled more easily from her side. She would never dare venture anywhere without her wajun, not even in the palace at the Capitol, but she had gradually settled into a state of relative calm. *I'm not expecting you now, Lokita, so will this be the time you come for me? You always seem to catch me off-guard, the very moment I get too secure in my surroundings... But you will not catch me off-guard again, sister...*

She sighed and turned around, forcing herself to check every crevice and every alleyway with at least a quick glance. *She will* not *take me by surprise again*, she vowed to herself. An uneasy feeling began to creep up on her, so she turned and made her way back to the house. *Paranoid*, she chided herself as she walked, though she knew that her paranoia was warranted.

She slipped back into the house and into bed without being noticed. She took the note off of her pillow, lovingly fingered the name she had signed to it, and then crumpled it up and disposed of it. Then she slipped back into bed, more awake than she had been before.

Chapter 43:

The next few days passed quickly. Akinia spent most of her time playing with Gevra and packing her few possessions. When the morning finally came to leave, there were tearful, and angry, goodbyes to be had. The lengthiest conversation was between Ko-Pau and his boys, explaining to them why they couldn't go on a mission with him. Gevra clung to Akinia until the last moment, tearfully extracting a promise to contact her very, very soon.

"Is it always that hard to leave?" Akinia asked curiously once they were well away from the house.

"Harder, usually," he sighed. "Most of the time they're all begging *me* to stay, because I don't have you to distract them."

Akinia elbowed him, which incited a troubled chuckle from him. "Don't be sad, Master," she begged in an all-too-innocent tone, "You still have Nath and I with you."

"I thought you were trying to cheer me up?" he grumbled, grinning.

This time when she elbowed him, he laughed in earnest. "See," she teased, "I knew there was a laugh in there somewhere."

The journey back to Paméd was quick, and uneventful. Akinia and Ko-Pau played cards most of the time. The nearer they got to Paméd, the more nervous Akinia grew.

"I'm sure he's not quite as mad anymore," Ko-Pau tried to assure her, but neither of them believed it enough for it to help her relax.

When the ship finally touched down, Akinia took a deep breath as she waited for the door to open. She hesitated uncertainly as she saw Khee-Lá waiting for them.

He didn't look happy.

She swallowed heavily, trying to decide whether to speak to

him or not. A smile crept onto her lips, quickly growing into a grin as she saw her uncle hold his arms out to her. She darted to him, relief flooding through her as she let him hold her.

"I'm sorry," he whispered in her ear. "Welcome home."

"I missed you, too," Akinia laughed, kissing his cheek.

"Come on, let's get you settled in," Khee-Lá said, as he wrapped an arm around her shoulders and led her into the base. "So how did you enjoy meeting Ko-Pau's family?" he asked as they reached her room.

She walked inside and plopped down heavily on her bed, exhaling in relief as she laid back. "It was great. His kids are so sweet," she replied without sitting up.

"Ko-Pau is a lucky man," he agreed.

"After all the other family that has been sprung on me, I suppose now you're going to tell me that you have a wife and a dozen kids somewhere?" she guessed.

Khee-Lá laughed. "No, I don't have a wife or children," he promised.

Akinia propped herself up on her elbows. "Why *did* you never get married?" she asked curiously. If children were the honor status on Náto, Najee or not, Khee-Lá should have been dying to get married and have kids.

"I was in love, once," he admitted. He sat in the small chair in the corner.

"What happened?" Akinia asked.

"I was only sixteen when I first met her, and she was two years older than I was. Even so, we both loved each other more than we cared to admit. Shortly after I turned eighteen, she gave birth to our son. We were ashamed to tell anyone about it because we were so young, and unwed. We planned to get married on a small planet that I had to get to anyway. It would only take a brush of my thoughts to cause the date on the marriage certificate to change to a year beforehand," Khee-Lá informed her with a sigh. "We were going to tell our parents that we had hidden it because we weren't sure if they would approve."

"So why didn't you get married?" she asked, confused. Had he gotten cold feet? Or had she?

Her uncle's expression darkened and he looked away. "Their transport wrecked. It was a freak accident, and no one's fault, but no one survived. I only found out after being ordered to help investigate. I never had any desire afterwards to fall in love or get married, or to have children of my own again," he smiled, "I was perfectly content to watch my brother and sister raise families, especially after you came along and I inherited you as a daughter."

Akinia smiled. That was the first time he had actually called her his daughter, in so many words. She had known that, as her Protector, he was legally her father since both of her parents were dead. Still, it felt nice to hear him call her such. She rose and walked over to him before bending down and giving him a quick kiss on the cheek. "And I'm perfectly content to be your daughter, so long as you don't try to keep me locked up on Paméd," she laughed.

Khee-Lá laughed with her. "I would appreciate you not telling anyone, though. You are the only person besides Lo-Kí to whom I have confided that particular bit of information," he requested.

"Of course," she agreed instantly, wondering all the while how many secrets she could be expected to keep.

"I should let you get some rest, you've had a long journey," he said, pushing himself up from the chair.

"No, I'm not tired. You don't have to go," she assured him.

He gave her a wry smile. "Actually, I do. I have some things that I have to take care of. I just wanted to put things right between us before any more time passed," he explained.

Akinia smiled in response. "I love you."

"I love you, too," he replied before walking out and leaving her alone.

Sighing, Akinia looked around her room. *Now what am I going to do?* she wondered, pursing her lips as she tried to think of something to do. She glanced down at the com-link on her wrist and smiled. It only took her a moment to type in the orphanage's keycode.

Chapter 44:

I wish that I could see Laani before I go, Akinia sighed to herself as she wandered up the hallways.

The Lyndop girl was still on a mission, and it would be over a month before she returned.

Sighing, Akinia turned down a side corridor, one that she knew led to the library. Plucking a random book off of one of the shelves as she walked past it, she settled into one of the many plush armchairs. She didn't even have a chance to open the book, though, before she noticed Lo-Kí approaching.

"May I have a word with you, Akinia?" he asked, by way of a greeting.

"Of course, Master Lo-Kí," she replied at once, setting the book aside. "Please, sit down."

He carefully lowered himself onto one of the armchairs before continuing, "We need to discuss the details of your mission."

Akinia's stomach twisted nervously as she nodded.

"Tomorrow morning, you will travel to the Capitol Planet, disguised as a soldier in Master Treemuth's squadron," Lo-Kí began. "Once there, you will report to Colonel Amistead."

"You said that I would be disguised as a soldier; who am I supposed to be?" she asked curiously, when he did not continue.

Lo-Kí smiled approvingly. "Your name is Lieutenant Ashma Fonden," he informed her. "You are nineteen years old. You got into the army on a tech permit when you were fifteen. You were chosen for this assignment because you are extremely proficient in all forms of technology and programming, and you'll be taking the place on an entire tech crew. You grew up on the Capitol, you have no siblings, and your parents are merchants. I will send you your full profile, along with some other pertinent information, later this evening."

Akinia hesitated. "May I ask you one more question?"

He motioned for her to continue.

"What happens if I don't learn to control myself before I get back?" she asked, grimacing.

Lo-Kí sighed. "I have some ideas, and we will leave it at that for now," he promised her. "You will be prepared to face Jade and Lokita, when the time comes for you to do so."

"What if they are at the exchange?" she asked worriedly, lowering her voice so that no one but Lo-Kí could hear her. "They'll recognize me. What if I can't control myself enough to escape?"

He regarded her curiously for a moment. "That is not what you are truly concerned about," he said knowingly.

In spite of herself, Akinia felt a smile cross her lips as she shook her head. "It feels like my life has become a game," she admitted. "I'm trying to win, but I'm still learning how the pieces move."

"It is a game, a very dangerous game, and the stakes are high," Lo-Kí agreed. "Win, and you will restore peace and harmony to our people; lose, and you will have doomed us all to a life of misery and discord."

Akinia tried to keep her breathing calm and steady as she listened to the old man's words. He was right, she knew... and that terrified her.

"However," he continued after a moment's pause, "as to your assertion that you are still learning how the pieces move across the board, I believe that you know more than you think that you do. I spent more than a century learning the things that you have absorbed in a single year. Sometimes I think that you know this game better than any of us."

Akinia didn't respond as she absorbed his words.

Lo-Kí stood and gave her a tense smile. He placed his hand on her shoulder as he walked past. "You will know what the right move is when the time comes for you to make it. Only be sure to fully think through the consequences before settling upon a course of action," he whispered as he walked away.

I will, Akinia silently swore, unwilling to extend her thoughts to the ancient Najee. *I must.*

Chapter 45:

"Lieutenant," the Colonel said sharply.

Akinia jumped, startled. "I'm sorry, sir, I didn't hear you," she apologized.

He sighed heavily, grumbling under his breath for a moment before motioning sharply to her. "Come with me," he ordered simply, not waiting for her to respond before he turned and walked off.

Nodding, Akinia grabbed her bedroll and darted after him. She couldn't help but gaze around in wonder at the massive military base as they made their way through. It was far less elegant than Paméd, and nowhere near as beautiful, but there was still something majestic about the professional simplicity of the base.

"You're no soldier," the Colonel groused, scowling.

Akinia's steps faltered. *How did he find out?*

The Colonel didn't seem to notice as he continued, "I don't hold with these tech permits; I never have. As far as I'm concerned, you're just a child that someone handed a gun to. War is no place for children."

Relief swept through Akinia as she nodded.

"You are here for one reason, and one reason only: the Najee liked your performance record, and thought you could leave more room for the real soldiers," the Colonel groused. "You'll have a gun, and you'll walk with the squadron, but you are not a soldier. Are we clear?"

"Yes, sir," Akinia replied at once, biting her tongue to keep from smirking. *No, I am certainly not a soldier*, she silently agreed.

They walked in silence for several minutes before arriving at a large hanger bay. The Colonel led the way over to a PT864 Cruiser, giving a sharp whistle that halted the work of a handful of soldiers. "Listen up, soldiers," the Colonel called. "Here's our last arrival, Lieutenant Fonden."

"Our techie?" a young woman, an Adamian who looked to be in

her late twenties, questioned.

"That's the one," the Colonel agreed. "Take her in, put her to work, and let's get this bucket ready to move." Without another word, or even a glance at Akinia, the Colonel turned and walked away.

The other soldiers all immediately turned and went back to work; no one wanted to be the last one hanging around to take the newbie on.

The young woman who had spoken, a lieutenant by the markings on her uniform, casually strolled over to Akinia. "What's your name, soldier?" she asked, smiling pleasantly.

"Ashma," Akinia replied after a moment's hesitation.

"You sure about that?" the woman teased.

Akinia grimaced. "I was this morning," she hedged, laughing grimly.

The woman laughed as well. "Yeah, this place can be a bit overwhelming at first. Where were you stationed before?"

"Tyne, in the Edging," Akinia replied at once, grateful that Lo-Kí had included that information in the profile that he sent her. She had spent he last week memorizing every detail of "her" life.

The woman nodded contemplatively. "Yeah, I've heard of that one. Nice place, a little small, though," she mused. "By the way, I'm Lieutenant Dodge. My given name's Eimma, but you can call me Eim."

Akinia shook the hand that she offered. "Nice to meet you, Eim."

"You, too, Ash," she grinned in return. "Come on, let's get you put to work before the Colonel gets a rock in his boot."

Chapter 46:

Akinia took a deep, nervous breath as she quickly shoved her wajun into the sleeve of her uniform. She glanced around, making certain that no one had seen her. *I can't afford to blow my cover now.*

"Ash, come on," Eim called impatiently, sticking her head into the room. "The Colonel's going to freak if you're the last one on deck."

"I'm coming," Akinia sighed, grimacing. Eim was right, she knew.

Since the beginning of the mission, the Colonel had been riding Akinia's case, making it perfectly clear how much he disapproved of her being included.

Grabbing her blaster from where it lay on her bunk, Akinia turned and followed Eim into the hallway. Eim's expression was grim, and Akinia knew that she was anxious about the prisoner exchange.

It was a valid concern.

Another three dozen soldiers, of varying ranks, surrounded a group of twenty-four prisoners.

Akinia and Eim fell into place where there were gaps. They exchanged a worried, nervous, and reassuring glance as the door of the ship opened. It amazed Akinia how close the two of them had gotten over the course of the two-month voyage. From time to time, it had been dangerous; Eim's innocently prying questions had nearly uncovered the truth more than once. *I will tell her who I really am once we return to the Empire*, Akinia had decided. *Maybe I can put in for her to be transferred to my squadron?*

She grimaced at the thought of returning to the Empire. Nath was right; she hadn't been able to use her abilities at all since the mission began. The quarters of the ship were too tight, and there were too many people; there would be no way to avoid detection. *I hope Lo-Ki has another plan in mind*, she sighed guiltily, *because I don't know how to make this one work.*

I don't need to be thinking about that right now, Akinia chastised herself a moment later, shaking her head to clear it. *I need to focus; this is Sigadia's Capitol!* Though she tried to maintain a calm, measured appearance, Akinia couldn't help but gape at the city around them. What had she been expecting?

Certainly not this...

Instead of the dark, war-ravaged streets that she had always imagined would fill the Sigidian Capitol, the city was bright, elegant, timeless. There was a strong and angular beauty which rivaled even the Imperial Capitol. No more than a hundred yards ahead of them stood the massive, imposing figure of the palace. A hundred metal turrets, shined to a blinding finish, stretched towards the skies. The tallest of these turrets was more than four-hundred meters in height.

The hairs on the back of Akinia's neck prickled, and she was extremely aware of her wajun brushing against the skin of her forearm, as she saw all of the Sigidian soldiers spread out among the crowd. She started to extend her mind, to determine their intentions, but stopped before she put her blockades down. *What if they are here? They'll sense me if I extend, and then it will be over,* she reminded herself.

Swallowing heavily, she forced herself to look at the children that had gathered around, as well. Some hid behind their parents, afraid to look at the Imperial soldiers. Others made faces, sticking their tongues out and crossing their eyes. The tension radiating from them all was unsettling. *Could we expect anything different? Our people are at war...*

The Imperial troops entered the front doors of the massive palace, a platoon of Sigidian soldiers falling into step around them. A wave of nausea struck Akinia, and she had to fight to keep from vomiting. There was something oddly familiar about the sensation...

Her eyes widened as the group was led through another set of massive doors, these ones leading to the throne room. It startled Akinia to realize how similar the Sigidian and Imperial throne rooms were, but it startled her far more to see the man sitting upon the Sigidian throne.

Emperor Caylon was a tall, muscular man. Even sitting on his throne, somewhat casually reclined to one side, he exuded a strength and power that dwarfed anything she had ever seen from Alania. He was young, only a few years older than the Imperial Monarch, and very handsome. His hair was very dark, paling his already pasty features even further. His eyes were a startling, electric shade of yellow which was easily visible, even from the other end of the throne room.

Akinia glanced over to Eim, and realized that they were thinking the exact same thing: *We could end the war. We could kill Caylon.* Her body ached as she fought against the instinct to grab her wajun. The soft, curving edged of the metal seemed to be as sharp as blades against her skin. *I can't; they would kill us all, and the Empire would suffer. It would only heighten the war, not end it,* she snarled to herself, taking a deep breath to calm her anxiously racing heart.

The Emperor stood and motioned with one hand.

A guard opened a pair of side doors, and a group of Sigidian soldiers entered, surrounding a handful of starving, half-dead Imperial soldiers. The group stopped at the base of the throne dais, the Sigidian soldiers bowing to their emperor.

The Colonel stepped forward, giving a quick and half-hearted salute to the Emperor before speaking. "Emperor Caylon," he began, "the Empire thanks you for your cooperation in the matter of this prisoner exchange. Princess Alania sends her hope that we may look upon this act as the first in a long path to peace between our nations."

His words hung in the air for several long moments, no one daring to move or breathe. Finally, the emperor smiled. "Your message has been heard," he said slowly, his voice low and mesmerizing. "Now I have one for your Princess."

Akinia felt as though she had been punched in the stomach; it was all that she could do to stay upright. Horror swept through her as she realized what was happening, a half-second before her comrades did.

A wave of blaster bolts swept through the throne room, striking each of the Imperial soldiers held captive by the Sigidians. There was a pause in the fire, just long enough for the Imperial soldiers to realize what had just happened.

Akinia's comrades pulled their weapons out, firing in all directions. Eim immediately put the Emperor in her sights and pulled the trigger, but a thick force field deflected the bullet. Screaming angrily, she loosed another half-dozen bolts in the Emperor's direction before three Sigidian bolts struck her in the chest. As she fell, she turned to Akinia, fear easily visible in her eyes. That fear was replaced by shock and confusion as she saw the wajun in Akinia's hands.

"With me!" Akinia ordered, deflecting a handful of bolts.

Only three of her companions remained, but they circled with her, the four keeping their backs together as they slowly made their way to the door.

A blaster shot took out one of the three soldiers, and the other two quickly closed in the hole his presence left.

We're going to die, Akinia realized, fear coursing through her, but she kept fighting.

Another Imperial soldier fell, leaving only one alive. As they reached the doors of the throne room, the last of Akinia's companions was struck and killed.

An infuriated scream escaped Akinia's lips as she lowered the defenses around her mind. She could feel the power surging through her, longing to escape. There was no way to control it; it was too much, it was too strong. She didn't bother to fight it; she just let it escape.

Every Sigidian with a hundred feet of Akinia crumpled to the ground, screaming in agony. Most were dead, a handful were dying.

She met Caylon's reptilian gaze for a moment, as her subconscious mind flung a piece of debris in his direction, striking the force field with enough power to make it shudder and power down.

Had that same amount of power stayed in her system, Akinia would have stayed and destroyed every Sigidian present, including Caylon, but she could already feel her power quickly waning. She hesitated a moment, torn between the desire to stay and fight, to avenge her companions' deaths, and the desire to escape.

Your family, a soft, wordless voice whispered in the back of her mind.

Turning, Akinia ran from the palace. She fought her way through lines of enemy soldiers, escaping through a series of alleyways and rooftops. Barely paying attention to where she was running, she simply allowed her instincts to guide her. When she saw the small ship, unattended and its cockpit open, she didn't even hesitate; she simply leapt into it, closed the cockpit, and launched into the skies. The ship was fast; it took her only seconds to escape the atmosphere of the Sigidian Capitol Planet.

She looked around the expanse of space at all of the planets and moons shining in the distance amongst the shimmering stars. Which one would offer her a chance of surviving? She stared at her hand, or rather, at the mark on it. What was it the Nrell had said? Oh yes, *you will always be able to find help when you need it.* "I could sure use some of that help now," she griped, wondering what the Nrell could have meant by that. She had been concentrating so hard on the mark, trying to figure out how to interpret the complex twists and lines in a way that might give her an idea of where to go, that her words seemed to have triggered the mark into taking action of its own accord.

It glowed white-hot, like it had when she had first received it, and she could feel her mind shoot out in all directions. She couldn't stop it, she couldn't control it. Suddenly she felt her mind connect with that of a strange being that was definitely not any she normally encountered. She watched a stream of memories of what had happened to her fly through the connection to the being. *Degru, hurry*, it ordered. It rescinded the contact before she could say anything. The mark cooled again as her mind settled back within its walls. Degru? She had never heard of a 'Degru' before.

Akinia wondered absently if this was a trap. *I have no choice but to try*. After all, she was dead anyway if she stayed out here. Searching through the ship's navigation file, she quickly found Degru. It was a small, sparsely populated planet only a few minute's leap from there. She programmed it into the computer and watched with baited breath as the ship took off again.

Chapter 47:

The few short minutes that it took Akinia to reach Degru seemed to last several hours as she anxiously waited. Her breath caught in her chest and her stomach clenched as she relived the slaughter over and over again in her mind. She kept seeing Eim's face, the shock, the confusion, the fear. Eim had been her friend, and now she was dead.

Akinia had once thought that she knew what war was, what it meant, but she hadn't. *This* was what war was. War was watching those you love be hurt, killed, ripped away from you in the most painful and torturous ways that Fate could think up. War was a friend killed, a child orphaned...

Eim was married. She had two little girls, one five, one three. Did they know that their mommy was dead? Had the Empire received word yet of the slaughter? How would Eim's husband ever tell their little girls that their mommy wasn't coming home? How could those innocent children understand?

And what about Akinia's family? Surely the entire Juntoby clan would soon know what had taken place. Would they think that she was dead, too? Would the Sigidians tell them that the young Najee had escaped? Would Akinia escape to return to the Empire, or would the Sigidians catch her?

Who was the voice that contacted her? It wasn't Jade or Lokita, she knew, but who was to say that they didn't have other Najee working with them? Surely the Sigidians had to have Najee born amongst them, too; it couldn't be a phenomena that only occurred in the Empire and Motúk.

Could it?

Was the Degru system a trap?

Her fears were eased some as the being's thoughts brushed against her consciousness again. She couldn't sense any danger from it...

It took control of her ship, carefully guiding it to the far side of the small forest planet in front of her. A large mountain range seemed to grow even larger as she neared it.

I'm going to crash! Akinia realized, startled, before she noticed a large crevice cut into the side of the mountain that she was approaching. Something metallic glinted inside of it. *It's a hanger bay?*

The being guided the ship to carefully land within the massive cavern.

Akinia's eyes opened wide in surprise as she saw a Nrell walk out into the middle of the hanger, pausing in front of her ship. She opened the cockpit and leapt to the floor, reflexively grabbing the end of her wajun as she stood, though she did not move it from its holster.

This Nrell was obviously male, his facial features being much rougher than Antia's had been, though he was still quite beautiful. He clasped his right fist to his left shoulder, bowed, and then extended his hand palm-forwards to her. "I am Ruegon of the Meigdhor clan. May peace reign in your heart," he said, pausing a moment and looking at her expectantly.

She shifted her weight uncomfortably. What was he waiting for? Curious, she looked as his extended hand. The mark on it was slightly different than hers.

"Forgive me for taking over your ship as such, but I wished to guide you in safe from the eyes of the settlers spread thin in our forest," he apologized as she stepped closer to him.

She nodded, but was looking in wonderment at her palm. How had the mark been able to guide her here? She couldn't extend her mind that far on her best day, so how had she contacted the Nrell so many light-years away?

The Nrell walked closer. "May I?" he asked, motioning to her hand.

She nodded and held it out towards him.

"Hmm, Devura clan. I have never heard of one being adopted into that clan before. Who are you?" he asked as he released her.

"I am Akinia Juntoby," she managed.

"That is a very rare and powerful name among my people. How is it that you came by it?" he asked.

She pulled the necklace from her shirt.

The Nrell recoiled at the sight of it.

"This was given to me at birth. My mother liked the name on the back, and gave it to me," she explained.

"Who gave such a thing to you?" the Nrell demanded angrily.

"The Najee Master of Masters when I was born gave this to my uncle, another Najee, to deliver to me. It was to mark me as the child of the prophecy written by the Nrell Efgor," she replied, tucking it possessively into her shirt.

"I see," he stated in surprise, "It is an honor to meet you, young Akinia. You shall stay here for as long as you desire."

Akinia hesitantly thanked him, her thoughts somewhat distracted. *I may not be here for long... I should ask him about my surges; it may be years before I see another Nrell!*

"May I offer you anything?" the Nrell asked.

She hesitated, about to voice her question, but then remembered a more pressing issue. "May I have access to a comm. system? My Master and my uncle will be worried about me," she asked hesitantly.

"Of course, follow me," Ruegon replied at once. He led her through a hallway that was also carved from the rocks and earth, the same as the hanger bay was. A small room sat just a few feet in, on the right-hand side of the tunnel. "I believe you'll find this comm. system acceptable."

"Thank you, so much. They'll be very worried about me," she said gratefully. She had to let the Council know what had happened, and that she was safe. Just as she began to type in the destination, she paused and erased what she had. She would just contact Jaynine and have him deliver the message. Khee-Lá would overreact if she told him, and she wouldn't be able to get him to quit talking to her.

"Of course, Mistress," came the droid's standard reply when she had given her orders.

"Master Lo-Kí," she began, "something has gone wrong. The prisoner exchange was a trap as you feared, and I alone was able to escape. I am unable to leave Sigadia for some time, due to increased activity by the patrol ships as they try to locate me. I am in a safe place where I will not be found by the Sigidians. Send no one for me. I will stay here for a few weeks and then once they have settled down enough that it is safe, I will return home. Tell Khee-Lá not worry, Ko-Pau to just go on with life as usual and not wait to hear from me, and Nath that I'll miss him, but I'll be back soon and safe. Lokita and Jade were not present, otherwise I may not have been so lucky. There is no message this time, do not send a rescue. I will return when it is safe, and contact you in a few weeks." With that she ended the message.

"Is there anyone else you wish to contact?" Ruegon asked.

Akinia shook her head. "You have been very kind, thank you," she replied.

Ruegon looked her over for a moment, regarding her curious eyes and blank expression.

I must ask now... "May I ask you something?" she queried shyly.

"Speak," he directed.

She slowly explained to him about her lapses in control, from throwing the cylinders across the room all the way up to nearly killing Khee-Lá, including the conversation she had overheard between him and Lo-Kí. Ruegon seemed only slightly concerned.

"It is not unheard of among the children of the prophecy," he informed her dismissively.

Akinia paused and thought for a moment about what he could have meant. Not finding a suitable explanation she asked, "What do you mean 'children of the prophecy'?"

The Nrell considered her for a moment before answering. "This is the fourth time the prophecy of Efgor has been born. The first was killed as a baby; the second renounced the Najee and violence in general after watching her family be murdered, refusing to ever take a blaster or wajun in her hand which effectively ended the possibility that that one could become the child; the third was an excellent Najee but was killed in a freak accident. We feared the prophecy to be dead after a thousand years had passed without your arrival. The others had all come within a couple of centuries of one another," he explained.

Akinia felt her eyes widen in shock. Her heart lurched, twisting painfully in her chest. "Are you telling me that all of the children born of the prophecy die or something happens to make them stop being Najee?" she demanded quietly, her voice shaking.

The Nrell laughed. "If that were so the prophecy would be about the deaths of several youths, rather than a restoration of peace. No, it is not hopeless. Do not fear or worry too much over it. You are safe here, at least," he promised.

She hesitated, struggling against herself as she decided whether to continue pursuing the matter. Finally, Akinia sighed. "Here, maybe. But how am I to protect myself from myself? I can't control my powers, so how do I know I won't harm or kill those I love?"

"If you like, we can show you how to master your powers in such a way that you will have complete control over them in more ways than Jade and Lokita could imagine, both awake and asleep. We can teach you to heal wounds and to render yourself invisible. We can show you things that the Council has never heard of, things that they could not teach you even if they had heard of it because of the level of power required. Once you leave here, even if you stay but a few weeks, you will know what you need to know to complete the prophecy," he offered after considering her problem.

Akinia's eyes widened as she heard this. So long as they could teach her to keep herself from hurting anyone, she would try whatever it was that he intended for her to learn. "When can we start?" she asked.

"If you like, we can begin first thing in the morning."

She nodded eagerly. "I don't want to be afraid of myself anymore. The quicker you can teach me to control myself, the better."

"I warn you now," he cautioned, "What we will show you cannot be performed in front of other Najee except in the most drastic of cases. Most of this will kill those weaker than you, and some of this will require most of even your strength."

She nodded, grimly aware of the consequences of using her gifts. "I understand," she agreed.

"Good," he nodded. "But for now it is late. I will show you to the room you will occupy during your stay. It will be in my household. Come."

Akinia obediently followed the Nrell farther down the hallway and gasped in shock as they entered the main area of the Nrell citadel.

The chasm was several miles long, and she could not even see to the bottom of it. Here and there, flimsy bridges of rope and planks had been stretched across the three-hundred meters to give the Nrell ways of getting across. Hundreds of thousands of paths and tunnels could be seen on the far side, and she was certain it looked the same on the side she stood on. Nrell packed the crowded pathways, but there was no sense of hurry or bustle that she had encountered in surface cities. Despite the fact that in places the Nrell could barely move because there were so many of them, there was no sense of crowding to their gatherings. It was a peaceful and harmonious atmosphere that Akinia had never encountered in large groups before; it almost frightened her.

"Mind you don't get too near the edge," Ruegon cautioned,

noticing her pause.

Akinia nodded dumbly and hurried over the uneven stone floor of the pathway to follow him. She watched wide-eyed as dozens of Nrell walked past, and once she caught sight of a Fronkutian child playing in one of the many doorways. "This is amazing," she breathed as Ruegon led her into one of the long tunnels that led away from the chasm.

"I am glad that you can appreciate its beauty. All too many are too blinded by their shallow ideas to appreciate the beauty of the natural stone and dirt. Even these roots that have somehow dug their way so far down into the earth have a certain beauty that is missed by many," he mused, gently fingering a web-like tangle of roots hanging from one corner of the low-ceilinged tunnel.

"My master once told me that a girl who would rescue and raise an orphaned Ceffre cub has got to be able to see beauty in things that no one else can see. Maybe he was right. At the time I assumed he was just teasing me," she laughed.

"He may well have been, but that does not make his observation less true," he corrected gently. "Here is the hall my family resides in," he said a moment later, motioning to an archway which seemed to lead into another long hallway.

Akinia looked around in amazement. The hall was five stories high and well over three hundred feet long. Arched doorways, some of which led into more tunnels, were carved into the sides of the halls.

Ruegon led her up a series of roughly carved stone stairs, well worn by many feet over many years, and into one of the short side-tunnels. He stopped at the third door in. "You will reside here for the duration of your stay," he informed her, opening the door and motioning for her to enter. "I will have a tray of food brought here for you later. For now you will rest. Come morning you will begin your training."

Without another word he turned and let Akinia to explore the small bedchamber on her own. It was of simple design, just a bed and small wooden chair in the main room and a small bathroom just off of it, and even simpler in decoration. Everything was very simple and very plain. The bedframe was of roughly-hewn timber, the blanket was a simple white throw, the wooden chair was unadorned and did not even seem to have been lacquered, and the rough stone floor was covered only by a woven rug made of rag scraps.

Deciding to take Ruegon's advice and rest, Akinia lay down on the bed, wincing at the hardness of the slender mattress, and closed her eyes. The faces of the soldiers she had been traveling with ran through her mind, and she grimaced as she thought about the fact that they were dead. *Eimma, I am so sorry...* Her face contorting into a mask of pain, she fell into a troubled sleep in which she relived their deaths over and over.

Chapter 48:

"Najee Akinia," Ruegon called through the gap in the slightly-ajar door.

Her eyes snapped open immediately. "Yes?" she questioned, only partially awake, as she sat up and rubbed her eyes.

"You wished to be trained, did you not?" he reminded her. "Come, and we will begin. You will find a new change of clothes on the chair. Put them on and join me in the hallway."

Now more fully awake, Akinia jumped to her feet, pushed the door shut, and grabbed the pile of cloth hanging over the back of the small wooden chair. She held it up in front of her for a moment, discovering it was a knee-length leather dress with tank-sleeves. There was also a pair of plain black leggings. Quickly pulling them on, she hurried to meet Ruegon.

He balled the hands of his right arms into fists and clasped them to his left shoulder before opening his hands again and extending the higher right arm towards her, palm outwards. "May peace reign in your heart," he said again, waiting expectantly as though he was waiting for her to say something.

Akinia hesitated, uncertain how to respond.

He regarded her curiously for a moment. "You have never been taught our courtesies?" he queried.

Akinia shook her head. "I have never spent time with any Nrell before now," she admitted. "Antia, the Nrell who gave me the mark, found me while my master's other apprentice and I were in the middle of a battle. We only spoke long enough for her to give me the mark, and tell me that I would find help whenever I was in need of it."

He pursed his lips as he considered this. "I see," he stated simply. "It seems to me as though we need to begin with teaching you the courtesies, then. Come, we will go to a place more private." He turned and walked away.

Akinia struggled to keep up with the Nrell, though by extending her stride she found she could keep up better than she had by walking more rapidly. She paid little attention to the other Nrell and Fronkutians that they passed, but focused instead on not tripping over the uneven surface of the stone floors as they walked through a maze of tunnels. Every ten feet down the tunnel a large red lantern hung on the wall.

"The red tint of the light ensures that our vision will not need to adjust so much when we emerge to the main caverns and to the surface," Ruegon explained as they walked. "It is kinder on Nrell eyes."

Akinia nodded to show that she had heard, but otherwise didn't respond. After what seemed like miles, they slowed to a stop. She followed Ruegon into a doorway and they emerged in a brightly lit room. A large desk sat against the far wall, and several tall, thin bookshelves rested against the other walls in a seemingly random fashion. A thick rug that seemed to be hand-woven covered the floor, giving some guard against the rough stone.

"Now," Ruegon began, "The rapid meeting between you and Antia, who, if I remember correctly, is a Settlement Head of the Emran clan?"

"That sounds right, but I couldn't swear to it," she cautioned when she realized that he was asking her to affirm that.

"The rapid meeting between you did not leave time for you to learn the courtesies of Nrell society. There are a great many small things to learn, most of which I will point out to you as we continue your psychokinetic training. However, there are some larger things which must be addressed now. To start with, you must learn to properly greet one of your brethren," he began. "Now, in your society, how do you greet your brethren?"

"Um, usually we say 'hello' and shake their hand, or we hug if they are close family or friends," she shrugged.

Ruegon nodded. "Our greetings are much the same, yet different. When greeting a stranger, without being introduced by a mutual friend, both parties would clasp their right fist to their left shoulder, bow slightly, and then they would stand upright and hold their hand palm-outwards to display their mark. That is followed by stating your name and clan, in the form of, 'I am Ruegon, of the Meighdor clan.' Whoever is the guest speaks first, or if they are both on foreign ground the lower-ranking person speaks first, unless of course a host wishes to honor a guest or a higher-ranking person wishes to honor a subordinate. Now, show me," he ordered.

Akinia hesitated for a moment before balling her right hand into a fist and laying her arm across her chest as he had, so that her fist touched her left shoulder. She then extended her hand to him, palm outwards, and said, "I am Akinia, of the Devura clan."

Ruegon nodded approvingly. "Very good. Bear in mind that if you were to meet a Nrell on ground foreign to you both, unless the Nrell is a Minister, a Clan Leader, or a Settlement Head, you rank above them as the Child of the Prophecy. You are, in essence, of a rank equal to our highest, but you are still outranked by our highest because you are not a Nrell by blood."

Akinia nodded, interested by that revelation. She hadn't realized that the Nrell regarded the prophecy so highly.

"Now, if the two Nrell know one another they do not speak their names, but go immediately into the second part of the greeting, strangers would come to this part after introductions. Again, the lower-ranking person or guest speaks first, unless the higher-ranking person or host wishes to honor them. Whoever speaks first will say, 'May peace reign in your heart' to which the second person responds, 'May your mind stay sharp'. If the two are close friends or family, or if they have already greeted each other that day, the greeting may end there. If one is greeting a stranger or if the occasion is important or formal in some way, the first will speak again and will say 'May your enemies quake before you' to which the second will respond 'And may the stars always light your path'. Now, show me," he ordered, waiting expectantly.

Akinia's eyes widened. "Um, could we work on just the first part for a few minutes? I can't remember which order they all come in," she requested, her face turning red.

Ruegon smiled. "As you wish," he agreed. "Let us assume that I have decided to speak first. I will now say 'May peace reign in your heart'. How do you respond?"

Akinia thought for a moment. "May your enemies quake before you?" she guessed.

"No," Ruegon reprimanded, shaking his head. "You would respond 'May your mind stay sharp'. Again, may peace reign in your heart."

"May your mind stay sharp," she responded confidently.

"Good," he smiled, nodding approvingly. "Again. May peace

reign in your heart."

"May your mind stay sharp."

"May peace reign in your heart."

"May your mind stay sharp."

For several minutes they practiced, Ruegon speaking the first line and Akinia quickly following with the second. Once her responses became more automatic, he made her say the first line while he responded with the second. The first several times she stuttered and spoke cautiously, uncertain if she had the words right. After the first few tries she was speaking more clearly, and a few times more and the phrase seemed to fall almost naturally from her lips.

"Now, I do not wish to confuse you, so if this will be too much for you to comprehend at this time we can postpone this lesson for a few days," he cautioned. "The greeting I have just taught you is the translation to Main, a language many of our people now use. However, if you wish to gain much respect by the ancients of our race, you can learn Nrelnalna, our language from times before we learned to ride the stars. I do warn you that the words can be difficult for humans to vocalize, but with practice you may well become fluent in our tongue. If you wish, I can teach you not only our courtesies, but also to speak our language during your time here."

Akinia's eyes widened. "Nrelnalna? I thought even the Nrell had forgotten the language?" she gasped. "All of the stories said it hasn't been spoken in eons."

"It is perhaps because we speak it only around our own kind in recent centuries. However, as I am revealing to you the rest of the secrets of our kind, I feel that the secret of our language will be safe with you," he mused.

"Why do you keep your language secret?" she asked curiously.

"Our language holds a certain power to direct your innate psychokinetic powers. It is how that necklace you wear became charmed to hold such vast reserves of energy that you can draw on at will, and how it came to mark the bottom of your wajun," he explained, motioning to the wajun hanging around her waist. "The Nrell Akinia charmed the pendant herself, and even we do not know what powers it holds. Truthfully, we thought the necklace to have been lost in eons previous. She was particularly skilled at charming items, and most of her personal belongings held secrets from her practicing. She uncovered hundreds, if not thousands, of abilities previously unknown, and many of which were lost with her. Now, let us not get off of the subject at hand. You will finish learning the courtesies in Main, and once you have them in your mind we will teach you the courtesies in Nrelnalna."

"What do you mean my necklace holds energy in it?" Akinia asked, puzzled by his statement.

He regarded her curiously for a moment. "Perhaps your knowledge of psychokinesis is less thorough than I had imagined. Have the Najee truly lost so much knowledge through the centuries?" he mused, but she could tell that he was mostly talking to himself. "I will answer your question at a later time. For now, we should get back to the courtesies."

Akinia proved to be a quick study. Less than a week had passed before she had memorized the majority of the subtleties of Nrell society; Ruegon then turned his attention to her instruction in Nrelnalna, of which she also proved to be a quick learner. She did not know enough for extensive communication, but Ruegon forbid her to speak Main, unless asking for a translation of a certain word or phrase.

He rarely praised her efforts, and sharply corrected her frequent mistakes, yet he was unfailingly patient and never lost his temper. She had been among the Nrell nearly a month when he turned to her in the middle of their lesson and said, "Tomorrow we will begin your psychokinetic training. You know enough Nrelnalnian that my tutelage will be instructive. Go to your room and rest; later you must contact the Najee and let them know you are still safe."

Shocked, amazed, and relieved, Akinia clasped her right fist to her left shoulder and bowed. "May the fortune of warriors smile upon you," she bade.

"And on you, my friend," he replied with a wry smile.

Chapter 49:

Nearly two months had passed since Akinia first arrived at the Nrell settlement. Every day of her visit was spent locked away in Ruegon's study, carefully executing various psychokinetic tasks under his patient tutelage. The power and control of what he asked her to do were far beyond anything she had attempted before, and her own reluctance to use her abilities didn't help her efforts.

Within the first few days Ruegon realized that she had subconsciously placed a series of powerful psychic blocks around the portion of her mind that controlled her abilities. After delving into her mind to carefully examine them, he decided that the powerful rudimentary walls had been there since her infancy.

"Can you take them down?" Akinia asked worriedly.

The Nrell sighed. "No, it would be far too dangerous. Your powers are so strong, and you have so little idea of how to control them, that the only way to safely remove them is to have you slowly work the blockades away. I have no doubt that's why you were having trouble controlling your abilities: they were breaking free of the barriers as you tapped into your power. We must be very careful how we proceed..."

The following weeks were spent carefully increasing the level of power Akinia used in her control exercises. Several times she lost control of herself, and Ruegon was forced to contain her in a cocoon of his own psychokinetic energy until she could get a firm grip on herself.

It was very hard to get used to the idea of controlling the energy, rather than forcing it back behind her mental walls, as she had done so many times before. Eventually, however, she began to learn to grasp the power and shape it how she wanted it to be used; and now she had enough control over herself that Ruegon decided it was time to proceed with her training.

For days they had been working on psychokinetic shields, and now he was teaching her a skill she desperately wanted to master: the ability to stop blaster bolts with her mind. They had already been at it for several hours…

"You are not concentrating," he chastised, letting another half-dozen bolts fly towards her.

"Hey!" she protested, cussing under her breath, as each of the stinging practice bolts hit her in the neck or chest.

"Mind your tongue," he snapped.

She glowered at him. "I'm sorry," she finally sighed. "My…companion, Nath, seems to have rubbed off on me. I don't normally curse."

"Your brother's tongue should not affect yours," he corrected quietly. He smiled at her startled expression. "I examined your mind, if you remember. I know your secrets, Akinia Enbrilth, and I know your brother's. Be not afraid. I do not hold your heritage against you, and I will keep your secret so long as you do. Now, again, put the shield up and dissolve the energy into yourself."

"Wait!" she requested. "Can you please show me again? It may help if I could see inside you while you do this, because I have no idea what to do."

Ruegon sighed. "It would be only a vague picture of what you seek, as your mind could not be bonded to me while I did this."

"A vague picture would serve me better than groping blindly," she protested. "If I even could see how your mind holds itself…"

"It would do you little good. The minds of each race work differently. To try and make an Adamian mind work like a Nrell mind would be futile," he corrected with forced patience. "Try again. Place an ordinary shield around yourself, but then focus on it in a different way. Use your mind's eye to see the world around you as energy, moving and flowing as part of a whole entity rather than as distinct items. When you see the universe in this manner, you will be able to control it more fully than before. The energy of the blaster bolts will pass into you and rather than disrupting the energy of your body, they will morph and join your body as fuel for your efforts. See that in your mind's eyes, picture it and control it. Now, ready yourself."

Akinia took a deep breath and held her hands out slightly above her head, using them to draw the flow of energy stemming from her body down into a barrier between her and Ruegon. His instructions echoed in her mind and she closed her eyes, slowing her heart rate and breathing as she observed the world around her with a second sight.

This was different than meditating with Nath had been. Then, they were seeing the life-forces of plants and animals, using their various consciousnesses to see the landscape around them. This form of meditation was something she had never experienced before, and her mind shrank back from it with a hidden thrill of terror. She shuddered and her shield dropped. "That was horrible," she whispered as the blood drained from her face.

Ruegon seemed intrigued. "What did you see? What did you feel?"

Still shaking, she whispered, "It…It was like static. The noise and the power…it was frightening. I felt so…so…inconsequential. It was like my life, my very existence, it was nothing…it *is* nothing," she paused searching his face with wide frightened eyes. "My life…to see the universe…like that… How can I be who I am said to be? How can that be possible? I…I'm nothing; a speck of dust seems larger than I am. Importance is an illusion we've created. How can I make any sort of difference, when I'm so insignificant?"

The Nrell smiled and nodded, seeming rather pleased. "What you have just seen, what you have just realized and reasoned, the level of wisdom and knowledge behind your acknowledgment is beyond most beings. Few ever truly recognize it, even after seeing and feeling the universe as you just have, and none that I have encountered have ever realized it so quickly. I am impressed, and it takes much to impress me," he informed her.

Akinia still stood there, shaking. She did not speak or acknowledge his praise, she only fought to calm her racing heart and steady her ragged breathing.

Ruegon tilted his head slightly as he watched her. "Now that you know what to expect, your next visions of the energy will be less traumatic and you will be able to see the beauty in it," he promised.

"How can anyone not feel that vastness that surrounds you when they see the universe like this? How can anyone not realize immediately how unimportant they are in comparison?" she demanded, finally steadying somewhat.

"It is as you said, isn't it?" he laughed. "We have been raised and surrounded by an illusion of grandeur. It is only the rare few who can release that illusion and see beyond their false assumptions. Now, again, put up your shield and see the energy of the universe through your mind's eye. This time, watch carefully around you. You will look to me, see the blaster in my hand, feel the energy begin to unfurl, and control the energy coming towards you. Make it change, make it morph, allow it to flood your body and become a part of it, but keep the energy of your body in control."

Akinia nodded and took a deep breath. Once again, she used her hands to draw a shield of energy between her and Ruegon. Taking another deep breath, she closed her eyes and let her mind see the energy flow of the universe. She fought against the urge to draw back into herself, and make her mind look towards where Ruegon stood. She could see the outlines and basic forms of everything around them for miles and miles. It was all vaguely transparent enough that she could see children playing in the Adamian settlement on the other side of the planet, and Nrell walking through the corridors all around her.

Despite her fear, she could see the beauty of this strange sight. She could marvel at her own skin, which also had the appearance of static, and how she could see every cell, every hair, every groove and curve of not only the skin, but of the muscles and tendons and ligaments and bones beneath the skin. She realized that if she focused her attention on anything, every part of it became painfully clear in her sight and in her mind, down to the last molecule it was both overwhelming and intoxicatingly beautiful.

She realized as she looked around that she had been wrong before. She was looking at the energy as though she was separate from it, a distinct entity to be judged beside it. That wasn't true. Every cell, every molecule, every miniscule thing had just as much significance as the largest building or mountain or planet. She wasn't an impossibly small being judged beside the universe, she *was* the universe. She was just as much a part of this incredible flow of energy as everything else that she saw, and it was all a part of her.

The moment that thought entered her mind and she realized its truth, her perception changed again. She was a part of the energy, and it was a part of her. She could control her body easily, and the entire universe was just as much a part of her as the body she had laid claim to. Just as she could tell her finger to scratch her arm, or her tongue to taste the food on her table, or her lungs to breathe in the air they needed, she could command the energy in ways it had never considered to move.

These realizations hit her in a split second, and by the time

282

Ruegon shot the practice bolt towards her she knew how to control it. She could see the energy racing at her, but more than that she could *feel* it. She was so connected to the world around her that she could feel the bolt's progress. She *was* the bolt, and as it approached her she simply allowed it to meld into the rest of her energy. It dispersed and sent a chill up her spine, but it was a pleasurable sensation. A dozen more bolts shot at her, but she paid them little mind as they simply dispersed throughout her body.

As she returned to her ordinary sight she looked over herself in amazement and smiled. She felt a tingle of electricity race up and down her spine several times and every cell in her body felt rejuvenated. "You know what I saw and felt this time," she accused as she noticed Ruegon smiling at her.

"You realized your connection, and you abandoned your disconnection. That is the only way you could have dispersed the bolt throughout your body, rather than simply sending it off into the air around you," he noted casually. "Do you think you are ready to try with real battle ammunition?"

She nodded instantly. "I am, but we've been at this for hours. Is it not close to time to eat?" she wondered, feeling her stomach ache for food.

"Do you feel weak?"

"No, I feel great, actually, but I'm hungry," she corrected. "I can't live off of borrowed strength, I know this. I still need to keep food in my system."

He nodded approvingly. "Maybe you are not so ignorant as I thought," he decided, "It would seem that you have had some experience with energy transfers."

"When my uncle found me in Jade's base I was near death. He gave me a little bit of his energy so that I could last until he could get me to help, but the process of giving it to me wore him down quickly," she explained. "It did nothing to bring my strength back, though; it just bought me a bit more time before I collapsed."

"I will teach you to share energy with someone, without wasting yours or theirs to perform the transfer, but not today," he promised. "It will work best with your brother, as your minds can meld most closely, but it will work to a certain extent with anyone. However I am wasting time by telling you of that lesson. Go and eat, and then rest in your room for a time. After dinner we will see if you are able to perform as well with battle ammunition as you do with practice bolts."

"Thank you," she grinned, "I'll be back here as soon as I finished dinner, I promise."

"I know you will be," he assured her. "Oh, and do take a few minutes to send another relayed communique to the Najee. It has been some time since the last one."

"I will," she promised. She clasped her right arm across her chest. "May the fortune of warriors smile upon you."

"And on you, my friend," he replied, clasping his own arm across his chest and inclining his head slightly.

Without another word, Akinia left.

Chapter 50:

The two white-haired warriors sat in silent contemplation, each one's thoughts drifting in a separate direction. The man sitting behind the ornate wooden desk clutched a slender datapad in his hands, reading and re-reading with increasing desperation. The reports from the war front were uniform in their message: Sigadia had grown more powerful, and the Empire's troops were struggling to hold their ground.

The woman rose from her chair with a power and grace that defied her advanced age and approached the man. "You see?" she questioned, her voice a hoarse whisper. "It is as has been foretold."

The man frowned, his brow furrowing. "You knew of this?" he asked, equally as quiet. His voice was low and coarse, worn from age, but there was a new weariness behind it as he struggled against the hopelessness their situation was bringing. Setting the datapad aside, he raised a shaking hand and brushed aside a stray strand of his long hair.

The woman gave a single curt nod and turned to pace the room. Her footsteps were slow and steady, confident and sure.

"You knew, and you did not see fit to warn me?" he demanded, outraged. He pushed himself from his chair, pausing as his balance wavered, and then made his way to the window that overlooked the training fields. A grim smile edged onto his lips as he watched the children practice. She would be nearly the same age now, in these same barracks had he not stolen her. Forcing those thoughts away, he turned back to the woman to demand an answer.

"There now, Master Lo-Kí," she reprimanded, a smirk playing upon her lips, "It was known to you as well as I that the situation would grow dire before her appearance. I did not think I would have to remind you of that."

He watched her, marveling at how calm she could appear in such a time. Though impressed at her even temper, his own rose in annoyance. *"The time is not yet come for her to appear,"* he snapped. *He motioned out the window he had just left. "Which of those children is the warrior we have waited for? Which of those children is the Child of Prophecy, if the time is so near for her to appear? All Najee children have been sought out, every corner of the Empire has been searched trying to find her, so which of those children is your prophesied hero?"*

"She is not among them," the woman answered evenly, and without hesitation. *"The child is alive now, however."*

Lo-Ki's eyes snapped from his desk to the woman's smug face. He searched her expression for any sign of teasing, but found only confidence spread across her features. "Where?" he demanded.

"That is not a question for me to answer," she shrugged, picking up a small trinket from his desk and twirling it in her fingers.

"Are you or are you not the eldest of our Gifted? Who but you has the power to answer?" he demanded, annoyance rising again. *He turned sharply to stare out the window once more. Gaining control of his emotions, he gently asserted, "I know that I am not Master Orthin, but I am the Master of Masters now, and you will respect me, Tanlaish. Answer me: where is the child?"*

She smiled. "I know perfectly well who you are, Lo-Ki. Do not forget, we were once Apprenticed together as children. As to your question, I cannot answer because I do not know. None of the Gifted have seen her since her birth, at least none who were able to ascertain her location," she explained, standing to join him at the window.

"Then why don't you search for her? I have seen you do so many times in the past for others, why have you not yet done it for her?" he demanded bitterly.

"I have forbidden it, for her own safety. To search for her would awaken her mind, and Enbrilth would surely sense it," she explained with a sigh.

"He does not know what to look for," Lo-Ki protested.

Tanlaish smiled. "He does not need to, it would be a natural sense."

"Surely he is not a Gifted?!" Lo-Ki exclaimed, fear of the thought paling his already pasty features.

"Not in the least," she promised.

"But then, how? The only other way..." his face paled again. *"You do not mean to say that she is..."*

Tanlaish sighed and nodded, her smirk replaced by a worried frown. "Aye, but she is Imperial, and he is of yet unaware that she exists. But if we touch her mind before she is in our custody, and she begins to wake, he will know of her existence."

Swallowing audibly, he asked, "But then how are we to locate her? It may not be safe, but you must find her. We will have the nearest Master protect her until she can be brought here."

"It is not necessary," Tanlaish shrugged, her impish smirk returning.

"It is not necessary?" he echoed, flabbergasted. A curse escaped his lips before he could stop it. "We need her, if she truly lives. Our entire force is unable to drive back one man and one child, and you say it is unnecessary to find the one being in existence that can stop him?"

"No."

"'No'?" he demanded, exasperated, turning to face her again, "'No', what?"

She motioned for him to sit as she returned to her own chair. "No, I do not think it unnecessary to find the child. However, I do think it unnecessary to place her in danger when her location is perfectly well known," she explained quietly.

"Known? But you said not five minutes ago-"

"-that none of the Gifted knows her location. I would not allow it. That is not to say that her location is unknown by any Najee," she corrected.

Lo-Ki suppressed a growl of irritation, wondering to himself why he continued to consult the woman when she irritated him so badly; she seemed to enjoy infuriating him with her riddles! Nevertheless, he played along with her in the interests of solving this puzzle. "Who does know?" he asked simply.

"He does," she replied, brushing a crumb off of her robes.

"Who?" Lo-Ki asked with forced patience, biting back his frustration.

"Him," she replied without looking up from her search for more crumbs.

A soft knock on the door interrupted Lo-Ki's half-formed demand for a name. "Enter," he called sharply.

After a hesitation, the door opened and a young man uncertainly stepped through the entryway. "You summoned me, Master Tanlaish?" he spoke hesitantly, casting curious glances at both elder

287

warriors.

"Enter, and close the door behind you," she ordered, rising to her feet.

"What is this?" Lo-Kí demanded, looking back and forth between them. He knew well who this young man was: the young Master Khee-Lá Juntoby. He had been friends with the Juntoby family for many years, and had known many of the young man's ancestors. Now Khee-Lá was the last warrior of the Juntoby line that remained alive.

"Tell him," Tanlaish ordered the young man simply.

"What am I to tell him?" he wondered, uncertain what this was about.

She smiled. "Tell him where you sent Ko-Pau, and the purpose of the trip."

Lo-Kí frowned as the young man paled. "What is this about?" he wondered aloud, trying to determine if he could remember young Master Ko-Pau Klie's latest assignment. Nothing came to mind except a variety of memories that let him know Ko-Pau would willingly serve his Master in any request, despite the fact that he had now been promoted from an Apprentice to a Master himself, and had his own young Apprentice nearing Mastership.

"Master Tanlaish!" Khee-Lá protested, his mouth falling open.

"It is alright. I have told him what she is, if not who she is. He must know. We have kept him in the dark far too long. Master Orthin would not have approved of this secret, and we have both long known it. Speak, and be honest," she instructed.

Casting his gaze from one to another, and not daring to oppose an edict from them both, he took a deep breath and began his tale.

Lo-Kí sighed as he recalled the conversation, occurring mere days before Ko-Pau had taken Akinia from the orphanage. His anger and indignation at being kept in the dark had long since faded, but at the memory it seethed once more. In truth, the child would have been around seven years of age at Orthin's death, of age enough that he would have allowed her to come and begin her training. Khee-Lá's secrecy had hidden her from them for far too long.

And yet, a part of him understood the young Master's apprehension at having her on Paméd so young. As the Child of Prophecy, which would quickly have become known (or at the least, suspected), the poor girl would have been assaulted with constant demands for her presence on the battlefront. A premature death would not have helped anyone, and would have robbed the Najee of a charming and beloved child. No, he could no longer be angry that they had kept this secret. Now he could only wish they had perhaps kept the secret longer.

Sighing, he stood and looked out of his window to watch the children training. It was very early, so few had ventured out into the training fields, but it was these hardworking few that earned his greatest respect. They were not all the best of the best, most were at the bottoms of their classes, but they were diligent in their efforts to improve and that earned them notice and respect by the Master of Masters. The advanced students that joined them, taking time away from their own time of relaxation to help those lacking, had also earned his respect through their selfless assistance of their classmates. He would take particular care to assign them himself; they needed a firm but generous hand to guide them to Mastership.

A soft laugh escaped his lips as he watched a petit Dwarvian girl correct a tall Núnto boy's form, but the sound was laced with anxiety and concern as his thoughts returned to Akinia. There had been no word since her first message, nearly two months ago, despite her assurances that she would remain in contact. A twinge of guilt pierced his heart as he considered that *he* was, in fact, the one that had sent her alone into Sigidian territory.

His intentions had been good: he wished only to give her time to work through the difficult stage of mental control she was in, and that set his conscience somewhat at ease. Still, each time he saw Khee-Lá or Ko-Pau, inquiring after news of her, the guilt returned. He hid it well from them, but hiding it from young Nathaniel? That was a different matter entirely.

The boy had long cared for Akinia, that much was clear to any who had seen them together, but the agony and pain in his eyes as he spoke of her now led Lo-Kí to believe that his feelings were much deeper than previously thought. The guilt he felt while speaking to the child's uncle and her Master was nothing compared to the guilt the boy's eyes made him feel. If he were angry, or even passively aggressive, it would be easier to face him, but the Apprentice was simply inconsolably depressed behind an ill-disguised façade of dim hope.

Sighing, Lo-Kí thought back over all of his conversations with

Akinia, few though they were. In such a short time of knowing her, it was clear that she was a sweet child with a sharp wit and strategic mind. Her eyes pierced into the souls of those whose gaze she met, and within moments she would look away satisfied that she had found the answer she sought; but what was the question? Often he had wondered this, pondering her chain of thought as she analyzed any piece of information she received, yet he still could find no answer.

Would he ever get the chance to, now?

Enough! he chastised himself. It would not do to think that way. A part of him wanted to assemble a team of Najee to find Akinia and return her, but both she and Tanlaish had advised against it. Akinia would return when it was safe, and no sooner; dwelling upon her situation would not help.

Turning his mind away from the child, no easy task these days, he forced his thoughts to run through a list of the young Full Najee. He would spend his time doing something constructive, like pairing young Apprentices with appropriate Masters.

Jeshkir is due for Mastership before much longer... it seems only yesterday I was observing him in the training fields! I think he would do wonderful for the young Lyndop; what was her name, again? Oh yes, Av-Ki Luneck. The girl is a bit shy, but one of our best Learners, and Jeshkir is anything but shy. Yes, I think he would do well with her. Now what of Learner Pashten? I suppose he would do well with...

Chapter 51:

Several weeks had passed since Ruegon taught her to dissolve the bolts into herself, and now his promise to teach her about energy transfers was to be honored. The lessons that had taken place in the meantime varied greatly. One of her favorite topics thus far had been healing wounds; a skill of Lokita's that had startled even Lo-Kí. Yet at the same time, it was also one of her least-favorite lessons, as it involved repeatedly slicing her finger open to allow her to practice.

"I am torn between two beliefs," Ruegon admitted as their lesson drew to a close one night. "I do not wish you to heal any wounds in the presence of your comrades; however, for you to grow proficient enough in the skill for it to benefit you, then you must practice! Therefore, my orders on this front are for you to exercise discretion."

Their limited time together had not allowed for greatly detailed instruction in any skills, but she dutifully memorized the fundamentals and swore to practice them until perfected once she returned to Paméd. Now Akinia waited eagerly, nearly bouncing in anticipation, for Ruegon to begin his instruction in this new area.

"I promised you that I would teach you this, but I warn you that it will not work as well with me as it would with another Adamian," he cautioned. "Close friends of other races may be easier to transfer with than strangers of the other races, but there is enough of a difference in your minds to cause some of the energy to be lost. However, this transfer will be less difficult than the one your uncle performed on you."

"Why does it work best with Adamians?" she wondered.

"Your mind is more closely compatible with your own species. Certainly, it will work well enough with other races, but the transfer is most efficient within your own race. Close relatives are even more closely compatible because the genetic link provides a greater similarity in consciousnesses," he explained. "The closer the relation, the better and stronger the link is. Your brother would be more closely compatible than your uncle because you share a father with your brother and the ancestor you share with your uncle is slightly more distant."

Akinia nodded. "I'm going to guess that it involves melding minds with the person in question?"

"Very astute," he praised, "What makes you say that?"

"Well whenever you start talking about similarities in mind that make things easier, its generally followed by a brief recap on how to properly meld minds, followed by a new skill involving some form of mind-melding," she shrugged.

He smiled, his eyes bright with silent laughter. "Well, I will pass over the brief recap of how to properly meld minds. I'm certain that, by now, you know the theory and practice well enough. So now we will begin with the new skill involving some form of mind-melding. Tell me, when your uncle transferred energy to you, he put it directly in your body, did he not?"

"Yes," she agreed, nodding.

"Now answer me this: why, when transferring images to another mind, do you send them through a mental link and not implant them directly into the brain?" he asked, watching her closely.

Akinia frowned, uncertain why he was asking this. "I would assume that it's because it would take more energy to alter someone's mind to hold the images than it would to think about them and let whoever you're giving them to see them," she decided after a few moments' thought.

He nodded approvingly. "Energy transfers work in much the same way," he explained. "The energy is sent over the mental link, much like you have sent confidence and emotional strength. Transferred in that manner, that is the only way strength can be received: emotionally. Now, when your minds are melded, even partially, as you did with young Nath the day you were dancing in your room, your minds and bodies are linked and can freely share thoughts and energy. In essence, the link is uniting you into a single entity for a few moments. Now, the link will never be complete or whole, as each mind is built with slight differences, but the union is strong enough to share energy between the two parties."

"So the closer the mind, the closer the link, correct?" she affirmed. "So would identical twins be able to meld completely, if siblings can meld so close to completely?"

"That is a very difficult question," Ruegon sighed, seeming to debate with himself on how to answer. "Theoretically it would be possible, since the genetic make-up of the two individuals would be the same, but theoretically it would also be possible for the union to be less strong than the bond between ordinary siblings. Much depends on the individuals involved. For example, not only would neither you nor your twin open up to each other enough to meld completely, it is also reasonably possible that due to your different upbringings her thought patterns may be different enough to prevent the meld."

Akinia nodded thoughtfully. "Ruegon," she questioned hesitantly, "Is it wrong that I want her back, and that I wish for her to come to me just as my sister and not my enemy?"

He gave her a pitying smile. "It is only natural," he assured her. "In the womb, especially among the strongest Najee children, a bond is formed between identical twins. It is a very strong bond, sometimes leading ordinary twins to find each other decades after being separated at birth. The fact that you and your twin are and were so strong could possibly have formed an incredibly strong bond between you that she herself may feel.

"The use that bond is put to, however, can vary greatly. It is not necessarily a bond of love, only a thin tether between your subconscious minds that allows you to have a vague knowledge of the other's present location. It can be a tool, if you learn to feel it and let it warn you to her presence. It is not something I can teach you, but a skill you must learn yourself," he sighed. "Now, we should get on with our lesson. Meld your mind to mine, and I will transfer some energy to you so that you can feel the part of your consciousness that controls the energy transfer."

"But I have already used the link to know her presence, Ruegon," Akinia protested, hoping to prolong this conversation.

The Nrell was surprised. "Tell me."

Akinia quickly related the two instances in which she had felt Lokita's presence. "Can I strengthen this link, do you think? Of yet it has only happened when I was physically close to her. Can I extend it like I have extended my telepathic reach?"

He paused for a moment as he considered her words. "I have no way to know this," he finally admitted. "It is reasonable to assume that this power can grow as well as any other, but it is also reasonable to assume that it may only work when you are within a certain distance of one another. I recommend attempting it carefully every night before you sleep, but only after shielding your mind from her touch."

"But how do I attempt it?" she wondered. "I didn't mean to sense her either time that I have; how do I initiate it?"

His right ear twitched slightly as he mused her request, a move Akinia recognized as meaning that he was concentrating. "You will have to experiment with it," he finally admitted with some reluctance. "I can only offer this advice: it is different than trying to contact her mind. You only want to sense her essence, her aura."

Akinia frowned as she considered this, but only for a moment. Ruegon's sharp command to continue with her lesson interrupted her thoughts, and she forced herself to push the intriguing idea away. She would consider it later, as she rested, but for now she needed to concentrate on the problem at hand.

It was several hours later when Ruegon called her to stop. "Go and rest now," he instructed. "In the morning we will not have our lessons here. Two young Nrell from my clan, the boy being my niece's eldest son, will attempt to be married tomorrow. I think it would be well for your education of our customs if you were to attend it with me."

She smiled and bowed, aware of what an honor it was to have been invited.

He bowed in return, clasping his right arms across his chest. "May the fortune of warriors smile upon you."

Nearly speechless for a moment as she reveled in the honor he showed her by speaking first, she quickly recovered and replied, "And on you, my friend." Without another word she left, making her way through the now-familiar halls and into the small bedroom she occupied.

She sighed as she lay down on the bed, staring at the rough ceiling. Her mind raced as she wondered what the Nrell wedding would be like... *Will it be anything like an Imperial wedding?* Akinia wondered. She closed her eyes, wishing Laani could see the wedding with her. *She would love to see the Nrell...*

Her thoughts drifted, as they often did, to her family. She wondered what Khee-Lá, Ko-Pau, and Nath would do when she returned to Paméd... What had they told Andrid and Katarina? Did her cousin know where she was? Were they all well? How was Leena's health? Had Katarina yet recovered?

As she slept, a smile crept onto her face. She dreamed of

soaring through the skies of Náto on Insheff's back, while Amalli raced beside her on Nilek. Ko-Pau and Khee-Lá stood and waved to them, while Nath sat beside Rofa and grinned…

Chapter 52:

Ruegon came for her early the next morning. He led her down a series of unfamiliar halls and into a large room, the interior of which had been plastered smooth white and decorated ornately. There were already a great many Nrell there, silently taking their places amongst several rows of chairs. Ruegon led her up the center aisle that ran between the two columns, silently motioning for her to sit in one of two seats near the center of the right column.

"Our weddings are much different from yours, young Najee," Ruegon whispered, his voice barely comprehendible, "I will do my best to walk you through the ceremony, so to speak, but you must remain absolutely silent throughout the entire thing, am I clear?"

She nodded. Her eyes wandered up to the front of the room, where a large empty area sat in front of the rows of chairs. A velvet two-seated bench sat just off of the wall on the far side of the room, past the empty space. A Nrell, who Akinia recognized as being the one they call Minister-Raing, stood behind the bench, holding a small book in his hands. She assumed it held the bonding words within its binding.

Suddenly, the whole room fell into an impossibly deeper silence, penetrated by an electric current of anticipation. Several young heads turned to look down the aisle as the large doors opened, but at a sharp glance from their parents they turned to face forwards again. Akinia was careful to keep her gaze straight ahead.

"The bride and groom now enter," Ruegon whispered. "They wear the traditional bonding garb that our kind has worn for millennia."

As the bride and groom passed, the bride on the right and the groom on the left, Akinia felt her face turn slightly pink. The groom wore nothing but a leather loincloth, and the bride wore a loincloth and a leather breastplate that hung from around her neck and was fastened with a thin strap tied around her back, which gave only the barest

297

covering to her chest. They did not look at one another, nor did they smile, and there was a cautious, no-contact space maintained between them at all times.

"Now they approach the minister and kneel to hear his words from the First Rite," Ruegon explained, his voice still barely comprehendible even in the silence.

As he said, the bride and groom knelt before Minister, on the audience's side of the bench, and waited expectantly for him to speak.

He cleared his throat, opened the small book, and in the beautiful bell-tone voice of the Nrell, read, "The First Rite. Marriage is a sacred union. Once the bonds of marriage have been entered, there is no undoing of the vows. As such, be certain that you truly wish to make the pledge of lifelong matrimony before you speak. Krefton, of the Meighdor clan, are you satisfied with the bride that has been chosen for you?"

"I am, Minister," he replied. His voice was strong and confident, matched by the determined set of his chin.

"And do you, Krefton, of the Meighdor clan, believe yourself to be evenly matched with this woman? To make whole and complete one another, your strengths must match her weaknesses, yet her strengths must balance out yours. Do you believe that this is the woman who will do that for you?"

"I do, Minister," he stated, still confident.

The minister turned his attention to the bride. "Neilahnna, of the Meighdor clan, are you satisfied with the husband that has been chosen for you?"

"I am, Minister," she replied quietly. Her voice held notes of both fear and a thrill of excitement, and Akinia wondered if all women sounded that way on their wedding day.

"And do you, Neilahnna, of the Meighdor clan, believe yourself to be evenly matched with this man? To make whole and complete one another, your strengths must match his weaknesses, yet his strengths must balance out yours. Do you believe that this is the man who will do that for you?"

"I do, Minister," she answered fervently.

"Then the First Rite is complete, and the Second Rite begins," the minister said solemnly.

The atmosphere changed drastically at that moment. Akinia's pulse jumped and her breathing accelerated slightly as the tension in the room increased to the point that it was nearly a tangible thing. Low murmurs crossed the room as the doors once again opened. Akinia resisted the urge to look back, but as the child that entered walked past she could see that he held a velvet pillow in his hands, upon which sat two well-aged wajun.

Ruegon leaned slightly closer, to ensure Akinia could hear him and quickly hissed, "Now comes the Second Rite. Though we do not fight as Najee, our people still teach our children the ways Akinia first taught us. The compatibility of this union must be proven. This is how we have chosen our spouses from the time before Akinia. The bride and groom will fight, and if their fight lasts ten minutes with neither gaining the upper hand for more than a few moments, then their union is considered compatible. They must put their best effort into the fight. The moderator, one of the women sitting in the front row, keeps her mind's eye on them, ensuring that they aren't trying to compensate for their potential spouse's deficiency by performing at a less-than-excellent level."

The child, a girl, carried the velvet pillow up to the front, kneeling as she reached the bride and groom.

The minister motioned to the wajun. "Each of you take a wajun, and ready yourselves," he instructed.

The bride and groom bowed forwards slightly, rose to their feet, and each took the wajun nearest them. The bride moved to the right side of the large clearing in the front of room, and the groom to the left. The wajun were held, unopened, by their side.

The minister looked to them in turns, now that they were so far apart from one another. "And now the Second Rite begins. We have all heard your testimony, that you believe your union to be compatible. Now, that belief will be tested. You will fight one another, performing your best. And we will know if you do not make your best effort," he paused and motioned to an older Nrell woman sitting on the front row of the column in which Akinia sat. "If your union is compatible, we will proceed to the Third Rite. Now, ready your weapons."

The bride and groom both opened their wajun at the same moment. Akinia watched as a new expression took over their faces. It was a look she knew all too well; they were about to battle, and they would be fighting to kill. The expression was enough to make her shudder, because it reminded her of the look she had seen in Lokita's eyes the day they had fought on Granta, just before she had poisoned

Ko-Pau.

The minister looked from one to the other. "Begin," he stated simply.

It seemed almost effortless as the two charged one another. She brought her wajun down over her head, he held his up to block. They pulled away and circled back around, their wajun meeting fiercely on the groom's right side. They whirled, and their wajun met again on his left. They backed away from each other a couple of steps and then began to slice and parry, lunging and dodging, knocking the blade to the side and dodging its thrust at the last moment.

As the groom lunged, his blade heading for the bride's gut, she dropped down onto her knees and lay back so that her heels touched her back and her head lay on the floor. She swung her wajun up and around, but he blocked it just in time. Her blow was strong, and it knocked him backwards a step, giving her just enough time that she could push herself back into a standing position and place her blade between his and her body.

Akinia watched, on the edge of her seat, as they ducked and dodged and parried and thrust around one another. It was a dance, a glorious dance that seemed to have been choreographed and practiced to perfection. Their steps were perfect, mirror opposites of one another. It seemed all too soon that the Minister held up his hands for the battle to cease; she could have watched them for hours and not grown bored of their battle.

The bride and groom instantly stopped, their wajun snapping shut in an instant, and placed the weapons back on the velvet pillow the little girl still carried. They returned to the minister and knelt before him again.

"And so ends the Second Rite," the minister stated. "It seems to me that this is an equal pairing, would you not agree?"

The gathered Nrell nodded, and Akinia quickly gave a single nod when Ruegon urged her to participate.

"So it is agreed. We will now continue to the Third Rite," he announced.

Ruegon quickly whispered. "In the Third Rite the bride and groom work as a team to battle a pair who will fight them, to judge how well they work united. Two will be chosen from the gathered witnesses by the minister's wife, the young woman sitting beside the moderator. She chooses the two strongest fighters, a man and a woman, to test the bride and groom. The testers are allowed to hold back some to keep from overpowering or harming the bride and groom, but they must be tough and fierce enough to push the couple to their limits."

Akinia nodded in acknowledgement, eager to see who the next Rite performed. She watched as the young woman Ruegon spoke of rose and walked down the aisle, looking over the assembled guests. Many of the young children sat up eagerly, straining to catch the woman's eye as she walked past, hoping desperately to be allowed to test the new couple. Akinia smiled as she watched them; they reminded her of young Charlotte and the other children she used to watch.

The young woman walked all the way down to the last row, and then turned around and walked back to the front. She paused in the aisle as she reached the front again, turned, and let her eyes run over the guests. "I have made my decision," she announced, her eyes still tracing across the rows and columns of chairs. "The two will be Aidern, of the Meighdor clan," she paused as a young Nrell man stepped forwards, inclined his head respectfully and walked to stand on the left side of the groom, "And Akinia, of the Devura clan."

Akinia froze, uncertain if she had heard correctly. She looked to Ruegon anxiously; she didn't know what to do.

"Walk up, bow slightly forwards to her as the boy did, and then stand by the bride, go!" he urged quietly.

Akinia tried to remember her aunt's lessons about maintaining composure in even the most startling situations, and by time she stepped into the aisle her face was a mask of calm, as though she did this every day. She bowed slightly to the woman and took her place on the woman's right side. Murmurs, whether of dissent or assent she couldn't tell, rose up around the room before settling back into a tense silence.

"Aidern, of the Meighdor clan, and Akinia, of the Devura clan, you will test the bride and groom for their ability to work as a team, even in the face of grave danger. You may hold back to keep from defeating them, but push them to the limits of their skill. Try to divide them, and they will try to stay united. Do you both have a wajun with you?" the minister asked

"Yes, minister," Aidern answered, pulling his wajun from its holster under his robes.

"Yes, minister," Akinia echoed, pulling her own from within the fold of her dress.

"Very well," he stated. "Krefton, Neilhanna, take again the

301

weapons in your hands, and ready yourselves for the Third Rite."

The bride and groom stood again and took their wajun from atop the velvet pillow the girl still dutifully held and walked together to the right side of the room.

"Testers," the minister said, addressing Akinia and the young Nrell man, "Take your wajun and ready yourselves on the other side of the room."

Akinia bowed, following Aidern's lead, and followed him to the other side of the room, where they stood in ready position and waited for the order to begin. A stray flicker of thought wondered what Laani would think if she knew that Akinia was about to fight Nrell!

As he stopped, Aidern turned to Akinia and sharply whispered, "I do not know how a weakling was chosen for this, but do not dare embarrass the bride and groom, or I *will* regain their honor. Are we clear?"

Akinia nodded once, meeting his harsh gaze with determined patience. "Have you any other words of encouragement?" she asked, equally as quiet.

His eyes narrowed, an expression Akinia knew to mean amusement, and he replied, "Yes, fight to kill, but don't so much as scratch her if you can help it. Blood is not to be shed if it can be avoided."

"Forgive my ignorance, but am I only to fight *her* then?" she wondered.

His eyes widened in annoyance. "Yes, but there will be times when we will fight them both together. I will try to touch your arm to warn you of the change," he sneered, giving Akinia the impression that it was only for the sakes of the bride and groom that he did not allow her to humiliate herself.

Akinia gave a single nod in response, her cheeks turning pink in embarrassment of her own ignorance, and she directed her gaze back at the Minister. She was acutely aware of the eyes of the Nrell on her, more than they were on the bride and groom. Did they all know she was the Child of Prophecy? Were they waiting to see if she lived up to their expectations? Or did they simply think she was an adopted visitor, a weakling as Aidern said?

The Minister backed away and said, "Let the Third Rite begin."

Akinia did not hesitate, but she followed Aidern's calm saunter to the center of the room, which was matched by the bride and groom.

As she saw the Nrell's faces harden to battle, she tried to do the same. She was fighting to kill. With a bit of imagination, she managed to put herself in the mindset of fighting her twin. No emotion, only action and reaction.

The two teams were ten feet from one another when the bride and groom snapped open their wajun. Both shone soft blue. Aidern and Akinia opened theirs as well, his blade glowing yellow next to her white.

Gasps and murmurs erupted in the stoic crowd as Akinia's wajun opened. If they had not known before who she was, they certainly did now.

Blades crossed in a furious display of speed and agility. The bride focused her attention on Akinia, while the groom tried to disable Aidern. Her heart raced and her breathing sped for the first few moments of the battle; the Nrell woman was so fierce! However, as she settled into the steps of the dance, clearing her mind of all thought, surrendering herself to instinct as Ruegon had taught, Akinia found herself more than a match for her.

She felt a light pressure on her arm, and knew it was Aidern's hand. They switched off for a moment, Akinia now fighting the groom, before she found both blades crossing hers. She leapt and ducked, dived and parried, all while exchanging a volley of blows heavy and fast enough to evoke gasps of surprise from the assembly. It took a great deal of concentration for Akinia to keep from ending the fight, and another part of her mind was wondering where Aidern had gone.

She caught sight of him, finally, trying to return the groom's attention to himself, but both bride and groom were too busy with Akinia to take much notice. In a daring move, Akinia leapt into the air, parrying their blades as she crossed over their heads, and landed near Aidern, who willingly stepped in to divide the couple's focus once more.

They divided, forcing bride and groom to put their backs together and shield one another. Finally, after what seemed like hours, the Minister said, "Enough."

Akinia hesitated. His voice had been soft enough that she couldn't be certain he had really spoken, but the three Nrell snapped their wajun shut and so she did the same an instant later. As she saw Aidern move to stand beside the kneeling groom, she quickly moved to the kneeling bride's side. As the Minister approached, Akinia mimicked

Aidern's bow.

"It would seem an equal pairing in all regards, would it not?" the Minister asked of the assembly. All but the four directly in front of him nodded, Akinia remained still upon seeing Aidern remain still. "Do any of the assembled have cause to deny them their union?" No one in the hall moved. "In the name of God, rise Krefton and Neilhanna, for you are now wed."

The bride and groom rose to their feet and quitted the room in the same cautious, no-contact manner they had entered. It was only once they were gone that Aidern moved, prompting Akinia to follow suit. All of the assembled Nrell began to make their way, silently, from the hall.

"Akinia-Tullek, wait a moment," Aidern implored as she began to return to Ruegon.

She froze, surprised to hear him address her so highly. Turning back to him, she silently waited for him to speak.

"Forgive me," he requested, bowing to her. "I was rude with no cause, fearing my sister's wedding was to be shamed by the presence of a weakling who's only right to be here was the favor of a Settlement Head. I had no idea who you were, nor what you were. I cry your pardon a thousand times for my ill behavior."

She was careful not to let her surprise show. So that was the source of his despise! Thinking back on Ruegon's teachings her first day, she bowed in return to him. "Aidern-Melsh, there is nothing to forgive. I cannot begrudge anyone being concerned for the welfare of their family. I apologize for having caused you such pain, and assure you that I had no idea I would be chosen to participate. I also cry your pardon for my ignorance, which can only have served to increase your pain, and thank you for explaining what was expected of me today."

The Nrell bowed once more. "Then we are both forgiven," he decided, rising again. He clasped his right hands across his chest and said, "May the fortune of warriors smile upon you."

Akinia clasped her right arm across her chest and replied, "And on you, my friend." She did not miss the fact that he had chosen to address her first. Turning, she hastily made her way to Ruegon's side, musing the interaction and believing that she had, perhaps, made a friend. At the least, they would most likely meet without animosity in the future.

"You did well," Ruegon praised simply as he led her out.

Knowing his simple praise had covered her actions throughout the wedding, as well as after, Akinia smiled and replied, "Thank you."

"Your time here is coming to a close, child," he informed her. "Soon you will return to your people, custodian of the secrets of our race."

"You may trust me, Ruegon," she assured him quietly. "You have given me so much more than I could ever have wished for. I will be able to destroy the evil ones now, of that I am certain, and I owe it to you and to the rest of our people before us."

He regarded her curiously for a moment. "No, not *our* people; you have not been truly adopted into our society, not yet," he informed her casually.

She frowned, blushing. "But Antia said that I was, in all respects, a Nrell now that I have accepted the mark," she protested.

Ruegon opened the door to his study with a flicker of thought. "Sit, and I shall explain to you."

Akinia continued to frown, but did as she was told. She waited with a semblance of patience for the Nrell to speak.

Finally, Ruegon sat in his own chair and said, "Your hurried visit to Antia's settlement did not allow time for you to be truly adopted. You bear the mark, yes, but did not complete the ceremonies. If you truly wish to join our society, then you will need to follow the traditions."

"What traditions?" she asked curiously.

"Vows of acceptance, as well as a demonstration of knowledge of our society," he explained. "Because of your reputation and your destiny, the Minister may require a demonstration of your skills with wajun and psychokinesis. Afterwards there will be a great feast in your honor, as well as dancing and music."

"Whatever I must do to be accepted here, to truly belong among you, I am willing to do," she agreed wholeheartedly. "You have taught me well, so I have no fear of failing either test."

He regarded her with some amusement before replying, "It does not matter how well I taught you, child; it matters only how well you learned. I would be better assured by your assertion that you had been a diligent pupil. Regardless, you handled yourself remarkably well throughout the wedding and I have no doubts about your readiness to join my people."

Akinia smiled at her teacher's praise; it was so rarely given! "Then I assure you that I have been a diligent pupil. The language we

305

now converse in should be proof enough of that," she laughed, reminding him of her fluency in Nrelnalna.

"You will do your clan proud, I am certain," he agreed with a reluctant sigh. "Devura will have gained a brilliant mind."

Akinia frowned. "If you were to adopt a Najee into your clan, he or she would become part of the Meighdor clan, correct?" she asked, waiting for his affirming nod. "How is it that Antia of the Emran clan adopted me into the Devura clan?"

Ruegon hesitated a moment before answering. "No one truly knows," he finally admitted. "We can only guess that your destiny, as well as your link to your namesake, altered Antia's gift. Perhaps in much the same way as your wajun was marked by the necklace, bonded to you by that mark, you were bonded to the clan of Akinia by her own design so many eons before your birth. So much of her knowledge has been lost to us that it is impossible to tell."

Akinia nodded, pursing her lips as she contemplated this new information.

The Nrell watched her for a moment before adding, "It will be several days before I will be able to arrange for your adoption ceremony. I must contact the Clan Chief of Devura and let her know what is occurring, as well as to discover which family line you will be adopted into. I would suggest that you spend your time practicing your interactions with us."

"As you wish," she agreed instantly, inclining her head slightly.

"You may explore the settlement as you wish; your days are your own until the ceremony," Ruegon decided.

Akinia frowned. "Will you not be teaching me any longer?"

He shook his head and sighed. "No, you have learned the basics of what you need to survive in this war. You have been a good pupil, and I am honored to have had the privilege of training you. I know that you are disappointed, but if you honor me as a teacher, then you will now heed my instructions: explore the settlement, interact with my people, learn our ways as best you can."

Akinia bowed. "As you wish," she agreed again.

He placed a hand on her shoulder. "Now go and rest. Savor your solitude; you have had very little of it of late."

For a third time, Akinia bowed and replied, "As you wish." She began to turn away, but then paused to face him again. "Thank you, Ruegon-Nagga."

"You are very welcome, Akinia-Tullek," he replied, "and may the fortune of warriors smile upon you."

"And on you, my friend," she replied immediately, feeling her heart swell with pride again. That was the second time within minutes that a Nrell had honored her so highly by speaking first! Without another word she turned and left, following the passages back to her room.

I'll soon be going home, she mused to herself as she lay down on her bed, *so why does it feel as though I'll be leaving home, instead?* Frowning, she rolled over onto her side and closed her eyes. *What are you doing, Akinia? This isn't your home, and it will never be! Even when you are adopted into the Devura clan, you will never have a home in the Meighdor clan! You've gotten too comfortable... Paméd is your home, Náto is your home, Degru is not!*

Chapter 53:

Akinia smiled nervously as she looked at her reflection in the mirror. The two tank sleeves of her new dress were connected by silver rings, which perfectly accented the silvery-blue of the silk-like fabric. The flowing material, its colors shifting in shimmering in the light, looked like it was woven from water and beams of light. The adoption ceremony would begin in half an hour, but for now she waited anxiously for Ruegon to come for her.

In a way, it felt wrong to allow herself to be adopted into the Nrell society; after all, Akinia had a family now. Yet, in another way, it felt exactly right. In spite of the many arguments that she had been having with herself over it, the Nrell settlement had become her home, as well. The Nrell were her people, as much as the Nátoans or the Najee were. In some ways, she felt far more at home among the Nrell than she ever could anywhere else.

At least I will no longer be afraid of myself once I return, she mused, watching in the mirror as her hair raised itself up, twisting into an intricate series of braids that would have taken at least four pairs of hands to style. Satisfied that her hair looked nice, she settled onto her bed. Giving a bored sigh, she glanced around the room for something to do, and then she smirked.

Akinia focused on the cup of water on her nightstand, smiling as the liquid rose up into the air in front of her. She manipulated it into a variety of shapes, each one more complex and convoluted than the last. As a soft knock sounded on the door, she guided the water back into the cup.

"It is time," Ruegon called simply.

She took only a moment to force the knot in her stomach to relax before replying, "I am ready." Opening the door with a brush of her thoughts, she stepped out into the hallway.

Ruegon nodded, motioning for her to follow as he turned and walked up the hallway. "I am confident that you will do well tonight," he informed her as she fell into step beside him. "Only, remember to speak in Nrelnalnian. Also, do not address your clan head unless asked a direct question. Greet him, of course, and you will begin the greeting, but otherwise do not speak. Do exactly as the clan head and the minister instruct, however silly it may seem. Also, when they ask you to perform a task requiring a demonstration of your psychokinesis, show off your strength. Do exactly as they say, but do it in such a way as exceeds everyone's expectations. Only, be certain that you do not exceed the limits of your current skills. A slightly less powerful display is far less embarrassing than losing control of yourself. Am I clear?"

"Yes, Ruegon-Nagga," she replied at once, absorbing all of his advice.

He sighed heavily. "When we enter these doors, you will walk to the head of the room. There will be a chair waiting for you; do not sit upon it. Stand in front of it, looking out over the assembly. You will sit upon it once you have completed the ceremony."

"Where will you be?" Akinia asked, an anxious note to her voice.

His eyes narrowed slightly in amusement. "I will be in the assembly, watching, and wishing you fortune," he mused.

There wasn't time for anything else to be said as Ruegon pushed open a pair of large wooden doors, motioning for her to enter.

Akinia took a deep breath and then stepped through. Her eyes widened in amazements as she looked around. This hall was easily three times the size of the hall that the wedding ceremony took place in, and the walls and roof had been solidly plastered and painted a brilliant shade of white. It was so much different than the natural dirt and roots that filled the rest of the settlement!

Remembering Ruegon's instructions, Akinia slowly and purposefully walked up to the front of the room, ignoring the eyes of the three-hundred Nrell that had gathered for the occasion. She stopped in front of the chair, turning back to face the assembly, and then she waited.

One minute passed, and then two... five minutes... eight minutes... ten minutes...

Finally, just as Akinia began to wonder if they were coming at all, the Minister and another Nrell walked through the doors.

The entire assembly bowed their heads in respect as the Clan Head passed, so Akinia did likewise as he approached. She clasped her right hand to her left shoulder, and the Clan Head copied the movement. Akinia's jaw dropped slightly in shock as the Clan Head extended his arm to her, and then spoke.

"May peace reign in your heart, Akinia-Nagga," the Clan Head said slowly and purposefully, carefully annunciating each syllable.

Startled, she cast a nervous glance to Ruegon, who motioned for her to reply.

"May your mind stay sharp," she forced herself to reply. *Why did he address me first? Why the suffix Nagga?*

The Clan Head turned to the assembly. "This day, we gather to honor the union of the Devura clan with the Child of the Prophecy, set forth by the Nrell, Efgor, who was also of the clan, Devura. In accordance with the ancient traditions, the Devuran Council has assembled to name the line into which the Tribute shall be adopted. It has been decided that she will be joined in lineage, as in name, with the Mother of our race. As the first Akinia possesses no living heir, the Tribute shall become head of her family line."

What? Akinia thought to herself, shock flooding her. Her eyes searched through the crowd until she found Ruegon.

Even Ruegon seemed surprised.

The Minister cleared his throat. "If a grievance exists with this decision, let the aggrieved speak now," he called, his voice carrying through the chamber.

Silence was the only response.

"Very well," the Minister said after a few moments, nodding approvingly, "let us continue."

Just as Ruegon had predicted, the Minister and the Clan Head of Devura required demonstrations of her skills, both psychokinetic and with a wajun. Akinia was careful to show off as much as she could within the limits of their instructions and her own skill. In one of the demonstrations, she was instructed to manipulate water into a variety of constructs. In another, she was instructed to lift and manipulate multiple objects in various ways.

Finally, after hours of this, the Minister called the demonstrations to a halt. "Tribute Akinia, you have demonstrated great skill in every area which was required of you. You have passed," he said simply. Reaching out, he took Akinia's right hand, as well as the

311

Clan Head's upper right hand, in his. The Minister then placed their hands together, so that the marks on their palms lined up. Still holding their hands in his own, the Minister bowed his head. "It is done."

The pain that coursed through her mark was nearly unbearable, but it lasted only a moment. A liquid warmth coursed through her blood vessels, traveling up her arms and into her chest. Akinia could feel a wordless, voiceless approval in the back of her mind. It somehow felt like she was both alone in her thoughts, and being touched by another consciousness.

"I present Akinia, of the clan, Devura," the Minister announced loudly. "Let the celebration commence!"

Chapter 54:

"Najee Akinia," Ruegon called from outside of her room, early the next morning.

Akinia groggily pulled herself from her bed, quickly slipping the leather dress and leggings on. She paused a moment to scratch her sore Nrell-mark before strapping her wajun-belt around her waist and stepping out into the hallway. "May peace reign in your heart, Ruegon-Nagga," she greeted, her words slurring slightly as she struggled to blink the sleep from her eyes.

"May your mind stay sharp, Akinia-Nagga," he replied in kind.

Akinia intended to continue with the third line of the greeting, but only succeeded in yawning.

The old Nrell seemed amused, but he did not comment. "Come with me," he said simply.

The Najee nodded, forcing herself to match Ruegon's pace. She didn't bother to ask where they were going; the Nrell most likely wouldn't tell her. They walked for what seemed like hours, and Akinia was fully conscious by the time Ruegon slowed to a halt in front of a large set of double-doors that looked vaguely familiar...

Ruegon paused only a moment as he flicked his hand towards the doors, and a moment longer as they creaked open.

Suddenly, Akinia remembered why the doors looked so familiar. *The hanger!*

"This way," Ruegon said simply, walking towards the outer edge of the well-hidden hanger. He halted in front of a small, one-man shuttle. "This ship is fueled and loaded with supplies," he informed her. "It will get you to Paméd without any stops, and the Sigidians will not suspect it. Can you pilot a T-Frig system?"

"That's the system I learned on," Akinia informed him, grinning. *I'm going home!*

Ruegon smiled. "In which case, you may leave whenever you choose," he informed her. "At the same time, you may stay as long as you wish. Whichever you choose, the ship belongs to you; it is a gift from your clan."

"Mine?" Akinia echoed, her eyes widening. "Ruegon-Nagga, how do I thank them for this?"

"You do not; it would insult them," he corrected quickly. "It is tradition for a clan to give a generous gift to their adopted members upon completion of the ceremony."

Akinia hesitated a moment, and then nodded. "I see," she replied simply.

"Have you any idea how long you care to stay, now that you have your way to leave?" the old Nrell wondered.

"I must go as soon as I am able," Akinia admitted, grimacing. "The Najee are worried about me; the longer I stay away, the more worried they become, especially my family."

"I understand," the Nrell assured her. "Your presence will be missed in my family's hall."

Akinia bowed slightly. "I thank you for your hospitality. You and your clan have been very kind to me in my time of need," she thanked him.

Ruegon gave her a wry smile. "Our people protect their own; you would do well to remember that in your travels," he advised. "That mark is not just to distinguish our clans, it is to unify our people. Help will never be far."

Akinia returned his smile and bowed again. "I had best leave now, Ruegon-Nagga," she hesitantly admitted, glancing at the shuttle.

"No, you had best enjoy one last meal with us before you go. It is best not to venture on an empty stomach," he corrected. "Come, it will not delay your journey too long."

Her smile widening, Akinia nodded. "You are right," she agreed. "I can never repay your kindness, both in caring for me, and in teaching me."

"Fulfill the prophecy; that will be payment enough," the Nrell asserted gently.

Chapter 55:

The tawny brown of Paméd's surface, dotted here and there by glints of silver, came into view as the shuttle left hyper-space. *I'm home!* Akinia breathed, scarcely daring to imagine it was true. She didn't move for several long minutes, half afraid she might wake up and find herself still in Sigadia. Finally, though, she knew she had to land and report in.

She quickly flipped the comm-device on, frowning as she heard the electronic voice of the automatic system, rather than the voices of the Najee usually on guard. They worked in teams, she knew, to ensure that someone was always present to watch the system and control access. *Where are they?* she wondered as she typed Ko-Pau's admittance code onto the keypad.

"Code confirmed," the electronic voice announced a moment later, "direct your vessel to the landing field."

The shuttle was a bit more difficult to manage than her fighter, and a lot more difficult than the *Hailing Comet*. It fought against her a bit as she passed into the atmosphere of Paméd. "Ow!" she complained to herself as the shuttle roughly landed, hitting her arms against the control panel.

She rubbed her arms, scowling at the control panel. She glanced up and the furrows in her brow deepened as she realized that no other ships were taking off or landing. In fact, the entire landing field was unusually still and quiet. No preparations were underway, no ships were disembarking; it seemed as though Paméd were deserted. "Where is everyone?" she wondered aloud.

She quickly pushed herself to her feet and darted to the back of the ship. A small voice in the back of her mind seemed to whisper, *Could it be Jade?* She snatched the black cloak from the chair where she had thrown it and whipped it around her shoulders. *Enough, Akinia,* she chastised herself as she fastened the cloak on, *that's ridiculous!*

She pulled the hood up around her head, letting the hem drape over her face enough to disguise her features; if it was Jade, or even if it wasn't, no one could know she was here until she found Lo-Kí. Pausing at the doorway a moment to take a deep, fortifying breath, she forced herself to push the disturbing thoughts away. *There must be a simple explanation*, she mused, wishing she believed herself. Shaking her head to clear it, she snapped, *Enough, Akinia! Just go and find Lo-Kí!*

She psychokinetically opened the door and hesitantly stepped out. Inhaling deeply, she enjoyed the familiar dusty-grass smell. *I have missed this place!* Her heart swelled in excited anticipation as she thought of Ko-Pau, Khee-Lá, and Nath; yet at the same time, the caution and fear she had learned to trust told her to keep her mind clear until she knew what was happening.

She searched with her eyes, afraid to extend her thoughts, as she navigated the winding corridors of ships and shuttles. A place that once held noise and excitement was now completely bare of living creatures. One thing that *did* reassure her was the fact that every ship seemed prepped to go; there were no supplies waiting to be loaded, no off-loaded supplies waiting to be taken to holding, and no fighters rolled outside to be repaired.

Have missions been suspended? she wondered, that being the only explanation she could find. She jumped, her hand on her wajun, as a pair of Lyndop children, no more than twelve years old, darted across the pathway in front of her. Her heart was racing and her eyes wide as she tried to calm herself again. A smile crossed her lips as she realized they were playing. *Lo-Kí must be keeping the Najee here... but why?*

The children hadn't seemed to notice her, so Akinia continued towards the base. She glanced over her shoulder as she reached the small secondary entrance she normally used, hoping for another glimpse of the two children, or anyone, for that matter. Sighing, she cracked the door open and peeked inside. The hallway was empty, but this one normally was. *You can look at the statues later*, she chastised herself as she paused to finger an intricately carved bird she had always been fond of. *You must find Lo-Kí!*

Shaking her head to clear it, she forced herself to keep moving. She followed the winding corridors through the base, finally arriving at the more populated ones. A handful of Apprentices were walking here and there, but none of them recognized her, and she didn't recognize

316

any of them. *I wonder...*

As this new thought struck her, Akinia closed her eyes and concentrated. *What did Ruegon say? Oh, right!* It was with a large measure of pride and satisfaction that Akinia opened her eyes again and reached with her thoughts for the nearest Apprentice, a young Adamian girl near her own age. She had no fear of touching the girl's thoughts, because she had used one of the many tricks Ruegon had taught her during their lessons: how to block her mind from being felt, just as she had subconsciously done in the Aftarn Trance.

How long will Master be in Council? the girl complained. Here Akinia saw a brief image of a scruffy Dwarvian man, which she assumed to be the girl's Master. *Every day, he just sits there and talks about who-knows-what with the other Masters... We should be home by now! He promised to take me home!*

She dug a little deeper, hoping to find a reason for the suspension of the trip, but couldn't find anything. Akinia pulled away a moment later, satisfied she hadn't been detected. *I've never felt a more egocentric tone in anyone's mind,* she mused, amazed. The girl's complaints may not have been unreasonable, but there was a distinct air of selfishness that permeated them... it was almost nauseating! *Well,* she decided, *it isn't my problem. Now I know where to find Lo-Ki!*

Her pace quickened as she navigated the vaguely familiar halls. She had been to the Council Room only once, and that had been near the beginning of her life as a Najee. She had seen the path often enough in Ko-Pau and Khee-Lá's thoughts, however, to have a pretty firm idea of the direction she should go. *I found it!* she happily announced to herself as she turned down a short hallway that led only to one set of doors.

She paused for a moment just outside of the doors. She lowered the hood of her cloak, wishing she had taken the time to fix her hair, and then laughed at herself for being so shallow. *They aren't going to care if your hair is a mess, Akinia! They'll be happy to see you alive,* she reminded herself, amazed at the necessity. Even so, she took a moment to smooth her dress and fluff her hair to where it looked halfway decent, wondering all the while if she should knock or just go in.

After a moment, she raised her hand and knocked; there was no reply. She tried again, but the masters were unable to hear her over the noise of their arguments. Feeling her stomach twist with nervousness, she opened the door just wide enough to slip inside.

That got their attention.

Her name was shouted and gasped across the room as the assembled Masters recognized her. Glancing around anxiously, she searched until she caught sight of Khee-Lá and Ko-Pau. It was only then that she noticed Nath was sitting beside them. *He's a Full Najee!*

Her amazement at that realization stunned her. A moment later, when she was able to think again, she glanced up at Lo-Kí. His amazed expression, matching what she was feeling, caused a smile to creep onto her lips. She met his gaze, wondering if she should say something.

Before she could decide, Lo-Kí announced, "The Council is dismissed. We will resume tomorrow at 13:00."

Akinia turned to leave, excited to see Ko-Pau, Khee-Lá, and Nath again, while at the same time scared what their reaction to her long disappearance may be; but as Lo-Kí called to her, she found herself having to push her excitement and worry both away.

"You stay, Akinia. I wish to speak with you privately."

She turned back to face him, taking a moment to smile at each of the Masters that placed a hand on her and expressed their thankfulness for her safe return as they passed. Khee-Lá kissed her forehead, and Ko-Pau and Nath both hugged her, but none of them spoke a word.

Finally, after several minutes, the enormous crowd dissipated, leaving only Akinia and Lo-Kí. He motioned to her with a single finger and she quickly made her way over to stand near him.

She sat in one of the chairs.

"Where have you been?" he asked.

Akinia opened her mouth as though to speak, but stopped, remembering her promise. She closed her mouth and averted her gaze, hoping Lo-Kí would understand that she couldn't answer.

He regarded her for a moment before reaching over and grabbing her right hand. He flipped it, palm up, and nodded. "As I thought," he said simply.

"What?" Akinia asked, pretending to be oblivious to anything on her hand, just in case it wasn't the mark he referred to.

"Don't pretend not to know, Akinia. I can see the mark," Lo-Kí ordered.

"But how?" she managed. Hadn't the Nrell told her that only the Nrell and those who bore the mark themselves could see it? Her eyes automatically leapt to his gloved hands. He slowly peeled the fingerless glove off of his right hand, revealing a mark similar, but not identical, to Akinia's.

"I have sought refuge with them on many occasions, but we must keep this between the two of us. No one else knows of my mark, and they mustn't know of yours either," he warned.

"How many of us have been marked?" she asked curiously.

"Only a small handful, perhaps a half-dozen or so. But this is departing from the issue," Lo-Kí said, "I assume that they have worked with you and taught you how to hone your abilities. What all did they show you?"

She took a deep breath and said in Nrelnalnian, "If I were to list it all, we would still be here by time tomorrow's Council meeting abated. But I've been taught at least the fundamentals of everything that the Nrell have ever discovered the ability to perform. Some things they warned me not to show anyone because, if attempted, the amount of strength and power required would kill most Najee."

Lo-Kí's eyes brightened. "And are you afraid of your powers, now?" he asked, slipping into the ancient language of the Nrell as well.

Akinia hesitated. "I am, but I'm no longer afraid that I'll hurt anyone without meaning to. The Nrell taught me how to shield my mind before I go to sleep so that I can't extend unless I consciously remove the block. They also taught me how to block my mind so that no one can sense it, like I did in the Aftarn Trance," she replied, returning her speech to Main.

"Might I have a demonstration of that?" he asked, once again following her lead on the language.

She nodded once and focused for a minute as she struggled to put up the block. Once she was satisfied it was in place, she motioned for Lo-Kí to try and touch her thoughts.

Lo-Kí extended his mind towards hers. He frowned as he stretched farther and farther, groping with his mind, and still felt nothing. His frown was replaced with a pleased smile as he pulled his mind back into itself.

"I can't hold it for very long," she admitted. "Ruegon, the Nrell that taught me, told me that I had to keep practicing the various blocks so that my strength would grow. He said that it would take a while, but eventually I'd be able to keep it up for hours or even days at a time without thinking about it. Right now I can only keep it up for a few minutes." Another thought entered her mind as she considered the Nrell and the Najee, and she could feel her face drop into a worried grimace. *Should I tell him?*

Lo-Kí regarded her for a moment. "If I am to judge by your expression and your hesitation, you are also about to tell me that they informed you of the other Children of the Prophecy. Am I correct?"

"Yes, Master Lo-Kí," she admitted, nodding slowly. She could feel the fear creeping up from the pit of her stomach, and wondered if Lo-Kí could see it as strongly as she felt it.

His face twisted into a mask of concern and he stared at her intently. "I want you to listen to me, Akinia, and I want you to listen carefully: there can only be one *true* Child of the Prophecy. The other children he referred to were *possibles*. This means that they had the *potential* to fulfill the prophecy, though there was uncertainty as to whether or not they were the *true* children. The fates they met and the choices they made removed all doubt and led us to know that they were not the one intended to fulfill the prophecy. You, however, have already fulfilled portions of it.

"'Two halves of a whole life, once separated by pain and strife, reunited grow thrice as powerful'. You were born a princess, and also a Najee, but when your parents were killed and you were hidden in the orphanage, your life was separated. You were left only with the Najee half of yourself. When you discovered your true identity as Queen Leonora's daughter that was also the time your psychokinetic strength grew so drastically strong. You see, the first portion of the prophecy has already been fulfilled. That is more than any of the other children could say.

"This leads us, meaning myself and the Gifted Ones, to believe firmly that you are the *true* Child of the Prophecy. You are the one Efgor spoke of when he wrote this prophecy those many millennia ago. Do not fear that something will stop you from accomplishing your destiny, yet do not grow overconfident and become reckless. Trust in yourself and know that you have the ability to fulfill this destiny. Their fate is *not* yours," he promised.

Akinia was overcome for a moment with a relief so profound that her eyes filled with tears for a moment before she blinked the haze away. "Thank you," she managed to whisper.

Lo-Kí smiled. "Now go and rest and reunite with your loved ones. We will speak more in a few days, but for now you need to recover. Go," he bade pleasantly.

Akinia hesitated before hugging him and quickly darting off.

Lo-Kí smiled as he watched her go, his eyes twinkling with delight. *She has grown so much from the child I first saw,* he sighed to himself. *She has finally become a warrior worth Akinia's mighty name. May the fortune of warriors smile upon you, little one!*

Chapter 56:

"You're choking me," Akinia gasped as Ko-Pau and Khee-Lá crushed her in a hug, threatening to cut off the air to her lungs.

"Don't you ever do anything like that again!" Khee-Lá growled, pulling away to look at her before pulling her back into another tight hug.

Ko-Pau voiced his agreement. "I knew I should never have let you go."

"It was never your decision," she corrected softly. "And I'm glad I went."

Nath watched, a bit amused, with his arms crossed. "It is so nice to hear them griping at someone else for a change," he sighed with satisfaction.

Akinia stuck her tongue out at him. "Let me show you why you'll never get me to regret going," she offered, pulling back from them slightly.

They lowered the barriers around their minds, thinking she was going to touch their thoughts and perhaps share a memory, but they gasped as every loose possession in Akinia's room simultaneously rose into the air.

"I had a lot of time to work out my difficulties," she explained with a laugh as she sent the objects flying in a completely controlled manner across her room, each moving and traveling in a different direction. "I'm not afraid anymore."

Khee-Lá and Ko-Pau watched with pride for a moment more before she returned the objects to their original locations, not appearing to have grown any weaker for her efforts.

Nath grinned and shook his head. "I gotta say, Kiddo," he teased, "you're something else!"

I've missed you, my dear brother, she sighed, carefully

shielding the contact from her uncle and Master.

I've missed you, too, Sis, he replied earnestly, gently brushing her thoughts in return.

"You could have done that here," Ko-Pau noted solemnly, though his eyes were bright with delight at her newfound control and power.

"Actually I couldn't have," she disagreed. "I would never have allowed myself to use my abilities here, not when it placed you in danger. I needed the solitude."

"We can argue about this until the end of time, but what's done is done, and she is home safely," Khee-Lá sighed a moment later.

Ko-Pau winked at Akinia, "Did you ever think your uncle would be the one encouraging us not to argue?"

"I can't say that I did," she grinned.

Nath cleared his throat. "Do I ever get a hug, or are you just going to keep teasing Master Khee-Lá?"

Akinia pulled away from her Master and uncle. She darted the few steps to Nath and wrapped her arms around his neck.

He picked her up by the waist and swung her around a couple of times before setting her down and pulling her into a tight hug. "Now that's more like it," he teased.

She swatted his arm and pulled away. "Can we get something to eat? I'm starving!" she asked.

"Well, dinner is still a couple of hours away, but I see no reason anyone would protest to feeding you," Ko-Pau teased.

"Good," she grinned. "Now you three get out and let me change. I'll be out in five minutes," she ordered, waving them all towards the door. As the door shut behind them, she darted into her closet and pulled down one of her favorite halter-top dresses, the dark green floor-length, and quickly changed into it. She ran the brush through her hair, though it took a bit longer than she had thought it would, and slipped her shoes on as she walked back out to the main area of her room. Pausing a moment, she looked around her room at all of her things. It was good to be home!

"I'm ready," she announced as she joined them in the hallway.

Khee-Lá wordlessly offered her his arm, which she readily accepted, and led her to the Dining Hall.

Masters and Apprentices crowded the hallways as they walked, each wanting to get a look at her, to touch her arm and express their thanks for her safe return. She smiled and replied to each of their greetings, touching each of their hands in turn, with a calm patience that she felt Katarina and her mother would be proud of.

When they finally made it to the Dining Hall, Nath ordered her to sit while he got her tray.

"You're spoiling me," she warned with a grin as she turned to find a seat.

The greetings and words of encouragement came just as steadily, and dozens of Masters and Apprentices made their way to her table to speak with her for a moment. She knew very few of their faces, and none of their names, but greeted them all with the same casual familiarity and innocent grace she showed to her close friends.

Conversation with Nath and Ko-Pau and Khee-Lá was impossible due to this. Every moment that she could avoid speaking, she was filling her mouth with food. More and more people streamed in, hoping to have a moment of Akinia's time.

I am going to hide in my room for the next week, starting as soon as I finish this last bite, she warned her three companions.

I do not blame you, Nath laughed.

Akinia, there is a package in my room for you. It was sent to you, in my care, from a mutual acquaintance while you were in Sigadia. Why don't you go and get it before you retire? Khee-Lá suggested.

Alright, she agreed with a smile, wondering who it could be from. She gave a wordless apology to them each before pulling her mind away and hiding it under thick barriers. There were too many eager minds hovering around them for her to comfortably keep her thoughts linked with them. She could have blocked their conversation from eavesdroppers, but didn't feel like explaining how she had learned to do that. Hiding her thoughts was simply easier.

"Goodnight," Khee-Lá murmured, a sentiment which was soon echoed by Ko-Pau and Nath.

"I'll probably fall asleep as soon as I lay down, and I may not wake until late tomorrow," she cautioned.

"Long trip?" Nath guessed.

"Long, lonely, anxious, etcetera, etcetera," she laughed as she stood. "Goodnight."

"Akinia," Ko-Pau called as she started to walk away.

"Yes?"

He smiled. "Welcome home."

Smiling, she inclined her head. "I'm glad to be home," she replied earnestly before turning again to leave. By the time she got to Khee-Lá's room her patience was wearing a bit thin, but she remained polite and friendly. She let out a sigh of relief as the door closed behind her, and set out to look for the package.

She no sooner glanced around the room than she noticed a large package with a short note attached to the top. After making certain this was the package Khee-Lá had mentioned, she pulled the note off and read:

Princess Akinia Juntoby-Zanoratta,

Please accept these tokens of appreciation for the friendship you have shown me these past years. I hope that you will enjoy them! I wish that I could write more, but at this time I find myself quite occupied with matters of business. I will contact you shortly after you return from your mission, at which time you will be reading this letter. Your uncle, Prince Khee-Lá Emmeda-Juntoby, will send word to me when you return, so you needn't concern yourself with that.
Until then, my dear friend,
-Princess Alania Princeshian

Akinia gasped with delight as she finally discovered who had sent this to her. She read the letter once more before folding it up, tucking it under her arm, and reaching for the box with her mind. Though the majority of the weight was lifted with her mind, she supported the base of the box in her arms as though she carried it. In this manner she walked out of the room. Very few people stopped her, seeing the load she carried, and so the trip to her own room was very short.

She could hardly wait to open the box, which was very large, but instead she set it on her bed and went through her nightly routine. When she returned to the main area of her room, she clambered onto her bed and eagerly ripped open the box.

In the very top was a small, purple silk throw pillow covered in tea stained beaded lace. Akinia's eyes widened as she pulled it out and gently fingered the adornments. It was beautiful! Carefully setting in beside her, she turned her attention to the other items in the box.

She frowned as she pulled out a large bundle of fabric that

326

looked large enough to consist of several thick blankets. When she unrolled it, however, she let out a cry of surprise as she realized that it was the most beautiful gown she had ever seen! The entire gown was made of delicate pale blue silk and trimmed in white lace. The off-set sleeves would fit tightly down her arms, edged with lace cuffs that would cover her entire hand. The sweetheart neckline was also trimmed with a thin border of lace and a beautiful pink flower the size of her fist was nestled between her breasts. The bodice was tightly fitted with a low-cut waist. The skirt was very full and gathered, with a thick, built-in, lace petticoat beneath it. None of her old gowns could hope to match this one!

"Oh, Alania!" she gasped, resolving to ask her aunt what a proper response to such extravagant gifts would be. Carefully folding the gown back up, she laid it in her lap while she extracted the last gift from the box, all the while amazed at the princess's generosity.

The last of the presents from the box was a beautiful silver tea service, large enough to serve eight people, with a large teapot, sugar bowl, honey dish, nectar decanter, and creamer, all of which rested on a large silver platter detailed in a matching pattern. Akinia's hands shook as she lifted it out, and her breath caught in her chest as she hardly dared to believe that it was *hers*!

Tears streamed from her eyes as she looked at the beautiful gifts, overcome with emotion for the woman that cared so deeply for her. Ever so carefully, she carried the gown to her closet and placed it on an empty clothes hanger. It took her a moment to clear enough space for the gown to hang, and then she admired it for a moment longer before returning to the main area of her room. She placed the tea service on a small desk on the corner of her room, resolving to re-activate Jaynine in the morning and tell him the good news: Paméd's 'inadequate' dishes would no longer have to suffice!

Alania, my dear friend...how will I ever thank you?

Psychokinetically turning her light off, she climbed into bed and quickly curled beneath her blankets. She clutched the small throw pillow in her arms and fell asleep holding it close to her chest.

Chapter 57:

"What's this?" Akinia asked the next afternoon as she sat down beside Ko-Pau. She took the datapad from his hands and quickly scanned over it.

"Give me that," he ordered, laughing as he snatched it back. "It's this week's news reports. The public's version, anyway. I guess I should be used to how much they change these stories by now."

"Change?"

"Yes," he nodded. "They always change the stories so as not to worry the public, that or to make them more excited over something that was not really that dramatic. Here, read this one." He handed the datapad to her and she read:

A Rescue Mission

When a Najee child was captured and held for questioning by Jade Enbrilth, the Najee Council of Masters immediately arranged a rescue. It is reported that two Najee Masters and one Apprentice were sent in to rescue the fourteen-year-old girl. It would seem that Jade Enbrilth was not present at the aforementioned rescue, since all four Najee made it out of the base alive. The rescued Apprentice was injured, but there is no word as to whether or not she will recover. It is assumed that she is someone of importance, as this is only the second rescue of its kind to be attempted on the Najee Council's order.

The Najee Council made no comment, but Princess Alania can be quoted as saying, "The Imperial Council is relieved to hear that this Apprentice has survived her time in Jade Enbrilth's power, and is grateful to the Najee Council for rescuing her. We hope that her recovery is swift and that nothing of this sort occurs again."

At that point the story shifted to speculation of how this rescue would affect the war, and how Emperor Hurnith and Jade Enbrilth would respond to the Najee Council's 'brazen attack'.

Akinia rolled her eyes and passed the datapad back to her Master. "Why are they only writing about it this week? It's been months since that happened," she wondered.

"They didn't, I just used this old story as a comparison for you. They provide basic details, make it look as though they know something, and then spoon feed it to their readers. They are only guessing at your importance, and only guessing at the details. The official Najee report stated only that a female Apprentice of fourteen years old was captured, and that two Masters and an Apprentice retrieved her from one of Jade's bases. And from that they speculated that Jade was not present, you were someone of great importance, that you were injured, that you were held for questioning, and if you read all the way to the end they also speculate that you are a close acquaintance of Princess Alania," he shrugged, continuing to read.

"If they get everything so wrong, then why do you read them?"

"Because I like to know what the public is saying and thinking about certain stories, and since they say and think pretty much whatever the media reports tell them to, it's the easiest way of determining what's being said," he explained. "Their speculations were not too far off track here, but most of the time stories are either completely ignored or they are shifted greatly enough that you have to truly know what you are reading to correlate it to the actual event."

Akinia nodded. "And here I always thought I was getting the real story," she grimaced.

"Well, you got a better picture than you would have, seeing as how you hacked your way into the media reports hidden from the eyes of you innocent little orphans," he laughed. "Would you like me to get the media reports sent to you? I'll have to get you a datapad, but I've been meaning to get you a birthday present anyway. Do you realize that you will be sixteen in three days?"

"Really? I thought it was still a month off!" she said, amazed.

"That's because the headmistress under-estimated your age when you were abandoned. She thought you were two months, remember? You were three months. You'll be sixteen in three days and we are going to go and celebrate," he decided.

"Celebrate how?"

"Well, the traditions of my homeworld make a girl's sixteenth birthday a very special occasion. Other than the seventeenth birthday, when they come of age, the sixteenth is the only birthday truly celebrated," he explained. "Usually the entire family and a few close friends join together and have cakes, give the girl gifts, and play games. Pretty much it becomes a once-in-a-lifetime holiday."

"Why is it so important? I mean, you said seventeenth is the year they come of age there," she wondered.

He grinned. "It is an old tradition, from the days when a girl came of age at sixteen. Of course, that's been several centuries, but everyone loved the sixteenth birthday celebration so much it disappointed them to wait another year. Now the sixteenth birthday serves as a celebration of her last birthday as a child. On Náto, you come of age at eighteen, but they tend to celebrate every birthday. I wouldn't blame you if you wanted to go home, but if you didn't feel like a planet-wide celebration, the four of us could just go and celebrate by ourselves?"

"Mmm, sounds good. Of course, Uncle Khee-Lá may have other plans already. You two work it out, Nath and I will go along with whatever," she decided.

Ko-Pau gave her a wry smile. "Such a diplomatic answer... Katarina would be so proud of you."

Akinia snorted. "Just read the biased media reports," she ordered teasingly, motioning towards his datapad.

"Well, whichever we end up doing, I *will* buy you a datapad for your birthday. They have a new model you'll absolutely love. I had probably better find Khee-Lá and see what we're doing so I know how I'm supposed to get it," he mused, standing and walking away.

Laughing, Akinia quickly swallowed the last couple bites of her breakfast. She tried to stop smiling as she swallowed the last of her drink, but her stomach quivered with excitement. She had always wanted a datapad of her own, but the only ones she had ever been able to use were property of the orphanage or property of the Najee as a whole. Twice she had used Ko-Pau's datapad, which was much nicer than any other she had used, but to have one of her own?

She bit the corner of her lips in her excitement. Even Ko-Pau's datapad had been a year old when she had used it the first time, and that had been nearly two standard years ago. Now she was going to get a brand new model? Her mind reeled as she imagined the speed, and the features that must be included.

"Hey, Akinia!" a familiar voice called.

Akinia looked up, surprised to see that she had already gotten outside of the Dining Hall. She had been so lost in her thoughts that she hadn't realized she had left her table. "Laani?" she questioned, startled, as she recognized the voice. She turned to see the green-skinned Lyndop girl running down the hallway towards her.

"Hey, I heard you were back," she grinned as she came to a halt. She grabbed Akinia left arm in a forearm embrace with her own, holding it for a moment before releasing it.

"I can't believe you're here," Akinia gasped. "I thought you were on a mission?"

"Ha! Not quite. I was home, can't you tell? I haven't had a chance to change," she grinned, motioning to her clothes.

Akinia stepped back to look at Laani's outfit. The top looked like vines, twisting and curving in an intricate pattern hanging around her neck. The vines wound and swirled into an almost solid cover over each of her breasts before snaking away and curving around behind her back. Every so often along the vines a small green leaf, shriveled from having been away from its roots for so long, was apparent.

The skirt was a pale yellow cloth wrapped around her waist. A pleated rectangle of fabric hung down to her knees from the waistband in the front and back, tapering into a rounded end at the bottom. More of the vines that formed her shirt wound around her waist three times before weaving in and out of the pleated hangings, forming more of the same intricate swirling patterns that the straps of the blouse had made across her skin.

On her feet were shoes that looked as though leaves had been pressed together and dried, becoming about a quarter-inch thick throughout. More of the same vines wound up from the sides of the sole to wrap across her feet before twisting and curving around her ankles and up her legs, stopping at her knees.

Her hair, usually wildly twisting and sticking out in all directions, was pulled back into a tight plait down the back of her skull. It was held tight by more vines that seemed to twist in and out of her hair from the beginning of her hairline down to the tip of the braid.

"Wow," Akinia laughed, looking her over, "I don't think I've ever seen you in that before."

"Well, I haven't gone home in some time, and whenever I get back you're usually away," Laani grinned. "Come on, I want to get out of this but I don't want you to get away. You're coming with me."

Laughing, Akinia let Laani grab her hand and drag her down the maze of hallways and to Laani's room.

Akinia gasped in shock as they entered. The walls gave off an appearance of rough wood, and vines like the ones Laani wore wound around it, their leaves large and full with deep blue veins crisscrossing the fuzzy surfaces. Several small pots of soil set here and there along the bottom edge of the wall seemed to be the source of the vines. The floor looked and felt like moss, she noted as she bent down to stroke it. The bed seemed to be a large red-brown fungus with a quilt of leaves draped over the top of it; more moss formed semi-flat pillows on one edge of the oblong bed.

"This is amazing," she breathed, still gazing around in wonder.

"We're allowed to personalize our rooms," Laani shrugged. "Haven't you gotten yours yet?"

"Um, not really," she managed, now seeing the wide branches crisscrossing the roof, their papery brown bark peeling in places to reveal ebony-white boughs.

"You should. I picked this out soon after I got here, with Nath's help. He thought if I made my room remind me of home I'd get less homesick and less depressed."

"Did it work?"

"For the homesickness, but when I'm depressed very little cheers me up anyway so I kept it," she shrugged. "The only part of his advice that day I didn't listen to was wearing this all the time. Ledenellian fashion has lost its appeal since I started seeing clothing from other cultures."

"I can understand that, but I really do like that outfit, though," she promised her friend, assuming Laani was referring to her homeworld. "How do you get it off and on?"

Laani grinned. "Look here in the back," she said, turning around to let Akinia see. "The vines back here, two around my neck and three on my mid-back, well they aren't actually a whole vine like they look. Each one breaks apart in the middle. One side is hollow, the other side is carved to be more slender, and so they hold together. See?"

"That's cool. I've never seen anything like that before," Akinia mused, fingering the connections where she could just see the hairline fissures that marked the joint.

"Have I ever told you about Ledenell?" Laani wondered, thinking back over their conversations.

"No," Akinia replied instantly, shaking her head. "Is that your homeworld?"

Laani nodded, grinning, as she walked into her closet. She left the door open, but Akinia remained well away from it to give her friend some privacy. "Yeah, it's great. The trees there are enormous, some are well over twelve-thousand feet tall. The bases will be a mile wide or more, depending on how the tree grew. There are several different cities on the ground, but the majority of them are centered in hollowed Ancients," she stuck her head out of the closet, "That's what we call the *really* big trees," she explained before pulling her head back in.

"They *must* be ancient to be that large," Akinia murmured, her eyes widening at the thought.

"Well, our atmosphere is much higher than that of most other planets. On most planets, the trees can't grow that tall because there just isn't enough room for them to grow. Actually, we have such a large atmosphere that you can breathe almost as easily on the top of the ancients as you can towards the bottom. I prefer the tops, since the air is so thick down below. I rarely walk on the ground when I'm there," Laani explained.

She walked back out of her closet, now wearing a pair of tight black pants and a red strapless top. Her feet were bare. "When the Ancients get past a hundred years of age or so, they hollow themselves out. My people live in the living trees. It's actually quite amazing when you think about it, especially when so many planets have switched to artificial buildings. They destroy the landscape to put up a substitute for nature's providence, and my people think it's horrible."

"I'd love to see it someday," Akinia sighed.

"I'd love to see Náto," Laani laughed. "I've heard that it's beautiful."

Akinia smiled. "It's the most beautiful place I've ever seen," she sighed.

"Well then here's what we'll do," Laani decided, "Once we are Full Najee, we'll celebrate by taking two months off to visit each other's homeworlds."

"Sounds good to me," Akinia grinned. "But if we're going to get that much time off, we'd probably better keep our vacations short for the next few years."

"Probably," Laani agreed, sighing. "So have you killed Nath yet?"

"Actually, not yet. I came close, though."

Laani laughed. "Maybe one day you'll get him."

"Maybe," Akinia agreed, smirking.

The girls feel silent for a few moments, still smiling at one another, relieved to be back together. After a moment they sat down heavily on Laani's bed.

"How long are you staying?" Akinia asked quietly, not wanting to think about being apart from her anytime soon.

"I don't know," she sighed. "Master still isn't back from her visit home, and she'll want to rest for a few days before heading back to the front. It could be a while, or it could be the end of the week. There's really no way to tell. By the way, where is Rofa? She couldn't be separated from you last I saw her."

"Oh, she's probably doing one of three things: bugging Nath, following Skyler, or sitting around the Dining Hall begging for food. She's getting rather good at pretending I don't feed her," Akinia mused dryly.

"Can you call her? I'd love to see how much she's grown."

"She's quite a bit taller. Her back is slightly above my waist. According to the references I've been able to find, her growth will slow down about now. She'll be seven or eight standard years before she finishes growing. By then her back will be even with my shoulders, give or take a few inches."

Laani let out a low whistle. "Will you be able to keep her still?"

"Lo-Kí said it's alright, so long as I have her firmly in hand. He was telling me about a special saddle that people who raise Ceffres developed. Once she's almost six her back will be about even with my shoulder and then she'll be able to carry me around. Of course, as fast as she runs I'm not sure if I want to ride her," Akinia grinned. She reached out with her mind, trying to find the cub, and was surprised to find her asleep in her room. *Wake up, silly. Laani wants to see you. Come and find me*, she called softly. She could feel Rofa's eager response.

Laani laughed. "I doubt I'd want to ride her, either."

Akinia grinned and telepathically opened the door. A moment later Rofa bounded in excitedly. "Calm, Rofa," Akinia said firmly, backing up the order with a mental reprimand.

The cub immediately became still and lowered her head apologetically. A soft and dejected whimper escaped her lips.

"You're not sorry, and you know it," Akinia chastised, kissing the cub on her forehead. She rubbed down Rofa's spine, and then traced down each of her hind legs before rubbing down her chest and onto her single front leg.

Laani approached slowly, not wanting to excite her, and gently entwined her fingers into Rofa's thick black hair. She walked down the side Akinia wasn't standing on and traced down her backbone as Akinia had done. As she got to the base of Rofa's long, bald tail, her hand closed around it and felt down to the tapered tip. She laughed when a shiver raced down Rofa's spine. "You are a silly thing, aren't you?" she asked, returning to trace the planes of the cub's face.

"Did you ever have a pet, before you came to the Najee, I mean?" Akinia asked curiously as she absentmindedly flopped Rofa's large limp ears back and forth.

Laani shook her head. "No. Do you remember me telling you my parents knew that I would be a Najee as an infant, and didn't want to get too attached to me? Well, they would never let me have pets or anything that they would have to care for when I left. My brother had a Chicher Ape, though. It was adorable. I'd play with it when my parents were gone. They didn't want me to get too close to my brother, either."

Uncertain how to respond, Akinia asked, "What's a Chicher Ape?"

"Well, they're about the size of a three-year old child, except with four arms and four legs. They have six eyes, on each side of their face they have one large one and two progressively smaller ones that set on a diagonal to the outside of their heads. They have small twisted ears set on the sides of their heads just below their chins. They have two mouths, a smaller one just above the larger one, and their noses look like a squashed fruit with about two-dozen tiny nostrils. They have long tails with a thick tuft of purple fur on the very end. They don't have fur anywhere else, but their skin is dark red with black swirls on it. They're native to our planet and pretty common pets," she explained, using her fingers to map out the ape's features on her own face.

Akinia nodded, trying to picture the ape in her mind. It sounded pretty cute, except for its nose.

"I didn't tell you the most important thing that happened while I was home," Laani said casually, still gently rubbing Rofa's face.

"What?" Akinia asked curiously. She could see pleasure in her best friend's face, and hear a note of excitement hidden in her voice.

"My little brother, the one I wasn't supposed to get too attached to, but did anyway, showed me that he could hear my thoughts. I guess my prying into his mind kind of woke up his telepathy early, and now he knows he's going to be joining me soon," she explained happily. "Poor kid was scared to death when he realized we would be a Najee, since mother and father were so horrible when I was. He made me swear not to tell them."

"When will he come?" Akinia asked. "How old is he?"

"Well, right now he's eleven. I'm hoping no one finds him until I'm a Full Najee next year, and then I'll take him," she whispered urgently. "I'm really hoping that he isn't found until I'm a Master, and then I'll try to get him as my Apprentice."

"But isn't there a rule…"

"Against family training family? Yes, but I was never allowed to be around him so I'm hoping they'll make an exception since I don't even know him," she admitted, still whispering.

"Laani, I," Akinia began before pausing. "If they would, don't you think they would have made the exception for Khee-Lá to train me?"

"Kinny, I know it's a long shot, but I have to try. I know you're an only child, but think about that girl at the orphanage, Charlotte, wasn't it? If she became a Najee you'd want her, right? It's the same thing. Yeah, I share blood with him, but I've never been his sibling. Our parents never allowed that. He's like any other little boy I know there, and I would take any child from my village. I want him, more desperately than you can imagine.

"I don't want him because I want to protect him, I want him because I want to know him. I want to speak to him more than once a year, under close supervision by our parents. I want to know what he likes, how he speaks, how he behaves. Even when I lived with him, I only interacted with him once or twice without mother or father being right there overtop of us. He's not my brother, he's just another little boy from my home world, and I hate that," she finished, sighing.

Akinia walked around Rofa to embrace her friend. "I know," she murmured, "I just don't want to see you hurt if they refuse, which is very likely."

"I do have a favor to ask you, though," Laani said sheepishly,

337

pulling back to look at Akinia. "If they don't let me have him, will you take him? That way I'll still see him and be near him."

"I would, you know I would, but I can't," Akinia apologized, swallowing a rising lump as she saw her friend's dejected face. "Laani, I had a lot of time to think while I was in Sigadia. I won't be taking an Apprentice, not until I've killed Jade and Lokita. I can't put a child in danger like that, and I can't give Jade and Lokita another handhold to grab to when they try to force me to surrender. If they weren't in the picture, you know that I would take him in a heartbeat for you. I can't put us, or him, in that dangerous position. It wouldn't be fair to either of you, or to me."

Laani sighed and nodded. "I understand," she promised, not quite smiling. "I should have thought about that myself, but I can't even imagine not taking an apprentice. Ever since I got here, that's been the goal to work for. I should have known you would have been taught different goals, what with the prophecy and everything."

Akinia gave her a wry smile. "It will work out alright. I'm certain that, even if you don't get permission to train him, whoever does will surely let you be with him. It's wrong to keep family apart too much, everyone I know seems to be of that same consensus. It will work out alright."

"Thanks," Laani smiled, "I hope you're right."

"I'm always right," Akinia teased. "So have you heard from Master Junop lately?"

"Not for a couple of weeks. She doesn't contact me much when we're visiting our homeworlds. So is everyone in your group still conscious? No one in the medical ward?"

Akinia rolled her eyes. "Yes, everyone's awake and healthy. To the best of my knowledge, my family is safe, too. Katarina still isn't entirely over Lee's death, though."

"Whose death?" Laani questioned, puzzled.

"Oh, goodness, I forgot I hadn't told you," Akinia apologized. "When I went home before my Sigadia mission my aunt Katarina was pregnant with identical twins. They were born prematurely and the oldest, Lee, was unhealthy and died a few hours later. The younger, Leena, was uncertain for a while but she eventually pulled through. The medic said she'll be sickly, for the rest of her life though."

"How horrible!" Laani gasped.

Akinia grimaced. "Well, the medic advised that she not get

pregnant for at least a year. We nearly lost her as well. That's almost the hardest part for her, not being able to have another baby for so long."

"Why? How many children does she have?"

"Eight now, but she's wishing desperately to be allowed to have children again. They want a lot of children, my uncle especially. Uncle Andrid only had Uncle Khee-Lá and my mother as siblings, because my grandmother got really ill when mother was born and couldn't have any more children. Most well-off Nátoans have at least nine children, many have more. The poorest have at least two," Akinia shrugged.

Laani's eyes widened. "Lendellians generally only have two or three, at the most. Unless, of course, they have multiples. But why would the medic have to tell her to wait a year before having another child? You can only get pregnant a year and a half after giving birth," she laughed.

"Lyndops have to wait that long," Akinia specified, "Adamians can have a child every year."

"Every year?" she gasped. "I didn't think that was possible."

Akinia grinned.

"Why do Nátoans have so many children?" Laani asked before she could comment.

"The more kids you have, the more respected you are," Akinia shrugged. "I don't know why, but it may have something to do with whether or not you're able to feed so many children. Few children mean you're poor, many children mean you can provide for them. The only thing more precious to Nátoans than children is Nátoan Najee, since we're so rare."

"Wow. Our status is judged by our prowess in the Games," she mused.

"What 'Games'?" Akinia asked curiously.

Laani grinned. "I would say I'd take you to see, but that's what I just came back from. I go home every year at this same time to compete. It's a series of races and athletic tests where you compete against others in your village, then your sector, and finally the sector finalists from all the sectors combined. I made it to the sector championships."

"What kind of athletic tests?"

"Well, for the final events where the champions of all sectors compete, the challenge is a race to the top of one of the uninhabited ancients, but you have to climb up on the outside of the tree. They

339

change what tree they use every year, so there's no telling which one it is and no way to prepare for it. Luck is a big part of the games," she explained, grimacing at what appeared to be a memory.

"So how old do you have to be to compete?"

"If you can walk and talk, you can enter. Children never win, though. If I wasn't so strong from my training I wouldn't get close. My brother did come in fifth in the local event, though. He was so proud of himself! It was funny to watch him. I would say that you should enter, but outsiders are forbidden. Besides, you wouldn't stand much of a chance. You're strong, but you aren't used to climbing or running through trees. It's definitely an acquired skill," she sighed, seeming disappointed that Akinia couldn't compete.

"One area you can still beat me in?" she teased, grinning.

"Yes, one area. And I will definitely hold on to it for my pride's sake," she laughed.

"Speaking of areas that I can beat you in, would you like to spar? I haven't had a good spar in a while," Akinia offered.

Laani grinned. "Sounds good. Maybe I'll get my title back for a while if you're so out of practice."

"Don't count on it."

"I'm really not, honestly," she laughed.

"Rofa, why don't you go and lie back down?" Akinia suggested, reinforcing the suggestion telepathically to make sure the cub understood.

Rofa whined and rubbed against Akinia's leg.

"I know, girl, but I'll be back before long. You'll get bored watching me spar," she laughed, rubbing Rofa's head.

The cub hesitated for a moment before lowering her head submissively and leaving.

"You know," Laani mused, "It really is amazing how much she understands you."

"Spoken words aren't as clear, but she gets my meaning well enough when I touch her mind," she shrugged. "Come on, let's get going."

"You're going to spar in that?" Laani questioned, motioning to Akinia's dress.

"Hmm, I could, but I would hate to mess up mother's dress," she mused, suddenly remembering what she was wearing. "Should we go to my room so I can change?"

"Most definitely," she agreed. "Come on, I'll race you."

Akinia grinned as they started running. The hallways were mostly abandoned, but a couple of Masters laughed and pressed against the wall to keep out of their way as they saw the girls coming. The girls laughed and pushed each other gently, trying to slow each other down, as they ran. Neither seemed to be in the lead, but as they neared Akinia managed to get a step ahead. "I win," she grinned.

"Big surprise," Laani laughed. "But you only won by about a foot."

"A win is a win," she reminded her as they closed the door behind them. "I'll just be a minute. Sit down if you like."

"We definitely need to get your room personalized," Laani mused, looking around at the plain metal walls. "The only thing you've done different than normal is the bedding and this jewelry chest."

"Oh yeah," Akinia called from her closet, "Aunt Katarina insisted I take that bedding set. It was a gift from Senator," she hesitated a moment, "Merivan's wife. I can never remember their surname for some reason. I always have to think about it for a few minutes. That small purple pillow that doesn't match any of the others is one Alania gave me. I got the jewelry chest from my mother. Some of the things in it were hers but the majority of them were gifts from Nátoan diplomats while I was home."

"Princess Alania gave you this throw pillow?" Laani echoed, impressed.

"Not personally. It arrived last week along with a tea service and a silk gown she gave me for some reason. She's supposed to contact me tomorrow, but I'll need to look at her letter to remember what time," she laughed.

"She must really like you."

"I think she does. She's really sweet. She thinks my life is fascinating, like something in a book she once read. I told her she needs to find more interesting books. No one would want to read about my life," Akinia shrugged, emerging in her favorite brown pants and off-white halter top. She strapped her wajun belt back on and asked, "Ready?"

"Yeah," Laani agreed. "You know, I've never met Princess Alania. Actually, you and Master Khee-Lá are the only royalty or diplomats I've met."

"You'd like her. She's so sweet and kindhearted, she just makes you feel at home."

"Well of course you feel at home, you're royalty."

"Not when I met her," Akinia reminded her friend, closing the door behind them on the way out. "When we first became friends, I was just a no-account orphan that didn't even have a surname. She didn't even know I was the Child of the Prophecy until after I left to go to bed that night."

"She sounds great," Laani admitted.

"I think she'd like you, too."

"Even if I'm not Adamian? I heard that sometimes diplomats don't like people not of their race," she wondered.

Akinia laughed. "Some of her closest advisors are of other races. Her dearest friend is a Meshder, Princess Inzan. Despite the political front they keep in public, they really are quite close."

"Inzan… isn't she King Zyrig's daughter?"

"That's her," Akinia nodded.

"Akinia, Apprentice Akinia," someone called.

Both girls stopped and looked behind then to see a young boy, no more than thirteen, running after them.

"Yes, what is it?" Akinia asked diplomatically, hiding her annoyance at being interrupted.

"Master Lo-Kí requests you come to his office immediately. He says it is urgent, but to come calmly," he reported timidly.

Akinia sighed. "I'm afraid our spar will have to wait," she apologized.

Laani grinned and grabbed Akinia's left arm in a forearm grip. "We have plenty of time once you're finished. Find me once your meeting is over. I may go bug Nath for a while."

"Smack him for me. I'm sure he's done something to deserve it," Akinia laughed.

"Don't think I won't," Laani winked before releasing Akinia's arm and continuing down the hallway.

Chapter 58:

Akinia followed the boy silently through the unfamiliar passages in the ancient Elders' Hall, where the Council Elders each had an office that adjoined their bedchambers. "Thank you," she said softly as he pointed out Lo-Kí's office.

The boy made a clumsy attempt at a bow before turning and walking away.

Akinia raised her hand and knocked on the door.

Lo-Kí's mind brushed hers momentarily before he called, "Come in, Akinia."

She opened the door and stepped inside, trying to hide her surprise at seeing a small holo-table in the middle of the room. Alania's figure rose from the center of the table.

Akinia's eyes darted around the room, seeing a thousand different places in a second. She saw the large ornate desk and carefully carved chair sitting against the far wall. She saw the large bookcases that stretched along the length and breadth of the room, covering the walls so completely that she didn't know what color they might be. She saw the lighting panels on the ceiling twisting and morphing in a strangely bright and multicolored collaboration with no rhyme or reason to the colors or their changes, and she wondered how the room wasn't painted in swirling colors. She saw the thick mahogany carpet stretching from wall to wall. She could see the small wooden carvings sitting here and there on shelves and on top of the desk, some holding down papers or holding up rows of books that would otherwise have fallen. She saw a small multicolored bird sitting in a metal cage along the back wall and absentmindedly wondered what kind of bird it was.

She forced her eyes to turn back to Lo-Kí and Alania's holographic-self. "You sent for me?" she questioned, hesitating in the doorway.

"Yes, close the door and join our conversation," he offered, motioning to another sensor-port on the edge of the table.

Akinia nodded and stepped towards the sensor after closing the door. She knew the moment she was close enough because Alania's holographic eyes focused on her.

"Oh, Akinia, how lovely to see you. Did you receive my gifts?" she asked pleasantly.

Akinia smiled. "I did. They were wonderful, thank you," she replied earnestly, knowing that the words did not even begin to touch her gratitude.

"I know I said I would contact you tomorrow, but there was no way that I could wait. Master Lo-Kí, if you could show her?" she asked, suddenly growing solemn.

"Of course," Lo-Kí agreed. He began playing with a few knobs and pressing some buttons on the holo-table. "Ah, here it is," he said. Alania's figure temporarily disappeared and was replaced by a datafield. "The letter wasn't originally in Main, but we translated it as best we could. The threats against Alania's life are becoming more common and more severe. This is the fourth letter of its kind she has received in the past three days alone, all from different people, it seems."

"There are ways of tracing them, if they were sent through a device, but it can only take you to the original device, not to the person that wrote the letters," she mused, squinting to be able to better see the small lettering.

"Yes, and therein lies the problem," Lo-Kí agreed. "But that isn't why I called you here. We have several Najee working on following the origins of these threats, and trying to determine who may have written them, but we need something more done. Alania is no longer safe, and her guard is not going to be adequate protection if an assassin decides to make an attempt on her life."

"Akinia," Alania said gently, "I know you must be tired after your mission, and that long time hidden in Sigadia, but I would like you to consent to join me in the Capitol for a few weeks or so, just until this issue is sorted out."

"We think that you would be the best choice for this because very few people in the Empire, including Jade Enbrilth's people, know of your existence. You would be going as a princess of Náto, and not as a Najee. You have certain abilities recently mastered that make me think you are quite qualified for this," Lo-Kí informed her, being careful to keep his tone light and stress the words only with his expression.

"Of course," Akinia replied, understanding immediately what Lo-Kí was saying. "I'd be glad to."

"Wonderful! I knew you would be," Alania exclaimed, delighted.

Akinia smiled at the princess's joyful expression as Alania's holographic image once again appeared on the table. "When will I be leaving?"

"We'll need you to go to Náto first, and then to leave from there in a Nátoan ship with a Nátoan guard," Lo-Kí explained. "I have already been informed by your uncle that you will be leaving for Náto tomorrow afternoon, to ensure you are there in time for your birthday. You will have three days to visit with your family and make arrangements for an official invitation from Alania, for your guard to be arranged, and for the documentation to be altered to give the appearance that you are a full-time Nátoan royal, which, of course, Khee-Lá and King Andrid will be handling."

"Of course, Master Lo-Kí," Akinia smiled. "So will I be permitted to wear my wajun? I'm good at hiding it."

"I wouldn't send you without one," he promised. "I will be writing a letter to your aunt, which I want you to deliver. It will tell her to give you instruction in certain diplomatic performances. Princess Alania can help you through the rest."

"What will I do with Rofa? And my droid?" she asked next, suddenly remembering her cub.

This time it was Alania who answered. "It is not uncommon for you visiting diplomats to have a menagerie of unusual animals. Rofa will be welcome, though I recommend finding some sort of decoration such as jewels and fine fabric collars and such. Queen Katarina will be more than capable of outfitting her appropriately, as she'll know some things other diplomats do for their pets. As to the droid, I assume you are referring to J90-5?"

"Yes, Khee-Lá made him. He told me that Jaynine was my mother's droid," she explained quickly.

"Then he'll have been programmed for diplomatic rendezvous such as this one. Just make certain that you instruct him to treat you only as a princess, and not as a Najee," Alania decided after a moment of thought.

"Is there anything else I should know?" Akinia asked them

both.

They both thought for a moment before Lo-Kí said, "I will give you some more information on the case once we are finished speaking with Princess Alania, but that is really all of the information in my half of this mission. Have you anything to add, Princess?"

"Only that you would do well to seek Queen Katarina's advice on any questions you may have about the diplomatic portion of this assignment. You are very good with diplomacy to the best of my knowledge, but we are trying to pretend that you have been raised to be a full-time Nátoan royal. Oh, and also note that we are going to say to those who have heard of it that the Najee hid you the night Jade killed your parents and grandparents to preserve the Nátoan royal line, and we will imply that soon you will be named as heir apparent to the Nátoan throne," Alania cautioned. "You should be familiar with the tale before you arrive. My staff have been carefully screened and rotated so that none that saw you the last time you visited will be present."

"Perfect. The Nátoans are so loyal to my mother still that they will be no problem so far as discretion is concerned. Will I need to inform the Nátoan Senators and Representatives of our plan, or will they not be present?" she wondered.

Alania considered that for a moment. "There will be the matter of my coronation, which will take place shortly after you arrive. The Imperial Council has decided that it is well past time that I be crowned as Queen in my parents' place. Minor rulers from all corners of the Empire and Motuk will be gathering to witness, and most will have an entourage of diplomats escorting them. I am uncertain what plans the Nátoan family has in regards to this, but I am certain that your opinion will be regarded with great weight."

"I'll discuss it with my aunt and uncle, and ask their opinion," she decided immediately.

"Well said," Alania praised. "I'm afraid I must go now. I have much to do. Remember, ask Queen Katarina if you have any questions, but do not ask them over a com-device. They can all wait until you are safely on Náto. Farewell Master Lo-Kí, Apprentice Akinia." Without another word her figure disappeared from the holo-table.

"Well, Akinia, do you have any questions for me?" Lo-Kí asked as he waved his hand and the holo-table slid across the room to sit neatly against the wall.

She thought for a moment. "When you said I had skills that

enabled me to be the best one for the job, what were you referring to? I mean, obviously something the Nrell taught me, but did you have something specific in mind?"

He smiled, his aged cheeks wrinkling with the action as he sat in the ornate chair behind his desk. "Ah, Akinia, you are always so sharp. It makes me envious of your youth. Old eyes don't see as much as young ones, but an old mind may be able to unravel the mysteries better. You seem to have been gifted with an old mind behind your young eyes, yet a mind still young enough to learn so rapidly it's nearly beyond belief. It is quite a conundrum, I will say."

Akinia smiled and blushed, dipping her head slightly as she gazed across the room to avoid meeting the old man's stare.

"It's no surprise to me that the Nrell chose you, and I would bet that the Nrell who marked you did not realize that you were the Child of the Prophecy, either," he continued, seeming oblivious to her embarrassment at his praise. "Ah, well, the truth is that I did have a specific skill in mind. Do you remember the Nrell teaching you how to watch an area for danger? I fear that the assassin, whenever he or she comes, may have his mind closed off to where you will be unable to sense him or her, much like you did to your companions when they rescued you from Jade's base. Using the skill of searching for danger, and danger only, you can sense the moment an attacker with foul intent comes near the one you are watching, even if his or her mind is completely closed away beyond the ability to be felt."

Akinia's eyes widened. "I didn't realize it would work even then, I only knew of being able to sense danger. He never went into details about how well it would work, and under which circumstances it would work. He seemed to be under the impression that it wouldn't help me much since I would be in danger most of the time," she explained.

Lo-Kí pursed his lips as he contemplated that. "Hmm…this makes me wonder what else this Nrell did not think was relevant to your life that may have been useful. At some point in time I may take you to visit a close Nrell acquaintance of mine and have her test you, but there is no time now," he chastised himself as he realized he was considering it too strongly. "You must also remember to put a shield around Alania if you sense danger near her. Did he at least teach you how to make the shield draw its strength from the attacker?"

"He explained the principle and I tried it a couple of times, but he focused more on teaching me to dissolve blaster bolts and deflect wajun. He said those would be put up in a split-second and there wouldn't be time to turn them around to pull strength from Jade or Lokita. I did manage to do it successfully the second and third times I attempted it, but I only tried it three times," she explained hesitantly.

Lo-Kí sighed. "I want you to return here after dinner tonight and we will go over the principle again. For now, why don't you go and relax? Enjoy your evening, because we have a lot of work to do by time you leave tomorrow night. You may not get another chance to have time to yourself."

Akinia smiled. "Sure," she agreed, turning to leave. She in the doorway a moment and asked, "Why do you trust me so much, with missions so important?" She turned to face him, wanting to watch his face as he answered.

He regarded her curiously for a moment before he answered. "I ask nothing of you that you haven't demonstrated the potential to perform. I make your tasks difficult because you need me to. You need a challenge to rise to, and you need to rise to them well enough that it builds your confidence, and then you need to rise higher.

"Your greatest fault, and your most precious virtue, is your inability to trust yourself fully and completely to do the right thing. I trust you because you do not put too much trust in yourself. The fact that you doubt yourself enough to check your decisions before you act upon them makes me trust you to find the best course of action available at the time, and your willingness to put others before yourself is a rare virtue that is even more precious and more sought after when I look for someone to give an important task to.

"When I look at you I see a strong and powerful Najee, a sweet and innocent child, a selfless and honest soul, a skilled diplomat, a faithful friend, and a broken heart still trying to heal from the loss of so many who were close to you. You ask me why I trust you? I trust you because you have never given me a reason not to," he explained quietly.

Akinia considered that for a moment before turning again. "I…" she hesitated and then sighed, "I'm glad…to understand." Without another word she walked out, turning slightly to get a last puzzled glance at Lo-Kí before the door slid shut. Her lips twisted into a troubled smile as he met her gaze.

Maybe someday she *would* understand, but for now his words just puzzled her. She would think about them tonight, certainly, and probably several nights more. Later she would let his words invade her thoughts, driving all others from her mind, but not now. Now she would find Laani and enjoy the evening with her. After all, it could be the last time they saw one another for many months. She would unravel the hidden facets of Lo-Kí's unsettling assurances later, but for now she drove all thought of it from her mind.

Laani, meet me, she murmured, sending a mental image of her favorite training field. *Let's have some fun.*

Coming Soon:

Najee:
A Queen's Ransom
(Book 3 of the Najee Series)

Disguised by the protective umbrella of her maternal lineage and her carefully hidden identity, Akinia finds herself immersed in center of one of the biggest political events of the last several decades: the coronation of Queen Alania Princeshian. It is an event which has spawned a gathering of loyal allies, and dangerous enemies.
As one attempt on Alania's life leads to another, Akinia struggles to keep the soon-to-be queen alive long enough to accept her crown. And the addition of a new, but very familiar, face could be the choice that guarantees her success...
Or her failure.

About the Author

Sarah Y. Westmoreland has been writing since before she started kindergarten. She began outlining the Najee Series at thirteen, the same time that she began writing *A Glimmer of Hope*. Having graduated from high school at the age of sixteen, Sarah devotes a part of each day to her writing. Sarah, now eighteen, is attending college. She hopes to earn a double-major in Creative Writing and Spanish.

Sarah loves to hear from her readers! Connect with her via:

Facebook - www.Facebook.com/NajeeAGlimmerofHope

Email - NajeeSeries@gmail.com

Twitter - @NajeeSarahW

or through her Website - www.NajeeSeries.yolasite.com

www.ingramcontent.com/pod-product-compliance
Lightning Source LLC
Chambersburg PA
CBHW032203190626
46810CB00017B/33